Praise for

DOMINION: ASCENSION

"While this debut novel may be reminiscent of popular dystopian tales like The Divergent Series, D.A. Murray infuses the genre with a fresh signature voice through well-drawn characters, careful storytelling, and vivid world-building. Murray's work provokes lingering thoughts about gender expectations, class, ambition, romance, and impossible choices, with the nuanced poise of a writer clear-eyed about the disturbing social implications of the Dominion worldview. This is a stylish and timely read you won't soon forget."

—**J.H. ELLIS**, author of *The Seven Gates of the Kingdom* trilogy

"D.A. Murray delivers a riveting tale set in a chaotic dystopian world led by women with a formidable discrimination against men. This intriguing plot interweaves evil, greed, and unexpected twists that have you questioning everything until the very end. Get ready for a thrilling ride of emotions, romance, ethical decisions, and heart-wrenching choices."

—**KATRINA MACKRIDES**, author of *The Salty Swan* trilogy

"Murray's debut novel unfolds in a gripping dystopia, brought to life through cinematic prose and a cast of complex, compelling characters. I couldn't put it down—and I can't wait to read more from this powerful new voice in speculative fiction."

—**NATACHA BELAIR**, award-winning author of *A Stellar Purpose* trilogy

"D.A. Murray creates a world we've all thought about but have never seen: a world run by women. But with all things, nothing is ever as easy or as good as we imagine. The world of Dominion explores just such a world. Dominated by women, the overlying peacefulness belies the struggles for power and dominance that lies just underneath. In Dani Matthews, we find a heroine that uses her reporter instincts to ferret out the truth behind Dominion and her natural sense of empathy to champion those who have been relegated to servitude. All while unraveling the mystery of who is the power behind Dominion. An intriguing read set in a fantastical new world. Can't wait to read more."

—**DARRIEN MICHELE GIPSON**, executive director, SAGindie; filmmaker

"Bold, intense, and full of heart, *Dominion: Ascension* dives into a future where rebellion means everything—and freedom comes with a price.

"D.A. Murray's unforgettable characters and thrilling story will grab you from page one and never let go."

—**J. A. COLLIE**, author of *Grays of Novart*

DOMINION: ASCENSION

Dominion: Ascension

by D. A. Murray

ISBN 979-8-88824-772-3

Cover art and design by Lauren Sheldon

Published by

köehlerbooks™

3705 Shore Drive
Virginia Beach, VA 23455
800-435-4811
www.koehlerbooks.com

DOMINION

ASCENSION

a novel

D. A. MURRAY

VIRGINIA BEACH
CAPE CHARLES

Don't just read this thrilling tale from D.A. Murray . . . get the full *Dominion* immersive experience by accessing the curated collection of materials in the *Dominion* companion guide!

Check out the glossary at the end of the book and visit damurrayofficial.com/companion to get exclusives like a *Dominion* book club kit and to learn about events with the author.

CHAPTER ONE

It's been twenty years since the rise of Dominion, and the truth about my father's death is still a mystery to me. My mother told me that he died from a heart attack, but I had doubts. Over time, doubt became resentment. My mother, who was once my refuge from the harsh realities of this world, became a stranger to me.

I can't pinpoint exactly when I knew my mother was lying to me, but my obsession with discovering what really happened to my father was the reason I became an investigative reporter. Uncovering the truth, at all costs, is my North Star. I'm willing to face the unknown regardless of where it leads.

This should be one of the most exciting nights of my life, but I'm dreading it. The feeling that at any moment I will crack from the inside out intensifies as the Ascension Gala inches less than two hours. This night of remembrance and celebration marks the death of things once familiar, and the rise of a world run by science and the unbridled ambition of a new government.

When the Great War ended, most males became infertile and cognitively impaired from all the biochemical weapons. That was twenty years ago. Since 2030, women have assumed leadership. Males are assigned to one of six societal roles based on an IQ test. That test was pioneered by my mother. And tonight, she will receive the Effigent award. I don't understand how she can be proud of creating a system that steals a person's right to choose their path in life. The thought of attending this annual event for the first time sickens me to my core.

My hands are cold, and my mind is restless. Refusing to let my anxiety get the better of me, I get up from the chair, walk over to the full-length mirror, and stand confidently in front of it. My body is slender and delicate. I'm five-three, and sometimes I wish I was tall like my cousins on my father's side of the family. I look a lot like my mother, Linda, who is East Indian and Creole. We both have medium-brown skin with warm orange-red undertones and eyes as dark as coal. My high cheekbones, full lips, and thick, curly hair run in my family. I saw pictures of my maternal grandmother. She was fair-skinned and curvaceous. I wish I had a curvy figure like my mom. Everything she wears hugs her hourglass frame perfectly. I have to contort my body in a provocative pose to achieve the same effect. Otherwise, my clothes just loosely drape my rectangle-shaped figure.

My father, Karl, was of East Indian and African descent. He had a slender, athletic build and a deep cocoa complexion. His hazel eyes were the softest brown infused with green and rimmed with dark lashes. And he had a broad nose with an arcing profile, the kind that kept him from being too pretty. I remember how he smelled of cologne and tobacco.

My name, Danielle, means "God is my judge," according to my parents. My dad told me it was the perfect name because, when he held me for the first time, he felt like he was holding a piece of heaven. He believed that he'd been redeemed from all of his past wrongdoings. After leaving the military, he started a private militia that provided armed combat services for money, and he was ashamed of that. After I was born, he shuttered his company and went to work for the government as a military advisor. He would occasionally go on high-priority assignments.

Life before Dominion seems so long ago. I remember how I used to curl up in my father's lap while he told me stories about his life in the military. He led dangerous missions in faraway places like Nicaragua and Iran that were destroyed during the Great War and are now barren wastelands. In many ways, Dominion is like a barren wasteland of missed opportunities, lost hopes, and forgotten dreams. Men aren't human beings with unlimited potential but rather vessels with the explicit purpose to serve the women of Dominion. Their potential is strangled at the vine before it can grow. That is what tonight is about, and I don't know how to be a part of something I loathe.

The clock says there is less than an hour left now. The spider dress in my closet is freshly steamed. I slip it on and adjust my body-glam dial on the back of my dress. I need to pull in my stomach and hide the late-night binging I've been doing since the invitation to the Ascension arrived four weeks ago. I am standing in my favorite provocative pose, which involves standing on one leg, with the other bent at the knee, while balancing on the ball of my standing foot in heels, both hands on my hips. This pose accentuates my curves.

Staring at my stilettos with sharp black-and-gold-beaded spiked heels, I can't help but think, *How clever to design something both so beautiful and deadly.*

I wish I could congratulate my mother and tell her that I am proud of her, but I am conflicted. Her way of life represents everything I am against. Dominion has changed her. Her work today is so different than earlier in her career. In the beginning, she revolutionized IQ testing methods. Her methodology eliminated inherent biases that reinforced social and economic disadvantages for marginalized groups. Those same testing methods are now used to restrict the males of Dominion. She became rigid, uncompromising, and indifferent toward the negative impact of her testing methodology, now called IQ fencing. And this is what achievement looks like in Dominion.

After blotting my lips with plain bamboo tissue and carefully applying cherry-flavored lip glaze, I exit my bedroom and make my way to the living area. As I descend the staircase, my dress, the glass organza in tones of dark purples and turquoise covered with translucent bubbles, shimmers under the silver pendant lights. I see my mother staring at me disapprovingly. She's always so critical and unforgiving about my choices. I can tell by the way she sighs. She picks up her purse and rushes to the front door.

"Hurry up, Dani. We're late," she says.

"The reception begins in thirty minutes," I say, "and we're only fifteen minutes from the shrine."

"Yes, but I want to arrive early," she says. "I want to savor every moment of this night."

Look at her. She looks so confident and composed. I can't deny she's beautiful. Her long, black hair covers her bronze shoulders, and her turquoise dress hugs her perfectly. Her makeup is flawless, eyes seductive and framed with shadows of green and gold.

"I wish I could congratulate you," I say. "I really wish I could . . . but I can't."

"We're not hashing that out again. I realize that as a reporter, you're trained to question everything, but . . . I'm your mother!"

"What's wrong with questioning things?" I say.

"You're criticizing something you just don't understand," she says.

"You're right. I don't understand forcing young boys into a caste system based on a manipulated test that you created!"

Mother is getting angry now. "You don't know how it used to be between men and women, prior to the Ascension. You've only known the advantages of being a woman today. This manipulated test, as you call it, was necessary to save our country. Women were left to piece back together what remained after the Great War. There was no way that men could continue to lead when the majority of them were cognitively impaired and sterile. Dani, everything as we knew it was destroyed in an instant. You can't begin to understand what that was like. You were just nine years old, and your father and I protected you. You didn't see the death, women and children suffering from hunger and fear. Parts of our nation were uninhabitable, and when the migration to the north started, intrastate wars started."

Before I can respond, she turns away, slides on her shiny black coat, and heads to the stretch limousine waiting outside. I follow her. It's times like this when I struggle to understand my mother. Such composure and strength, yet so misguided.

Sunset is approaching, and the flashing sheets of rain become drizzling raindrops. I cover my head with the hood of my black coat.

The chauffeur gets out of the black limo, opens the passenger door, and guides us inside. The black leather interior is illuminated by high-tech LED lights and sports bench seating that can fit up to six people. There's a gold emblem stitched into the headrests of the leather seats and a silver ice bucket with a bottle of champagne chilling.

"Oh, my favorite!" Mother says, reaching for a glass flute. "Join me, Danielle."

She pops open the cork and pours us each a glass. The effervescence tickles my nose. After two sips, I tilt my head back and close my eyes. I can feel my mind drifting into a state of mild euphoria when, suddenly, a sharp bump on the road jolts my head forward. When I look up and glance out the window, I see it—a Dissident bus.

"That's strange . . . a Dissenter bus traveling through the city," Mother says.

"You're right, the Dissidents are usually transported via back roads and typically late in the evening to avoid attracting too much attention. This does seem odd."

Mother remarks, "The transport may be delayed due to the riot in Hansen. I heard that the roads were closed for most of the day."

We slow down for a red light. I see the dark cloud of exhaust spewing from the rear of the bus as it comes to a lazy stop. The outer frame of the bus is dark blue, and there is a dark orange emblem of the Harken, a symbol of duty and courage, on the side of the bus. The sign is faded, and the edges are weathered away. The top level of the bus is reserved for the officers and medical personnel. I know Dissident camps are nothing more than prisons. The only difference is that Dissident sentences are for life.

The first level of the bus is full of men and women, all standing packed together. They're wedged like spoons, with no room to even turn around. The windows of the bottom level are steamy, and I can imagine the foul smell of sweat, vomit, and blood. The light turns green, and as we accelerate past the bus, a hand grips the side of a cracked window.

How did it come to this? My mother tries to distract me from looking at the bus by pressing the 3D holographic TV button directly in front of us. The TV is showing the rebellion by the separatist organization, National Freedom League in Dennering, the far north corner of the Second Quadrant, what used to be Crescent City, California.

"So much civil unrest. You realize that you helped create this mess," I say. "How can you celebrate your role in this?"

"These men refuse to accept their reality. They hate that we live in a society led by women. What they refuse to accept, they want to destroy. So, I have no compassion for anarchists," she says as she waves her hand to dismiss me.

We both watch the holographic TV intently as the rebels invade the Dennering Illegis facility, where IQ testing occurs. You can see the rage etched in the rebels as they bum-rush through the metal barricade surrounding the stairs to the front entrance. The intensity of their chanting—"DEATH TO DOMINION!"—drowns out the warnings from the Illegis police blaring through the bull horns. Rebels run quickly, covering every square inch of the stairs until bodies are heaving up in great swells against the front entrance.

A silhouette of three young male children, hand in hand, appear on the lower right of the screen. The boy in the center is leading the way while the other two are gasping for air and attempting to look back at the rage and destruction. Translucent ribbons of smoke lurk like clouds above the multitude of bodies lying motionless on the ground. Their ripped, raw flesh is red with blood and mingled with gravel.

The roaring flames engulfing all five sides of the pentagon-shaped Illegis building come back into view. The fury of the mob seems to explode onto the screen—primitive impulses intermingled with flesh and bone. The gallows are on the east side of the Illegis building, and the Dominion flag flies at half-mast, the stars representing the twenty-six republics stained in blood. The screen reveals an eerie, misty gray while the cries of oppression are muted by the sound of sirens, the helicopters overhead.

I shake my head in frustration and notice my mother sipping her champagne and looking out the window. She seems completely unfazed by the mayhem directly in front of her. This was just another day in Dominion, where demonstrations of rage were frequent and public. After all, storming is necessary to forge a stronger nation.

CHAPTER TWO

Linda

Dani was barely five years old when the world turned upside down. The ashes are no more. The scarlet hue of the sunset fades away in the distance as the limo travels along the main boulevard. Many cities, after the Great War, were dark like charcoal and stripped of their beauty and purpose. This road was populated by charred, limbless tree trunks stretching on both sides. Vaporous clouds of black ash enveloped the sky, and the metal wires that hung from the burnt traffic lights blew wildly in the wind. Dilapidated buildings and blackened digital screens littered the ground as far as the eye could see. In the light of dawn, the heat engulfed the city. Sometimes, the fiery rays of the sun burned the skin until it was red and inflamed. It scorched the ground, forming deep cracks and fissures.

Mothers, ravaged by war, were broken, and the innocence of their children was murdered in an instant. Nothing was left but cold indifference and defective hearts. Then destabilization efforts pit one group against another, and lawlessness prevailed. The death toll teetered just over one million. Millions more wandered the streets malnourished.

I press the remote to crack the window open so I can breathe in the cool breeze that fills my nostrils with a fresh pine and floral scent. This smell is the promise of a nation reborn. No more of the smoke or death that filled each day with despair. We resurrected a country where no aesthetic diversity within the city was possible. To do so, we alleviated diversity amongst nongovernment employees. So, along the drive, there are rows of gray and white buildings, one identical to the other. The life of the city dwellers, which are made up of the working class, is no different than the life of another. Their language, societal norms, laws, residences, and places of business are the same. Private property is reserved for the Dominion cabinet members and their staff as a means of protection. The Colonies ensure the propagation of our society and are the incubators of our technological advancement.

As we drive by the School of Phoenix, I see a congregation of young women scholars walking into the outdoor pavilion, sitting on the steps and perfectly manicured lawn. They are students of science, philosophy, engineering, law, and many others. These women are our future. They will inherit our legacy of courage and compassion and continue to build a great nation. I am so proud of the beauty we've created from the ashes of the past.

CHAPTER THREE

The limousine stops in front of the shrine, a large 100,000-seat amphitheater with fifty levels and a retractable, ringlike roof. The vibrant lights cast all the colors of the rainbow.

Armed guards are standing along the perimeter of the amphitheater, closely watching the protesters of the Men Against Oppression movement. MAO members are dressed in black and holding posters with statements like "MEN'S RIGHTS ARE HUMAN RIGHTS," "MALISM DESTROYS LIVES," "MY SEX IS NOT A CRIME," "MALE RIGHTS ARE NOT OPTIONAL," and "FREEDOM FOR ALL." The anger of the mob rages as they chant, "RESPECT EXISTENCE OR EXPECT RESISTANCE!" Their bodies seem to contort, strike, then retract in unison. A man runs away from the angry mob and stops in front of a metal post a few feet away from our limo; he leans against it. He clings to the post so forcefully that I can see the whites of his knuckles. Tears spill from his eyes as grief and anguish seem to surge with every breath. Watching the relentless determination on this man's face makes me angry, and I want to explode.

Exiting the limousine is difficult. My heart feels like it is about to pound out of my chest. Gold-plated statues flank each side of the entrance to the theatre. One of the statues is a woman holding the butterfly, representing transformation and the nature of womanhood. The other statue is the phoenix, the ultimate symbol of strength and renewal. A red carpet leads up the stairs to the entrance. Blinded by the flashing lights, I stand to the side as my mother exits the limousine, reporters buzzing around her and snapping pictures. She is polite as always and charms them with her smile. She says that she hates the attention, but I know that's a lie. She thrives on public adoration, and tonight she's in the spotlight. She glides up the steps, and I walk slightly behind her, diminished in her shadow.

The lobby of the theater is filled with women wearing designer dresses and jewels. They seem almost like mannequins, their perfection artificial and removed from anything real or human. The program director, Sharla, greets my mother and escorts us to the private reception on the sixth floor.

The elevator is full. I stand as close to the far corner as possible and look down to avoid making eye contact with anyone. The compartment grinds to a halt, and the doors open to a large, modernist room. The white marble floors seem to stretch on for eternity. The room has floor-to-ceiling windows with a 180-degree view of the skyline and a stunning panoramic view of the sun as it sets, casting a pink and copper glimmer across the city. The walls are almost bare, with the exception of architectural holograms of the Angkor Wat Sunrise star burst, Pyramids of Giza, the Taj Mahal, and the Hanging Gardens of Babylon.

Glancing across the room, the handsome men look like statues wearing tuxedos that accentuate their tall frames and chiseled physiques. They're so polished and charming—almost perfect. This can't be what I think it is. I focus more closely and notice the Singletary band (also known as *S-bands*) around their necks. Each band is a different color, representing each of the Singletary classifications. Most of the men are S6, otherwise known as *Seducers,* and their band color is red. These bands rest firmly around the necks of each male in Dominion society and remain there until reassignment or death.

Since the S-bands must be visible at all times, the tuxedo is designed to reveal them. The traditional tuxedo, which includes a black or dark-blue jacket with satin facing on the lapels, dark trousers with silk stripes down the sides, and a cummerbund, remains the same as it was prior to the Ascension. The main difference is the design of the shirt and bow tie. The shirt has a wide, deep V-neck, and the collar around the neck is turned up to expose the collarbone so the S-band is prominently displayed. The bow tie, which is now a sheath of black satin with designer detail, is attached to the center of the collar.

I lean in and whisper softly to my mother, "Most of these men are Seducers. I've never seen so many of them at one gathering."

"Yes," she says, "I do believe you're right. It's not surprising though. Seducers are so much more amiable—they know their place, and you know what you're getting at the end of the night."

"What do you mean that Seducers are more amiable?" I ask, peering at my mother with an expression that could melt a rock.

Pulling me close while maintaining a smug smile, Mother whispers, "Benignants are cause-driven and feel deeply about caring for the world around them; they would sacrifice their lives for what is right. Have you ever seen a selfish minister, social worker, or teacher? I haven't."

Scanning the room, Mother directs me to look over at the man with a white band around his neck, wearing a black cassock. "You see the Benignant over there? Of course, he seems pleasant enough, but challenge his convictions, and that mild-mannered creature becomes ferocious." She smiles wickedly as she picks up a glass of champagne offered by the server.

"What's wrong with that?"

"Well, nothing when you are in a place that caters to their sensibilities, but at a function like this, where vanity is on display, Benignants can be judgmental and hard to tolerate."

Mother continues to look around the room, lets out a boisterous laugh, then says softly, "Now Assiduites, on the other hand, can be engaging. They exemplify the strength and creativity of the human form and mind. They bask in the glory of their physical and mental prowess. They don't particularly care about pleasing others. Assiduites expect to be adored."

Drawing my attention to the man wearing a purple S-band and dancing on the stage, Mother points out his muscular extremities and the synchronicity of his movements in harmony with the music.

Tapping my shoulder, a server wearing a brown S-band says, "Excuse me, miss, would you care for a roasted grape crostini?"

Again, Mother's eyes gaze whimsically at the server. Nodding inconspicuously at me as he walks away, she says, "Now, he's a Formalist. And it's surprising that you don't see too many green S-bands. Expeditors are very similar to Formalists, as they're hardworking and friendly, but they tend to be a bit rougher around the edges and avoid events like this. Formalists and Expeditors have ordinary, everyday jobs compared to the other Singletary groups. I must say, I've never desired to remarry, but if I did, these men are the easiest to domesticate. They can be resentful toward the other Singletary groups, particularly Breeders, since they are reliant on their *contribution* to sire their children. The Formalists and Expeditors, who refuse to accept their purpose, become rebellious, and their mood and demeanor reflects that."

Walking toward the bronze statue of the male form on the marble pedestal directly in front of us, Mother says, "No Singletary group exemplifies the depth of Dominion's favor more than Breeders. Their black S-bands signify power. They are highly regarded for their contribution and sacrifice, but they can be pious and standoffish. So, when you want someone whose entire focus is on providing female pleasure, it's not surprising that this room is full of Seducers tonight. It is befitting that Seducers S-bands are red, the color of sexuality, passion, and joy." Mother snickers, drains the last bit of champagne from her glass, and flags the server for another.

"I've never ordered a Seducer," I say. "I just don't feel comfortable with any of it."

"It's nothing to be ashamed of," Mother says. "It's so simple and convenient."

I lean in close and ask, "How often do you use it?"

"Oh, maybe once a week. When I'm in the mood for uncomplicated companionship, I peruse the Carousel for whatever I want. They usually arrive in less than thirty minutes," she says dismissively.

She lets out a wicked laugh and abruptly walks across the room to a man standing near the buffet table. She taps him on the shoulder and lets out an exuberant laugh as he embraces her. I can only see his back from here. He is tall and appears to have a brown S-band.

"Danielle!" my mother calls to me from across the room. "Come here, sweetheart."

You have got to be kidding me, I thought. *She only calls me Danielle when she is putting on airs. Who is she trying to impress?* Her face tightens, and she begins waving me over impatiently. She looks like she's about to explode with impatience. When I finally join her, I see she is talking to Stephen. We met at a charity event last month. He appears to be enjoying her company. She motions for me to stand closer to him. My shoulder brushes against his arm, and I smile gingerly as I maneuver to be an arm's length away from him. Her agenda is clear; she thinks Stephen is coupling material, and she wants me to take an interest in him.

In Dominion, marriage is considered "old-fashioned." If a woman wants a family, she chooses a man to have a child with. If she wants, she may marry or simply retain a domestic agreement with her mate, otherwise known as partnering. Standing almost motionless and flushed with embarrassment, I start to imagine my hands clamped tightly around her neck and pressing her trachea with my thumbs until she begins to choke. The harder I press, the more powerful I become, until I start to tower over her. Tightening my grip even more causes her to lose consciousness and drop to the floor. She's still alive, and as she gasps for breath, her eyes open. Her piercing stare frightens me. It's as if she can see through me and knows my shame. I quickly fall to my knees and cradle her head in my lap. She's moving in my arms, and with each gesture, I begin to weaken and feel small again.

"Danielle, are you listening to me?" Mother nudges my shoulder as she gives me a condescending sneer. I snap back to the present, and while scanning the room for any distraction, I notice a man standing next to the hologram of Victoria Falls. He is stately, his gestures subtle as he admires the hologram. He turns away from the hologram and studies the room. He seems to be searching for someone. What will capture his attention? Suddenly, I feel warm and uneasy. He's looking at me. His gaze is mesmerizing and so intense, it feels like it's piercing my flesh.

"Excuse me," I say to my mother and Stephen and begin walking toward the bar. Placing my hand on the countertop, I motion to the bartender. "Meridian cocktail, please."

"I noticed you were staring at me a moment ago," the man says, having approached me from the side.

"Staring?" I ask. "You must have confused me with someone else."

"No, it was you," he says, smiling. "There's no way I'd forget such captivating eyes and luscious lips."

I look away and gently shrug to appear shy but alluring. As he steps closer to whisper in my ear, his cologne begins to seduce me. It's a masculine scent of spicy lavender and amber, with a hint of clove and something crisp and clean like grass. As his hand presses firmly against my waist, I close my eyes softly.

"My name is Colin, Colin Cordova. How about you?" he asks.

"Me, what?"

"Your name." He smiles warmly.

"Danielle, but most people call me Dani."

He looks around the room again and says, "It's getting warm in here. Care to join me on the terrace?"

Looking over at my mother and Stephen, I notice they're still talking. More precisely, she's still talking. "Sure, why not?" I say.

He takes my hand and guides me toward the large concave doors that open onto the terrace. It's a beautiful night. The terrace overlooks the harbor, and myriads of moonbeams reflect off the water, making it shimmer with soft, golden waves.

"Your hands are cold. Let me warm them up," Colin says. When he touches me, it feels like electricity shooting through my body. I feel alive and engulfed by the moment.

"So, Colin," I begin, "clearly, you're not escorting anyone to this event, so what brings you to the Ascension tonight?" Typically, there are very few unattached men at these soirees, and they are usually here to work.

"My mother is the host, and I'm here as her guest."

"Your mother is Valentina Cordova?" I ask.

"Yes," he replies.

"Impressive black band," I say. "You are an S-five. Tell me, Colin, do you like being a Breeder? I haven't met many Breeders, but the few I have met seem very aloof and keep their conversation brief. Why is that?" I ask.

"I suppose many Breeders feel somewhat insecure about how society perceives their role, and they don't want to be treated like carnival freaks," he says. "We're regular guys who, like the military or law enforcement, protect and serve our country. The only difference is that our service is protecting procreation and providing the genetic contribution necessary for the evolution of our society."

"Would you do it if you had a choice?" I ask.

"Yes," he says without thinking. "The life of a Breeder is quite satisfying. It's not just about donating specimens. Because Breeders are permitted education beyond the *Standards*, we are highly educated, and our expenses are funded by the government for life," Colin says.

"Well, regardless of the educational advantages, I am sure there are Breeders who don't find their lives as satisfying. You're subject to the same limitations as other men—the inability to choose your work or creative self-expression," I say.

Taking a few steps closer, toward the railing facing the moonlit water, and putting his hands in his pockets, he replies, "Who's to say that I don't find creative self-expression as a Breeder? Dani, you have a narrow view. Why don't you visit the Colony so you can see how Breeders live? Our lives are much more robust than you think."

"I'll definitely take you up on that invitation," I say as I raise my pod to connect with his. "Also, judging from the gold plate on your S-band, when you reached thirty, you chose to stay in the Colony instead of leaving. What's that like, to know that as long as you remain a Breeder, you can't marry or sire children of your own?" I ask.

"Well, this life isn't for everyone long-term, but for those of us who recommit, the sacrifice is worth the reward," Colin says, unflinching in his response.

"I don't question the value that Breeders provide our society," I say, "but I *do* question the recruitment methods. You were assigned to be a Breeder at the age of twelve. You didn't have a choice and couldn't have understood the gravity of the commitment you were making."

Colin says nothing. He seems to be waiting for me to continue. *Did I offend him?*

"I'm sorry," I say. "I don't mean to come off judgmental or disapproving. I better join my mother. I'm sure she must be looking for me."

It is starting to get very cold outside, so I make my way back to the reception and head toward one of the bars. Even though there are at least five people ahead of me, the bartender does not seem particularly hurried. The lights are dim, making it a bit harder to scan the room for a familiar face.

"Dani, Danielle Matthews?" A gentleman taps me on the shoulder and smiles.

"Yes, I'm sorry," I reply. "Do I know you?"

"Dani," he says, grinning. "It's been a while, but I would never forget those beautiful dark eyes. It's me, Robbie! You remember, we were neighbors? We used to play cops and robbers when we were little kids." He takes a beat, watching my face for recognition. "Let's see, the last time I saw you, you were eleven and I was twelve. You always wanted to be the cop, and I was the robber who got caught and jailed every time."

"Robbie!" I say. "It's been so long. You look so different. You were tall and really skinny. Oh, and you wore these thick black glasses with Coke-bottle lenses. And you had braces. Wow, you've really changed!" I say while looking him up and down as surreptitiously as possible. "You're so handsome and definitely not that scrawny twelve-year-old."

"Well, it's been eighteen years," he says. "One optical transference and dental reconstruction later . . ." He puffs out his chest comically.

And then I saw it, a black S-band—*he's a Breeder*. Looking down into his eyes, I hoped he didn't sense the sadness that I felt. "So, what have you been doing for the past eighteen years?" I ask.

Suddenly, Robbie's mood seemed to shift. He went from excited to somber and pensive.

"Well, Dani," he says. "You know I was assigned to S5 when I was twelve and have been at the Colony ever since. I'm here for the *Release* Tribute."

"Wow, that's wonderful!" I say. "So, you chose to leave the Colony? That must be exciting and terrifying. How do you feel about it?"

"Listen, we have so much to catch up on," he says. "Why don't we plan to connect when I'm released from acculturation training in six weeks?"

"Sure," I say. "That sounds great. Let me give you my contact information."

I pull out my pod so we can tap the corners of our devices to exchange contact information, but before we can, he says, "Unfortunately, my contact information will change after I complete acculturation training." He leans in closely and, with a solemn expression, whispers, "We'll be transported to the training locations immediately following the *Release* ceremony tonight. So, why don't you scan your information on this?"

He pulls a pod out of his jacket pocket and hands it to me. It doesn't look like any pod I've ever seen, but I am so excited to see him that it doesn't seem to matter right now.

"Okay," I say, taking the pod. "Here you go. Please make sure you contact me. I'd love to see you again."

"You bet I will," he says. "Have to go now. See ya soon." He gives me a wink and walks away.

Sipping my drink and walking slowly, I take my time rejoining my mother since I don't want to make an appearance until Stephen is gone. After all, he seems more her type than mine, younger and much too eager.

The lights begin to dim in the reception hall, and Sharla whispers in my mother's ear.

"Danielle, it's time to be seated," Mother says.

We get on the elevator. As it ascends, I am filled with dread. The elevator opens on the ninth floor, and we walk across the glass bridge to the huge amphitheater. We find our seats in front. All of the award recipients and their families are seated near us, closest to the stage.

The crowd has a life of its own. Swarms of women descend the concrete stairs in the faint light. The uniform tapping of feet makes a rumbling sound in my ears. One by one, they head to the entrance that leads to one of the eight cabinets on the main floor surrounding the stage or upstairs to public seating. The second tier above public seating is occupied by the Breeders dressed in black suits, with the gold plates on their S-bands glistening. There must be at least 100 of them moving carefully like chess pieces. Once in their seats, they look straight ahead, never looking away from the stage.

On the ground floor, the chatter is so loud, I can barely hear the music playing. The vivid colors of the cabinet members' garments are dazzling and create a brilliant rainbow as the spotlights glaze blinding white light across every section of the theater. Each seating tier is occupied by women who have risen to the top of their fields in one of the eight cabinets: Law, Science, Commerce, Transportation, Religion, Military, Art, and Politics. They are in rich hues of purple, gold, red, blue, orange, green, bronze, or gray, depending on their cabinet. Like soldiers, they line up and sit in their designated seats according to their rank. They are Dominion's leaders and look so strong and confident, but the homogeneity of these women just further confirms that I will never become one of them.

At exactly 8 p.m., the lights begin to dim, and the stage curtain rises. The spotlight finds a beautiful soloist who begins to sing a cappella before the orchestra starts to play the Dominion anthem. When the music fades to a faint echo, everyone stands to face the flag with the Dominion butterfly symbol. We place our right hands over our hearts and recite:

"I pledge allegiance to the Dominion butterfly, a symbol of strength and renewal. Bonded in blood and ingenuity, we rise to our calling as leaders, protectors, and educators of our nation. As women, we are saviors and judges. Saviors of those who seek wisdom and life and judges of those who seek to destroy what God has made above all else. We will endeavor to create a great nation and help other nations discover true freedom through the natural order of humanity. What science has destroyed, so shall it be reborn as it was meant to be."

Looking around, I see these women, standing tall, with a look of stoic resignation. There is vengeful indignation for the past indiscretions of men. Everyone sits at the same time as they are ordered to do. No one questions anything anymore. They just stand, bow, and sit on command like trained seals. *I am not a seal.*

Following a moment of silence, Valentina Cordova, the leader of the Science cabinet, approaches the podium at the center of the stage to deliver the opening address. She looks intently into the audience and smiles.

"Welcome to the twentieth Ascension ceremony," she says. "Tonight, we honor the anniversary of restoration, peace to our nation, and the end of global unrest. Twenty years ago, women resumed our natural place in society as leaders, protectors, and educators of our future. We balance on our shoulders the responsibility of giving and ensuring that all citizens of Dominion can serve society in a way that guarantees our survival and allows us to thrive as a nation. The fate of our world is no longer left to chance or to the carnal lust and power-hungry desires of men. It is a new world, and we are here to celebrate the birth of Dominion!"

As Valentina speaks, my mind begins to wander. I remember being a young girl before Dominion. I remember sitting on my dad's lap while he read bedtime stories to me. He always disguised his voice for each of the characters. He loved me more than anyone else did, including my mother. He never criticized me or made me feel inferior, like my mother did. In his eyes, I was always "good enough." His love gave me confidence, and

I knew I could do anything, be anything. When he died, I lost my way. My protector was gone, and I was left with only my mother. She, just like Dominion, wasn't enough. I needed to stretch my wings and learn how to fly, but all she did was tell me I couldn't. My mother weighed me down with her pragmatism and conceit. At times, I struggled to breathe because I felt so imprisoned by her ego. In many ways, my mother and Dominion are the same. I yearn for something better.

Valentina leaves the stage, and the lights dim. A panoramic screen descends from the ceiling, and the story of Dominion is retold. The horrors of military warfare: death, hunger, and destruction; sexual discrimination and assault; sex trafficking; and hundreds of thousands of children abused, neglected, and living without the love of a family. All of it is highlighted to show the past degradation of women and the rise of a female-led society ushering in peace, harmony, and justice.

As the retractable screens disappear into the ceiling, Valentina returns to the stage and continues her speech. "Women govern this country by leading social reform, protecting the environment, and strengthening the sociopolitical safety of every human being through the eight cabinets. In this new dawn of womankind, women are the policymakers, law enforcers, captains of industry, spiritual leaders, preservers of our nation's history, science, language, and currency, and givers of life. Men serve their vital purpose as domestic partners and public and domestic providers of goods and services essential to the well-being and propagation of the human species. Women have advanced reproductive technology. Now, through genetic editing, we have eradicated some of the deadliest diseases that ravaged our world. Also, we can provide 150 genetic options that have enriched the productivity and societal equilibrium necessary to ensure long-term peace and prosperity for every citizen of Dominion."

"We are deeply grateful to our Breeders. These men are our heroes. They provide the genetic contribution needed to further modify and perfect our offspring. At this time, I ask that the Breeder initiates present for tonight's celebration stand up."

A brilliant light shines on eight Breeders. With their heads bowed, they slowly rise in unison and begin a slow and steady march from the first row to the stage. Each step is cautious and controlled, and their arms are pressed tightly against their sides. The women from each of the eight cabinets stand and applaud.

My face feels hot with shame, and my mind begins to race. This system works for us now because of what we suffered as a nation. But it won't last. Men will not accept their fate for much longer. No one dares address this because we are all afraid of another war. Why do we have to fight to hold onto power when we know that it will not last? Why can't men and women work together as equals?

The ceremony continues to give tribute to the accomplishments of all the cabinets. When the time arrives for the science accolades, my body tenses, and I close my eyes, hoping that my mind will transport me to any place but here. My mother props up in her seat. Her eyes are fixated on Valentina as her body stiffens in anticipation of the adoration she is about to receive. I press my hands together and begin wringing them tightly.

Valentina Cordova is my mother's cabinet leader and close friend. Glancing at the program on my lap, I begin to read the acknowledgment about my mother and her contribution to society. "As a member of the Science community, Linda Matthews is being honored today for developing IQ fencing, the nucleus of our male assignment protocol, *Illegis*. It enables the men of Dominion to fulfill their genetically assigned Singletary roles and become valuable contributors to society."

My mother rises slowly. She squints her eyes against the spotlights that guide her to the podium on the stage. The panoramic screen hanging from the ceiling drops down slowly and begins to display each of the six Singletary groups. The film presents the first group of men who are part of the S1 group, the Benignants. They are teaching and caring for the young and old, giving comfort and hope to the sick, and guarding the helpless. The S2 group, the Assiduites, follow. Their bodies are strong, flexible, and lean. They are dancing, singing, running, playing instruments, and writing. They are bending, twisting, and extending their limbs. Their faces, some sensuous and some fatigued, are vibrant and alive. Their suffering is depicted as their joy. The S3s, the Formalists, are shown attending to clerical details and ensuring the safety of our communities, while the S4, Expeditors, are laboring in public works and building with their hands.

As my mother steps onto the stage, the S5 group, the Breeders, appear in the film. They are holding the gift of life—a baby, swaddled in a white blanket. And lastly, the S6s, the Seducers, are standing tall with robust physiques and gentle smiles, partially hidden in darkness. They are holding the symbol of pleasure, a red apple.

Mother takes a deep breath and waits until the applause dies down.

"Thank you so much. This is truly an honor," she says. "Over twenty years ago, when I developed the assessment prototype for Illegis, I could not imagine that it would become such a pivotal tool in shaping Dominion. Before Illegis, many men and women were barred from opportunities because of standardized test results. Those tests were racially and economically biased. Illegis technology and protocols eliminate these biases and give our citizens choices that weren't available to them before Dominion. Tonight is also about the freedom to choose. The eight men here tonight have chosen to end their service as Breeders, and that's okay. They have provided an invaluable service to our country, and I wish them good fortune and success in their future endeavors.

"I am deeply grateful and honored by the recognition bestowed upon me tonight and the new journey that our eight Breeders are about to begin. I look forward to another twenty years of peace and prosperity for Dominion. Thank you and God bless."

The audience stands, and their applause is deafening. My mother returns to her seat. As she rests her award at her feet, I notice a single tear trailing down the side of her face.

"Mother, what's wrong?" I ask.

"Receiving this award is a great honor, but it reminds me of something I gave up to get it." A cold chill goes through my body.

What are Mother's secrets about? I dare not ask at this moment. For the next two hours, I watch and listen to countless speeches and media footage aggrandizing the success of Dominion and its leaders. I feel more deflated and melancholy. All this talk about peace and prosperity is a lie. There's no mention of the thousands of men and women who live as outcasts, or Dissidents, because they refuse to be labeled or forced into a role they don't want. These people live in desolate communities, with no viable means to make a living, so they steal and kill to survive.

It's a mockery that Valentina is now wearing a long white flowing robe with a hood. She makes her way to the center of the stage. She stands alone, surrounded in darkness.

The stage is soon illuminated with red light, and a spotlight beams on each of the eight men standing on the stage in white robes, with hoods covering their bowed heads. "The men you see standing before you are our heroes. They will be ending one phase of their lives as Breeders to start a new journey as civilians. Let us begin the Release Tribute!"

I stare intensely at each of the Breeders, trying to figure out which one is Robbie. Their hoods are covering their faces, and at a distance they appear almost identical. Sometimes, I wonder what it would be like to date a Breeder. I assume most are reserved, given their sheltered lives in the Colony. But Colin doesn't seem to be that way at all. In fact, he seems quite the opposite. I can't wait to see him again. I wonder what he is like as a man, as a lover. Will he tease me and demand attention, or will he shower me with affection? And then there's Robbie. I can't believe I ran into him after all this time. He still makes me tingle inside. I suppose not much can happen there until he finishes his six-week acculturation training.

The men turn counterclockwise to face the west end of the stage and then again to face the back of the stage. Valentina says, "From water you were born, and it is from water that you will be reborn!"

One by one, each of the men walk toward a large, clear tank filled with water. The first man begins to ascend the thirty steps, each step signifying a year of his life. Once the first man reaches the top of the stairs, he removes his hood, steps into a harness, extends his arms so his body forms a perfect cross, and leaps into the tank.

The crowd yells, "Through water, you are reborn!"

One by one, each of the Breeders plunges into the tank and reemerges with his arms extended upward. Cables pull him up until he disappears above the stage. The eighth and final Breeder walks up the thirty steps and repeats the same act. Finally, all eight Breeders have vanished from the stage.

Valentina returns to the center of the stage and says, "We are proud to release these men into the world. Long live Dominion!"

The crowd replies, "Long live Dominion!"

The lights slowly start to change back to soft white. Valentina turns and exits the stage to thunderous applause.

Looking around, I notice that everyone is leaving quietly. The noisy chatter at the beginning of the evening is gone. My mother seems unusually melancholy. *What happened?* I turn and look up at the guest seating area above the main floor. The Breeder section is flooded with security guards. They seem to be searching and questioning the Breeders. Also, dangling from the skylight is a red flag. The last time I saw a red flag was during the riot in Pearson, Quadrant-Five. At least fifty people died that day, and even more were severely injured.

As we make our way toward the aisle leading to the exit, my mother receives a pod alert. She grabs my hand and urges me to follow her to the back stage. Once again, I am expected to follow without question.

CHAPTER FOUR

The sounds of shuffling feet and busy chatter fill the backstage. We make our way to Valentina's dressing room.

My mother knocks. No answer. As she knocks again, she says, "Valentina, are you in there? It's Linda. You messaged me a few minutes ago to come back and meet. What's going on?"

Valentina slowly opens the door. She appears shaken and distraught.

"Val, what's going on?" my mother asks as she enters the room and gently closes the door. I remain outside, closely peering through the long, narrow slit in the door. Their voices are faint, but I can hear them.

"Oh, Linda! Thank God you're here. I was just informed that one of the Breeders has escaped. Security is looking for him right now." Val sighs and begins to pace the room.

"Why would a Breeder escape?" my mother asks. "That doesn't make sense. He's essentially guaranteed a life of comfort once he reenters civilian life."

"Unless he plans to join the resistance instead," Valentina says. "You know there have been instances of Breeders escaping, but it's usually while they're in the Colony."

She sits down in the vanity chair.

"Well, I can't imagine he'll get very far unless he's being aided by someone on the inside," my mother says. "Maybe that's why he escaped now. His accomplice was here tonight."

Unable to understand what they are saying, I step into the dressing room. There are four bare beige walls, with a vanity against the wall to the right and one open window above a chair. Directly below the window, there is an object wrapped with a gray towel on the chair and shattered glass on the floor.

"Excuse my interruption. It's becoming very hectic in the hallway outside. I hope you don't mind if I join you," I say.

"No, not at all. Your mother is such a wonderful friend. I don't know what I would do without her," Valentina says and fondly embraces my mother.

As my mother consoles Valentina, a security guard steps into the room.

"Ms. Cordova, we have not located the Breeder yet. We noticed glass fragments on the floor beneath that window," he says while pointing.

"I believe the Breeder wrapped your portal with the towel to bust open the window and escaped. We scanned the window, portal, and chair for prints and DNA. We'll know more shortly. It might be best if you allow us to escort you out of the theater."

"Is a security detail necessary?" my mother asks the officer.

"Linda, it's okay. Let's go," Valentina says.

She makes her way toward the dressing room door when a woman enters. She is tall and intimidating, rather husky for a woman. She is wearing black pants and a black leather jacket. She introduces herself to Valentina, my mother, and I as Detective Monahan and begins to ask Valentina a series of questions.

"Ms. Cordova, I am sure all of this must feel quite unsettling. For now, it appears that the escape occurred in this room." Detective Monahan's disposition is calm and direct. Like a hawk, she is able to zero in on the inconspicuous clues.

"What time did you arrive here?" Detective Monahan asks.

"Just before 2 p.m. I remember my pod alarm sounding as I entered the dressing room," Valentina says as she sits in her vanity chair and begins fiddling with the gold tassels on her dress.

"Was your arrival time planned?"

"Yes, I was scheduled for a program run-through at 2:30 p.m."

"Who else was aware of your schedule?" Detective Monahan stands completely still, delivering a piercing stare as she observes Valentina's responses.

"Well, my assistant, Drina, and the program planners here at the shrine. Possibly others. I am not aware of them all," she says as she begins to breathe rapidly and wring her trembling hands.

"Ms. Cordova, besides the broken glass on the floor and towel wrapped around the portal, is there anything else that seems out of place?"

Valentina looks around the room slowly. Sucking her teeth, she abruptly stands up and begins pacing. "No . . . I don't think so," she says with an uncertain tone.

"I know this must be frustrating. You are focusing on the physical space and what you see around you, but what about something you were supposed to see?"

"What do you mean?" Valentina looks confused. Before Detective Monahan can respond, Valentina screams, "The VIP keycard . . . the escape key card is missing! The keycard was supposed to be delivered to my room by the time I arrived. I noticed it wasn't here and informed the event planner. I remembered when I reported it, he noted that the keycard was delivered just minutes before I arrived. He said that he would follow up, but I never heard back from anyone about it."

"What's the keycard for?" Detective Monahan asks.

"It's for leaving the premises through a secured exit route. My assistant, Drina, suggested I get one in case of emergency. The MAO riots are becoming increasingly violent, and she noted that it would be a reasonable safety measure."

"Did Drina accompany you to the shrine?

"No, she arrived early to make sure my accommodations were in order and left shortly after I arrived."

"So, surely, if Drina was making your arrangements, she would have noticed that the keycard was not present yet. She didn't report the matter to you or the security team?" Detective Monahan says while recording a message in her pod. "Ms. Cordova, I'd like the contact information of your assistant, please."

"Of, course. You don't think she had something to do with this, do you?"

Detective Monahan responds, "At this point, we are just gathering information."

The heavy knocking on the door reverberates throughout the room. More personnel begin to arrive, so I step out of the dressing room. The hallway is flooded with police, event security, and onlookers. I find a secure corner to stay out of the way of the frenzied crowd, but I can still see the entrance to the dressing room. Before I can become too comfortable in my sequestered corner, I see Colin bustling through security only to be stopped by a guard and begin conversing with him. I try to rush over to him, but I'm blocked by a group of security guards just a few feet away from him.

"Colin, over here!" I blurt loudly.

"Dani!" Colin quickly rushes toward me. "What's going on? No one will tell me what happened."

After a few seconds, Colin grabs my hand and leads me with him to the security officer he was speaking with just before I called for him. We approach the dressing room.

"Sir, this is a restricted area. I can't let you in," says the guard at the door.

"This is my mother's dressing room. What happened?" Colin asks again.

"Sir, stand aside, please. Detective Monahan is in the room now, but I will let her know you are here. I'm sure she'll want to speak with you."

"What happened? Tell me what happened!" Colin says, growing frantic.

Before I can catch my breath and explain what I know, the detective appears. "Mr. Cordova, I am Detective Monahan. May I have a word with you?"

Colin slowly responds nervously, "Of course." She leads Colin away from the crowd, and he waves his hand toward me to follow them.

Moving to a private corner, Detective Monahan continues asking questions. Her gaze is intense. "Do you know Robert Cummings?"

"No, I don't know him," Colin replies.

"Did you notice anything unusual this evening?"

"Nothing I would consider unusual," Colin says. "I'm afraid that I'm not going to be much help with this investigation." He looks sheepish. "Detective, I don't understand why there is heightened security for my mother and why you're questioning her. Do you think she's in danger?"

"We don't know for sure, but with the spike in protests, especially on Ascension Day, we can't rule out the threat of kidnapping," the detective says. "Your mother is a high-profile person, so her safety may be in danger."

Detective Monahan becomes fixated on the security camera mounted next to the overhead sconce, directly across from Valentina's dressing room.

"Is there anything else you want to ask me, Detective?"

"Not at this time, thank you."

Colin rushes into the dressing room.

"Excuse me, Ms. Matthews," Detective Monahan says, "I need to speak with you as well."

"Of course," I tell her. "Whatever I can do to help."

She nods. "Earlier this evening, at the cocktail reception, you were seen talking at length with the escapee, Robert Cummings."

"Wait," I say, trying to make sense of what she said. "You're telling me the missing Breeder is Robert Cummings? You make him sound like a fugitive."

"Breeders are expected to follow a very strict code of behavior, and they must return to the Colony following the Ascension ceremony." The detective pulls out her pod. "What did the two of you discuss?" Detective Monahan asks, her tone accusatory.

"I knew Robbie, I mean, Robert, when we were kids. I hadn't seen him since he was twelve. We were catching up. He told me that he'd been in the Colony since then and was going to be part of the Release ceremony tonight. He seemed excited to move on to civilian life."

Even though Robbie seemed somewhat agitated when I asked him about his plans after the six-week program, I think but don't say.

"Did he happen to mention any friends he planned to get in touch with or plans following his release?"

"Nothing I can remember," I reply.

"Ms. Matthews, I realize this is a shock," she says, her face a mask of concern. "If you happen to think of anything, give me a call. Here's my contact information."

She holds out her pod to scan and share contact information.

This is too much. In seconds, my headache went from annoying to obliterating. Rubbing my temples and trying to focus on Detective Monahan's actions, my mother joins us.

"I hope I am not intruding, but Dani, I think we should leave."

"Please, Ms. Matthews, before you leave, can you tell me what Ms. Cordova told you when you met her in the dressing room?" Detective Monahan asks.

As my mother begins to recount every detail, I watch Colin out of the corner of my eye. He's talking to someone on his pod.

"Excuse me for a moment," I say as I walk across the hallway. The crowd has thinned out a bit. Only a few security guards remain standing at Valentina's dressing room door.

"Colin, is there anything I can do?" I ask when he ends the call.

"The security team is escorting my mother home tonight," he says. "She doesn't want my sister, Deanne, and I hovering over her for the rest of the night. Deanne will stay with her tonight, and I'll visit with her tomorrow morning. Let's get out of here. The air is stale here, and I can't breathe."

Looking over at my mother, she is still in deep discussion with Detective Monahan. I message her that I am leaving with Colin, the limousine is parked in Gateway Seventeen, and I will contact her in the morning.

Colin and I walk past security and take the back exit. The cold, biting wind feels prickly against my face as we hurry down the alleyway toward the main street. By the time we reach the sidewalk, a black limousine stops at the curb.

"This is us. Shall we?" he asks.

Exiting the gated parking area, the limousine moves deliberately through the swarm of people gathered at the perimeter of the theater. Their faces, agitated and unyielding, reveal a fierce determination. Some of the protesters remain perfectly still while others move restlessly through the crowd, chanting, screaming, and carrying signs among the police barricades securing a safe exit for the people leaving the theater.

We remain silent for most of the limousine ride until it stops in front of a restaurant. The lights are dim, and it appears closed. Colin takes my hand and guides me out of the limousine. As soon as we approach the entrance, a short, pudgy man, dressed in a chef's coat and black trousers, opens the door.

"Colin! My friend, it is wonderful to see you! And who is this enchanting woman?" the man asks, beaming.

"Franco, this is Dani," Colin says. "I'm sorry for keeping you past business hours, but I need a quiet place away from the public right now, and I'm absolutely famished."

"Of course, my friend," Franco says, waving away Colin's apology. "You are welcome anytime. How about my famous Greek salad and eggplant Romanesco?"

"That will be great." Colin looks at me, and I give an approving nod.

Franco leads us to a quiet booth in the private dining area and disappears into the kitchen.

"None of this makes sense. Why would my mother be so shaken up about an escaped Breeder?" Colin says.

"I'd never met your mom before, but she and my mother are good friends. Perhaps my mother will have some answers?"

His pod begins to vibrate, and he glances at it.

"Do you mind if we get dinner to go?" he asks. "I need to check in with my sister to find out how my mom is doing. And will you connect me with your mom tomorrow? I'd like to find out what she may know about what involvement my mom may have in all of this."

"Sure," I say. "I'll call you in the morning with details. And again, I'm sorry."

Colin excuses himself to speak privately with Franco. A few minutes later, Colin returns.

"Well, that seemed pretty secretive," I say, scooting in next to him.

"No, nothing secretive, just wanted to tell him about tonight. Franco is well connected with the police in Sector Five. I asked him to share any information about the investigation that he can get. I don't trust Detective Monahan to tell us everything she knows.

"How has Franco come about such strong alliances with the police?"

"His niece is a detective. She works out of another quadrant and is well connected."

Franco rushes out of the kitchen with two cotton mesh bags. The aroma of fresh baked bread, tomato, and basil takes over the air. Colin steps away from the table to exchange a sentimental hug with Franco. I join him in thanking Franco for his hospitality, and then we exit the restaurant and head toward the limousine.

As the limousine pulls away, Colin is quiet again. He stares out the window and barely speaks for most of the ride to my place. He places his hand on top of mine and starts to stroke my wrist with his thumb. I slide closer to him and rest my head on the side of his left shoulder.

I am exhausted by the turn of events tonight but also beguiled by this man. He is a delicious mystery I want to uncover repeatedly. I can't stop imagining what it would be like to be with a Breeder. *He's made his choice to remain a Breeder, so what else is left?*

The black stretch limousine pulls up in front of my apartment, and Colin opens the door and steps out. My hands tingle as he guides me to the walkway. His arm pulls me in closer as we walk up the stairs to the entrance. I stop and turn to him.

"I'm glad we met," I say, but before I can say anything else, he brushes the side of my cheek and kisses me, first softly, then long and hard. His lips are warm and soft, and all I know is that I want that again.

CHAPTER FIVE

The traffic is brutal on my way to my mother's house. I was supposed to be there by 11 a.m., and it's already 11:16 a.m. No doubt, I'll hear the usual recriminations about how I'm always late and how it annoys her greatly.

My AV parks in the circular driveway of my mother's Tudor-style home with the perfectly manicured lawn. The walkway is lined with lush ornamental grasses and colorful flowers like daffodils, coneflowers, rhododendron, and begonias. There are also large green containers brimming with greenery. The fragrance delights my senses, and I am excited to see Colin again.

I hope Colin finds the place. It's sequestered by tall camphor trees and Japanese boxwood shrubs on a no-outlet street. I gave him the address: 2034 N. Windsor Lane.

Walking into the house, the foyer is filled with the familiar aroma of blueberry lemon zest Belgian waffles, exotic fruits, and Florentine omelets with spicy tomato basil sauce.

"Mother, I'm here!" I call out.

"Danielle, must you always be late? Join me in the sunroom," she says.

"I told you last night that ten was a bit too early since I had to stop by the office to pick up supplies for my next assignment before I got here. But, as usual, it had to be your way," I say. "Why is that, Mother? Why can't you ever compromise?"

"Never mind about that," Mother says. "Is this new assignment dangerous?"

"Not at all. It has the potential to be one of the biggest stories of my career. I would tell you more about it, but I am sure it would just bore you to tears," I say sarcastically.

She looks at me with a disapproving sneer and takes a sip of her Velvet Eclipse chocolate cocktail, her favorite brunch drink, while settling in the green cushioned patio chair.

"So, what did you think about the event last night? I still can't believe it took this long for you to attend your first Ascension ceremony. I guess I will need to win more awards for you to agree to go again," my mother says with a sarcastic tone.

"It wasn't far off from what I expected. Before you even ask, I have not changed my perspective, but I will tell you what really shocked me." Mother leans in closer, her posture almost electrified by the intrigue. "You'll never guess who I ran into last night," I say.

"I am not going to guess. Just tell me!" Mother says.

"Robbie!" I say.

"You mean little Robbie who used to live next door? Sharon and Idris's son?"

"Yes, can you believe it? And that's not even the most shocking part. Robbie is the escaped Breeder!"

"You're kidding! I never knew that he became a Breeder." And, within seconds, the energy in the room goes flat.

My cheeks flushed fever-hot as I watched the blank stare on her face. Mother's memory is never lacking when she wants to express her disappointment in me. But, conveniently, she claims ignorance to the one thing that broke my heart and forced an indelible wedge between us. She wouldn't let me say goodbye to Robbie before he left for the Colony.

"How can you say you didn't know? Of course you knew, and that's why you betrayed him and me. And, for what? For Dominion. Everything is for Dominion! Why, Mother?" I ask, but she just looks away and continues to drink her cocktail without a sign of emotion.

Adjusting her posture in the seat, Mother responds, "Betrayal? Don't you think you're being a bit overdramatic? Do you recall that I caught you planning to run away from home? Did you expect me to just turn the other way and let you do something so ridiculous?"

Trembling with rage and fisting my hands to steady them, I respond, "This isn't about not letting me run away. This is about you preventing me from saying goodbye to Robbie. You knew he was going to the Colony and that I wouldn't see him for years, if ever. You knew how much he meant to me, and you just stood there, ice cold, unfeeling, and determined to keep me from him.

"What do you want from me, Danielle? I don't recall finding out that Robbie was a Breeder. You never shared that with me, and his parents told everyone that he was going away to boarding school. Anyway, that was years ago. You are an adult now. Act like it!" Mother says.

Realizing that I'm not going to get anywhere with her, I sit in the chair, gazing out the large bay window. I feel frozen with resentment, but I can't just walk away. Colin will be here any second, so I need to save this for another day.

Tucking away my hurt, I give a disparaging little shrug, crack a half smile while delivering a piercing stare, and say, "Anyway, thanks for agreeing to meet Colin. Of course, he's in shock about the escaped Breeder, but he's hoping that Valentina may have shared something with you. His mom is really shaken up about it. He thinks there may be more going on than just this escape. That there's something she's hiding from him because, when Detective Monahan asked her if she was aware of any reason someone would target her dressing room for the escape, he could tell she was lying. Apparently, she has a slight stutter when she is not telling the truth. He also noticed that she slipped a note in her robe pocket, and when he asked her about it, she refused to answer.

"Well, like I said last night, I have—" She's interrupted by the doorbell. Frowning, she leaves the sunroom to answer the door. I can hear her greeting Colin with a warm, hearty introduction and inviting him in for brunch.

Following behind my mother, Colin steps into the room and seems delighted to see the buffet. "This looks amazing!" he says as he greets me with his gleaming smile. He's even more handsome than I remember. While his tall muscular frame, sharp facial features, black curly hair, and dark piercing eyes are appealing, his calm, unassuming demeanor is equally attractive. He takes off his black sports coat to reveal a seafoam-green casual button-down shirt, dark-gray slim-cut trousers, and black loafers. He gently kisses me on the forehead and sits beside me.

"Ms. Matthews," he says to my mother, "I appreciate you taking the time to meet with me this morning."

"No need for such formality. Call me Linda," Mother says, grinning from ear to ear.

"My mind is still reeling from the shock of last night. I sense that there is something more going on than just the Breeder escape that is upsetting my mother. I could tell that she was withholding information to the detective and wouldn't share the contents of the note she slipped in her pocket. My instincts tell me she's keeping something from me. Do you have any idea what else could be going on?" Colin scoots his chair a bit closer to my mother.

"Colin," my mother says, "there is something your mother is not sharing with you. I think it is her way of trying to keep you and your sister from worrying, but she's been receiving death threats. She started getting anonymous calls a month ago. Apparently, her chief of staff had been shielding her from a recent slew of anonymous letters, criticizing her recommendations to deny Singletary reassignments. The letters were escalating from criticisms to outright threats, and she was advised that security would be amplified. She believes the letters were sent by members of the resistance, Polix-Five."

"The militant group that's been bombing Illegis centers around the country?" Colin asks.

Leaning forward to pour a cup of coffee for Colin, Mother says, "Yes, their tactics are violent, and their numbers are scaling rapidly. The letters were sent to the FBI for analysis. I informed Detective Monahan about this last night."

"Also, Detective Monahan thinks that her assistant may have something to do with the Breeder escape. That possibility is deeply disturbing. Drina has been with her for over ten years."

"Mom, don't worry about that now. It sounds like the detective is just questioning everyone. Of course, it only makes sense that she would speak with Drina."

"I will contact Detective Monahan," Colin says, stretching his arms and settling into his chair.

"I'll go with you to see her," I say. "I want to be there for you, and I also want to find out who is behind this. Whoever helped the Breeder escape may be responsible for the threats." Without thinking, I reach out and take hold of his hand.

"Danielle, this is not a news story for you to exploit," my mother says with a hint of concern. "Val is a dear friend, and I don't want these threats to become front-page news."

"I'll be discreet, I promise. Besides, the news is about the Breeder escape. There's no evidence to suggest that it's related in any way to the death threats. My priority is to support Colin and find out who's been threatening Valentina."

I turn to Colin and look deeply into his eyes. "Colin, are you okay with me working on this?"

"Yes, I'm okay with it. The more resources working to solve this, the better. Thank you."

"Well, I guess that settles it," my mother says, sighing before finishing her cocktail.

CHAPTER SIX

Maneuvering through the bustling traffic, Colin and I finally arrive at the Sector Five police station. It's my first time visiting this precinct since the renovation. It's a large building consisting of intersecting blocks clad in concrete, metal, and glass. The station is surrounded by polished concrete planters containing evergreen shrubs. The inside of the police station is organized around a six-story central atrium filled with natural light and partly landscaped with plants and trees. We head toward the security checkpoint. There's only one agent working; he directs us to scan our national IDs and walk through the laser scanners. Detective Monahan's office is on the fifth floor. We walk up the stairs because the elevator is out of service. When we arrive on the fifth floor, also known as the Dissident Investigations Unit, we're met with a frenetic scene.

"Detective Monahan, please," Colin says to the officer sitting closest to the entrance.

"Do you have a name?" the officer asks.

"I'm Colin Cordova. I called her an hour ago, and she asked that I come by."

As we wait, I notice a young man in a chair bobbing his head back and forth and mumbling profanities. Seated next to him is an older man dressed in a tattered brown coat and dirty jeans. He's digging a pencil into the palm of his hand and crying. The data screens are flashing while the officers buzz around the room, moving people to private holding areas, shuffling tablets, and taking statements. Among all of this, the lights in the corner of the room flicker on and off near a dingy window with a large crack.

"Mr. Cordova and Ms. Matthews," Detective Monahan says, emerging from the back. "Glad to see you. Come on back."

We are ushered into a tiny, dimly lit room with a long table and four chairs. There's no window, just four gray walls sporting water stains. The air is stale, even though the wall air-conditioner unit is humming.

"Detective Monahan," Colin begins. "I understand that Ms. Matthew's mother, Linda, shared some information about the threatening letters my mother received. I need to know what you know about who sent them." He speaks without blinking.

"Well, Mr. Cordova," Detective Monahan begins, "all we know at this point is that the letters were mailed in envelopes with local postmarks and were sent over the course of the past month. We've sent all the letters to our lab for residue, fingerprint, and ink testing. Results should be back in a week."

"A week!" Colin exclaims as he leans forward and darts a pensive look at Detective Monahan. "That's a long time. Surely a high-profile case warrants faster testing?" He is clearly agitated. I don't blame him.

"The letters are being evaluated by the FBI, and I have put a rush on it," Detective Monahan explains, "but I can't do more than that. One week is the average, but I expect I may receive the results within the next few days. I don't want to promise something I may not be able to deliver." She takes a deep breath. "Is there any additional information you have to share with me?"

"No, not at this time," Colin says and relaxes back into the chair.

I hesitate at first, then ask, "Detective, I understand the threats are in response to recent recommendations Ms. Cordova made regarding Singletary reassignments, correct?"

"Just one moment," Detective Monahan says and begins thumbing through her tablet.

"Valentina is the head of Singletary Administration, which is the sole decision-making authority when it comes to codifying and executing Singletary assignments. Reassignments are limited to

Breeders awaiting release from the Colony and petitioners claiming extreme hardship as a result of their Singletary assignment. Petitions for reassignment are rarely approved, and the public response to these decisions was becoming increasingly violent. In the most recent incident, Hangar-Eight, one of the major resistance groups, set off one of the deadliest riots to occur in a single year, claiming five lives and injuring twenty-three," I say.

"Yes, that's right," she confirms.

"Then I would expect that you're looking into the resistance groups such as Hangar-Eight and Polix-Five?" I ask. A dull knock at the door distracts Detective Monahan, and she excuses herself for a moment. Colin looks worried. He pulls out his pod and begins messaging someone.

"Who are you messaging?"

"Franco. He can get me the information I need. Detective Monahan is very guarded. She's not telling us everything she knows," Colin replies.

I hope Franco can provide more information for Colin. Resistance groups like Hangar-Eight and Polix-Five move in the shadows. Their underground network is expansive and keeps them well hidden from the police. Their origins date back to the days following Dominion's national charter. Their members include Dissidents and male and female Dominion citizens in good standing who support the Men's Movement. Their rebellions go beyond violent protests to include financial market manipulation, federal and republic security interference, and military weapons theft—the list goes on and on. They won't stop until their version of male equality is established and Dominion is destroyed.

Detective Monahan reenters the room, her demeanor unsteady. Her facial expression is stern, and when her eyes meet mine, she immediately looks away as if she wants to conceal something from me. Sitting back down in her chair, Detective Monahan clears her throat and responds, "So you were asking if we are looking into Hangar-Eight and Polix-Five, and we are. Besides the threats to Ms. Cordova, what else do you know about these agitators?"

"Detective," I explain. "I'm a journalist for the *Beacon*. I did an interview with the leader of Hangar-Eight a year ago. Of course, his true identity was hidden from me, but I'm aware of their agenda to create chaos and destruction. The most important thing you must know is that Hangar-Eight will stop at nothing to overthrow our government. What they want to achieve is well documented. It's how they want to do it that deeply concerns me. About a month before the interview, I covered the bombing of the Illegis Center in Quadrant-Three. Surely you saw the live footage of the eruption of fire and smoke as it engulfed the entire thirty-thousand-foot compound. Ash and metal covered the ground as hundreds of civilians poured out of the dense streets like ants fleeing a collapsed hill. They packed into the train station to escape sheets of glass spiraling from the exploding windows and the black smoke that burned their eyes and tasted like singed metal. Nearly two hundred people died or were injured that day, and Hangar-Eight was responsible for that. The interview details are in the article I wrote. I'll send it to you."

For just a few seconds, Detective Monahan's eyes squeeze shut as if she is trying to concentrate on something. Then she manages to nod.

"Well, Detective, I look forward to hearing from you soon. Thank you," Colin says.

Colin motions quickly toward the door and exits abruptly. I exit alongside him, and we hurry to the stairs.

Once we make it outside of the police station, I squeeze Colin's hand and kiss him on the cheek. He looks down at me as he grazes my cheek with his fingertips and tucks a few of my escaped tendrils back into my topknot.

"Look, last night was a bust with all the commotion. Why don't we try having dinner again tonight?" Colin asks.

"Sounds great, but there's only one condition," I say with a mischievous smile.

"Oh yeah. What's that?" Colin asks as he leans in close. He presses his lips into mine and softly sucks my tongue into his mouth, drawing me into a slow, deep kiss. Lightly, he nips my bottom lip with his teeth, and I feel weak in the knees.

After steadying my stance, I say, "Dinner will be at my place. I love to cook, and I am dying to share a wonderful bottle of wine I bought at the vintage auction in Quadrant Two last month."

"Sounds perfect!" Colin replies as we part ways, and he heads toward his EV.

I head in the opposite direction, and after languishing in the daze of that incredible kiss, I begin thinking about how I can reconnect with Hangar-Eight.

CHAPTER SEVEN

Everything tonight has to be perfect. Preparing for my date with Colin unsettles my nerves. My hands are a little jittery, and it's hard to fasten the clasp of my silver necklace. At least I don't have to worry about my black dress. It hugs my slender frame in all the right places. I hate wearing heels. They seem to slow me down, and that's annoying. As an investigative reporter, you have to stay alert and move fast. I slip on my three-inch black slingback sandals so my five-foot-three self isn't dwarfed by Colin, who is a foot taller than me.

I head down the pale-green hallway outside my bedroom and descend the stairs, thinking of Colin's kiss. Yes, that kiss took me by surprise and left me wanting more.

Colin excites me. Seeing him for the first time was exhilarating. We seem to have an instinctual rhythm that holds me captive and turned on, but I never thought I would seriously date a Breeder. Mother always says a Breeder's future is service to Dominion. The only chance a Breeder has to change his vocation occurs at age thirty, and Colin chose to remain a Breeder. How can I build a future with him?

Heading down the staircase, my senses are overtaken by the light that bathes my living room in the sunset's warm pink-amber glow and the aroma of truffled mushroom lasagna that I slaved over for two hours, making sure everything was perfect. I hurry to the kitchen and take it out of the oven so it can rest before dinner. I don't know why I am so nervous and fidgety. Part of me is excited about the possibilities, and another part is tired of starting over. I've never dated a Breeder before. They seem reclusive and almost above everyone else, but Colin wasn't like that when I met him. He had a warm and inviting smile. He didn't shy away from talking about himself. He made me feel at ease and not like an outsider. Was that just a disguise? Is underneath just a man who is loyal to Dominion and nothing and no one else? Maybe Mom was right. Am I wasting my time and setting myself up for another heartbreak? She says Breeders are conditioned not to desire romantic partnerships because they must procreate for the multitude, and monogamy opposes that. Is he more interested in what I can do to help his mom, or does he really want to get to know me?

The intercom buzzes, and I go to the monitor. My hands feel warm and jittery. I can't wait to see him again. I can't stop thinking about his touch, his mouth, and indulging in him. My lips quiver as I press the button to let him in.

"Come to the tenth floor," I say.

When the door opens, Colin steps into my apartment, and again, his smell of sage and amber intoxicates me. Even though I am a bundle of nerves, surprisingly, I start to feel calm in his presence. He gives me a smoldering gaze, takes off his black leather jacket, and places it on the hallway table. I notice a short, raised, jagged scar snaking across the side of his neck. It was hardly noticeable when I first met him at the Ascension, but for some reason, I am acutely aware of every square inch of his body. More vividly, through his open button-down navy shirt, I see his strong arms and chest. I imagine his chiseled abs and his deep-brown skin stretching down to his adonis belt and disappearing into his black denim trousers that hug his quads so perfectly.

"Come here," he says.

Biting the corner of my lip, I step in closer to him, inhaling his scent even deeper. His hands are strong and pull me in gently. Ghosting his lips over mine, he whispers, "I've been waiting for this all day," and kisses me with a warmth that incinerates my inhibitions.

His caress leaves me wanting more, but I resist and step away to welcome him into my home.

"What a great place. Somehow, I imagined your place a bit differently," he says, looking around.

"Oh yeah, what did you expect?"

"Um, just something more bohemian, with bright colors and a free-spirited vibe."

"Well, as you can see, the color is toned-down, and the structural elements, like the high-beamed ceiling, are artistically unique. But I like that you see me as a free spirit. Care for a drink?"

"Sure. Can you make a Crimson Spell?"

"I believe so. That's made with whiskey, pomegranate juice, and lemon juice, right?"

"Yes, and add a hint of spicy maple syrup if you have it. I'm not drinking much these days, but a few sips won't hurt."

Colin sits in the center of the sectional and adjusts his neck against the headrest.

"You know, I never got to thank you properly for coming to the police station with me earlier today," he says. "I appreciate your support."

"You did thank me. I remember you thanking me just before we went to our EVs." I place our cocktails on the console and sit close to him, adjusting the hem of my dress to show off my toned legs.

"I didn't thank you properly," he says.

He moves close to me and touches my shoulder, then begins to trace his hand down my back to my waist. He embraces me and kisses my forehead and cheek while caressing the small of my back. His scent is intoxicating. When our lips meet, I feel limp in his arms. He kisses my neck and then slowly loosens his embrace. "Thank you."

"How about dinner?" I say as I stand up slowly, giving my knees time to recover.

Colin makes his way to the dining area and sits in the chair facing the kitchen. He looks at me as I prepare our plates. He is so charming and seems to say all the right things, but *Is this real? Is this just a seduction, or is it more than that?* Well, I need to know if he can be more than just a lover—*Where can this go?*

During dinner, he teases me with his smile and hypnotic gaze that slices through me like a razor-sharp blade through butter. He is stupidly irresistible, so I periodically find myself looking away to disrupt this force of nature pulling me in.

I find myself becoming more intrigued by this man. His life as a Breeder fascinates me. He didn't have to accept this fate for himself. He's the son of a cabinet leader. He could have chosen any of the Singletary roles for his vocation, but he accepted the assignment to be a Breeder and serve his country.

The other Singletary assignments are not as honorable. They are roles with little to no distinction other than the fact that they are needed for order, peace, and abundance in Dominion. Once assigned, male children are educated and trained to meet their obligations as workers. Since their paths are known and regulated by the Dominion government, males attend trade schools while the universities are restricted to females. Females are allowed to pursue roles in science, law, politics, literature, just to name a few. This creates a societal divide that's destroying gender equality and human liberties as we once knew it.

"You look deep in thought. What's on your mind?" he asks.

Hesitancy evaporates as my courageous heart forces me to ask, "What was it like for you when you found out you were going to be a Breeder?"

Colin crosses his arms tightly across his chest, takes a deep breath, and responds, "I can remember listening to my teachers explaining the Great War, and the retribution that ensued frightened me at first. I was afraid that I would be condemned to a life of misery and shame, but when I was chosen to become a Breeder, my entire perspective changed. I was not going to be punished but allowed to live a purposeful and comfortable life. Becoming a Breeder was never a burden. It was my salvation, and I am grateful for it."

"Did you know you had a choice?" I start to squirm in my chair and begin circling the outer rim of my glass with my finger.

"What do you mean?" He takes a deep gulp from his glass and sets it firmly on the table.

"You're a cabinet minister's son. You could have rejected the assignment."

Straightening his posture and tilting his head to the side to loosen the stiffness in his neck, he replies, "Yes, but being a Breeder is the greatest honor a male can receive. Valor is demonstrated by helping our nation procreate for survival and not just giving our lives selflessly on the battlefield."

"What about the males assigned to other S-bands? Shouldn't they be honored for their sacrifice as well?" A stony silence creeps into the room.

"Why so many questions about my status? Does it bother you?"

"No, it doesn't bother me. I'm just curious. After all, I am a reporter. It is my nature to probe. I am preparing for an interview with the chief superintendent, Tobias Ludlow, in a few days at the Transformation Center in Keelan, and I am trying to do as much fact-gathering as I can. It took years to get the approvals and clearance for this interview."

Newly assigned Breeders are sent to the Transformation Center for acculturation training before they are deployed to the Colony. Since its inception twenty years ago, no one outside of Dominion government officials, Breeders, and a select group of men have been allowed inside the Transformation Center. Men are sourced from a small town managed by the Dominion military near the Transformation Center. There's so much secrecy about the Breeder training practices at the Transformation Center. There are rumors that extreme isolation, starvation, mind-altering drugs, and torture are used to train the Breeders, but no one has been able to confirm it.

"I've been cleared to explore the entire facility and get an in-depth look at how Breeders are acculturated before they are placed into the Colony. What was it like for you?"

Colin appears pensive, then shrugs it off, stands up, and says, "Let's change the subject," as he heads toward the living room.

We snuggle close to each other on the couch while Neo-jazz plays in the background. I want to get lost in my feelings for Colin, but I keep fighting the urge to understand if being with a Breeder is the right choice for me. Pulling back from his embrace, I lean against the sofa pillows. Struggling with the hesitancy in my voice, I ask, "Is this all there can ever be between us?"

"What do you mean?"

"From the moment I met you, Colin, I felt a strong connection. As much as I want to let go and just fall into these feelings, I am afraid."

I've had only four past relationships. Each of them lasted no more than two years. The sex was great—maybe too great—and that made me stay longer than I should've. But there was always something missing, a closeness, a sense of intimacy that I longed for but never got. It seems like every time I meet someone I care for, there is a barrier to our relationship—my career ambition, fear of commitment, or just outright selfishness. So, I became a serial dater; it is convenient and shields me from getting hurt. But I don't want the fear of getting hurt to deprive me of the love I want. Sometimes I think I want the kind of love that devours my heart and soul; then fear sets in. Fear of becoming too dependent on someone else for my happiness haunts my desires. Also, what it takes to become a "we" from an "I" scares me, so I hold back my heart in anticipation that he will do something to justify my fears.

"So, Colin, is this all we'll ever have? I mean, you live in the Colony, separated from everyone else. You can't marry, have children of your own, or even work outside of the Colony. As much as I like you, all I see are roadblocks to having any kind of future with you. Am I mistaken to feel this way?"

Moving in closer, he strokes my hair and grazes his lips against my neck, then starts to suck my ear lobes gently. I begin to quiver all over, the warmth of his mouth scrambling my brain.

"I'm serious, Colin. Answer my question," I say as I pull away again.

"Dani, you are not wrong to feel the way you do. Dating a Breeder does come with limitations, but you seem to think that I can't choose to leave."

Looking lost, I reply, "I don't understand. You're saying that you can end your Breeder status anytime you want?" My eyes and ears suddenly perk up.

"Well, yes and no. I can petition for a change in my Singletary status, and if approved, I can exit. The catch is that if I leave, I lose all of my benefits."

I grab my wine from the console and sit up straight, my back barely touching the sofa pillows, and ask, "What do you mean?"

"Dani, when I turned thirty and chose to remain a Breeder until recommission, I relinquished my rights to the 'New Life Benefits,' which are granted to released Breeders in their thirtieth year. Released Breeders are set up with a whole new life: new residence, Singletary position, and retraining. They also receive a monthly stipend for twelve months following their release. Breeders who recommit at the age of thirty and then revoke their commitment get nothing but a meager release bonus, Singletary reassignment, limited retraining, and temporary housing. The standard of living is a far cry from what a Breeder is used to in the Colony, which is why few Breeders revoke their commitment. But the point is that it is possible for me to leave." Staring at the subtle glimmer of the patio light tracing through the window, Colin says, "Look you do have reasons to be hesitant, but it isn't as hopeless as you think. There is a way, if that is where this goes."

"You've given me a lot to process. I think I just need some time to settle in with what you just told me," I say as I drain the wine from my glass and settle back into his arms.

"Look, we don't have to rush this. I think this may be a good time to end the evening. I really like you, Dani, and I hope you will be okay with seeing me again. I like that you feel comfortable enough to tell me how you feel. It's refreshing," Colin says as he regrettably pulls away from my embrace.

"You don't have to leave," I say. "I want you to stay." I pull him close to me again and kiss him passionately.

"You have no idea how much I want to stay, but I better leave before this goes any further," he says hesitantly.

"Well, okay, but tell me why," I say as I sit up and straighten my dress.

"Have you heard of the *Contribution*?" he asks.

"Sort of. Doesn't it require Breeders to donate their seed for testing and reproduction?"

"That's part of it," he says. "The *Contribution* occurs four times a year. Breeders are required to observe strict dietary, fitness, and mental agility goals to ensure the highest potency and quality of our seed for the reproductive panel. I must abstain from sexual intercourse a minimum of seven days prior to the *Contribution*. It's tomorrow."

"Ah," I say, understanding. "So, besides controlling when you can have sex, what are the other constraints?"

"That's just a minor inconvenience that only occurs four times a year. It's a small price to pay for the lifestyle we have. We live in luxurious, state-of-the-art living quarters and have healthy, gourmet meals. There's daily housekeeping, holographic entertainment, and rewarding work. We not only contribute our seed but also work within the system to secure and support our way of life."

"What exactly does that mean?" I ask. "What you describe almost sounds like confinement with a few luxuries to keep you quiet. Is that enough for you?"

"Confinement? Not at all. My choice to serve Dominion comes with certain obligations, just as your work does. I live in a community that recognizes my commitment and rewards me for it. That hardly sounds like confinement. Clearly, you envision our life at the Colony to be rigid and confined. If that was the case, I wouldn't be here."

"I know that my inquisitive nature can be a bit overbearing at times, so I'm sorry if you feel like I am attacking you. I'm not. I've had very limited experience with Breeders on a personal level, so be patient with me?"

"Listen," Colin says. "The best way to help you understand is to let you visit the Colony. How about I arrange a visit for you the day after tomorrow?"

"I would love to visit, but it is going to have to be after I return from my assignment."

"There's something I want you to keep in mind. The next time I'm alone with you in close quarters, I have every intention of finishing what we started tonight."

Giving away control is not something I like to do. Whether we fall in love or not, I still want to fuck him tonight. The idea of defiling the Contribution is arousing me. He's not fooling me with that little "good boy" act. I feel his desire to seduce me, and right now, that's the most seductive thing about him. Seduction is what I do best. Moving in closer with just the right amount of intensity in my eyes, I touch his warm lips with my hands. I kiss his neck gently; then he brushes my hair back from my shoulder and moves in so close, I can feel his lean body pressed up against me. When I feel his resistance crumbling, I continue to tease him until I know he will give in; then, I pull back. I'll let him leave, but I want his body to ache all over for me so he knows I let him leave on my terms and not his. Besides, I may decide not to fuck him at all. One of the cardinal rules of journalism is "Never fuck your source." On the other hand, he's not an official source yet, so for now, I am okay. "I will see you soon," I say with a mischievous smirk.

"Can't wait," Colin says. He walks toward the front door, picks up his jacket, and kisses me before he leaves.

"I can't believe I'm falling for a Breeder," I say quietly to myself as I close the door behind him.

CHAPTER EIGHT

The next morning, on the way to work at the *Beacon* office, I contemplate the possible angles for the Breeder escape story. I've been nervous about eating anything this morning. Just the thought of food nauseates me. My mind is jam-packed with several possible culprits behind the Breeder escape. My first hunch is to follow up with my contacts in the resistance groups, Hangar-Eight and Polix-Five. As my EV glides on the blacktop road, I screen through my pod, searching for the multiple aliases I used to identify the resistance POCs. My mind is scrambling for what to say once I call. These people will sniff out bullshit in a minute, so my reason for calling has to be legit. I'm not sure they'd cop to helping a Breeder escape. I need more time to figure out my approach, so I redirect my thoughts to possible connections with Valentina's personal life. I remember Valentina swaying back and forth nervously, rhythmically tapping her foot on the floor, and sounding agitated when responding to Detective Monahan's questions. She appeared as if she was concealing something. Colin doesn't believe she has any enemies, and my mother seems dumbfounded as well. Thinking about how I might get in touch with Valentina's assistant, my EV pulls into the garage and parks in a space just below the office building.

The underground parking garage of the *Beacon* building is pitch-black except for a few security lights illuminating the entryway. I rush to the elevator, and during my ride to the twenty-fifth floor, I keep replaying how I'm going to pitch this story to Samantha, my editor.

She's a hardcore newswoman, and chances are she's already assigned someone to investigate this story.

Stepping out of the elevator, I can hear the random gabble of reporters as they exit the elevator next to me and move fast across the hallway and into the *Beacon* office. Following a few feet behind them, I enter and make a beeline for Sam's office. Even though her door is closed, I can see through the large floor-to-ceiling plate glass wall that she's on the phone. Sam is a woman of few words. She's all about getting things done and doesn't shy away from a challenge, no matter how difficult. She sat in jail for several months because she refused to disclose the name of her informant in a case that could have significantly advanced her career. When Sam is agitated, she doesn't rant or rave; she speaks with focused intention and authority.

Right now, she is rubbing her temples while pacing the floor, so she must be livid about something. I lean next to Sam's door, hoping to overhear why she is so angry. As I wait for her to finish her call, I walk over to the end of the hallway, and the door to the corner office is open. I overhear Amanda Peterson, one of *Beacon*'s lead journalists, requesting information on the Breeder escape story. She's trying to speak to the head of security at the amphitheater.

While on hold, she says to her assistant, "I am getting nowhere with this. The police are stonewalling me. My inside contacts don't even know what's happening. All I could get from them is that some new detective is handling the case, and they don't know the name."

She hands her assistant the tablet and snaps, "Stay on hold while I look for another source, and hand me the tablet when someone finally answers!" Amanda begins anxiously rummaging through her rolodex. Sounds like she isn't getting very far. As I sigh with relief and chuckle at the prospect that I have the edge on Amanda, she glances at me through the glass wall with a condescending sneer. Since she won the Sidney Journalism Award for exposing an underground vigilante group that was trafficking male minors out of the country, she acts like she's the Queen Bee and we are her drones around here. Well, I am just as good as she is—actually better because I have an ease with people that makes them comfortable enough to tell me just about anything. Amanda has to resort to bribery and blackmail to get what she wants. She's not respected. She's feared, or some folks would even say hated. One day her mouth is going to write a check that her ass can't cash, and all I know is that I want a front-row seat to see the fireworks. I immediately make a beeline back to Sam's office and lean over to see what she's doing.

"Dani, whatcha got for me?" Sam says as she opens her door and rushes back to her desk.

"Listen, Sam," I say, following her inside. "I was at the Ascension Gala Saturday night and already have the inside track on the Breeder escape. The lead detective is talking to me. And I have a direct connection to one of the suspects. It's my story, Sam, and I want it!"

"Well, well, aren't you ambitious," she says with a sly smile. "I'm actually a bit surprised that you are putting a stake in the ground on this story almost two days after the escape. You're kinda late to the party. That's not your MO. What gives?"

"I just needed time to validate my leads and their stories. So far, I've visited Valentina Cordova in her dressing room, which was the location of the crime scene. I met with the lead detective and know that she thinks this was the work of one of the resistance groups. I also have reason to believe that Polix-Five or Hangar-Eight may be involved, and you know I have contacts with both groups. You remember, after the bombing of Illegis Center in Quadrant-Five, I wrote the piece, 'The Reign of Terror'? I interviewed the leaders of Hangar-Eight and Polix-Five. It took months for me to get the connection for that story. I still have those contacts. Just let me pursue this route, and if my hunch is wrong, I will step back," I say with an unwavering look of confidence.

Sam says, "Well, I'll tell you, Dani, one thing I like about you is your hunger for a good story. You like to get in the trenches, and I like that. It certainly sounds like you're making headway. The problem is, Amanda is already all over this. Not sure I want to pull her off right now."

"Come on, Sam," I plead. "You've reassigned jobs a million times. Besides, Amanda just started. It doesn't sound like she's making much headway, and I have the inside track!"

"Just a minute. Wait here," Sam says.

She darts out of her office, closes the door, and approaches Amanda, who is talking to Sam's admin, Olian, whose desk is directly outside of Sam's office. I can't hear what they're saying, but Amanda is clearly upset. Sam pats Amanda on the shoulder and makes her way back to her office. Through the plate glass window in Sam's office, Amanda glares at me with a stone-cold look of disgust and walks away.

Sam is back at her desk. "Okay, it's yours, Dani," she says. "I want an update in seventy-two hours. Now get out of here!" She smiles smugly and shoos me out of her office.

I head to one of the unoccupied community offices and slip in quietly to make a call. About a year ago, I interviewed the leader of Hangar-Eight, Kalix. I suspect that if Hangar-Eight had anything to do with Valentina's threats, Kalix will claim it. He wants the world to know that Hangar-Eight is a major threat and will seek retribution by any means necessary. I send an urgent message to Jetzen, the middleman I worked with to secure the Hangar-Eight interview. I hope I can connect with him soon.

By the time I make it to the lower level of the parking garage, my pod rings. "This is Dani," I say anxiously.

But no one speaks. There's just heavy breathing mixed with the sound of an engine revving up in the background.

"What do you need?" a voice says forcefully while an engine cranks up even louder.

"Is this Jetzen?" I ask.

Still no response. Just more heavy breathing, and then a voice blurts out, "Get to it!"

"This is Dani Matthews from the *Beacon*. I called this number a year ago to arrange a meeting with Kalix," I say clumsily. "I am researching the recent Breeder escape from the amphitheater and the death threats made to Valentina Cordova. I want to confirm if Hangar-Eight is behind the escape, the threats, or both." A few seconds of dead silence precedes an undistinguishable response. "I can barely hear you. What's that?" I say, urging him to speak clearly. I can sense the trepidation in his voice as he starts to utter his response.

"No, it's not Hangar-Eight for the escape or the threats," he restates impatiently. The engine roars then releases a faint hissing sound.

I can hear a voice in the background shouting, "Hey, Jetz, are you coming?"

"Shut up!" Jetzen yells.

"Why did you hesitate before you answered my question? How do I know you are telling me the truth?" I say. "Is this Jetzen?"

"Hangar-Eight doesn't back down from anything. We own what we do," he responds unapologetically. "If you have to guess my name, you have no business calling this number in the first place."

Next, I hear the sound of a disconnect buzzing in my ears.

After shuffling through my rolodex, I find the contact number for Polix-Five. I dial the number, and within seconds, the call dies. I try again and again, and still no live connection.

Well, I guess I am back to square one. Only this time, I have a deadline.

CHAPTER NINE

The commute from the *Beacon* offices to my apartment takes about ten minutes. Rushing into my EV, I get in and launch the command "Home." The EV pulls out of the parking garage and begins the journey. While staring out of the window, my mind drifts to my chance encounter with Robbie. It was so random, and I was completely unprepared. So many times, I imagined what it would be like to see Robbie again. Instead of saying what needed to be said, I was a coward. So many questions swirled around in my head, and I just couldn't think straight, so I smiled to hide my feelings. I doubt he could tell how badly I wanted to hug him and tell him how much he meant to me. Feelings of regret haunted me whenever I thought about Robbie. I regret not saying goodbye when he told me he was going away to live in the Colony eighteen years ago. At that time, I was just eleven years old, just two years after I lost my father. I felt stiff and hesitated to speak. I just shook my head in agreement when Robbie asked me to run away with him, but I didn't do it. *She* took him away from me just like she did with my father.

As my EV passes by a field of naked trees, their dormancy reminds me of the stiff, almost petrified look Robbie had on his face when I asked him about his plans after acculturation. I could sense that he wanted to say something, but he hesitated. Why didn't I probe the matter? My mind was focused on getting back to my mother since the cocktail party was ending and I knew she wanted to make a beeline to the seating area. I let her needs pull me away from Robbie then, and now it happened again—I won't let her take Robbie away from me again.

The EV parks in my underground parking space, and I hurry to the elevator and take it to the tenth floor. By the time I make it through the front door, all I can think about is taking off my shoes, making a Shadow and Smoke cocktail, and relaxing on my balcony while the sun sets. The feeling of my bare feet on the cool, dry surface feels liberating. It reminds me of my childhood when I ran free on grass or the beach. As soon as the sun sets, I start to feel chilly, so I go inside to grab a sweater. While running up the stairs, I hear the sound of a door creaking open. Looking to the left toward my bedroom, then to the right, I'm startled to find Robbie standing in the doorway of my guest bedroom.

"Robbie!" I nearly scream. "What are you doing here?"

"I'm sorry I scared you, Dani. I just need a place to stay for a couple days. Is that okay?"

"How did you get in?"

"You'd be surprised by the banned security devices people like me have access to."

"Okay, something tells me that is a conversation for a later date. There are more important matters to address." Rushing toward him, I place his hand in mine and deliver a pensive stare. "The police are looking for you," I tell him. "Does anyone know you're here?"

"No, I was staying at a friend's place, but the police snatched him up and took him in for questioning. He sent me a warning to leave right away. I barely got out before the police showed up. Listen, if this is too much for you, I can leave. I just didn't have any other safe place to go."

"No, it's okay," I say. "I knew something wasn't right when you practically froze up the other night when I asked you about your plans after leaving the Colony. I'm so sorry, Robbie."

"Sorry for what?" he asks.

"Sorry for doing the same thing the other day that I did when you went away to the Colony eighteen years ago," I say, not meeting his gaze.

"Dani, you didn't do anything wrong." He put his hand on my shoulder reassuringly.

"Exactly, I did nothing then, but it's going to be different now, Robbie," I say. "You can stay here as long as you need. You can stay in the guest room. Just freshen up, relax, whatever you need. I'll make us some dinner. You must be hungry."

This is my do-over, a chance to say what I was too scared to say the other night. I will tell him everything, and this time *she* can't hurt us again.

CHAPTER TEN

I prepare two trays, each containing a plate of herb-roasted portobello mushrooms in a truffle butter sauce, mac and cheese, collard greens, and Frostbite lemonade. I remember when Robbie and I were kids, he always liked my mother's roasted mushrooms and mac and cheese; it was his favorite. Our family picnics were one of my fondest memories with Robbie, so I spread a large picnic blanket on the living room rug and set the trays on it. I hurry up the stairs and knock softly on the guest room door. Robbie answers, "Come in."

"I hope you're hungry," I say. "I made all your favorites." I smile.

"That must mean there's some mac and cheese!" He laughs.

"Come on down," I reply.

We sit on the picnic blanket in the living room, enjoying our meal. As the golden haze from the sunset kisses our faces, we revisit every funny prank, mischievous deed, and fond memory we have of our childhood together. Memory is a strange thing. Recollections make their way in and out of my mind, drifting endlessly, and this time, with Robbie, they feel so special. The memories of our childhood are sweet and then tainted by the harsh disappointment of him leaving for the Colony.

Gripping the red-and-white checkered napkin tighter in my hand, I gaze into Robbie's eyes. They are so different from what I remember at the gala—softer and reminiscent of what we shared when we were younger. I can feel that our zest for adventure and restless spirits remain untamed. Life almost seems suspended in time when our eyes lock.

"Robbie, I regret so much about the way we parted. I was angry at you for leaving, and I let that anger prevent me from reaching out to you." Suddenly, sitting on the floor feels uncomfortable, so we move to the couch while our gaze at each other remains uninterrupted.

I continue, "It wasn't until you left that I realized that I loved you. I loved how I felt when I was with you: safe, unafraid. I knew that we could accomplish anything together. Being with you gave me a sense of security, and you took that away when you left." Moving closer to me, Robbie gently takes hold of my hands. "For the past eighteen years, I have struggled to find the kind of undeniable connection we had, and each time I failed, I told myself that the next time would be different. Until finally, I told myself that what we had was rooted in childish fancy and not realistic now. Am I right to think that, Robbie?"

A hazy, moonlit glow fills the living room. "Dani, what we had wasn't childish. We were lucky enough to find each other when we were kids, and what we shared was special. I feel a strong connection to you, but a lot has happened over the past eighteen years, and we have to give ourselves the chance to get to know each other again. Is that okay with you?"

"Absolutely," I reply as I cuddle next to him and lean my head on his shoulder.

"Robbie, why did you escape?" I ask softly. "You were about to be free and live your life as you choose. Why throw that away by doing this?"

"Dani, what do you know about the life of a Breeder after he chooses to be released?" he asks with a perturbed look.

"I know that Breeders are reassigned and prepared for civilian life, which, from what I'm told, seems pretty comfortable. Breeders are provided with a safe and stable livelihood when they leave the Colony, a generous stipend, a place to live in a secure, high-end community, and they can marry, sire more children, and live a successful and gratifying life." As I spoke, I realized I was reciting what I'd been told over the years and what Colin reaffirmed.

"Just as I feared," he says. "You know nothing. Or rather, you know what Dominion wants you to know. You think being set up in a nice house with a stipend and the right to marry and have a job that the government assigns to me is gratifying? My right to a gratifying life was taken away from me the moment I was assigned to become a Breeder. The life of a Breeder, Dani, both in and out of the Colony, is manipulated and engineered to be anything but gratifying. Breeders aren't treated like men—we're robots doing Dominion's bidding. Everything that makes us unique individuals is taken away from us, and all that's left is the shell of a man. I want out now while I have the chance. I don't want to live the life I'm allowed to live but the life I *want* to live. Dani, I escaped because I want to join the resistance and fight for justice." Robbie takes a deep breath and gives me a hard stare.

"The resistance? You mean Polix-Five or Hangar-Eight? Robbie, that's a death sentence."

"No, Dani, it's freedom, and, more importantly, it's the chance to live," Robbie replies.

"What do you mean by a chance to live?" I ask as I nestle my head squarely on his shoulder and gaze directly at the silver ceiling light.

"Most of the Breeders who choose to be released are not acculturated back into civilian life. They're sold as Breeders on the global black market. After the war, many foreign countries were not as fortunate as Dominion. Most of the male population was severely hampered intellectually, and their source for quality breeding was significantly limited. Dominion supplies these countries with Breeders for genetic modification and propagation. Only a few are allowed to live as civilians—the male children of wealthy and powerful women. The released Breeders are used to perpetuate the falsehood that released Breeders are happy and living well in our society, but in reality, most of them are sold like slaves and dead within five years."

I feel numb and unable to move. This can't be real. "How do you know this?" I ask.

"One of the squadron leaders of Polix-Five is a Breeder who was sold on the black market and escaped back to Dominion to join the resistance. He's helped hundreds of Breeders escape their fate. He's also been the driving force behind driving change within the Singletary reassignment process. It's just another method Dominion uses to control and diminish the value of men."

"Speaking of the escape, why did you exit from Valentina Cordorva's dressing room?"

"It was meant to send a message that she can't prevent the inevitable—that Breeders will be free and there's nothing she can do to stop it."

"So it was Polix-Five behind the escape—I knew it!" I say triumphantly.

"Well, yes, why are you grinning from ear to ear?"

"Well, Robbie, I am an investigative reporter, and I am covering the Breeder escape story, but don't worry. I have no intention of interfering with your escape plan. I do, however, want to uncover this Dominion conspiracy you are telling me about, and I want to interview the Dissidents behind the threats on Valentina Cordova's life. It sounds like Polix-Five."

"Dominion cabinet officials keep their deception hidden from the public so they can continue to feed you lies and give you a false sense of security about this new world order we live in," Robbie says.

At that moment, any sense of doubt I had vanished, and I was left with the gnawing, aching truth that I was living a lie. I knew I couldn't be a part of this any longer. I took a deep breath, looked into Robbie's eyes, and asked the question I should have asked eighteen years earlier: "What can I do?"

CHAPTER ELEVEN

Lying in bed that night, I feel numb all over. Robbie's account of the Colony was so vastly different from Colin's. Clearly, as the child of a prominent family, Colin was afforded opportunities that most Breeders weren't. I must know what Dominion is hiding, no matter the cost. My burning desire for the truth has been with me since my father died and became even stronger after Robbie left all those years ago. No one's explanation—including Robbie's—seems adequate.

I stumble out of bed and head to the bathroom. The coldness of the hard tile stings my feet, and as I look into the mirror above the bamboo vanity, I am startled to see the face of someone who looks like me but is different. My eyes are still round but not quite as soft in appearance. My skin is still smooth and taut but not quite as dewy. The look of innocence is beginning to fade, and this adult child I see is becoming someone I have waited for. Facing the truth about Dominion, Robbie, and myself is changing me into the woman I am meant to be.

After a hot shower, I am refreshed and ready to tackle the illicit truth. I rush down the stairs to the kitchen and see Robbie standing in front of the sliding glass door, staring into the azure-blue sky and the soft morning light.

"Good morning," I say in a chipper, lighthearted tone.

"Mornin'," he responds. He turns to face me. "When I came here yesterday, it was my intention to lay low for a day or two until I could reconnect with my contact and leave." I nod, waiting for him to continue. "Well, it appears he's being detained indefinitely by the police, so I need to find another way. This is going to be dangerous, and if we're caught, I don't have the resources to protect you. Are you sure you want to help me?"

"Robbie, we can help each other. I can help you get to your final destination, and when we get there, you can help me get in so I can get the story. There's so much more to this than I thought. So, yes, I'm in. What do you need me to do?"

"Without my contact, I'm unable to arrive at the connect location as planned. The password changes every five days, and with two days already gone, I'll need to get the new password in the next seventy-two hours so that I can travel to the connect location."

"Password?" I ask.

"Escapees travel via the passage to Haven, the settlement of Polix-Five, using passwords that change with every stop along the way. Without it, I won't be able to make contact with the first connect on my journey, and I'll be stranded. I need the new password before we leave, but with my contact in police custody, there's only one other source for this information."

"What is it?" I ask.

"He's called The Broker," Robbie explains. "He's a Breeder who lives in the Colony. I need you to make contact with him and get the password. If I go back there, I'll get caught."

"Okay," I say. "How do I get in?"

"I saw you talking to a Breeder at the Ascension reception," Robbie says. "How well do you know him?"

"Well enough to visit him at the Colony," I say. "As a matter of fact, he invited me to visit him tomorrow. How can I make contact with The Broker and get this password once I'm there?"

"Perfect. My contact is expected to connect with The Broker daily to confirm the status of the escape," Robbie explains. "That contact didn't connect with The Broker yesterday since he was in police custody. The broker will be on the lookout for a connect with the *recovery* password, which notifies him that another password is needed to resume the escape plan. He will be working in the Architectural study room of the library."

"So, now all I have to do is get the new password. Somehow, I suspect that will not be easy," I say.

"I always plan better when I eat," Robbie says. "Breakfast?"

Moments later we head to the kitchen, and, over hot bourbon coffee, beignets, and Indian Marsala omelets, Robbie and I draft a plan for me to connect with The Broker and begin his journey to Haven.

CHAPTER TWELVE

It's now just seventy-two hours until Robbie and I have to reach our first stop on our way to Haven. Before we can start our journey, I must complete an assignment and travel to the Colony to get the password from The Broker. There's no room for error—timing is everything. This is typical. I'm usually under pressure to deliver, and this assignment is shaping up to be no different. The escape is only a small part of a much bigger story. The real story is what I will confirm about the Transformation Center. I will expose the truth that Breeders aren't free to choose, and Dominion is involved in a cover-up.

I'm traveling to the airport to take a helicopter to Keelan, a small community located in the Third District. Keelan is the location of the Transformation Center, where all twelve-year-old males, newly assigned to the Breeder class, are sent for training before moving to the Colony. Recently released Breeders, at the age of thirty, also come to the Transformation Center to prepare for a new life outside of the Colony. In both cases, the Transition is rumored to be long and harsh despite the Dominion account that it is kind and humane. Tales about mind-altering drug use, brainwashing, heat stress, and sleep deprivation are the most frequently cited incidents. Also, the Colony is heavily guarded. The people who work there are completely devoted to the mission to ensure the preservation of Dominion. Everything about the Transformation Center is shrouded in secrecy, so it is not surprising that it has taken almost two years for the *Beacon* to get an exclusive interview with the chief superintendent, Tobias Ludlow.

Of course, the *Beacon* will send its most tenacious news team, which is why Trevor and Isaac, the production crew, and I got the assignment. I waited years for a break like this. This story is a challenge that I gladly accepted. I am known for being unrelenting, thorough, and—most importantly—a risk taker. I don't let fear conquer my pursuit of the truth. I know that I can get behind all the political rhetoric about the Transformation Center and expose the hypocrisy.

Everything I've ever read or saw about the Transformation Center is always so perfect . . . almost too perfect. There are seven Transformation Centers across the twenty-six Dominion Republics. Each one is located in remote areas, only accessible by aircraft or boat. The Transformation Center in Keelan is the largest and was the first to be established. The people who work at the Transformation Centers are required to live in the Center or its nearby surroundings. It is rumored that once a person dedicates their service to the Transformation Center, they never leave, and that is hard to verify since the workers are never officially disclosed to the public. Of course, people who live in the surrounding communities know more about what really goes on, but their livelihood is dependent on the Dominion government. Not many people are willing to risk their health and security to expose the secrets of the Transformation Center, and even if someone was, they wouldn't expose their families and loved ones to the consequences.

I dive headfirst into uncovering every piece of research I can about the establishment of the Transformation Center, but I soon find that I have to dive in well before that time. The realities that shaped the purpose and role of the Transformation Center occurred well before it was established, and in some ways, those realities remain a mystery. Male infertility and cognitive impairment, which affected the majority of males, were unexpected outcomes of the war, as were pollution, depleted resources, defaunation, etc., and with the millions reported dead, panic ensued. A deadly bacterial plague, called "The Crippler," caused full-body paralysis, then death, and our leaders decided to quarantine the sick. The quarantine locations were located at twenty ports of entry and land-border crossings. The ban on entry to the United States and domestic migration was instituted and lasted for one year. During that time, the states were reconfigured based on geographic borders such as rivers, mountains, and the construction of the new hyperloop trains powered by maglev technology and active suspension systems designed to travel through all twenty-six republics. The female senators and congresswomen at the time bonded together to form the eight cabinets, and Allura Yakubu was elected by the governing body as interim president. To solidify her power as quickly as possible, Allura led the establishment of the Colony. It was positioned as a fundamental solution to obtaining stability. It was also the gateway to many technological advancements, like Illegis. Allura built her entire campaign on the success of the Colony and the Singletary structure.

As I board the helicopter, the cold, stubborn wind causes my eyes to well with tears, prickling my cheeks. The sound of the chopper blades pierces my ears as they tear into the sky. The engines roar relentlessly while the wind buffets and rocks us like a sky-born cradle. I hold my pod tightly and begin reviewing my notes while snuggling in my goose-down coat. After a while, the golden rays of the sunrise begin to cast a rosy hue across the sky and pour through the windows. Just for a moment, I close my eyes and imagine warmth radiating over my entire body and the turbulence replaced by the morning stillness.

Finally, the lift and drag become less choppy as we begin to descend slowly and land on the helipad. We quickly exit and begin walking briskly toward the sign indicating the path to the wait station.

The chill in the air cracks against my skin like a whip. Sounds of branches creaking, leaves rustling, and our feet shuffling through the harsh underbrush hastens my pace. There is a heavy fog, and the air is thick with moisture. As we move swiftly through the forest, early-morning beams of light barely streak through the boughs, illuminating the sequoias looming over us like giant skyscrapers, their cinnamon-red bark glistening from the misty rain. The dense underbrush is wild and gnarly, scraping and twisting against my boots. The pathway veers up a steep incline, and we struggle to maintain our footing while slipping and sliding along the muddy trail. My breathing is shallow, and by the time we reach the top of the incline, I am gasping for air. Just ahead, we see a run-down building; its sides are covered with foliage, and the roof is unleveled. We stop to look for our guide, who is supposed to meet us at the wait station, but there is no one here. Trevor and Isaac look almost frozen in place as they wait with their equipment dangling awkwardly from their shoulders.

This trail is hard but not as challenging as the security clearance we needed for the interview with Tobias Ludlow. But it really doesn't matter how hard they make it. I know there is a story here, and I am going to get it!

The frigid air keeps me in the moment, devouring our body heat. My breath rises and forms tiny clouds that dissipate into the defiant wind. Just ahead, I see someone making his way to the wait station. He is tall, with unusually broad shoulders. He is dressed in black from head to toe, and as he gets closer, the stoic expression on his face, which is likely meant to intimidate me, simply reinforces my resolve to get the story no matter what.

Standing about a foot in front of me, he says, "Ms. Matthews?" The corner of my mouth wrinkles up, and I reply with a slight hoarseness in my voice, brought about by the chill in the air, "Yes." I turn to Trevor and Isaac as they confirm their identities.

"I am Farlan, your guide. Follow me," he says as he turns abruptly and begins walking toward the wooded path. I keep moving, hoping that the warmth of my blood will rescue me from this bitter cold. Again, we pass grudgingly through the thicket. The trees look weathered and their bark scarred. Rocks, broken branches, and acorns cover the ground. They lay almost frozen on the soil against the dark, rain-soaked ground. Several minutes later, my limbs are stiff and aching, and my face is chiseled from the brisk wind. As much as I want to know how much further we have to go, I refuse to show any degree of intolerance to Farlan. I am tough, and I will not be intimidated by any challenges he puts in my way.

Farlan points to an opening to what looks like a tunnel just a few feet away. I hasten my pace, glad that I can at least escape the chill that is gnawing at my jaw and biting the corners of my eyes. Once inside, I notice that the tunnel is perfectly straight and lit with dim lights. By the time we reach the end of one tunnel, we climb up the stairs to another. We move quickly from one level to another, and I start to perspire and feel a band of heat overtaking my body.

"We're almost there. That red light ahead marks the exit," Farlan says as his voice echoes throughout the chamber. I hear a high-pitched whistling sound.

"We need to stop! Trevor needs his inhaler," Isaac says forcefully, and I turn around to see if he is okay.

We stop moving, and Trevor looks at me passively, reaches for his inhaler, removes the cap, breathes in deeply, then begins to breathe out, pushing as much air out as possible. He then starts to breathe slowly and steadily.

My limbs are weary and fatigued. Trevor keeps moving his head from side to side as if to release tension, and we're breathing heavily. Farlan appears almost unaffected.

"You'll be okay once we reach the altitude adjustment chamber. We went up a few thousand feet, and it affects your oxygen intake," Farlan says with a slight smirk.

My legs feel like they are about to buckle when Farlan announces, "Here we are!" He looks directly into the retinal scanner, and the door opens. Once we enter the chamber, a wave of warmth envelopes my body, and I begin to feel the tension in my shoulders dissipate. The chamber leads to a long hallway that is cool, empty, and smells of disinfectant. I can hear muffled angry voices in the distance. I look straight ahead in anticipation, but before I can get a glimpse of the havoc, Farlan directs us to veer left toward another interlocking chamber. The bright light becomes darker the further we walk. No way out, just this endless pathway leading to another nondescript location.

"Where are we headed again?" Isaac asks with a worried expression.

"The altitude adjustment chamber," Farlan replies with an irritated tone. Farlan stops abruptly in front of a flat iron door with a rectangle of glass just a few inches above my head. "This is where you will rest for roughly an hour." Farlan opens the door again by looking directly into the retinal scanner. We walk in, staring at radiant blue light pulsing from all four corners of the room. In the center are four large pods.

"I've never seen something like this before. What are they?" I ask.

Farlan walks to the far right side of the room, pushes a button, and responds, "These are your equilibrium pods." The hatch of the pods open wide, and Farlan invites us to settle in. "An hour in this, and you'll feel refreshed and energized. There is balancing fluid in the pod that you can drink to optimize your electrolytes and masks you can place over your nose and mouth to treat oxygen deprivation."

I step into the pod, carefully observing the austere inside compartment. Just as I secure myself in the seat, the hatch closes quickly. The blue lights begin to fade, and after I drink the fluid and place the mask over my nose and mouth, I begin to relax my body within the warmth and serenity of the metallic cocoon.

CHAPTER THIRTEEN

"Time to wake up!" Farlan announces as the hatch starts to open and disturbs my slumber.

"How long have I been out?" I ask.

"Just an hour."

"Feels like I've been sleeping for hours," Isaac states as he steps out of the pod.

"Where's our equipment?" Trevor asks quietly.

"We moved it to Coventry. That's where Tobias will meet you. Follow me."

I stumble out of the pod, grab my bag, and ask, "Can we head to the restroom first?"

My pace is lagging far behind Farlan and the others, and my thoughts are a little foggy. We finally reach the restrooms, and I dart straight in.

At first, I need to squint as I transition from the dark hallway into the brightly lit room. It is a natural space with the scent of lavender soothing my senses. I freshen up my makeup, slick my hair back, and tighten my ponytail. After reviewing my notes, I tuck them away in my bag and head for the exit with my head held high, exuding confidence and ready for whatever comes my way. My heels make a clacking sound with a confident rhythm as I walk across the wooden floors with a rich maple hue and glossy surface. My determination is undeniable.

Farlan escorts us into the reception area of Coventry. Bright lights encircle the entire room, and I can smell the faint scent of mint and sandalwood. The room is large and sparsely furnished. In the center are two light blue armchairs with high flared backs and small cushions cradled in the center. An oval-shaped wooden table with a reddish-brown glaze occupies the space between the chairs; it has a pitcher and two glasses beside it. The smell of disinfectant and the large floor-to-ceiling steel cabinets occupying one side of the wall reminds me of the interrogation room where Colin and I met with Detective Monaghan, cold and impersonal.

"So, the interview is here?" I asked.

"Yes, Mr. Ludlow will be here shortly," Farlan replies. "Your equipment is in the bottom storage cabinets over there." Farlan points to the far east corner of the room. Isaac and Trevor make a beeline to the cabinets.

I continue to stand so that when Tobias enters the room, I will look confident and prepared. After ten minutes, my feet begin to tire.

"Ms. Matthews, you're more than welcome to sit."

"Thank you, but I prefer to stand," I say kindly.

Isaac and Trevor move in closer, and I begin my stand-up when I hear heavy footsteps in the room. I turn around and see a very tall, slender man moving with a rather bold stride. His dark brown eyes suggest confidence born from experience. His salt-and-pepper thinning hair is slightly disheveled, and despite the cool room temperature, his forehead is beaded with sweat.

"Ah, Ms. Matthews, welcome to the Transformation Center." He smiles as he greets me. His hands remain at his side, betraying his kind facial expression.

"Hello, Mr. Ludlow. Pleased to meet you. You can call me Dani." I turn around and point in the distance. "This is the production crew, Isaac and Trevor." They extend a simple wave.

"I thought it might make sense for me to provide you with a tour of the facility before we sit down. Is that okay with you?"

"Yes, that would be fantastic," I reply.

Isaac begins to detach the camera from the pod when Tobias says, "Recording and film devices are not permitted outside of this room."

Isaac reattaches the camera and places the equipment against the wall, and he and Trevor proceed to follow Tobias and me.

Before we exit Coventry, Tobias states, "Just to confirm, the article requires my approval before it can be released. Are we clear on this matter?"

My cheeks feel warm and flushed. "That's right," I say and nod my head in agreement.

The smell of disinfectant lingers in the air as I walk side by side with Tobias. The narrow walkway seems to close in on us as we turn the corner. Muffled voices vibrate throughout the confined space and become louder and more defined as we approach a wide doorway that appears to be a portal to something exciting and new. My heart is racing, and I have to remind myself to remain calm and aware of everything around me. Like a savant, I dissect the physical space surrounding me with my five senses and move at a rhythmic pace.

Before we walk in, Tobias says, "This is the first of four zones you will see. This first one is our Purification Zone."

I enter the room and then Trevor follows. A black case falls from Isaac's backpack and hits the floor with a loud thud. He stumbles clumsily to retrieve it.

"Why name it Purification?" I ask.

"The minds and hearts of newly assigned and exiting Breeders must let go of the past and be retrained to embrace a completely new life. Those who are new to breeding must understand the enormous responsibility they are tasked with."

"You mean being bound to produce children?"

"We prefer to think of it as ensuring our survival. Millions died during the Great War, and with the onslaught of male infertility and cognitive impairment, we needed a solution quickly. I sense the reluctance in your voice, Ms. Matthews. You think another solution would've been better?"

"Well, the solution was so quick, there didn't appear to be a period to consider other options."

"Ms. Matthews, when a house is on fire, you don't wait; you simply take the fastest and safest route to survive. The breeding program was our fastest and safest solution."

"Well, I guess we'll never know now, will we, Mr. Ludlow," I say with a hint of sarcasm.

We venture further into the zone. The air is so dense and muggy, and with each breath, I think I might snap. Everything looks stark and aesthetically bland. The walls are light gray. Above, several white pendant lights, suspended by metal rods, hang from the ceiling. The bright light cascades over the entire room, and when I stand directly underneath the light, I can feel an intense heat. There are ten rows of desks that extend from one end of the room to another, no more than twenty males sitting at them, with another person sitting directly across from them. A man, standing at the head of the class, sounds a buzzer, and a stream of low-pitch chatter fills the room.

"What happens here?" I ask.

"This is the beginning of our twelve-day Purification phase for our Breeder initiates who you see sitting at the desks, wearing white dogi uniforms, the black lapels, and belts. The man at the head of the class, wearing a dark blue robe, is the procter. He monitors the session. The man in the pale-blue robe, sitting across from the Breeder initiate, is the recorder. He administers the surveys and records the Breeder's responses. A survey is administered for five hours, and three hours of teaching occurs for each of the eleven days, and on the twelfth day, there is an exam covering learnings from day one."

"What type of questions are in the survey?" I ask while raising a quizzical brow.

"Practical questions like, 'What's your favorite food?' to the most deeply personal questions like, 'What is the worst thing you ever did to another person?' The idea here is to purge anything that taints a Breeder's calling to live a clean and selfless life."

"Why are the lights so bright and hot?" I ask as I look up at the ceiling above me and squint my eyes.

"The heat from the lights helps to rid the body of toxic elements. This program is combined with exercise, dietary supplements, and physical cleansing in our detox saunas."

"Is all of this necessary? You know it's been suggested that the methods at the Transformation Center are long and harsh and, some have suggested, even cruel. What can you share with me to refute this claim?" I ask. Tobias loosens the collar around his neck.

"I've heard those accusations as well, but I assure you that can't be farther from the truth. To protect the sanctity of our process and the safety of our Breeders, we must be highly protective of their activities here. Our strict privacy policies prohibiting access cause many people to imagine the worst. Even our restrictive policies for new Breeders regarding outside contact while training is misconstrued as cruel and inhumane for lack of knowing the truth. It isn't. If anything, our work is patriotic in the truest sense of the word."

"So, is dispelling the rumors the reason you agreed to do this interview?" I ask as I zero in on Tobias's crepey skin crumpling as he rubs his chin. He takes a long pause and stiffens his shoulders.

"Yes and no, Dani. Yes, I want the public to be reassured that our work at the Transformation Center is for the good of our nation and not hurtful in any way, but this wouldn't have been the way I would have chosen to address the matter. Needless to say, the *Beacon* didn't give us much of a choice," Tobias says in a snarly tone.

"What does that mean?"

Tobias was slow to respond. "Just that it would be more costly to avoid this interview." Tobias checks the time and notes, "We are falling behind schedule. We better move on."

"Mr. Ludlow, with all due respect, you didn't answer my question."

"Ms. Matthews, with all due respect, you didn't like the answer I provided. There's a difference."

CHAPTER FOURTEEN

As we leave the classroom area of the Purification Zone, Tobias's gait is fast and determined. I move hurriedly with short, quick steps. He is silent and gives a cursory nod in the direction of the sauna area. Tobias initiates another retinal scan at the security gate, and the front door swings open. A short man, wearing a dark-blue robe, walks into the hallway and leads us further into the interlocking chamber. His militaristic stride is precise and controlled. Soon, the clip-clopped sound of our hastened footsteps is overpowered by the intense roar of water as we enter a dark hallway. I can't see where it is coming from, and it is getting louder. The darkness soon begins to subside as a flurry of white light draws us closer to what Tobias refers to as the Rain Room, the culmination of the Purification process. I am literally standing in awe of what looks like a wall of rain falling from the ceiling like a rainstorm. The water emits a rainbow of playful sky-blue amid gold and copper-red. I reach out to touch it, but it is not wet. The drops just disappear on my skin, and once I fully immerse myself in the falling rain, I walk to the other side completely dry.

"When a new Breeder completes the Purification phase, he is made anew in the Rain Room. The act of passing through the rain symbolizes a Breeder beginning to release old fears, shame, and regret. Learning to surrender his complete self to his calling is taught in the next twelve-day phase, the extraction phase." Tobias stands completely still as he gazes at the top of the rainfall.

"Why call the next phase extraction if the Breeder is made anew via the Purification phase?" I ask while expressing a hint of cynicism.

"Purification is only the beginning of the Breeder's journey to understanding and commitment. Even after Purification, the will is still vulnerable to old habits that weaken the spirit. During the extraction phase, the Breeder is completely removed from the shell that withheld his true spirit and embraces his duty to Dominion."

The entrance to the extraction area is showered with flickering light beams spreading like petals on the ceiling and walls. Tobias's mannerisms remain stoic as he opens the door. Even though the room is not very big, the bare, pale-white interior gives off an illusion of a large space that seems much bigger than the Purification Zone. Tobias points toward the far-left section of the zone where there are about thirty to forty desks arranged classroom-style. A floor-to-ceiling screen is directly in front of the desks and a large podium is next to the screen. The dry heat is less stifling, unlike the Purification room, where the air is hot and humid. The ceiling beams are dull and rusty, and above them are beams of red light piercing my skin. I put my blazer back on so the sleeves can protect my arms. I try to protect my face by looking down at the floor, but there is dry heat emanating from it, so I squint so hard that my eyes quiver uncontrollably and my cheeks tighten.

The instructor immediately stops speaking, and the initiates fall silent and rise to their feet in unison, their hands clasped behind them and their heads bowed down.

Tobias notes, "Notice that the Breeder initiates are wearing a white dogi with gray lapels and belts. This phase is also a time of intense learning."

Tobias motions for us to keep walking. He appears frustrated, but I try to ignore it.

"What is the purpose of conducting classes in a hot room?" I ask while trying to keep up with his fast pace.

"The heat purges the body of mental and physical impurities. Retention increases exponentially when purging is combined with learning," Tobias relays, only looking back briefly before charging ahead.

I want to look around and ask more questions about this room, but I feel like I am burning from the inside out. Trevor and Isaac look miserable, so we walk quickly to the exit, which leads to a much larger room. Once inside, I ask, "What lesson requires such extreme methods for retention?"

Tobias gazes at me for a moment, motions for us to sit in the chairs nestled in the corner of the room, while he stands, then responds, "The truth," his voice cutting through the room like a blade, sharp and precise. Tobias paces slowly, breathing heavily, then clasps his hands together tightly.

"The truth, according to the Breeder Doctrine, is a series of absolute facts that legitimize the Breeder's role in society. Facts like the death toll of twelve million and over one-hundred-and-fifty million males who became infertile after the Great War. But there is so much more that you can't get from the writings." Tobias moves in closer, with a cautious ease; his stoic demeanor begins to crumble. "It was easy to screen for infertility right away after the war since it was one of several potential side effects caused by chemical warfare. Cognitive impairment was harder to diagnose, so the numbers are less precise.

"The annals confirm that ninety-nine percent of males were cognitively impaired. Social chaos ensued. The spread of false information was rampant. In addition to the crippling plague, rumors of the deadly virus, israe, swept across the country. People feared for their lives. Israe was a man-made infectious disease caused by a synthetic parasite, but the belief that it was a plague sent by God to punish evildoers consumed the masses. Thousands sought redemption through suicide and even murder. Centralized containment camps were set up to separate the sick from the healthy, and people feared the secret police, who enforced extradition.

"Tens of thousands of our military forces were decimated in the Great War, and our government officials fought for absolute power instead of protecting the people. Dozens of military factions took over cities, and localized wars were used to seize power, resources, and wealth. But people continued to suffer under the weight of the military factions who were nothing more than oppressors. In some areas, people were starving and in desperate need of medical attention." Tobias raises his eyebrows and lifts his index finger to move his glasses further up the ridge of his nose. He is a man who is set in his ways. Now, when simple eye surgery can eliminate the need for corrective eyewear, he continues to wear spectacles just because that is what he is used to.

"After much bloodshed and the consolidation of power, only twenty-four factions remained, but they were weak and fragmented. They wasted time fighting against each other instead of trying to unite our country, and they abused their authority with warrantless wiretapping, kidnapping, and detention to suppress uprisings. They lost sight of the fact that authority and power are not the same. True power lies in truth and not coerciveness. The Doyennes understood that. This collective of women were our nation's top scientific, legal, economic, spiritual, and political minds, and they unified the people.

"The Doyennes knew they held the future of our country in their hands, so while local militia created chaos, they reestablished the rules and regulations, policies, and decision-making processes needed to centralize power. They knew the pain of being marginalized, oppressed, and hidden, and they used that to build their relationship with the people and eventually establish Dominion and occupy the seats within the eight cabinets. Allura Yakubu was able to seize power as Dominion's highest-ranking official by wielding her enormous influence to establish Illegis as a societal stabilizer and bring hope back to millions. Creating the Breeder classification allowed her to restore a sense of control for the millions of males who felt dejected and angry. Her words were passionate, and she surrendered her heart when she said, "The future of our nation lies beneath your feet, and only you can choose to let it thrive or die; it's your choice!" Noticing Trevor's fascination with the Dominion timeline on the wall, we rise from our chairs and walk across the room and join him.

"Imagine how inspiring Allura must've been to convince mobs of angry men to relinquish their power to a woman," Trevor says with a bewildered tone while studying the engraved metal tablets on the wall. The tablets represented the timeline of key events and statistics outlining the rise of Dominion, with particular attention to the rise of the Breeder class and the early establishment of the seven Transformation Centers in Dominion.

"Not too surprising, since Allura clearly had to pander to the male ego by stating that the key to survival lied with them, and only they could choose. There never was a choice, just an understood acquiescence based on the fallacy of control," I say begrudgingly while motioning to Trevor and Isaac to keep up with Tobias and me.

There is an office in one corner, with three obstacle courses located at each corner of the room, and directly in the center is the Dominion flag hanging from a silvery metal pole. The hues of purple, gold, and white look vibrant and pristine under the blazing lights.

Tobias passively walks by the classroom area. His gait seems strained, and I begin to notice a slight limp. He stops in front of a high roped wall with tall steel poles on both sides, two large barrels flanking each side of the poles. I carefully peek inside and see belay devices crammed in tightly. Tobias smirks bitterly and refers to this obstacle course as the place where renuevering begins.

"Renuevering?" I ask.

He glances at the top of the wall then back at me with empty, forlorn eyes, as if he's remembering a secret too painful to bear.

"Renuevering?" I ask again.

Dead silence grips the room; then he replies, "It helps Breeders reframe their source of logic and truth through education and meditation." His hand displays a nervous twitch as he guides our attention to the starting point of the first obstacle course, which he references as the easiest of the three. "The Breeder's physical journey of extraction begins with challenging his core strength. The objective here is to brave unstable surfaces that challenge balance and speed."

The challenge begins with stepping stones, each of different sizes and shapes, dispersed along a path surrounded by hot stones and steaming hot liquid underneath. At the end of the path is a wooden climbing wall. Its surface is unleveled and appears to become increasingly narrower toward the top. About six feet from the opposite side of the wall is a thick rope hanging from the ceiling and a platform at the very top. Climbing this rope, which dangles roughly 100 feet from steel rafters, is the only way to access the platform. It seems almost impossible to climb higher up the rope and still endure the heat and glare of the red lights that blanket the ceiling. Close to the top is a platform that leads to the monkey bars, which stretch over a pool of ice-cold water. We walk slowly by each contortion of the course. Isaac trips again, and this time, the crash of his backpack echoes loudly. My neck and shoulders start to tighten, and my limbs feel numb, as if they really don't belong to me. By the time we make it to the end of this obstacle course, exasperation overwhelms my body.

"You look tired. Should we walk quickly past the next two courses?" Tobias asks. He, too, looks tired but numb from all feelings. The ability to sustain unrelenting pain, at any cost, comes from the experience of deep adversity. Perhaps, for him, the Transformation Center is more of a refuge from the past than a call to duty.

I look back at Trevor and Isaac. Their walk is slow and exaggerated, as if each step is a negotiation rather than an order, and their faces look desperate for a break.

"No, let's keep going," I say under my breath, my throat dry and scratchy.

"All right,"

We continue walking along the smooth concrete floors. The *click, clop* rhythm of soles upon the walkway hastens until we stop in front of a large, black, oval-shaped steel door. A glimmer of light shines from the ceiling and illuminates the security pad. Tobias leans his shoulder against the wall, with his back to me, and enters a code.

"This next zone we will enter is called Instruction. This is where Breeders build a sense of kinship and trust in their purpose," Tobias says while saluting the metal plate of the Dominion flag on the wall.

Looking at the way he lingers in deference to this next zone, it is clear he is a man of deep conviction. Every move he makes seems intentional and profound. Instead of moving with him, I decide to wait until he motions for me and the crew to step into the chamber.

Upon entering, everything feels different. The air is cool, fresh, and easy to breathe, unlike the prior zones. The space is expansive, with sections of cedar-brown benches arranged in concentric circles around what Tobias refers to as the "Learning Tree." Its branches stretch skyward, and its glossy leaves coil around it like a lace of silent bark, and the flora surrounding the tree looks like a jubilant festival of vibrant hues.

As we get closer to the tree, the scents of cinnamon and citrus frolic with my senses. Large water coolers are dispersed throughout the room.

"Care for a cup of water?" Tobias asks with a mischievous half grin.

"Yes, thank you."

The water is icy, and I feel a chill running down my throat. Almost instantly, I feel rejuvenated, and the tension in my body is gone. I turn around to see Trevor and Isaac enjoying the soothing effects of the water. Their facial expressions are joyful and relaxed, and their walking is now focused and energetic.

"What's in the water? I feel completely different, completely uninhibited."

"The water is infused with natural ingredients that elevate learning, retention, and memory. It also evokes euphoria and contentment. It has a more profound effect on you since your body has not adapted to it."

"Why are these benches surrounding the Learning Tree?" Trevor asks hesitantly.

"This place is both soft and hard, with the focus on learning. The design of this zone is soft and soothing. All the way from the cool, fragrant air, subdued lighting, and natural green plants. The water elevates these good feelings so the body is prepared for optimal learning. The benches are hard because learning requires a firm foundation, and a Breeder's commitment must be unyielding and strong. The Learning Tree is in the middle, as it represents the purpose of this environment, which is to learn and stretch beyond our comfort zones. The lessons are meant to help Breeders understand their duties and build confidence and conviction toward their societal role. Also, at this stage of the process, the Breeder's allegiance to Dominion is solidified."

There is something solemn and almost prophetic in the way Tobias describes this zone. His tone and posture are stiff, and he seems to be in excruciating pain.

"Tobias, are you okay? You seem to be in extreme discomfort."

No response.

Squeezing his left hand and cocking his neck slightly to one side, he responds, slightly irritated, "I am fine. Shall we move on?"

As we exit the zone, echoing sounds pervade the corridor. I press my hands against my ears as a piercing whistle sounds throughout the passageway.

"What's happening?" I scream and furrow my brows.

Trevor and Isaac cover their ears and lower their heads.

Tobias continues walking with a hastened pace but does not reply.

"Tobias!" I scream again.

"Keep your ears covered! We are almost there!" he replies loudly and authoritatively.

Without warning, the loud screeching goes away as quickly as it started.

Tobias stands firmly in front of the door of the final zone. He presses his hand against a sensor pad, and the door opens to a large auditorium with large, comfy, crimson seats in front of a stage with crimson and gold drapes. The hue of the seats is soft yet with a bright, energetic vibe. Silver and gold pendant lights with the girth of a sequoia tree dangle and emit a blanket of rich gold and copper hues.

"This final zone is called Transition. Each day, for eleven days, the Breeders rehearse for the Transition ceremony. During the first two hours of the Transition ceremony, the initiates glorify Dominion's principal doctrines, reenacting the battle of Carthesis that marked the final defeat of the anarchists and the rise of Dominion. The next two hours are devoted to displays of physical strength, usually single combat for ten to twelve minutes, with as many as ten to fifteen combats. Next on the program is a contest of core knowledge and thinking agility. We conclude with the Reaping, which involves each Breeder releasing his old self and embracing his new self, the assignment of names and the Breeder's oath, and the pendent ceremony on the twelfth day."

Tobias looks down at his pod and says, "Looks like we're behind schedule. We should return to Coventry."

"Sure, but why do I get the impression that I've only seen the tip of the iceberg," I hint slyly.

"There are no smoke and mirrors here, Ms. Matthews. I'm sorry that reality doesn't seem to measure up to what you thought you'd find. This way, please," Tobias says coldly.

The path leading back to Coventry is mysterious. Each step feels like an invitation to discover something unknown and tempestuous. The tunnel is dark and zigzags harshly across the uneven concrete surfaces. You can hear the rhythm of our soles as they crush the bits of rocks and metal beneath them. I am mesmerized by the possibility of what could end the bleak silence that consumes the moment. Tobias's limp becomes more pronounced as we enter the first corridor. When he stops walking to stroke his hip lightly, I notice a band of young males marching in the distance. They are dressed in black from head to toe, and their stride is confident and determined, each hand and leg movement in unison. I can hear a faint chant as they march across the ground. I also notice a boy following the troop at a distance and hiding in between the vacuous craters along the pathway. He moves reluctantly and looks afraid. His attention is strictly on the troop some distance in front of him, and he doesn't notice that I can see him. I don't know why I feel the need to protect his cover, but I do.

Seeking to distract Tobias from the boy, I ask, "Tobias, what is the purpose of these etchings on the wall?" He immediately stops stroking his hip and looks at me. His gaze is harsh. "The etchings, right there," I say, pointing to the corner just to his left side.

"Oh, that's nothing to concern you. Just an engineering plate. We are building another corridor near here." I distract Tobias long enough for the boy to move far beyond our purview.

"And what is that group of young men marching over there?" I ask.

Tobias responds, "Those are new Breeder initiates heading to the Purification Zone. Right this way."

We continue our journey in absolute silence, with nothing more than the sound of our unsteady pace.

My aching limbs rejoice when I see the entrance to Coventry. Everything is just as we left it, so I follow Tobias to the seating area while Trevor and Isaac rush to set up the equipment.

Settling into the soft cushions that push me up while hugging my lower back, I can feel the adrenaline flooding my system. My heart is pumping so hard, like it will explode, and my eyes are wide as I focus on Tobias. This is how it is for every interview. My body and thoughts are ready to pounce like a hungry lioness, eager to devour my prey. I relish every moment of this, and I don't try to quell it—coming here and facing Tobias Ludlow is finally about to happen on my terms.

CHAPTER FIFTEEN

Tobias carefully maneuvers his body onto the couch, and I can tell he is in pain even though he refuses to acknowledge it. His cheeks look blanched from the chill in the walkway, and his eyes give off a listless stare.

"Are you comfortable?" I ask Tobias as he wipes the lens of his spectacles then places them securely on the bridge of his nose.

"I'm ready," he replies with a look of apathetic resignation.

"Let's begin," I say softly. I follow Trevor's hand as he moves it directly in front of me, and then the red camera light comes on.

"We're live," he says as he moves in even closer.

I smile kindly, looking directly into his eyes, and say, "So, Mr. Ludlow, why don't you tell us how long you've worked at the Transformation Center and what your role is today." My fingers lace around my water glass.

"I am the superintendent of the Transformation Center in Keelan. I oversee the operational and financial management responsibilities here," he responds calmly.

"Would you say that you have ultimate accountability for all of the activities that occur at the Transformation Center?"

Tobias's cool composure appears slightly unstable. He grazes his chin with his hand and lifts his head up slightly, like he is trying to second-guess where my questions are going. "Well, not ultimate, but I definitely represent the leadership connection between feet on the ground here in Keelan and the Dominion government."

"So, since you are the point person in charge of what goes on at the Transformation Center, how do you respond to the allegations of brainwashing?"

Hesitating for a moment and loosening the band around his neck, Tobias responds, "I'm not sure I understand what you mean by brainwashing."

"There are accounts of forced isolation, debilitation, exhaustion, drugs, torture, hypnosis, and many other control techniques." I pause. "Surely, this is not a surprise to you," I say grimly.

"Much of what we do is within the confines of the Transformation Center. Our seclusion and unwillingness to divulge our methods makes us vulnerable to falsehoods and allegations," he replies without hesitation.

There's no rest for the weary, and Tobias is definitely breaking down. Like rapid bullets, each question weakens Tobias's composure. Small beads of sweat appear on his brow. Mounting my evidence with sworn witness statements, photos, and videos, he is unable to produce a single piece of evidence refuting my claims.

Straightening my posture, I lean in and ask, "My last question, Tobias." I take a long pause so I can savor the intensity of the moment. "You manage the acculturation program for the Breeders who return to society, but you have been reluctant to prove that these civilians even exist. Why is that? One would think you're hiding something." Trevor zeros in on Tobias's face.

I think about the irony. Tobias sits on a couche, a word used to describe a piece of furniture used for lying down. I sit in a chair that can mean a leader of a meeting, a mode of execution, and the French word for flesh. Tobias doesn't have the fortitude to lie, and I hold all the cards as his captor, willing to extrude a pound of flesh.

Recoiling in horror, Tobias rises to his feet quickly and responds, "That question was not on the approved list. This interview is over!" he shouts with harsh indignation.

He turns away, shuffles angrily toward the door, and exits. Standing in the center of Coventry, I wring my hands so tightly, my knuckles are pale. It's time for me to retract the predator in me. I have taken my pound of flesh, and it feels good. Now, if I am lucky, Haven will give me the answers I am looking for.

CHAPTER SIXTEEN

By 5:30, we pack up our equipment and begin walking toward the exit. Tobias leads the way, walking swiftly. His gait that was smooth this morning is faltering and unsteady. He keeps checking his pod and doesn't appear to care that Isaac and Trevor are stumbling to keep up. We finally make it to the exit when Tobias scans the door pad with the palm of his hand. Immediately, the door flings open. He ushers us out the door, points to the helicopter in the distance, and quickly disappears behind the heavy thud as the door shuts.

The punishing rainfall makes the two-minute walk on the tarmac feel like an eternity. The hard pattering of the rain feels like prickly ice against my skin. Rain like this makes you walk with your head down, shoulders shrugged, anxious to get somewhere warm.

The helicopter shines in the distance like a bright beacon. The storm winds are vicious, causing our umbrellas to turn inside out. Finally, the pilot opens the door, and we pile in quickly. The floor is freezing, and there's hardly any visibility through the windows. As the long, narrow blades begin to spin and rip through the air, we begin our ascent. First leaning forward, then back, our heads whipping back and forth until we reach altitude. I bend my head forward to stretch my neck when I notice the large black bag tucked beneath the cargo railing moving.

Turning to Trevor, I make eye contact and motion for him to look at the bag on the floor.

"Do you see what I'm seeing?" I ask. The sky is so dark that it is hard to see a few inches past your nose.

"Yes," Trevor says. He motions for me and Isaac to lean back. He unlocks his safety belt, pauses, and peers around. Without hesitating, he hurries and pounces on the black sack. The force of his body thrusts the bag forward. A head appears from the corner of the bag as Trevor draws his hand back and plunges his knuckles hard against the stowaway's cheek. As the stowaway rises to his knees, dazed and in pain, Trevor pulls a short rod from the floor and swings it against the stowaway's arm, then again against his torso. Plummeting to the floor, Isaac flashes a light on the body, lying motionless on the floor.

"Wait, don't hit him!" I scream. "That's the boy!"

"What boy?" Trevor asks loudly.

Moving in closer to inspect the boy's face, I notice that he's wearing a black garment with a black-and-red collar around his neck, the S-band colors of a Breeder initiate recently transported to the Transformation Center. He's the boy I saw underground following the new Breeder initiates marching to the Purification Center. He was hiding as he followed them. I distracted Tobias long enough for him to keep moving unnoticed.

"Why did you do that?" Trevor asks.

"I don't know. He just looked scared. I just reacted without thinking," I say solemnly.

Trevor picks him up and places him upright in the seat next to me. He's still unconscious, so I pat his left cheek softly, then hard. He starts to open his eyes. At first, he looks confused; then, within seconds, he sharpens his glare, stiffens his jaw, and says, "Please help me."

"Who are you?" I ask.

"I am Kazen. I know you saw me today following the initiates. You didn't report me. I knew then that you would help me." His vulnerability and blank stare pierce my soul in a way that feels familiar.

"Why did you stow away on our helicopter?" I ask.

Kazen hesitates for a moment, then says, "I need to escape to the Towers."

"The Towers. Where is that?" I wipe the blood streaming down his cheek with a cloth.

"On the outskirts of Quadrant 1. From there, I can travel to the safety zone. I need to get there. My brother, Azone, is waiting for me." Kazen's voice is twisted with guilt. "I am sorry for the way I involved you in this, but I had no choice. This was the only way out."

Isaac and Trevor shrink back in their seats while I question Kazen. He was placed as a Breeder and slated to begin indoctrination. Before he was taken to the Transformation Center, his brother gave him a map to memorize and use to escape. What are the chances that a twelve-year-old boy would remember an incredibly complex labyrinth-like pathway through a compound he's never seen? Kazen has a photographic memory and can consume significant volumes of information quickly. Once he reads or sees it, he remembers it. He is what we call a *super Breeder*. Super Breeders have the mental acuity and fertility that is at least ten times the level of the average male. These males are rare and coveted by the government. It is likely that Tobias and his team are already looking for him.

A sob finally builds up in Kazen's throat, a choking sensation, but he swallows it. Kazen elaborates, "Remaining a Breeder will surely mean death. I will be nothing more than a lab rat. Scientists will poke and prod me until there's nothing left. My brother says that Dominion wants to reverse the effects of the war, and the super Breeders are the key to that discovery. I had to run. I have to get to the Towers!" Kazen leans back in exhaustion.

"If you're what you say, Tobias may suspect that you're with us." I pause. "Look at me, Kazen," I say authoritatively.

Kazen lifts his eyes. "You're not going back to the Transformation Center. We'll get you to the Towers." Kazen's nose prickles. Tears threaten to burst while he strains to hold them back.

I flag the pilot, Gerund, and instruct him to change course. "We're going to make a quick stop at the Towers in Quadrant One before returning to the office. Don't record this on the manifest, and as far as you know, we had some technical problems that delayed our return, right?

"Right," Gerund responds. Then the helicopter swoops in low, changes course, and soars away.

CHAPTER SEVENTEEN

After almost an hour, I am completely oblivious to the sound of the blades rotating above me. Isaac and Trevor sit quietly while occasionally checking on Kazen as he sleeps. Without warning, the helicopter begins to fight violently through the dark, overcast sky. The turbulence awakens. Peering from the window, a sheath of blackness transitions into a gray, dense fog; then there's a blue and bright cloudless sky.

"Our destination is just ahead," the pilot calls out.

As we begin our descent, a woven tapestry of steel and concrete monuments stand among towering trees and vacant land. The Towers, formerly known as the Watts Towers, was once a symbol of the Black nationalist movement and Black Arts. After the Great War, it became the "neutral zone," also declared condemned property.

As we land on the bare concrete, everything is paling away into the murk. Soft ash blowing in loose swirls stick against the windows. There's nothing in sight except segments of road among dead trees.

"Where will you go?" I ask.

Lowering his glasses and wiping his nose on the back of his wrist, Kazen responds, "There are watchers here. I am sure, by now, they've sent word to my brother that a helicopter has landed."

"Will they come here for you?" Trevor asks.

Gathering a black knapsack across his shoulder, Kazen responds, "I must go to the Spectre Tower. It's going to be hard to navigate in the dark, but I can make it."

"Wait," I say, grasping Kazen's sleeve, "we're coming with you."

"No need. I'll be safe."

"Are you sure about that? I doubt that your brother's militia is the only one using this zone. You need protection, and I've got it. Let's go!" I say as I grab a gun from underneath my seat.

The concrete pathway is covered with dust and ash, charred and barren trees stretching away on every side. Farther along, we pass the first tower. Shards of glass and tile wrapped with wire stretch high and wide. Kazen continues to lead the way, his slender body bracing the heavy wind. Cold air rips through my nostrils like a knife, and my feet are numb.

Crossing a trench covered with tarp, we make our way up a slope through a cluster of rocks to another tower.

"This is it," Kazen shouts. "We can wait here. Someone will be here soon."

"Are you sure" I ask?

"Yes. Just wait," he responds confidently as he drops his knapsack on the ground and sits on it.

"Here, drink this. It'll warm you up," I say, passing a thermos filled with hot water and citrus to Kazen. He drinks, then screws down the metal cap and wipes the thermos off with a rag.

A light shines from the distance. Kazen stands and holds his arms directly up with his right hand balled in a fist. The band that was around his neck is now strapped to his wrist. He continues to jab his right fist upward, wait five seconds, then upward again with his thumb tucked into his palm. This continues for several minutes until the voice of a man can be heard in the distance. "Who are you?"

"I am Kazen, brother of Azone."

"What were you doing when you discovered your assignment?"

Kazen hesitates, then responds, "I was drawing."

"What were you drawing?"

A long pause supersedes a deep sigh; then Kazen blurts out, "Sea turtles!"

"And why sea turtles?" the voice says softly. The man draws in closer.

"Azone told me that no matter what the results, I had to exhibit the strength and persistence of a sea turtle."

"Kazen, my brother!" a voice shouts just a few feet away.

"Azone, is that you?" Kazen runs toward the dark figure in the shadows and embraces him.

Grasping Azone's hand, Kazen leads him to meet us.

We sit huddled together, wrapped in a blanket over our coats, the heavy winds subsiding and the cold air gliding across my nose like a gentle breeze.

"Azone, this is Dani, Trevor, and Isaac. They helped me escape from the Transformation Center," Kazen says as he tugs Azone's hand to move in closer.

Azone immediately asks, "Were you followed?"

"No, I suspect they may be searching for your brother on the compound. He was a stowaway on our helicopter, so we couldn't have done anything to tip them off before we left," I say.

Raising a puzzled brow, Azone asks, "Why'd you help him?"

"Well, what Kazen left out is that I am a reporter for the *Beacon*. I was at the Transformation Center to interview Superintendent Tobias Ludlow."

Azone leans in. "How'd that go?"

"He was careful not to say too much, but I rattled him," I say with a half grin. "I intend to expose the truth behind the exploitation of Breeders. What I learned today is only part of the story. There's much more." I pause. "I know you're Kazen's brother and part of the resistance, but that's all I know. I've interviewed militants like Hangar-Eight and Polix-Five. We can help each other." I wince as dry wind blows in my face. "I can help you get your message out, and maybe you can help me piece together what's really going on with Breeders."

Azone swallows. "How do I know I can trust you?"

"Look, I'm a reporter, and I protect my sources. All I care about is the story, so use me. You have nothing to lose," I say. A long pause ensues as he looks me up and down, as if to find some indicator of my integrity.

Sniffling, struggling to focus, with a large bruise blooming on his face, Azone sits on a large rock, rubbing his torso. He appears to be in pain.

"What happened to you?" I ask.

"I was part of the Illegis riots in Quadrant Two a few days ago. Many of my brothers died. I was lucky. Our fight for justice has been a choreographed dance of destruction for far too long. I'm weary from the struggle already, and there's so much left to do," Azone says as he tries to control the tremors in his hand.

"Fighting for justice is a lifelong struggle and will involve many toils and snares," I say.

"Yes, justice, but more than that, the truth!" he says.

Feeling the tension and intensity in his tone, I reply, "Tell me, what is the truth you want the world to know, Azone?" My throat is scratchy, and I can hardly breathe while waiting for his words.

Moving his head up slowly until his eyes meet mine, he says, "Illegis is a lie! Singletary assignments are manipulated to control us."

"What do you mean?" I ask. The chaotic pulse of the wind assaults my face.

"Cognitive impairment is not a permanent result of the Great War. It was only temporary, but Dominion found a way to extend it. It was the only way that power could remain in the hands of women."

"Wait, if what you're saying is true, how is this being done?" I ask.

"Singletary testing involves securing each twelve-year-old male in a brace to do the body scan, and it is at that time that the body absorbs a toxin that creates cognitive impairment."

"How do you know this?" I ask.

Taking a deep breath that seems to last an eternity, he responds, "It happened to me, but for some reason, the effects didn't last. I went underground shortly after I recovered my memory of the testing, and with the help of the Crusaders, I was able to piece together the truth. The Crusaders saved my life, and now I fight with them, shoulder to shoulder, against this cancer devouring our country."

Taking a long pause, I ask, "I am just curious. Were the Crusaders behind the threats to Valentina Cordova? After all, she administers Singletary assignments."

"Yes, she knows the truth and continues to enforce this lie. Illegis is weaponized to perpetuate a form of servitude. Men are prevented from understanding and pursuing their rightful place in Dominion, and this has to end!"

"What can you tell me about the Breeders? Is their status also manufactured?" I ask.

"It seems unlikely since there's no value in inducing infertility. But Breeders suffer the trauma of forced indoctrination at the Transformation Center, which is why I needed to get Kazen out of there. Thank you for saving my brother. Now, we have to go. Our check-in time is quickly approaching," Azone says as he grabs Kazen's hand, stands up, and turns away.

"But wait, how do I reach you if I need to talk to you?" I ask, seeing nothing but the back of their heads disappearing in a black stillness.

"You don't," Azone's voice says, fading in the distance.

CHAPTER EIGHTEEN

The crisp fall air whips through the open window of the limo as it skims along the landing strip, past the control tower. My limbs are still trembling as I reflect on my discussion with Azone. I try clearing my thoughts, but the image of Kazen's face riddled with fear and Azone's anger remains locked in my mind. I feel a deep sense of sadness knowing that Dominion is a lie.

The limo finally parks in front of the *Beacon*, and I struggle to exit, my head still pounding from the choppy return flight. Isaac and Trevor were silent all the way back from our meeting with Azone. They weren't permitted to participate or even listen to my discussion with him, but somehow they knew what we uncovered at the Transformation Center was just the beginning. Their stillness makes me anxious and unsure of my next move.

"I'll connect with you in the morning," I say as they start to exit the limo with their equipment.

I rush up to the twenty-fifth floor in the hopes that Sam is working late. Walking toward her office, I see the light scattered through the dark hallway. I compose myself and walk in.

"Sam, what a day. I didn't expect to learn as much as I did. I . . . are you okay?" I ask as Sam appears distracted.

"Sam?" I gesture my hand in front of her face.

Shaking her head and attempting to refocus, she looks up and says, "Sorry about that. I am still reeling from the execution today."

"That's right! Leo Cogsen. What happened?" I drop my satchel on the floor and move in closer.

"Ever since Dominion rescinded the abolishment of capital punishment, people have become so unfeeling and robotic about it. Hundreds of people turned out for it, like it was a spectator's sport. It was cold and rainy, but no one cared, not with their bodies pressed closely together. All the screens across the detention field went black before flashing the words, 'Cogsen Execution.' The crowd cheered. At seven minutes past five, the screens displayed Leo being escorted by two uniformed officers into the chamber. He looked disoriented and moved with a sluggish pace. His head remained face down. The crowd eagerly stomped their feet and chanted, 'Justice for Leah!' You recall, she was the woman killed by the explosion. Within seconds of being strapped in the chair, his body became limp and slumped over. Just like that, he was dead, and the screen went black again, and the sound of stomping feet and chanting ceased. People walked away as if nothing happened. The widespread apathy made me numb all over."

"Sam, that's why the truth about Dominion must be unmasked before it sucks the humanity out of each one of us."

"I'm afraid it already has," Sam says with a tone of fierce resignation.

Following a brief silence, Sam shakes her head vigorously, sits up straight in her chair, leans forward, and asks, "So, what do you have for me, Dani?"

"Here's the Breeder escape story. It's all here," I say as I hand her the thumb drive. "The Breeder escape story and the Transformation Center interview are related. I need time to dig deeper, and I will have to be gone for a while."

"What's a while?"

"Not sure yet, but Sam, this is big. This is *the* story we've been waiting for. The fallout from this could rattle Dominion at the very top."

Sam leaps from her chair and motions toward the window. A morbid tone creeps into her voice as she says, "I can see the screens in the detention center flashing, 'Cogsen Execution Complete!' as if it was a victory."

Her back is to me as she looks out at the city lights, the moon hanging low in the sky, casting a soft glow over the buildings nearby.

Sam steps away from the window and begins pacing vigorously. Something's wrong. I can tell.

"What's going on, Sam?"

Stopping in mid-stride and placing her hand on her hip, Sam says, "Look, I don't know if this will change your plans at all, but I have to tell you something. I'm just going to say it, and I'm sorry if I don't say this in a more delicate way. Valentina Cordova is not the only one getting death threats now."

"Okay, what are you saying?" My eyes lock in on Sam's with an unrelenting stare.

"I ran into my source from the precinct at the execution today. He's been tracking death threats against some of the honorees from the Ascension. He believes it's a newly formed militant group focused on destroying Illegis. He's interviewed many of the prospective targets, and I hate to say this." Sam takes a deep breath, then says reluctantly, "Your mother is one of them. She reported the threats and has been under twenty-four-hour surveillance over the past forty-eight hours." Sam examines my limbs for a reaction.

Grabbing my satchel from the floor and storming toward the door, I suddenly feel dazed and a little weak. "She hasn't said anything to me about this."

"I know. She was adamant that no one was to be informed of the threats, not even you. I'm sorry."

Bursting out of Sam's office and rushing to the elevator, all I can think about is how true to form this is for my mother. Her entire world is made up of secrets and lies. *Why should this be any different?*

CHAPTER NINETEEN

Traveling in my EV on my way to the Colony, my hands and feet keep fidgeting. *How am I going to get away with this without tipping off Colin?* While I continue to play out each possible scenario in my head, the EV pulls up in front of the security gate. The titanium walls tower at least 100 feet high and are surrounded by an invisible force field, as indicated by the warning sign affixed to the security gate.

I show my ID to the guard and wait for her to confirm the approval to proceed. Before I'm permitted to enter, I'm asked to open my trunk while the agent checks my EV for any prohibited items. While checking the back seat, the guard confiscates my camera and asks for my pod and glasses so she can disable my imaging and recording features.

"Why is it necessary to confiscate my camera?" I ask.

"Simply taking precautions to protect the privacy of the residents and medical personnel. You'll get it back when you leave. Thank you. You can move forward."

The path to the main building entrance is long and flanked by tall trees; their overhanging branches, with slender tendrils, gently glide over the windshield as I travel along the narrow driveway. The EV stops in front of the entrance, and a valet rushes to the driver's side to escort me out. The building is pristine and intimidating. The simplicity of the rough-cast, circular, monochromatic concrete building creates a contrast of light and darkness while it deflects the outside environment, and the sun casts its light against the translucent glass windows. The sharp clapping sound of my heels creates a faint echo as I walk up the stairs to the entrance, which is long, straight, and surrounded by vertical posts that hold up the handrails. The top of the stairs leads to a circular path arching over an aquarium of colorful fish and a mix of slate and lava rocks layered throughout the aquascape.

Once inside, I am met by more security agents confirming my identity. Satisfied, they direct me to walk through the body scanner and wait for Colin.

In the distance, I see Colin. His movement is confident and fluid, exuding a natural charisma that makes everyone take notice. He's dressed in a crisp, blue-gray shirt that fits his physique perfectly and sporty, dark trousers. I am immediately beguiled by his intense gaze.

"Dani, you made it," Colin says a few moments later. "I'm so glad to see you." He smiles widely. Again, I am consumed by his energy as he embraces me tightly. "I hope you're hungry. I had lunch prepared for us. I hope you like it." Colin takes my hand and guides me toward the escalator. As we ascend, the shine from the hard, white marble floors grows faint, and the glare from the sunlight beaming through the translucent glass panes is almost blinding; I turn away. When we reach the top floor, Colin leads me down a circular walkway with scallop-shell flooring that interweaves between thick, concrete interior and exterior spaces and opens onto an observation deck.

"Colin, this is amazing. You must give me a tour," I say excitedly.

"Of course," he replies.

Directing my attention to the building in the distance, Colin says, "The deck overlooks the amphitheater, which is east. On either side of it are restaurants, shops, and the Palarium, also known as our social space, which is in the center. The Science, Data Management, and Learning Centers are west, and the residences are dispersed throughout the Colony. It's early afternoon, so there are a lot of people relaxing and socializing directly below us. Follow me."

He leads me down the spiral walkway and instructs me to place my hand just above the sensor of the security kiosks as we enter the Palarium. The space is knitted together by a chain-link mesh canopy supported by a forest of wavering pillars over a sea of colorful benches and tables. It's at once playful and serene.

As we walk hand in hand, I can feel the warmth of the sun caressing my skin and the gentle breeze gliding softly across my face. When we reach the Data Management Center, Colin acknowledges that centralized record-keeping for many businesses both in and outside of the Colony is managed there. It is also the location where census information across all Dominion colonies resides. As we walk inside, light steel and glass walkways intersect and link the two lobes of the building, creating public spaces, while the central stairways and elevators provide easy circulation between the data entry areas on the left and data storage on the right. The design maximizes the natural light, which enhances the views from the sky bridge connected to the Science Center.

As we pass by the security entrance to the data entry area, Colin says, "This is where I work. I update consensus and project data in addition to my Breeder duties."

"Besides the Contribution, what are your other Breeder duties?" I ask, trying not to sound like I am interrogating him.

"I'm required to stay physically fit, maintain a goal weight, study political science, which is my chosen educational major, and keep my stress levels low through activities such as yogametrics and meditation," Colin replies, appearing relaxed and unaffected by my curiosity.

While I'm unable to go past the security checkpoint, I can see the workspaces of the security team. The space is minimalist. I see women in white jumpsuits, carrying sleek tablets and digi pens, with their phasers and climens tucked neatly in their pockets.

Just 200 feet past the Data Management Center is the Science Center. It looks like the Data Management Center from the outside, and between the two buildings is a steel walkway encased in glass. As we walk by the Science Center, named Apogee, I notice three men, dressed in blue jumpsuits, heading toward the entrance.

"What do the blue jumpsuits mean?" I ask.

"We typically wear normal attire when we aren't working," Colin explains. "But the blue jumpsuits are for testing days."

"Testing?" I ask.

"Yes, Breeders go through a series of tests to identify and validate genetic makeup and environmental influencers," he explains. "Thorough assessment of these characteristics is central to the genetically modified specimens developed in the labs. These specimens are reengineered to reflect close to one hundred and fifty selectable traits for breeding."

I glance back at the men. "I don't think controlling human reproduction through a genetically engineered reproductive process is right," I say. "We stand to lose what makes us human."

"And what is humanity, Dani, if it culminates in greed, destruction, and fear?" Colin asks. "What makes us human also cripples us and causes our destruction. We've evolved from the catastrophic temptations of our predecessors to become the makers of a compassionate and stable existence. Humanity as we know it is extinct. Genetic engineering eliminates disease and enhances desirable physical, emotional, and psychological traits. Of course, there are foundational traits like empathy that are required for all specimens, while traits such as greed and self-sacrifice are balanced in relationship to the other selectable traits, but the common directive is to maintain genetic traits that will ensure Dominion's survival." Colin speaks as though he's given this speech before.

"Do you know everything that's going on to ensure this new humanity, as you call it?" I ask sarcastically.

"What do you mean?" he asks.

I hesitate for a moment and reply, "Nothing. I just question if what we're doing to maintain our society is what's truly best for everyone. What you're describing is utopia, and frankly, that doesn't exist." Looking around, a foreboding feeling comes over me. If I wasn't certain of it before, being here and listening to Colin has convinced me that everything Robbie told me about the Colony being a place where Breeders are manipulated and engineered is true. "I'm surprised to see so many women," I say. "I thought only Breeders resided in the Colony."

"For the most part, that's true," Colin says. "The women here are the scientists, instructors, security personnel, leaders of our Data Management Center, and general managers of the Colony's business operations. Most of them live outside of the Colony. The few women who do live here are typically here for short periods of time, usually tied to critical project timelines."

"Besides providing the genetic material necessary for scientific purposes, what other roles do Breeders have?" I ask.

"Well, we do one-hundred percent of the maintenance, service, and hospitality work here," Colin explains. "The athletes and data entry professionals are Breeders. We also have a select number of Breeders who work in our Learning Center, which is essentially our extended education facility and library."

"Library?" I say, surprised. "That sounds interesting. Can we visit the library?"

"Sure. Follow me." Colin leads me along another circular pathway where we pass small, enclosed spaces and wide-open areas accented with traditional Japanese-style gardens. As we approach the library, it looks calm and serene and displays a beautiful interface of water and light. We follow a path along a waterfall lined with cyprus trees and pass a wall of rough granite blocks leading to the concrete plaza. Steps in the corner of the plaza lead down to a water patio with pools, cascading waterfalls crashing against the rocks on both sides, and a recessed walkway. Along the edge of the walkway is a central pond behind a curtain of water. Beyond is a rotunda. My head is almost spinning as my senses try to take in everything around me: the sound of water swirling and splashing and the sharp, aromatic smell of the greenery and flowers. I take off my heels so I can feel the sensation of the perfectly manicured lawn tickling my toes. A ramp inside the rotunda guides us to the mid-level entrance to the library. We pass through another kiosk, placing our hands just above the sensors, and enter the main lobby area.

"I've always been fascinated by architecture," I say, looking around. "This place is amazing. Can we go to the Architectural study room?"

"Yes, I believe that's on the third floor," Colin says. He is clearly delighted by my interest.

Once we reach the third floor, I begin looking around the room for someone who fits the description of The Broker. In the far-right corner, I notice a man scanning and recording books. He's tall, of medium build, with rugged looks. He is older than the other men I've seen here.

"Colin, when was the Colony built?" I ask. "Who is the architect, and what was her design aesthetic and philosophy?"

"Hold on," Colin says, smiling. "I don't know that level of detail."

"I'd love to learn more about the architectural design history of the Colony," I say. "Is it okay if I ask that gentleman over there to assist me?" I point to the man I'd noticed.

"Sure, I'll introduce you," Colin offers.

"No need. I'll be right back." Before Colin can respond, I quickly make my way toward the stacks, but the man is gone. *How did he disappear so quickly?* I pick up my pace and scurry around the corner before Colin can follow me. I slow down and walk lightly, my stride faint and restrained. At each corner, I look carefully down the row of books before turning into another narrow passageway. The sounds of the library are dull, and the air is warm. As I approach a steel-framed door, a hand touches the back of my shoulder. I'm startled and thrown slightly off balance, but I manage not to make a noise. I turn around to see the man I'd noticed earlier. He looks at me with a puzzled expression and asks, "How can I help you?"

"My name is Dani," I say. "Who are you?"

"I'm Sylas, the library attendant," he says. "What do you want?"

"I'm interested in a book about the architecture of the Colony, specifically regarding its ergonomic design. Can you help me?" I ask. I look for a sign of recognition as I say the password, "ergonomic," but his facial expression does not change.

"Wait here while I find what you need," he says before turning and disappearing down a row of books.

Moments later, he returns with a five-by-seven postcard. "This is all you need," he says with a stoic expression. I take the card and glance at it. It's just a postcard with the image of the bald eagle embossed in the upper-right corner. *This is it?* I shove it in my pocket.

I scurry back to Colin, shrug, and say, "He wasn't much help, but he did give me a visitor's postcard."

Colin smiles as if to say, "Oh well."

"I'm absolutely famished," I say, taking his hand. "What's for lunch?"

CHAPTER TWENTY

We walk to Colin's residence in the Litem sector. Litem is one of six distinctive curved glass buildings. His residence is compact. The door opens into a short, narrow hallway with a culinary bar on the right side. The bar has a stainless-steel surface and a digital console containing the week's menu. The items for the weekly menu are stored beneath the bar in a ready-to-heat-or-eat format. A larger room with a tufted leather sofa, end table, desk with a swivel chair, and a floor-to-ceiling liquidus media console occupies the space. The restroom is tucked away to the left side of the entryway.

Colin approaches the wall console across from the sofa and programs his digital window to display a scene of the sun setting behind four sloping blue mountains.

"Very impressive," I say.

"Let's take your jacket off," he says gently into my ear. He grips the collar and begins to slide the jacket very slowly down my shoulders. He presses closer as the jacket falls. He catches it and places it on the chair.

"Have a seat while I pour you a glass of wine," he says. "Blush, right?"

"Yes," I reply and sit on the sofa, sliding back against the plush cushions.

He strolls toward me. His eyes are confident and sexy, and he gazes directly at me. I begin to feel a warm sensation overtaking my body. He sits down next to me and places the glasses on the table. I stare down at my hands as I knot my fingers together. Reaching over, he takes one of my hands and gently kisses it. Picking up my wineglass and dipping his finger into it, he begins to trace the outer rim of my lips, pressing firmly, then releasing softly. My heart races. His hands are wide and strong. He starts to nibble on my earlobe, then kisses my neck. With each kiss, I begin to melt and lean further back against the sofa cushions.

"I have fantasized about touching, kissing, and devouring every part of your body, over and over again," he whispers. His breathing becomes shallow, and the tip of his tongue begins to trace the outer rim of my earlobe.

Every muscle in my body begins to tighten then release as his tongue strokes my neck. I feel so alive. All my senses feel raw and exposed. As he leans closer and pulls me in tighter, he removes the straps of my top and glides his fingers down the back of my arms. He peels my top off with his hands and softly kisses my breasts. He stands up and guides me away from the sofa, still kissing me hard, then soft. I feel weak when I stand, so he places his arms around me and supports the small of my back as I find my balance.

Once I'm steady, he stands back and gazes deeply into my eyes and says, "You are breathtaking. I am intoxicated by the warmth of your body, your smooth skin, and your supple lips. I want you to feel how much I want you." He guides my hand to the hardness between his legs.

I am so turned on by his eagerness and desire for me. He begins to remove the clip from my hair, which cascades gently across my shoulders. He reaches for the digital remote and presses a button, and a bed zooms out of the console and extends into the room. He wraps his arms around my waist and lifts me up while continuing to kiss me. He places me firmly on the bed. I moan deeper and longer while he teases me with gentle, then firm kisses on my breasts as his hands explore my behind and thighs. He squeezes, and I feel him getting harder and his breathing becoming shallower.

I whisper in his ear, "Take off your pants and get on your back." I am consumed with lust and playfulness, so when he lies on his back, I push him deeper onto the bed, gripping his muscular biceps, then releasing them. My body is astride his, and I begin to trace my tongue down his chest, twirling it around each nipple and biting him gently. I release the grip on his shoulders, run my hands down to the hardness between his legs, and begin to purr like a kitten. His hands press harder against my behind; then he begins moving his hands up my outer thigh, squeezing harder as his hips begin grinding against the warm, moist center between my legs.

Seeing him groan with pleasure is making me so hot. "You feel so good," he whispers and closes his eyes, and I melt even deeper into his chest. Holding me tightly, he massages my thighs, stares into my eyes seductively, and gently rolls me over on the bed. He removes my panties slowly, his deep, penetrating stare devouring my body, and I feel weightless from the passion. "Dani, you are so beautiful. I can't wait to be inside of you," he says.

I can't stop squirming from desire as he trails kisses down my torso, burying his tongue in my navel, then kissing the inside of my thighs. I am burning with desire. My legs quiver as the intensity of his tongue traces closer to the wetness between my legs. My skin is flushed as he kisses my lips and gently sucks and licks me so hard that I dig my nails into his skin and beg for him to go deeper.

He glides his hand up my torso and cups my breasts. My nipples are hard. As he rolls his fingers in a circular motion around my nipple, I start to groan, "I'm so wet. I want to feel you inside me." I beg and plead for this yearning to subside and to feel the intensity of him thrusting deeper and deeper.

"It's time to make you come," he murmurs and guides his hardness into me. First slowly, then harder, his sensuous assault makes me dizzy, and my body begins to convulse. The intensity of him easing in and out of me, grabbing my thighs and butt, grows more erotic. Our bodies are locked in a symphony of carnal pleasure. He kisses me hard and begins to stroke my hair. "Come for me, Dani," he murmurs softly. At his urging, I explode inside. Every sense in my body shatters, and for a moment, all I can feel is delirious ecstasy.

I am shaking and breathing erratically. "Dani, are you okay?" Colin asks as he gazes softly into my eyes. He holds me tight to stave off the tremors still traversing my body.

I stretch out beside him and gaze out the floor-length window. The brightness of the day is surrendering to the darkness, and the clouds linger amid the timid sky. The amphitheater is clearly visible from the window. The marble columns seem to change color from a blush pink to a milky white and then to gold as the sun finally sets. I am humbled by the beauty and wonder how far Dominion will go to replace nature with science.

"I hate to say this, but I have to leave," I say begrudgingly.

"Stay the night," he says.

"I wish I could. I have a business trip in the morning, and I have to pack tonight and prepare my notes."

"How long will you be gone?" he asks.

"I'm not exactly sure. It's a trip for a deep investigative piece. It could be days or even weeks, it's hard to tell," I say. "But I'll contact you when I return."

Colin pulls me in closer as we gaze at the setting sun.

CHAPTER TWENTY-ONE

The drive along the winding driveway toward the exit soothes me. My entire body is relaxed, and I feel euphoric. I can't remember the last time I felt this way, so I allow my heart to linger in this feeling. Pulling up to the security post forces me to come crashing back to reality. I'm not just here to help Robbie but to expose the truth about Dominion. For now, Colin will have to remain a pleasant dalliance. I've got work to do.

After the guard returns my camera, I lay it on the seat next to me and check my purse to make sure the card The Broker gave me is still in a secure place. I drive away.

Finally, while traveling on an empty road, the scenery of barren land transitions to tall buildings and a barrage of traffic lights signaling that I have reached the city limit. A heavy rain begins and turns to hail, leaving a dusty residue that my windshield is unable to remove—acid rain no doubt. The glaring beams of the construction trucks blur my vision as I exit the highway, and just as I reach the intersection, my ears are assaulted by the sharp screeching of the express train whizzing across the tracks. Taking shortcuts to avoid traffic, I notice a black truck following me. I dismiss it as a coincidence when I receive an incoming call. I feel a bit faint after traveling for almost an hour.

My ankles feel stiff, and I shake out my hands. As the EV slows down in front of my apartment to turn into the garage, I notice the same black truck edging slowly down the street. It slips into a parking space directly across from my apartment building. Could it be a coincidence that this looks like the same black truck that has been behind me for a mile? I stall at the entrance to the gate and wait to see if anyone gets out of the truck. Unable to see a face beyond the dark tinted windows, I edge into the parking garage and rush to the elevator.

I enter my apartment clumsily, dropping my jacket and keys on the entrance table and stumbling into the living area to find Robbie enjoying a bowl of popcorn and watching skizzer ball on the aqua screen.

"Well, you look cozy," I say with a half grin.

"And you look tuckered out from what appears to be a successful coup," Robbie says, sizing me up. "Do you have the postcard?"

I slip my hand into my purse and retrieve the postcard from the pocket. "Here. Although, I don't see anything special about it," I say, handing it over.

Robbie grabs a small flashlight from the coffee table. "This is a very special postcard," he says. "Watch." He holds up the postcard and skims it with the flashlight. "The UV light acts as a decoder when it's shone on the card," he says. As he speaks, letters begin to appear on the card, and I can make out the words *IFFMAN coordinates: 31.6598° N. 110.5254° W.* Robbie rushes to his phone and enters the coordinates.

"Have you heard of Elgin, Arizona?" he asks.

"It's five hundred miles west of here in the Third Quadrant," I say.

"I'm going to head out now," Robbie says in a hurried state.

"Wait," I say. "I wasn't exaggerating when I said I want to go with you."

He opens his mouth to speak, but I hold up my hand to stop him. "And before you object, hear me out. When you left the first time to go to the Colony, I never tried to check up on you to make sure you were okay. I just let you go, no questions asked. I regret that, and I'm not going to do it again." I look at him seriously. "Robbie, I need to know you're going to be okay." My palms are sweaty, and my heart is racing.

"This is not a vacation, Dani," he says. "This is a mission. It could be dangerous. The people who are looking for me will not hesitate to arrest or even kill you if they perceive you to be a threat of any kind. I can't put you in that kind of danger."

"I know the danger," I say. "I'm an investigative reporter. You think I haven't been in my share of life-threatening situations? Besides, there's a truth here that I want to uncover. You told me about this black market for Breeders. I want to expose that, and the best way for me to do that is to speak to the Breeders who've escaped, the ones who are at Haven."

"Dani, they may not let you into Haven," he says. Robbie continues to fumble through the room while packing his knapsack.

"Yes," I say, "but that doesn't mean they won't talk to me. I want to know the truth. Not just from them but from the people who are helping you escape. They're endangering their lives for this cause. I know there's more to uncover."

"I may not be able to protect you, and these people may not be willing to talk," Robbie says.

I shake my head, waving away his concerns. "I have quite the knack for getting information out of people, so don't worry about it. Just know that I'm not scared, and I need to do this."

He looks at me but says nothing, evidently resigned to the fact that he'll have company.

"Let's pack a few more essentials and head out first thing in the morning," I say and run to my room to prepare for our journey.

CHAPTER TWENTY-TWO

At sunrise, we move swiftly through the deserted parking garage. The air is stale and cold as we pack our things in the back seat. My hair is pulled up neatly and held by a single black and gray striped band. Robbie is dressed inconspicuously in a black and gray shirt and black running pants. I can't help but notice that he is smaller in build than Colin, but that is convenient given the journey we are on. He edges himself firmly into the trunk and lies down on his side, and I conceal him with a black tarp.

"The train station is about ten miles away, so you'll be in here for roughly twenty minutes," I say firmly as I close the trunk.

I exit the garage carefully and drive to the train station. I notice that black truck is two cars behind me, so I tear through the business quarter, weaving past office buildings and retail stores, finally racing out a side street, and taking a right turn onto the congested I-10 highway.

My adrenaline is rising, and my hands are gripping the steering wheel so hard that my knuckles stiffen. I override the auto-drive feature of the EV and lean into the steering wheel. I grip the wheel even tighter as I speed away from the truck trailing us. I get to the exit, and as soon as I leave the highway, I turn down a narrow alleyway. It looks like I've lost them as I serpentine through the sparse traffic and turn into the parking garage below my office building.

"Hurry, get out," I say to Robbie as I pop the trunk. "We're going to travel on foot to the train station."

"What's going on?" Robbie asks.

"Remember I told you about that black truck that was parked in front of my apartment last night? Well, it started following me when I left this morning. I knew I couldn't ditch it, so I drove to work. We're in the parking garage, and they won't be able to follow me in, so they're probably waiting for my car to leave. As far as they know, I was in a hurry to get to work this morning. There's an exit in the back of the building that leads to an underground walkway we can take to get to the train station. I'll leave my car here. Let's go!"

Feeling a shiver of anticipation, I grab Robbie's bag out of the trunk and lock it behind us. We disappear swiftly into the direction of the rear exit. Walking quickly through a desolate alleyway flanked by crumbling stone walls, we soon arrive at the train station. It's crowded with people bustling throughout the terminal. A motley assortment of backpackers almost engulfs us, their overstuffed duffle bags dangling from their shoulders.

"We need to buy tickets for the nine-twelve train to Elgin, Arizona, Quadrant Three," I say. Robbie nods, and I lead the way to the ticket counter, where I purchase two train tickets with cash. Cash transactions are longer and more complicated than paying with a pod card, which is genetically cued to your DNA and can be accessed via retina, finger, or skin scan. But cash is still used in a few places because social activists refuse to succumb to electronic monitoring.

While I wait for the agent to process my transaction, I watch Robbie carefully as he quietly examines the station. His head is tilted slightly down so you can see the "FREEDOM" emblem embroidered on the front of his cap. I feel a chill and wonder what other secrets a man like Robbie might keep. Since he was recruited into the Colony at age twelve, everything about him feels like a mystery. How is it that he could share so much about his life with me, but I still feel like he's a complete stranger? On the outside, he looks and sounds like the Robbie I knew so many years ago, but there is something different in his eyes, almost a quiet desperation. The longing I see in him frightens me and draws me in at the same time. I want to know about all the experiences that made him who he is today. Somehow, his truth feels like my salvation.

CHAPTER TWENTY-THREE

We have a fifty-minute wait until our train departs, so we follow the security lines to a transparent pavilion on the platform. The entire waiting area is made up of floor-to-ceiling windows that open to allow passengers to enter and exit. We sit in the far northeast corner of the pavilion, next to the snack dispensary. Robbie is quiet and seems unaffected by the possible perils of our journey. Blending cleverly into the background, he lowers his head and begins reading his pod. Unlike him, my senses are aroused by the close call of our daring escape.

Looking across the waiting area, I notice a man and woman sitting together and a baby nestled close to the woman's breast. Their clothing is functional but ordinary. The woman is wearing a loose-fitting, white button-up blouse and a dark gray skirt that reaches to her knees. Her black tights appear to sag near her ankles, and her hair is swept back from her face and confined in a tight bun. She moves from side to side, attempting to get in a more comfortable position to suckle her child beneath the white cotton cloth she layers over her left breast. Finally, settling in her seat, she leans back and lets out a solemn sigh as the baby lies weightlessly in her arms.

The man is also fully covered. He's wearing slightly baggy pants, a long-sleeved white cotton shirt, and a brimmed hat. He inspects the room with his hawkish eyes, looking for any signs of mischief or possible retaliation. His husky, strong frame is poised and alert. He, unlike many of his kind, chose to stand in the light and show deference to his religion and way of life. He is a Sandicist. The Sandicists are modern-day purists who live simply and peacefully outside of Dominion's social, political, and economic strata. They worship nature and live off the bounty of the land. Men are the leaders, and the women follow. Their procreation is controlled by Dominion, but outside of that, they are allowed to live according to their beliefs. While they are a peaceful community, there are people who resent their lifestyle simply because it is different, so they are often targeted by hate groups. They are allowed to coexist within the Dominion strata because they pose no political or economic threat. After the Ascension, Sandicists petitioned to hold on to their way of life, and in exchange for this privilege, they were prohibited from holding office or gaining access to government-funded economic aid.

My intense stare is interrupted by the sound of a beverage pouch being released from the snack dispenser next to me. A woman, wearing a form-fitting burgundy business suit, grabs the beverage and makes a beeline for a seat on the opposite side of the pavilion, where she continues to engage in conversation on her pod. She's tall and fit with a feminine strength and moves with an air of confidence. According to Dominion doctrine, she is the epitome of today's woman. She does not shrink into the background but makes her way in the world, going for what she wants and enjoying a quiet satisfaction when she gets it. Her ego does not rule her motivations or her integrity but serves to raise her up, as well as others around her. She stands with many as she works tirelessly to lift up womankind and demonize the treacherous and demoralizing ways of the past when men led society into chaos and destruction.

On one side of the Pavilion sits our past, ostracized in many ways, and on the other is our present. They coexist in an uneasy détente. Across from them is a man, sitting quietly as he waits for the train. His stature is almost limp and his eyes listless and dull. He represents the spirit of men who have settled into an uncomfortable but well-deserved mediocrity. He, too, buries his head in his pod, looking up from time to time to make sure no one can tell what he's really thinking—this struggle is far from over.

Finally, we hear the announcement that our train is ready to board.

Robbie and I make our way through the sliding doors to the train. Moving cautiously down the narrow aisle, we take seats next to each other. Once the train pulls away, both of us sigh deeply and sink into the comfy seats. We close our eyes to rest for what we know will be a long, harrowing journey.

CHAPTER TWENTY-FOUR

The train pulls into the Phoenix station, which is about seventy-five minutes from our final destination of Elgin, Arizona, Quadrant 3. Robbie leaps from the seat and makes his way to the lavatory while I scrounge around in my backpack for a salty snack and a juice pouch. My neck and shoulders are stiff, and I stand up to stretch and grab my jacket from the rack above our seats. It's quiet, almost too quiet, when two men dressed in what looks like Colony security uniforms board the train. I begin to look around for Robbie. I reach for my pod and send him a visual message: "Red sky." It's a code term Robbie and I developed after I returned from the Colony. We needed code to alert us to potential threats. It means "stay away, trouble is near." A few minutes later, the train pulls out of the station, but Robbie has not returned. I hope he got my message.

Almost thirty minutes pass, and there's still no sign of Robbie. He must have gotten my message, but what if he's been captured? Thoughts of his apprehension or possible escape cloud my mind, and I feel almost paralyzed with fear. I reach into my pocket and check my pod again—still no reply. I send another visual message, "Yellow sky?" which means "Are you safe?" It's now an hour later, and there's still no reply when, suddenly, I receive a message: "Confirming your order #3680 is ready for pickup."

Oh shoot—that's my dry-cleaning confirmation. I squint my eyes and yawn deeply. A few minutes later, I feel a virtual hug from Robbie via the clip-on he placed on my shirt this morning. I let out a sigh of relief, but now I have to wonder how we will connect when the train pulls into the station in less than fifteen minutes.

The two security officers are still sitting in my compartment. They seem engaged in a heated conversation, and I'm curious to hear what they're saying. I get up from my seat and walk casually toward the officers while pretending to listen to my pod, with echelon microbeads in my ear. As I get closer, I can hear them saying, "His last communication was with someone in New Mexico, and Carter confirmed the location. I don't think it's a ruse to throw us off the trail. Carter has too much to lose if this is a bust." The other officer scoffs and looks away angrily.

I walk to the end of the compartment and use the lavatory. On my way back to my seat, the officers both have their heads buried in a pod excursion, and I whiz by and sit back down.

As the train comes into the Elgin station, I begin to gather my belongings and wait for the signal to exit. My palms are sweaty. I'm not sure how I'll connect with Robbie, so I decide to let him find me. I exit the train and decide to wait in the transparent pavilion. Since everyone is sitting down, I remain standing in the center of the wait area and pretend to be talking on my pod. As I wait, I notice the two officers still sitting on the train as it pulls away from the station.

When I turn around, I see a man in a black cap trailing behind a woman pulling a roller bag toward the platform exit. He stalls for a moment outside the pavilion, turns toward me, makes eye contact, then starts walking toward the exit.

It's Robbie. I follow his lead and maintain a careful distance until we exit the station.

CHAPTER TWENTY-FIVE

The station is located on the outskirts of the city of Elgin. Both the entrance and exit face a large parking lot. The main street is barren, with nothing more than a yellow traffic light flashing on and off. The town itself is almost deserted, except for the retail center just west of the station and an EV charging complex on the east side of the street.

Robbie turns around and motions for me to follow him to the diner on the opposite side of the parking lot. It's small but busy enough for us to enter without being noticed. We walk in just as another couple exits through the silver metallic doors, joyfully laughing and holding hands. We scurry into a corner booth furthest from the front entrance and begin to peruse the menu.

"So, where did you hide out for the last hour of the trip?" I ask.

"As I was returning to my seat," Robbie says, "I noticed the officers boarding the train, so I followed far behind them until I saw where they sat. There was a vacant seat near the train exit. I had a clear view of them, so I sat there to keep an eye on them."

"Why did you wait so long to respond to me?" I ask, irritated.

"Sorry about that," he says. "But I couldn't risk them air scanning the pod frequencies on the train. I waited until we were about to pull into the station. Pod and haptic communications are typically canceled out by the station's receiving signal, so I knew that would be a safe time to communicate."

"How long do we wait?" I ask, rummaging through my backpack.

"The connect time is three p.m. We have almost two hours," Robbie says.

After devouring cheeseburgers, chips, and fruit juice, I pay, and we scurry out of the restaurant. There's a thick fog covering the edge of the city. We walk briskly across the main street and into the park, which is densely populated with many tall trees. There are several pathways throughout the park, surrounded by colorful flowers and grass. None of the benches along the pathways are occupied, except for the one closest to a statue of a woman holding a butterfly and standing on the neck of a serpent—this is the statue of a Paragonin, a symbol of Dominion's triumph over the callous brutality and destructive greed perpetrated by men. It has become the national symbol of freedom and justice, just as the Statue of Liberty once prevailed as the paragon of freedom and democracy for the United States.

It is at this bench that we are to meet our first connect. We carefully approach the bench where an old man sits slumped on the far end, his left hand hanging over the armrest; his face, inflamed with sores and rashes, looks haggard and confused. His pants look like they're tied up with a string, and his tattered shoes are badly torn and worn out. He smells of putrid sweat and urine. I am overcome by revulsion, then sadness.

"Sir, are you okay?" Robbie asks softly.

The old man does not move or say a word. He's nearly catatonic, completely unaware of his surroundings. We scan the area for any clue that might help us understand why he's here or who he is. Glancing at the ground, I notice a syringe with a needle crumpled among some damp leaves and a soiled cloth.

"Robbie—look," I say. "It looks like he's an infinity user." I move closer to him to confirm my suspicion.

"I think you're right," Robbie says, squinting at him. He takes in the despondent look on his face, the bulging eyes with a lost stare, and the hands clenched tightly into fists. "He's completely shut down. When he comes to, he won't even know where he is, let alone that we were here."

Stepping away from the haggard, old man, we notice a beam of light coming from the trees behind the bench. "This must be our connect," Robbie says. "Let's wait near that tree to see if he approaches." We huddle next to the tree and continue talking. The beam of light grows sharper and brighter as it narrows in on the bench next to the statue.

A tall, husky man, wearing a dark uniform and white cap, approaches the bench. Standing near the old man slumped over on the bench, the man in uniform pulls out his pod and begins to send a message. Robbie walks slowly toward him and asks loudly, "Excuse me, sir, I seem to be lost. Can you tell me where I can find the Phoenix?"

Watching Robbie just standing there, looking timid and unsure, I recall the word "Phoenix" being on the card The Broker gave us. The man looks up from his pod, takes off his cap, and motions for Robbie to come closer. I'm standing in the distance, unable to hear what they're saying to each other, but at one point, their voices become louder. I can't make out what they're saying. Obviously agitated, the man begins to walk away. Robbie stands still, and suddenly, the tall, husky stranger turns around and extends his arm, encouraging Robbie to follow him. Robbie turns to me and makes the same gesture, and I run to him; we follow the mysterious stranger together.

The man rushes to a dark pickup truck. It's a classic. It must be at least a couple decades old. There are a few tall boxes in the open cargo area, and he opens the door and starts the engine. Robbie and I scamper to the passenger side of the truck and get in. We sit quietly while the man stares intently at the open highway. The truck seems to hug the black tarmac as it travels over the uneven road. A loud thud startles me when Robbie's head hits the roof after a front tire barrels over a pothole. The dust billowing from the air conditioner fills my nostrils, and I start sneezing uncontrollably. Robbie begins to speak, and the man signals with his hand for him to stop. Unsure what is happening, Robbie stays silent, and I follow suit. After we pass a large tree with a hole in the center, the man says, "Now we can talk." He turns to me and says, "You're probably wondering what the scuffle was about in the park. I wasn't expecting Robbie to be traveling with a companion. It's highly unusual that I secure more than one traveler at a time. What's your story? Why are you here?"

I hesitate at first, then respond with conviction, "I'm here to do anything I can to ensure Robbie's safe arrival to Haven. I'm aware of the risks, and your intimidation tactics don't scare me!" I look at him intently. I release tension in my shoulders as I look at Robbie. I'm not going to leave his side. Robbie looks pleasantly surprised by my response. He smiles, brushes against my shoulder, then looks out the window.

"Well," he says, "you sound determined. Just know that the journey is hard, and you're going to have to hold your own."

"Not a problem," I reply, my cheeks getting warm as I glare into his dark eyes.

"And now that we understand each other—welcome aboard. I'm Ambrose."

CHAPTER TWENTY-SIX

The ride is long, and I begin to lean on Robbie's shoulder and rest my eyes. The trip has been exhausting, and not once did I let down my guard enough to take in my surroundings or relax my mind. Just for a moment, here in the relative safety of Ambrose's truck, I begin to drift into a light slumber. Awakened by a loud clunk, which slams me hard against Robbie's shoulder, I'm enamored of what I see; it's dusk and the golden shadows seem to kiss the departure of the sun.

The truck slows as we approach a towering gate. Ambrose turns off the paved road onto uneven dirt and says, "Welcome to Garland Vineyards. Five acres of the closest thing to heaven on earth." The dirt road seems endless as we pass rows and rows of grapes on the vine. The vines are dense and full. They tower with inexplicable authority and make me feel humble and grateful. I lower the window and take a deep breath, smelling the cold, crisp air as it blows across my face and tickles my nose.

In the distance, I see a large residence with several smaller homes flanking it on both sides in a U-shape. We pull into an enclosed garage attached to the main residence. Ambrose turns off the engine and says, "Follow me." Robbie and I climb out of the truck and follow Ambrose into the house. The garage—cold, damp, and dark—leads to an amazing large hallway. From there, we make a left into the dining room. It is alive with vibrant hues of the sunset flooding through the large bay windows. When I exit the dining room, I see a kitchen, a big open space filled with orange light. I can feel the warmth of the room and the nostalgic blend of freshly baked cinnamon rolls and a smoky, earthy aroma of dark roast coffee. I walk briskly through the kitchen to a large living room. Straight ahead are a set of stairs leading to the second floor, with five bedrooms and four bathrooms. "Follow me to the attic. This is where you and Robbie will stay," Ambrose says. Dusk is giving way to night, and our bodies are weary and ready for rest. Looking around, I can sense the tempered ambitions and fears of the people who came before us. Those seeking freedom and refuge from Dominion. To them, this place was safe, and now I, too, feel safe, at least until daybreak.

I lay my head on the soft pillow, which caresses my neck and envelops the back of my head. My shoulders grow limp as each muscle in my body is besieged by the stillness of the night. Robbie stays awake, keeping watch through the oval stained-glass window between our beds, as I drift into slumber.

In the morning, I'm awakened by a loud clacking sound outside. I look out of the window to see men dragging large burlap bags and tools from a nearby shed and loading them into the back of a pickup truck. As my eyes begin to take in the surrounding garden filled with what looks like flower bells, blue azaleas, forget-me-nots, lilies, and irises, Ambrose calls us down to breakfast.

The house is even more beautiful in the daylight. It reminds me of the pre-Ascension homes. It has full light windows rather than the UV light and AV particle blocking windows you find in cities these days. The house itself is made of brick instead of the characteristic recycled concrete, metal, and synthetic wood. The furniture is rustic, colonial, and lends a homey warmth rather than the minimalist, cold, and overly functional furniture of our modern-day city residences. But what really strikes me are the smells of natural food aromas and the sandalwood and citrus essence throughout the house. In the city, smell is largely manufactured and can be selected, much like light, scenery, or music. I often choose lavender and mint scent enhancement via my olfactory console, which permeates my home and drowns out natural scents. It feels artificial, but over time, I guess I just became used to it and forgot the delight of natural scents.

Ambrose welcomes us into the breakfast dining area, where three men and a woman are gathered around the table, talking and laughing. Ambrose introduces us to his wife, Sirah. She is slender, tall, and moves with grace and elegance as she plates the food on large serving platters and carries them to the table. He turns to his youngest son, Jason, twenty-one, who lifts his head to give us a brief nod and then returns his attention to his pod. Ambrose's middle son, Jaxon, twenty-four, is a bit more conversational and introduces us to his brother Jared, twenty-six. Jared acts like the oldest as he stares us down and looks like he's preparing to interrogate us. Lastly, rushing in the house with a bunch of fresh flowers in her hand is Josephine, as Jared introduces her. "Everyone calls her Josie," Sirah says, smiling as she grabs a vase for the flowers.

"She is sixteen," Jared interjects. She looks so innocent as she bats her gentle, doe eyes and smiles shyly at Robbie.

"What a beautiful family you have, Ambrose," I say.

"Well, thank you," he says. "I'm sure you can tell that my family is used to sheltering newcomers. Very early on, Sirah and I taught our children how very fortunate they are to live free from the judgment and limits in this society, where your entire individual value and potential is based on scientifically assessed value quotients. Just before the Ascension, I was fifty-three and a biogenetic chemist. My work was my life, and I had no wife or children. I ignored the outside world. I turned away from the horrors of war, greed, poverty, religious and political persecution, and leaders who sought power through racial and sexual demagoguery. After the war, I was temporarily infertile, and even though I became fertile again, I was deemed too old to join the Breeder Colony. Youth has the advantages of future promise but disadvantages of ignorance.

"The immediate impact of the war resulted in a temporary amnesia, which was diagnosed as mental and cognitive impairment. I regained my mental capabilities but hid my recovery in order to be perceived as nonthreatening. My parents owned this vineyard, and when they died, they left it to me. Because of the laws regulating business and land ownership, I had to share ownership of the vineyard with an adult woman. Luckily, I met Sirah in the hospital where I was recuperating. She was a nurse, and she gave me the courage and love I needed to start over again for a new cause. Sirah and I married, and she and her sons moved to the vineyard, where we began our new life." Ambrose looks up and smiles at each of his children. "So," he says, looking around. "That's enough of our story for now. Let me show you the vineyard." He stands and heads toward the front door.

Stepping outside of the house, I feel an immediate sense of calm and community as I walk along the dirt road with Ambrose and Robbie. Each row is tended to by laborers in straw hats, with bandanas covering their foreheads, jean coveralls, and sturdy work shoes. They seem content as they work diligently.

Ambrose introduces us to Josh, his foreman. Josh continues the tour and walks us through the manufacturing and curing facilities. As the Garland clock, which is visible from the main archway leading to the distillery, strikes ten, an alarm sounds, and the workers begin to leave the field to head home for their midmorning meal. I also notice children exiting a nearby structure.

"What's that?" I ask.

"That's our school for our children ages five through twelve," Josh explains. "Children in grades nine through twelve are homeschooled."

"Do the kids interact with children outside of the Garland compound?" I ask.

"They do," Josh responds. "Outside of their schooling, they have the same experiences as any other kids their age." He smiles at me. "We give our children as normal an upbringing as possible. Our way of life is not infected with the shackles of genetic selection and societal limitations."

Josh continues the tour through the warehouse, bottling lines, and laboratory. The heat from the sun overhead distracts me as I walk from one building to another. Unable to show any further restraint, I blurt out, "But surely you benefit from some aspects of Dominion society. Like Breeders to sire your children?"

Josh gives me a blank stare and pauses before answering. "We don't use Breeders," he says. "We denounce all constructs of Dominion society that degrade men."

"Are you telling me that none of these children were sired by Breeders?" I ask.

"That's correct," Josh responds.

"How is that possible?" I ask.

Before Josh can respond, the siren goes off again, and the late morning shift begins.

CHAPTER TWENTY-SEVEN

The day begins to wind down. There's a gentle stir in the trees and the sound of families congregating for the evening meal.

Dinner is a sacred time for Ambrose and his family. Promptly at sundown, the family comes down for the evening meal after showering off the day's work. They come together and share their lives in a way that reminds me of what life was like before my father died. My mother was so different then. We would gather at the dinner table, and there was laughter and joy. It was only when the war started that conversations became tense and my father seemed to carry the weight of the world on his shoulders. I still struggle with his death, and *she* blames the war for his heart attack. The birth of Dominion took so much away from me: my father, my way of life, and in many ways, *she* was no longer the mother I knew.

After dinner is the best part of the evening. The family rests in big, comfy chairs and on pillows in the great room. Their bellies full and eyes gleaming with contentment, Ambrose shares his memories of life before the Ascension and the days when men were free to live their lives as equals to women. I find his recounting a bit misleading in the way he describes the balance of power between men and women. His belief that the social dynamics between men and women achieved some sort of equilibrium is false. Women struggled with social and economic equality, and the political unrest was burgeoning into another Women's Rights Movement, like the fight for women's suffrage in the mid-nineteenth century. However, there is truth to his sentiment that people must be free to pursue their dreams, and no government has the right to dictate human potential and value.

While Ambrose is talking, I notice something peculiar. Josie is smiling and licking her lips amorously while ogling Robbie. Her deep stare at Robbie doesn't go unnoticed as Robbie glances down and then up again at her. From the corner of my eye, I notice Ambrose smiling as he observes this overt flirting between Josie and Robbie. He seems almost exhilarated by the attraction between them.

As the clock strikes 9 p.m., the family begins to disperse, and I motion to Robbie. I want him to ask Ambrose about an update regarding our next connect. All Robbie and I know is that it will be within the next twenty-four to forty-eight hours, but we need to know when and where to meet.

"Ambrose, have you received information regarding our next connect?" Robbie asks.

"Nothing yet, Robbie. I expect to hear something tomorrow," Ambrose responds.

Robbie and I head up to the attic to retire for the evening.

Lying awake in the darkness, my mind churns like a runaway engine. This sleeplessness is torture. I toss and turn as ideas of possible angles for the story, looming deadlines, and conflicting thoughts about Ambrose's stories occupy my mind. My eyes open and immediately fixate on the clock. It's 11 p.m. Just as a heaviness begins to overtake my consciousness, the clamor of people shouting outside my window startles me. I look over to see that Robbie's sleep is uninterrupted. Rather than continuing to toss and turn, I decide to make a call. Curling tightly underneath my blanket and covering my head, I grab my pod and dial the number of the one person I know will be up anxiously awaiting my call.

"Hi, Sam? It's Dani," I say.

"Well, it's about time. You're late checking in. What do ya have for me?" Sam asks in a zealous tone.

"Well, just as I thought—it turns out that the story about the escaped Breeder is peanuts compared to what I've uncovered so far," I say. "As I promised, there's a much bigger story here." I grab the pillow next to the wall and press it over my head to muffle the sound of my voice. "There may be a government conspiracy surrounding the release of Breeders, and the Transformation Center is part of it. Sam, this story could be big."

"Dani, stay on this," she says. "I like where this is going. In the meantime, I'm going to let Amanda cover any updates regarding the police investigation about the Breeder escape. Just stay on top of this. I want this story!"

"You got it," I say.

"By the way," Sam asks, "any inside info on the recent Accolade announcement?"

"What announcement?" I ask. "This investigation gives me limited exposure to what's going on in the outside world. I haven't talked to my source in several days."

"The Defense secretary announced that the Accolade will become the direct recruitment source for all government executive-level Intelligence and Defense positions," she explains. "It's just another way for the wealthy to exclude underprivileged females from positions of power. Over the years, the Accolade has become the most exclusive government training program. It only recruits the most elite females from prestigious schools. This decision only widens the socioeconomic divide between the women of Dominion."

"Wow," I say. "How can Dominion leadership not see that economic stratification breeds divide and inequality?"

"There are protests bubbling up at college campuses across the country," she goes on. "It's been national headline news for the past couple of days, and the media networks and virtual worlds are in a frenzy.

"Clearly, Dominion officials underestimated the impact of this announcement because there were no media containment policies enacted before the disclosure. The media content seizure policies are being enacted now, but it's too late. The groundswell is underway." The brisk wind outside blows louder, causing the tree branches to scrape and scratch against the window. "We've seen how institutionalized elitism and exclusion poisoned our country before the Ascension," Sam says. "A rebellion led by those who have no power can be contained, but creating division through manipulation and subterfuge among those in power, even if the power is controlled, is a slippery slope. Dominion can't survive this way."

"I remember my interview with a female member of Hangar-Eight," I say. "She recounted what Dominion was like when it began. Women were unified and working together, rich, poor, old, young, it didn't matter. We were women, and we did what was best to rebuild the country. We seem to be falling back into the trap that existed before."

"It does seem like it," Sam says. "Anyway, keep on with the story."

"I will," I promise and hang up.

The call ends on a somber note. The thought that we are recreating the same societal ills that destroyed our country before is chilling. The fact that leadership lies in the hands of women versus men doesn't change what is fundamentally unchangeable; we are humans first.

I try to snuggle back into sleep. The room grows cold as I slumber in oversized sweatpants and a long-sleeve T-shirt that I grabbed from a box of spare clothes underneath the bed. A dull, thumping sound awakens me from a sound sleep. It's 3:30 a.m.

"Robbie, Robbie, do you hear that?" I ask.

"Hear what?" Robbie says in an irritated tone as he buries his head deeper into the pillow.

"There's a dull, muffled noise—almost like a humming coming from downstairs," I say.

I pop out of bed, put on my sneakers, and begin to follow the noise.

"Where are you going?" Robbie asks.

"I'm going to find out where that noise is coming from," I say.

"Wait for me," Robbie says as he moves to put on his jacket and sneakers, then grabs his pod.

"Let's go," I say.

We maneuver quietly through the house, searching for the dull, throbbing noise, which grows louder as we get closer to the rear exit near the garage entrance. Making our way down the stairs, the noise becomes a distinctive humming sound.

"Wait," Robbie says as he presses his ear against the hallway door.

Turning the doorknob, he pushes the door open. It connects into another long, narrow, dimly lit hallway with concrete flooring. We sneak quietly through the hallway to another door. This one is a heavy steel with a security pad affixed to the lower right side of the door handle.

"Now we just need to figure out how to get in." I say.

"Let's try this," Robbie says as he retrieves a card from his pocket.

"Where did you get that?" I ask.

"Ambrose gave this to me when I had to get through the security gate to grab my jacket from his truck in the garage this afternoon, and I forgot to return it."

Robbie slides the card across the card reader, and the door cracks open.

We slip past the door and follow the increasingly loud throbbing noise. Finally, we reach a room with a plate glass window.

"I don't believe what I'm seeing," I say, peering inside. "This is odd. It's a laboratory with what looks like really high-tech equipment. This reminds me of the labs at the Colony."

Robbie says nothing. He just watches through the window.

"Wait, Robbie, these guys look really familiar," I say. "If I'm not mistaken, the guy in the white coat with the gray gloves is Josh, and there's Ambrose."

I take in the rest of the men. "It looks like some of the same guys who were in the field this afternoon."

Without warning, someone grabs me and Robbie from behind and pushes us through the door.

"Ambrose, it looks like your guests have been snooping," a man says as he holds a laser to our heads.

Ambrose looks up, signs a document, and approaches us.

"Well, it's just as well that you know what's going on here," he says as he removes his gloves and leans against the beveled observation window.

"As you can see," he continues, "we're doing more than just making wine here at Garland. For the past fifteen years, I've been leading a team of researchers to find a cure for the mental and cognitive impairment caused by the war. Some of the men here work in the fields during the afternoon shift and work in the lab at night. They're some of the brightest scientific minds working for this cure, and we are very close to a breakthrough." He states this all plainly, as though there is nothing odd about it.

"Who are the other people?" I ask.

"They're migrant workers who live close by," Ambrose responds.

"So, you're telling me those men have not experienced cognitive decline?" I ask.

"No, each of these men experienced it, and I invented a serum that temporarily restores their cognitive abilities, but the effects typically wear off after ten hours, and the side effects are still being tested. We're searching for a permanent restorative cure. Once we find it, we'll be able to disseminate the cure to the men affected by the war. In the meantime, I will continue to help men seeking freedom from the oppression of breeding or the Dissident camps." Ambrose clears his throat and leans back against the window.

Clearing my throat, I ask, "Is it possible that the cognitive effects from the Great War were only temporary, but Dominion purposely induces it through the Singletary assignment process? Do you know anything about that?"

There's something puzzling in the way Ambrose is looking at me. It's like the weight of his thoughts is torturing him. With a tone of deep sadness and melancholy, he replies, "Yes, the real purpose of Illegis is to disempower the male population, and that includes ensuring that the effects of the Great War continue. But we have a chance to stop this and set a new course," Ambrose says, peering at Robbie with a sense of indescribable longing, as if there was a secret that only he and Robbie could share.

"What about infertility?" I ask. "Are you able to restore their fertility?"

"Why do you ask?" Ambrose looks puzzled.

"I've seen at least a dozen children on this compound, and Josh mentioned that this community denounces the societal constraints that Dominion created. One of those is the establishment of the Colony for Breeders. If you don't take part in the Breeder program, how are you able to have children?" I ask.

"Josh is correct when he says that we do not support the Dominion way of life. But we have not found a cure for male infertility. The men at Garland are sterile and unable to sire children. Each child you see here at Garland is my own," Ambrose says.

"You sired every child in this compound?" I ask. "There have to be at least twenty!"

"Fourteen, to be exact," Ambrose says. "After the war, my cognitive abilities and fertility were temporarily compromised long enough for me to test out of the system and be reinstated to this vineyard."

"How are you accounting for children who are not conceived via a Breeder? Surely, the mandatory census would uncover the discrepancy?" I ask.

"We go through the Breeder process, but the actual contribution used for implantation is my own. Sirah works at the local fertility center, and she manages all the Breeder deposits. She simply substitutes my own contribution for the Breeder deposits," Ambrose says, watching me closely for any reaction.

"I see. So as far as Dominion knows, these children are bred via the Breeder process, but the actual contribution is your own," I say. Robbie is quiet as he stares at the clock just above the observation window.

"Listen, I commend your efforts to find a cure, but in the meantime, I need to move on to the next connect," he says. "We have no intention of telling anyone your secret, so when can we leave?"

"Soon, Robbie," Ambrose says. "Soon. I will take care of everything, so why don't you go back to sleep, and we can have a talk in the morning?" He reaches out and shakes Robbie's hand.

Robbie and I head back to the attic, not saying a word to each other. All we know is that we need to get out of this place soon. Something just doesn't feel right.

CHAPTER TWENTY-EIGHT

The next morning, Robbie nudges my shoulder and urges me to get out of bed. I feel a bit disoriented, and looking directly at him, I ask, "Did I dream that we're living in a house with a man who managed to survive the war, retain his cognitive abilities, restore his fertility, build a secret laboratory managed by field laborers by day and scientists by night, and sire all fourteen children in this compound?"

"That's about right," Robbie responds.

"Robbie, while I understand Ambrose's goals, something about all of this doesn't feel right. Did you notice the crazy look in his eyes as he told us what was going on? The way he looks at you, as if he wants more than to send us on our way. He's hiding something," I say declaratively. "My instincts are never wrong. We gotta get out of here."

"Listen," Robbie says. "I'll meet with Ambrose this morning and get the connect details so we can plan our next move. Don't worry." Robbie strokes my cheek. "Let's go have breakfast."

Walking to the kitchen, we notice that the house is silent. The sound of laughter and busy chatter is absent. We look beyond the great room and see only Sirah sitting at the breakfast table reading.

"Good morning, Sirah," I say.

"Good morning, can I get you some coffee? We have breakfast breads, cereal, and yogurt," she says pleasantly.

"Yes, coffee and yogurt would be fine," I reply.

"Just coffee for me," Robbie says. "And Sirah, where is Ambrose?"

"He went into town for a meeting," she says. "He should be back in a couple of hours."

Robbie seems a bit annoyed but retains his composure. "Why don't we head out for a walk?" he asks me, his tone casual.

I remember how much I loved to take long walks with Robbie when we were kids. We called them nature walks, and we would explore our surroundings, including climbing fences, smelling and tasting unknown plants, and running through wide-open spaces until we fell down from exhaustion and stared up at the clear, blue sky. We imagined ourselves flying, climbing a mountain, or swimming across the ocean.

As we head upstairs to grab our jackets, we hear a harsh knock against the front door. Sirah looks out of the peephole and says, "It's the police. Go upstairs." She waves her hand. We rush to the head of the stairs, where we are out of sight but can overhear the exchange and see Sirah from behind the stairwell.

"Who is it?" she asks.

"It's the Elgin police," a voice says.

"Hello, officers, how may I help you?" Sirah asks kindly as she opens the door.

"Hello, ma'am, we're looking for this man. His name is Robert Cummings." The officer shows Sirah a picture.

"He doesn't look familiar," she says. "What is this about? Should I be worried?" Her voice is calm.

"Yes," the officer says. "He's dangerous, and should you see him, it is imperative that you report it immediately. This is my code," he says, touching Sirah's pod with his.

"Do you mind if we make inquiries with some of your laborers?" the other officer asks.

"Not at all," Sirah replies. "But please keep the disturbance to a minimum. We're at the height of harvesting and can't afford any distractions right now."

"Thank you, ma'am," the first officer says.

Robbie and I rush from behind the stairs as she closes the door. "Sirah, if they ask around, someone is bound to recall seeing Robbie,"

I say.

"No need to worry," she says. "Our workers will not say a word. They fear the law and will not tell them anything. As for the others, they know to say nothing."

"Still, we need to be on our way," Robbie says. "I don't like this. They're on our trail."

"I'll call Ambrose," Sirah says. "He'll know what to do. In the meantime, stay inside."

We head up to the attic and begin packing our bags.

CHAPTER TWENTY-NINE

After packing our things needed to sustain an even deeper underground escape, we sit on our beds and wait for Ambrose to arrive.

"What do we already know about the next connect?" I ask.

"I know that we most likely have to get somewhere in Quadrant Nine by Friday. Jason told me that the next connect will be there. It may take up to two days. Ambrose mentioned lending us a car, but now I'm not too sure that traveling by car is a good idea. With them so close on our trail, the roads are bound to be staked out," Robbie says.

"The train does seem a bit safer at this point, but it's also possible that they've surveilled the train station for us," I say.

"Do you think they know we're traveling together?" Robbie asks.

"No, I don't think so," I say. "They only showed Sirah your photo. As far as anyone knows, I'm out of town covering a story."

"What we don't know is who the next connect is and what time we're supposed to meet them. That's what we need from Ambrose." Robbie looks worried.

The sound of tires screeching to a halt in front of the house distracts me. I look out the window and see Ambrose getting out of the truck. Robbie and I rush downstairs with our bags to meet Ambrose in the great room.

"We've got to go now," Robbie says. "The police are on my trail. Any idea how they tracked me down?"

"I heard there's a mole in the Colony," Ambrose says. "He may have intercepted a communication and informed the police. I need to reach your connect and inform him so we can change the location and time. Let me make the call."

Ambrose heads to his office while we wait.

I'm getting that uneasy feeling again, I think. "I'm going to grab a piece of fruit," I say.

On my way to the kitchen, I notice the door to Ambrose's office is slightly cracked. I move in closer to see what he's doing.

I watch as Ambrose picks up a piece of paper from his desk and writes something down on it. He secures the paper in his portfolio, and speaking to someone on his pod, he says, "Give me another day. I need time to work this out. I need him to stay here."

What does he mean by that? I quietly rush back to the great room, but before I can tell Robbie what I heard, Ambrose returns.

"I left a message and should hear back soon," he says. "In the meantime, Robbie, I need to speak with you privately." Ambrose begins walking toward the kitchen, and I notice he is holding a small book in his hand. In his haste, he drops it, and the earthy-hued cover opens. Inside, a few pages flutter in the breeze and then spill onto the floor. Ambrose picks up the book as I give Robbie an assertive look, signaling my concern.

Ambrose and Robbie exit through the back door and begin walking toward the large mesquite tree in the backyard. Its full, looming branches lightly camouflage Robbie and Ambrose in the distance.

I head to the kitchen to grab an apple when my pod rings. It's Robbie. When I answer it, I hear the rustle of the leaves in between the heavy pounding of footsteps. Robbie wants me to be aware of what's going on, so I listen and rush to the kitchen window to see what is happening.

"I hope you don't mind me insisting on a private chat just between us," Ambrose says. "What I have to say will be a bit unusual, and I want to make sure your immediate response is not influenced by anyone else."

"Ambrose, what is this about?" Robbie asks. Ambrose stops walking and firmly grips Robbie's arm.

"You recall last night, when I told you that we're close to completing the retrieval formulation that will reverse cognitive impairment?"

"Sure," Robbie says.

"Well," Ambrose continues. "That is not the case anymore. Recent results are not as promising as I would like, and we need to make some changes. These changes could result in a delay of close to a year, maybe more." I hear Ambrose clear his throat.

"That's a setback for sure," Robbie says. "But you appear to have a well-oiled machine here." Robbie jerks his arm back to release Ambrose's grip.

"Robbie," Ambrose says, "I don't know how else to say this, but I'm dying. I'm not expected to live more than six months. The disease has been progressing slowly. I was diagnosed with a rare intestinal fungus just before the war. Somehow, afterward, the disease wasn't present in my body. We thought it may have been destroyed by the effects of the war. What we didn't know at the time is that it was simply in remission, and it returned several years later. It's been slowly taking over my body. There is no cure. I've been working as fast as I can to deliver the retrieval formula and find a cure. We are so close but not close enough for me."

"I'm so sorry about that, Ambrose," Robbie says. "Do you have a backup plan to continue the work?"

"It's funny you should ask that, but yes, I do. Or at least I have a succession plan for the retrieval formula but not for the continued growth of this community. Once the retrieval formula is finished, cognitive dysfunction will be eradicated, but fertility could take much longer to restore. I need someone who can continue to sire children for our community. Robbie, I need you."

"Need me for what? I don't know exactly what you're asking," Robbie replies.

"I'm asking you to vacate your plans and stay in Garland," Ambrose says. "You are the perfect successor. You're young, fertile, familiar with the breeding culture and processes, unable to resurface in society, and you bring a separate gene pool, which is necessary to grow this community.

Also, I've seen the way you and Josie look at each other. There's chemistry there, and I'm sure, over time, love can grow between you. The two of you could marry and eventually run Garland." Stunned by what I am hearing, I walk outside to find Sirah and notice a man trimming the hedges near the fence. He looks a lot like one of the officers who came looking for us. Refocusing my eyes on Robbie, I see Ambrose making fists with his hands, and Robbie takes a step back.

"Ambrose," Robbie says, fighting to keep his tone even. "I truly appreciate your hospitality and help, but I can't stay here. I have to make it to Haven to be free and join the resistance."

"Don't you see, Robbie, that the resistance exists here on Garland as well?" Ambrose says. "We are fighting to restore balance to society through science. Haven will lead you to violence and further destruction." Ambrose steps closer to Robbie and grabs his arm more firmly this time. "Robbie, this is your destiny. Can't you see that?"

"I can't stay here," Robbie says. "My commitment to find Haven is as much for Dani as it is for me. She's counting on me. I can't turn back now. When that call comes in, you'll confirm the time and location of our next connect so we can get out of here. I am sorry, Ambrose, but this is the way it has to be." Robbie's tone is stern and unyielding.

"Of course, I understand your resistance. This is a lot to take in, and maybe you just need some time to digest what you've just heard," Ambrose replies.

"I don't need to think it over. I'm outta here," Robbie says and turns toward the house.

"Wait, before you leave, just read this." Ambrose attempts to hand the book to Robbie. Robbie turns away again.

"Please take it!" Ambrose says with a shrill cry.

Robbie grabs the book, looks at the cover, and thumbs through it.

"This looks like a journal. Is this yours?" Robbie looks confused.

Ambrose responds, "No, but I beg you to read it before you leave Garland. It has the answers you're looking for and will help you better understand why remaining here is the best solution for you."

Robbie tucks the journal under his arm and races to the house. Ambrose sits on the bench beneath the tree, his body limp and his head down, languishing in despair.

CHAPTER THIRTY

"You're right. Something isn't right here," Robbie says as he bustles his way back into the attic. "We've got to get out of here fast."

"I saw both of you and heard bits and pieces of the conversation, but the sound got a bit muddled in some parts. What does he want from you?" I ask.

"Ambrose is dying. He needs a successor to continue siring offspring for Garland. Apparently, I fit the job description. He even offered up Josie as a reward. Can you imagine how desperate he has to be to treat his own child like a pawn?" Robbie asks.

"You must've been flattered to receive such an offer." I brush my hair off my face.

"Flattered! Why would you say something like that?" Robbie asks.

"I notice the way you and Josie look at each other," I say. "There's no denying the chemistry you have."

"Chemistry! Did you and Ambrose discuss this earlier?" Robbie says. "The two of you sound like collaborators. I want out of here now. Chemistry or not, we're not staying!"

"I agree that we need to leave," I say. "What's that under your arm?"

"Nothing. Ambrose wants me to read it. He thinks it may convince me to stay. I'm not interested in any more of his mind games." Robbie throws the journal on the bed.

"Well, if you don't want it, I'll take it. It may be useful." I stash it in my backpack.

"Fine, but save it for another day. We need to figure out how to get the hell out of here." Robbie begins pacing the floor, his gait erratic.

"But I do sympathize with Ambrose's situation. He's trying to change the world. That takes courage. Often, that determination can push you to unimaginable places. Did you ever wonder how the officers came to inquire about us here? I thought it was odd when Ambrose told you there was a leak at the Colony. Then, while you and Ambrose were out talking, I went outside to find Sirah, and I noticed a man trimming the hedges near the fence. He looked a lot like one of the officers who came looking for us. Now that I know what Ambrose is after, it makes me think the officers weren't real. They were Ambrose's minions, doing his bidding. Ambrose wanted you to think that the officers were on your trail so you would stay here and remain shielded from the police. What are the chances they would return after being told you weren't here? And by not asking about me, it would make it easy for me to go back home." I reach for my backpack, pull out a piece of paper, and hand it to Robbie.

"What's this?" he asks.

"I overheard Ambrose talking on the pod, and he wrote something down. I thought it might be directions for our next connect, so I copied it while you two were outside talking."

Robbie examines the note. "This is it," he says. "These are the instructions for our next connect, and we've got a little over twenty-four hours to get there. We've got to go now, and we can't chance Ambrose trying to stop us."

"How do we get out of here without anyone knowing?" I ask.

"Ambrose keeps an old car just beyond the storage unit on the perimeter of the compound. It's a short walk from here," Robbie says. "We can drive it to the train station in the next town and leave from there."

"Let's go!" I say, not looking back.

The dust and wind whip across our faces as we run toward the storage facility. The weight of the extra supplies bears heavily against my shoulders and back as the adrenaline from this escape dulls the aching feeling near my ribs. When we finally reach the storage unit, we find it empty except for the old car parked near a dumpster near the rear exit.

"I haven't seen one of these since I was a kid," I say as I open the door. "I hope one of us can remember how to drive this thing."

"For one thing," Robbie says, "we need keys to start it, and we don't have them."

I begin searching in the car. I reach far underneath the steering wheel and locate a key. "Let's just hope this works," I say, pulling it out.

The car jumps to life, then, just as quickly, stalls out.

"I'm going to have to pop the hood and take a look," Robbie says. "I remember a little bit from when my dad and I used to work on his old sedan. Let me see what I can do."

Suddenly, in the distance, we hear a voice. "Robbie, Dani? What are you doing here?" Looking up, we see Josie walking toward us, a scowl on her face. "What's going on?" she asks.

"Look, Josie, it's time for us to move on to our next connect," Robbie says calmly.

"But Daddy told me you were staying here!" she replies, her tone anxious. She slowly walks toward Robbie, her hands almost glued to her side.

"Josie, what he told you isn't true," Robbie says.

The car roars to life and begins to purr. "I think we got it," I say.

"Look, Josie," Robbie says, his voice growing agitated. "We're in a hurry."

Angry and confused, Josie shouts, "You can't go. I'm gonna tell!" She runs away, and Robbie chases after her.

"Stop, you can't tell anyone!" Robbie shouts as he closes in on her. Grabbing her arm, he pulls her to him and urges her to calm down. "Josie, this can't be. We can't be. I can't stay here."

"You can't go. I want you to stay here." Josie throws her arms around him and gives him a passionate gaze.

CHAPTER THIRTY-ONE

AMBROSE

As I sit quietly under the cool leaves of the desert willow tree, replaying my recent encounter with Robbie, I begin to think.

How could Robbie not understand? I have sacrificed the last several years of my life restoring what is right and natural to this world here in Garland. I thought I finally found the answer when I allowed Robbie and Dani here. But he is willing to be a slave to a society that only wants him to advance the agenda of a group of female demagogues preying on the carnage of war. Robbie has been brainwashed. First by the Colony, and now by this intruder, Dani. She has somehow convinced him that his destiny is in Haven and not Garland. I will not let her destroy my last chance to save Garland and all the others who could flourish here.

My eyes are bloodshot from nights of working to find a cure. My limbs ache as much from this unnatural world as from the pain of this disease. My heart starves for days gone by that may never come again. My mind is my only ally, and it will deliver us from this mad world we have created, but I must first do what I have never done before.

I must kill. I must kill Dani.

Walking back to the house, I begin to imagine how I will do it. Should I poison her with the cyanide in my lab, or perhaps shoot her? Yes—that's it! Suddenly, I feel like I am in a trancelike state as I enter the house and head for the study. My surroundings seem distorted. The framed pictures of vibrant patterns and sweeping landscapes on the wall are closing in like they will consume me if I don't move faster. Bustling through the kitchen, I hear a sharp thud, followed by a screech as the chair legs drag against the floor before toppling over. My thoughts and emotions are free-falling like a meteoric shower drowning me into a weightless abyss. My mind is not my own.

Once Dani's out of the way, Robbie will want to stay. He resists my Josie because of his attachment to Dani. Robbie will be my successor. . . . He has to stay. . . . I have to believe that what seems impossible now is achievable.

I unlock the bottom drawer of my desk and retrieve a gun. There's no turning back. I trace the outside of the steel chamber with my stiff, swollen fingers and slip it into my jacket pocket. Everyone appears to be gone, except for Dani and Robbie, who should be in the attic. My hands break out in a cold sweat and become fidgety as I walk calmly to the foot of the stairs. With each step, I am playing out how I will lure Dani to the abandoned bunker a half-mile away from Garland. It's desolate, and no one goes there. It's the perfect place to bury a body. Getting Dani there shouldn't be a problem. She's fascinated by the story of Haven. The bunker used to be a temporary holding place for escapees traveling to Haven. Surely, her curiosity will get the best of her, and she'll want to see it. Robbie will have to stay here to await Sirah's return with the supplies he requested for their travel.

Rising to the top stairs at the entrance to the attic, I look around the room. It is almost barren, with only the twin beds, sofa, a nightstand, two floor lamps near the stained-glass window, and a trunk on the opposite side of the room. I shudder at the thought of my greatest fear at this moment. *They are gone.*

Feelings of rage and fear consume me as I stumble erractically down the stairs and head to the garage. The trucks are still there. I check for the truck parked behind the house, and it is still there, but just beyond the wrought-iron fence, I notice two people standing in the distance. They appear to be hugging. They begin to struggle and pull away from each other, and I can hear loud screams in the distance.

Moving in closer and narrowing in to focus, I see a female wearing a bright-red jacket with a black hood and sleeves. That's Dani, and she appears to be arguing with Robbie. *Clearly, there's trouble in paradise*, I think. Maybe I should just take her out now. Removing the revolver from my jacket pocket, I quickly aim and shoot.

Approaching the body, which is motionless on the ground, I start to grow anxious. Something doesn't seem right.

Robbie drops to his knees and begins pressing hard against her chest.

Suddenly, I see Dani rushing toward Robbie from the back of the storage unit. I finally stop just a few feet from Robbie and see him kneeling alongside the body.

"Robbie!" I call out. "What are you doing out here?"

"Why did you shoot?" Robbie screams.

"I thought you were thieves!" I say, quickening my pace and looking at him hovering over the body on the ground.

I reach the body, rubbing my eyes to make sure they aren't deceiving me. *That's not Dani running over here—No, it can't be Dani.* My eyes begin to close in on the body, almost petrified to scan any closer.

"No—Josie!" I scream, my voice riddled with anguish and my face filled with horror. "This can't be happening!" I drop to my knees to hold my Josie. I can barely see Robbie, my eyes overflowing with tears and my heart filled with anguish. "You could have lived in peace here and been happy," I say as I struggle to stand, but my limbs feel like stone. "You were my last chance to help Garland live on. You've taken everything from me—my hopes, my life, my child. How dare you?"

"How dare he? How dare you!" Dani yells. "How dare you lie, scheme, and trick your way into our lives? You know why we came here. We trusted you! I'm deeply sorry this happened, but this was of your own doing. The deception and abuse of power that you claim to hate so much, you employ for your own selfish ends. And now your deceit has rebelled against you. I'm sorry, Ambrose, but this is not the way to get back what you lost."

"Get out of here," I say. "I never want to see either of you again!" Falling to the ground again, I lay the side of my face against Josie's lifeless chest.

CHAPTER THIRTY-TWO

We speed away from Garland in the beat-up sedan, the road coarse and riddled with small rocks and ditches. Silent from the terror of our escape, I shake my head as tears stream down my face. I am becoming more restless, traveling just below the speed limit to the train station.

We park the old car behind the station in an almost full lot and enter via the rear entrance. The lobby is buzzing with people standing around or rushing to the ticket counter. There isn't an empty seat anywhere as passengers wait for the next train due to arrive in ten minutes. I stand in line while Robbie waits near the entrance to the platform.

My palms are sweaty as I make my way to Robbie with two tickets to Bixby, Oklahoma, in the Ninth Republic. He looks anxious.

"You look a little uptight," I say. "You don't want to draw attention to yourself."

"Dani, do you realize that we just left a crime scene?" he asks. "We don't know what Ambrose is going to do. Yes, he told us to leave, but that doesn't mean he won't try to retaliate in some way." Robbie leans against the post on the platform.

"What do you mean by retaliate?" I ask.

"How do you think it's going to go when Ambrose tells his family that Josie died from a gunshot wound? Do you really think he's going to confess? He was distraught when he told us to go, but by now, he's gonna want vengeance. Even if he doesn't, what about her brothers or the others at Garland? They could come after us." Robbie grabs his backpack and hikes it onto his shoulder as the train pulls slowly into the station.

In the distance, I notice three men rushing through the crowd toward the platform. They battle through the crowd, apologizing to people, clearly looking for someone.

"Robbie," I say. "Don't turn around, but Jason, Jackson, and Jared are here. They must be looking for us."

As the travelers board the train, we let ourselves be swept along with them. I look back, trying to catch a glimpse of our pursuers, but I can't see them. It's as if they've disappeared.

We grab two seats, and as the train begins to pull out of the station, I look out the window and see the brothers being detained by two security guards. I look straight ahead and start to count backward from 100 in my head. Finally reaching twenty, I squeeze my eyes shut tightly and grab Robbie's hand. The nervous sweat in the palm of my hands has dried, and all I feel is a hesitant relief and then a blissful calm, not because we just pulled off a narrow escape but from the feel of Robbie's hand in mine. Something feels right.

CHAPTER THIRTY-THREE

Several hours later, we arrive in Bixby. It is pouring rain, and the sky is dark and cloudy as we exit the train station.

"We barely made it on time," Robbie says. "We've got less than half an hour before contact."

Following the location tracker on my pod, we make it to the corner of Walmont and Daley streets. It's dark, and no one is around. There's a bench in front of a community garden, so we sit and wait.

I feel helpless as we wait for a complete stranger to take us to safety. Not knowing what Ambrose may have done to sabotage our journey sickens me. The bitter cold and mild nausea sieges my nerves and makes me question the soundness of my decision to accompany Robbie. Suddenly, the reality of this mission hits me: Before we reach Haven, we could be arrested or worse. We could be dead.

The rain continues to beat down, soaking me, chaotic and scattered. As a thin layer of water runs down my face, the cold wind freezes the tiny droplets clinging to my lashes. A black EV approaches and stops in front of us. The window rolls down, and we hear a man shout, "Get in!"

We hurry into the back seat of the EV. "You're drenched. Here, dry off," the man says, handing me a towel. "I am Malchior," he continues. "I was sent by Dr. Chavin to collect you."

"Thank you," I say, rubbing my hair with the towel. The car is warm, and we remove our jackets and pat our faces dry.

"Who is Dr. Chavin?" Robbie asks.

"That is not for me to say," Malchior says. "Dr. Chavin will tell you what you need to know. Just sit back. We have a long drive ahead of us."

The ride to our destination is calm as the rain falls on the black EV. I pat the hood of my saturated jacket with the damp towel and pull back my hair in a slick ponytail.

The rain seems to dissipate as we settle into the soft leather cushions and drift into a mild slumber.

"We're here," Malchior says as he pulls into the driveway. Stepping out of the EV, I study the exterior of the house. It's a pre-Ascension three-story, red-brick Victorian with large bay windows overlooking a perfectly manicured lawn. The stairs leading up to the wide veranda creak with each step I take. Malchior unlocks the door and invites us in.

"I hope you don't mind the darkness too much. Dr. Chavin likes the lighting dim. Follow me," he says as he leads us up the stairs. The air is stale and dry, and I pick up a peculiar odor that I can't quite place.

"Dani, this is your room, and Robbie, your room is the next door to the right. Why don't you get settled in? Dinner is at eight, so I will come to collect you at seven forty-five sharp."

"Will we meet Dr. Chavin for dinner?" I ask.

"Dr. Chavin may join you if he is available," Malchior replies, his tone revealing nothing. He turns on his heel to head back down the stairs.

The room is large and decorated in vintage Victorian. The cherrywood headboard is flanked with mahogany pillars and two nightstands with gold-leaf handles. The vanity is positioned in front of a large window overlooking the garden. I am fascinated by the furnishings and classic impressionist artwork on the walls. As I marvel at a crystal paperweight sitting on the nightstand, Robbie knocks on the door. "Can I come in?" he asks.

"Of course," I reply.

Robbie enters quietly and sits on the edge of the bed. "I'm still concerned about Ambrose," he says. "I think it's a real possibility that he may retaliate. Even though we escaped from the train station, he can still find us. He knows how to contact Dr. Chavin and the connect location." Robbie looks up at me with a worried expression.

"What do you want to do?" I ask calmly, ready to counter his suggestion if I don't like it.

"We need to tell Dr. Chavin everything. It's the only way we can protect ourselves in case Ambrose shows up," he says. "If this Dr. Chavin knows the whole story, then if Ambrose tries to subvert our plans, he may be able to protect us."

"But what if he doesn't believe us and Ambrose convinces him that we're killers on the run?" I ask.

"That's a risk we're going to have to take," Robbie says as he stands up. "See you for dinner." He closes the door behind him.

CHAPTER THIRTY-FOUR

True to his word, at 7:45 p.m. sharp, Malchior arrives and escorts us to the formal dining room. The room is dark with a single window and a cream-colored window shade rolled up. The walls are painted a deep earth-toned brown. A tall cherrywood china cabinet with beveled glass doors provides a pop of color and displays small art pieces. A serving table is positioned opposite the china cabinet. The colors rust, red, and black flow through into an adjacent sitting room.

Malchior seats us on opposite sides of a very long table set with three formal dinnerware settings. Two tall sterling-silver candelabras bathe the room in a soft, golden light.

We take sips of the Alzaiec wine Malchior pours and nibble at the individual vegetable crudité appetizers.

A man steps into the dining room. "Good evening," he says. "I am Dr. Chavin, but you can call me Alec. I apologize for my tardiness and for the rather mysterious introduction. Malchior can be rather obscure, but he is a loyal and reliable companion. I don't know what I would do without him. I trust you find your accommodations satisfactory?" Dr. Chavin says as he takes his seat at the head of the table.

"Yes, thanks for letting us stay here. I'm Robbie. This is Dani. She's coming with me to Haven."

"Yes, I was informed there would be two of you," Dr. Chavin says. "However, I must ask, while I understand why you are traveling to Haven," he says, gesturing to Robbie, "why are you going as well?" he asks me.

"Robbie is a dear childhood friend. I couldn't let him travel to Haven alone. I have two contacts who can help us should this journey prove more perilous than expected."

"I once underestimated the cunning ingenuity of a woman," Alec says with a knowing frown. "I will not do that again." He picks up his glass and inclines it toward me. "May your journey to Haven be safe and the realities of what you find live up to your expectations."

"What do you mean?" I ask. "That sounds ominous."

"Dani," Alec says, setting down his wineglass, "I have found over the years that most of the time, the things that we hold dear and those that we strive for are often the same things that bring us disappointment and regret. While I admire both of you for undertaking this mission, I am sure you will ultimately be disappointed on some level." He waves his hand in dismissal. "But enough of this talk. The point is that I wish you well, and that is what matters." Alec raises his glass again, and Robbie and I join in with timid reservation.

"Alec, thanks for your help, but we have to tell ya something." Robbie's voice quivers as he recounts the sordid details of Ambrose's plan. I squirm while I watch Alec's suspicion begin to change to curiosity, then disdain. "I'm telling you this in case Ambrose and his family show up here or try to contact you. Ambrose may know that we got the info for our connect with you." Robbie pauses for a moment and exhales deeply; then he looks at me.

"I respect your commitment to keep what you learned a secret," Alec says. "I hope you do the same when you leave here. As for Ambrose, I received a call from him earlier today, asking me to confirm when you arrived. He sounded agitated and impatient, but I assumed he wanted to ensure your safe arrival. While I wish to keep what I know to myself, I may have some idea of the matters that you speak of. No need to say anything more. I will not let Ambrose know that you are here. Now, it is late, and I must retire for the evening. We will have much to discuss tomorrow. Good night." Alec rises from the chair and exits the dining room. We watch in silence as he disappears down the long hallway.

CHAPTER THIRTY-FIVE

The morning sun shines through the red velvet drapes secured by a gold rope affixed to the wall. The sun's warmth cradles my face as I bury my head deeply into the soft fullness of my pillow. I awaken to the sound of a lawn mower in the courtyard below. My body still aches from the stiff vinyl train seats, and my skin is dry and chafed from the cold, blistering wind and rain from the night before.

I stumble out of bed, make my way to the bathroom, and turn on the shower. The warm water streams down my shoulders and back as I slick my hair back and tilt my head up to feel the water gush over my face. I begin to feel warm all over as I reminisce about my evening with Colin at the Colony. His hands caressing my breasts as he kissed me softly along the nape of my neck. Looking up and gazing into his eyes, Colin's sharp, chiseled features seem to fade away, and I begin to imagine Robbie touching and devouring my body. Weak from the intensity of my fantasy, I get out of the shower and return to the bedroom to get ready for breakfast.

At exactly 8 a.m., Malchior knocks on my door and invites me to join Robbie and Alec in the solarium for breakfast. I enter the library and am overwhelmed by the sheer number of books on the shelves. There must be hundreds. Tall wooden bookcases line each wall, and a large, oak desk sits in front of the window. A love seat, two end tables, and two chairs are directly in front of the desk. Walking slowly through the library, I am humbled by the first edition works of Tolstoy, Salinger, and Steinbeck carefully positioned and preserved on each bookcase.

I hear Robbie and Alec talking. It sounds like a lively discussion.

"I hope I'm not disturbing you," I say as I enter the solarium and head to the buffet table. I take a plate and begin to serve myself.

"Dani, your timing is perfect," Alec says. "Robbie and I were discussing Dominion's recent mandate requiring tracking implants for all citizens, including inclusions for visitors and unrestricted work-visa holders. I believe it's necessary to ensure that our citizens are safe. You may not remember this, but before Dominion was established, crime was rampant—murder, robberies, kidnapping, rape, and drugs were out of control. The first phase of tracking was tested on convicted criminals and people apprehended and suspected of criminal activity. Since then, crime has declined significantly, except for militant activity from the resistance. Anything that promotes stability for Dominion is necessary for our country to thrive." Alec looks at Robbie, awaiting him to state his case.

"I hear you, Alec. But you're forgetting that all of this is about control, not safety or crime. Today, the tracking implants are a trick to get citizens to trust the government. Tomorrow, they'll control our entire way of life—how we make money, how we communicate, how and when we travel . . . maybe even how we vote. Dominion leaders will do anything to make sure they don't lose control. They don't trust us to make our own choices because they don't want us to. I spent every day for the last several years being treated like a lab rat. Nothing was my own. Not even my thoughts. Escaping Breeder life is not just about resisting change; it's about facing my fears with courage and letting that courage show me the way to who I am." Both Robbie and Alec turn to me for my response.

"Alec, I have to ask," I begin, "if you believe that controls must be put in place to ensure that Dominion thrives, why are you helping us? Surely, seeing us safely to Haven empowers the resistance to overthrow this social order you seem to appreciate."

"The notion that trackers will somehow convert us to compliant zombies is ludicrous," Alec says. "The imbalance that exists between our sexes will continue to be challenged, and social unrest will be the catalyst for change, but we must not confuse the means necessary to deter criminal dysfunction with the inevitable evolution of social justice. Your participation in challenging the system is necessary; that's how things change. But a full-scale revolution isn't the answer."

"Why do I get the impression there's something else you aren't telling us?" I ask.

"Maybe later, Dani," Alec says dismissively. "For now, why don't you enjoy the gardens? It's beautiful outside, and I need to work for the remainder of the day. Malchior will attend to your needs. Enjoy." Alec stands and exits the solarium.

"Alec's hiding something," I say quietly to Robbie. "I'm going to find out what it is." My mind begins to wander as I sip the rest of my osmanthus tea.

CHAPTER THIRTY-SIX

The spectrum of bright colors and the smell of jasmine and lilac seduces my senses. Rows and rows of Gerber daisies, Peruvian lilies, solidago, chrysanthemum, dahlias, roses, and irises drink in the fullness of the sun and illuminate the greenhouse. I feel a familiar happiness just being in Robbie's presence, almost like a secret passageway opened into a wondrous world of dazzling lights and bright colors. From the laughs to the gentle smiles, we hold hands, exchanging sweet, silent glances. Walking alongside the rows of sweet dahlias, I feel Robbie's hand on my back. He massages my shoulders, relieving the tension and seducing me into a tranquil state. I take in the beauty and calmness of the moment as he pulls me closer and begins to stroke the side of my neck. His touch makes me warm all over. He teases my hair with his fingers and glides the back of his hand along my cheek, pressing his forefinger against my bottom lip. The temperature rises as our bodies sink into each other. My breasts press firmly against his chest, and our lips brush against each other, timidly at first, then firmly. The warmth of his breath teases me as I taste sweet cinnamon and honey. This moment feels precious, and just as quickly as it arose, it goes away. "What was that?" I ask.

"I don't know, exactly," Robbie says, pulling back. "I have to keep reminding myself that this time we have is only temporary. Soon, I'll be in Haven, and you'll be going back home. But right now, I can't stop myself, Dani. The way your eyes lit up as you smelled the flowers made me feel something. You take my breath away."

"Robbie, I don't know what to say," I say, suddenly shy. "All this time, I think I may have been fooling myself into believing that I needed to accompany you on this trip because I wasn't there for you eighteen years ago, but that's not true. I never stopped caring about you. Even when you were gone, I never stopped imagining that we would someday be reunited. When you came back into my life, I felt that fate had brought us back together, but I told myself that being with you would be impossible, so I deluded myself. I made myself play the role of the loyal, trusted friend. Robbie, I do love you—I don't think I ever stopped loving you—but I don't see how this could work."

"Dani, this is our time," he says. "If we don't find a way to make it work now, it will never happen for us."

Holding each other tightly, I feel a sense of relief mixed with sadness. My passion runs deep like a roaring fire that incinerates my sensibilities and bares my soul naked yet encumbered by fear. I can't release my inhibitions. I'm afraid of the possibilities. Looking toward the courtyard entrance, I see Alec staring at us. His icy stare seems empty, like he is in a trance. I can't help but wonder what type of pain or longing is behind those eyes. Just as our eyes meet, he appears startled, looks away, and quickly exits.

CHAPTER THIRTY-SEVEN

Descending the spiral staircase to the formal dining room for dinner, Robbie and I are somewhat distant with each other. We both want something greater than what we can find with each other, and it hurts.

Alec welcomes us to the dining room. He is dressed in formal attire, clean-shaven, and his thinning hair on his balding, mottled scalp is slicked back instead of frizzy and disheveled as it had been earlier that day. His wrinkled face crumples as he rubs it with his spotted hands showing bones and veins. He has a youthful smile, showing a gleam of white from his teeth, and his kind eyes sparkle even though his lids are heavy and weighed down with wrinkled folds.

The grandfather clock in the dark corner closest to the entrance strikes 8 p.m. The sound pierces my senses and lingers with a sharp ringing in my ears. The conversation is dull and unfamiliar compared to the exuberant exchanges we had earlier. It is as if our souls are mourning the end of something. There is no need to say more.

"So Alec, do you mind if I ask what inspired your love of the Victorian era? You have so many precious things," I say.

"Oh, I suppose I was inspired by my mother's love for it. This house has been in my family for generations, and I cherish everything about it," Chavin responds fondly.

"You've managed to carve out your piece of heaven here. There's no one around for miles, and I suppose you like it like that," I say smartly.

"Yes, you're right. I appreciate the solitude, but sometimes being alone with your thoughts can condemn your spirit," Chavin says, staring intently at his wineglass.

I gaze at the silver beam of moonlight spilling through the window. Its presence stirs me as it devours the darkness of the room. As Malchior clears our plates, I raise my glass to propose a toast when the doorbell interrupts my thoughts. Malchior goes to answer it. The voices are faint at first, but moments later, I recognize one of them.

"It's Jared, Ambrose's oldest son," I whisper to Alec.

Robbie jumps up from his seat and moves close to Alec. "Just tell them we're not here," he says. He takes my hand and pulls me through the door leading to the kitchen.

Once Alec closes the double doors, Robbie and I rush back into the dining room and peer through the entrance. Malchior escorts the visitors to the library and returns to inform Alec about the purpose of their visit.

This unexpected visit interrupts Alec's pensive mood and seems to energize him. His entire demeanor changes from tepid to hawkish within seconds. I am impressed. We make our way to the entryway from the kitchen to the library and peer through the slit in the door. Robbie's cheek feels warm and tingles against mine as we listen in.

Alec enters the library and greets them. "Gentlemen, this is highly irregular," he says. "I understand you're looking for Robbie and Dani. What is this about?"

Jared steps in front of his brothers, Jackson and Jason. His eyes are dark and intimidating. He presses his hands against the side of his coat and sinks his left hand into his pocket. Standing firmly, he responds, "We are here on behalf of our father, Ambrose. Robbie and Dani stayed at our home. Before they left, Robbie killed my sister, Josie. My father can't demand justice for Josie, but we can. We don't wanna hurt you. We just want Robbie. He needs to face up to what he did."

"And exactly who will deliver these consequences?" Alec asks as he moves in closer to Jared, chiding him for his combative tone.

"The law enforcement in our town, of course," Jared says.

Jason is seething with anger. He strains to contain his words, but the bulging vein in his forehead and swollen eyelids will not be tamed. Jackson appears to be staring off into space, unable to speak. His posture is erect, almost frozen, with no feeling.

"From the looks of you and your brothers, I have my doubts about that," Alec says. "But that is neither here nor there, as they're no longer here, and I do not know the whereabouts of their next destination."

"When did they leave?" Jared asks.

"Sometime yesterday afternoon," Alec says. "I was in my lab working through the day. When I returned for dinner, they were gone."

"How did they leave?"

"Malchior drove them to the train station. Malchior, did our guests share any information about where they were going?" Alec asks.

"They did not," Malchior says. "Although, I got the distinct impression that they may have been planning to head north since they made mention of the Dion, a statue in the Fifteenth Republic. Dani mentioned that she had always wanted to see it. I dropped them at the station near three p.m., and they made haste."

"Thank you, Malchior." Alec turns back to the brothers. "I am sorry this happened. I hope you find them. No one should get away with murder." There seems to be a hidden meaning to Alec's expression.

"May I ask, sir," Jared says, "how is it that you don't know the next destination? I know that the contact reaches out to the ascendant."

"That is typically the case, but the ascendant sent information via courier to my residence. Apparently, he asked to meet with Robbie directly to disclose the destination. Malchior knew the rules and asked for the password, which was correct, so he notified Robbie that the courier was here. Robbie met with him and left moments later."

Alec turned back to Malchior. "Do I have that correct?"

"Yes, sir," Malchior replies with firm resolve.

"There's nothing more for us here," Jared says. "Let's head back to the train station. Thank you for your help. If you think of anything else, contact my pod."

Returning to the dining room with a confident look, Alec says, "I trust you heard that?"

Robbie and I return to our seats at the large mahogany dining table. We sit with our hands folded on the varnished surface.

"It was Ambrose who shot Josie," Robbie blurts loudly. "It wasn't me."

"When I agreed to become part of the Elevator—"

I interrupt in confusion, "Elevator? What does that mean?"

Alec responds with an impatient tone, "Dani, this entire secret network is made up of people like me, and we refer to ourselves as Elevators because we are helping people like you and Robbie reach a critical destination. That's all I need to share for now." He pauses. "When I agreed to become part of the Elevator, I did it because I believe in a man's right to be more than what our society allows him to be. There are so many men like Ambrose—men who have lost their way in this new society. I'm sure when he first started this endeavor to find cures for cognitive impairment and infertility, he did it for all the right reasons, but somewhere along the way, those reasons became shrouded in darkness, and the ruthless appeal to dehumanize his intentions took over. His sense of humanity and what is decent became blurred, then died, and what resurrected in its place was something unnatural and evil. I believe you, Robbie."

I sighed deeply in relief and asked, "Alec, now I'm more confused than before. If you believe in a man's right to choose and are clearly facilitating that opportunity, how can you also support measures to suppress freedoms like the right to privacy? Your philosophy and actions seem contradictory. Forgive me, but I can't help but feel that there's something you're leaving out."

"How observant you are, my dear Dani," Alec says. "Yes, there is something. Something I feel tremendous guilt about. I never told you about the nature of my work in the lab. I've lived with this shame for so long. It's a shame that chokes me until I gasp for forgiveness. I have to make things right."

"What does this all mean?" I ask. I lean forward. I know what I'm about to hear will be a crucial part of this house of cards.

CHAPTER THIRTY-EIGHT

As he stands next to the window overlooking the southeast corner of the estate, Alec's demeanor grows mournful and deflated. He grips the edge of the velvet drape and pulls it further away from the window. Tilting his head up as if to take in the sheltered glow of the moonlight, he begins his story:

"Our world is changing at an ever-faster rate, taking in the ills of yesterday yet regurgitating the same transgressions," he says. "We plan to do better, turning the impossible into the possible, but there's a risk of discovering something we can't handle. We delude ourselves into believing that our exploration will save lives and eradicate systemic ills that are destroying our civilization. The risk of science diminishing our humanity is real. The use of genetic technologies has evolved to the point where it has usurped control of our destinies and, inevitably, our humanity. As scientists, we did what was necessary to ensure our survival. We rebuked what was natural, replaced it with genetic engineering, and called it natural evolution. But there's nothing natural about an idea that stands to destroy what makes us human. We knew the risks, but we couldn't resist it, so we gave in to reckless abandon and changed the course of history in a way we never anticipated." He takes a deep breath but does not turn away from the window.

"Before I moved my lab and took up residence here," he continued, "it was roughly two years before the Great War began. I was the lead biophysicist at Glausomon, Inc., a biotech company located just outside of what was then Berkeley, California. One morning, like so many others, I walked through the lobby of the BioGenome wing to the lab I shared with a fellow scientist, Eva Newsomb. When I arrived, I unlocked the cryotech storage component in the main working area and withdrew a long tray of frozen protein to be used for genome editing. It can alter the DNA of any cell in any organism.

"Eva was there already. She was holding a small metal tray. She said, 'It's amazing to think that such a small thing could alter the course of humanity in a way we never dreamed possible.'

"We headed to the workstation to record the work plan for the day. I watched Eva inject the waygate specimen into the radioactive culture. Everything seemed normal. The cold, hard surfaces that housed millions of specimens in tiny jars and the sterile workspaces seemed to blend into this perfectly planned world that she and I had built over the previous year.

"Eva told me the culture was too warm. 'We need to cool the temperature by ten degrees immediately,' she said.

"'Yes, the link test will fail again without the targeted temperature at the time of release,' I agreed.

"I handed Eva the specimen and watched as she returned it to the cooling area. Her white coat gently draped her figure and clung softly to her curvaceous silhouette. Her hands always showed the right amount of control—so precise and unyielding as she closed the incubator door. Her face was oval, her facial features flawless—her almond-shaped brown eyes, narrow nose, high cheekbones, and full lips perfectly adorned with a very bright shade of red lipstick. She was a woman of distinctive natural beauty, and her walk was pristine and confident.

"Returning to the work area, Eva began to record the morning's activities while I prepped for the next trial. Together, we were the perfect duo—precise, dedicated, and uncompromising in our resolve to create the neutralizer. This biochemical cocktail had the capability to reverse the effects of nuclear radiation on all living cells. It was a solution desperately needed in the event of a bionuclear attack.

"By day, we were consumed with perfecting the neutralizer, and by night, our passion for each other was insatiable. I loved her deeply, perhaps more than any woman before or after. There were times when I could smell the lilac and mandarin scent of her hair or feel the warmth of her breath against my neck. I craved her body and soul, and our work satiated my hunger to achieve what we had been working toward for so long. I wanted to save the world, and all she wanted was me. At the time, her goal seemed so insignificant next to my lofty endeavor, but it didn't matter. As long as we were together, I knew I could create what the world would need after devastating destruction: a second chance.

"We worked tirelessly for almost two years, knowing that in another year, our creation would be complete. That was until we received notice that we had only three more months to deliver the neutralizer. At first, that seemed impossible, but I knew it could be done. Our work in the lab stretched long into the night. I was like a machine, requiring little sleep and minimal food to sustain my health, and Eva became nothing more than a lab instrument to me. My ambition and drive began to starve and then strangle our love for each other. After a month of what seemed like endless tests, monitoring, and retesting, Eva cornered me in the stock closet. My eyes ached, and my hands were stiff. I flinched as she touched my shoulder. She told me about her recent visit to Dr. Klegg. She stared at me with an intense longing that was unfamiliar. I couldn't move, and when I edged backward to gain some distance, she shouted, 'I'm pregnant!' in a high-pitched voice. I stood petrified as I tried to understand what I was feeling—fear, then relief, excitement, joy, anger, and then the return of fear. I walked away. I refused to accept any possible distractions, including my own child. It was at that moment that I lost my humanity, and that is why I know that somewhere along the way, something happened to cause Ambrose to lose his way. We both started with good, noble intentions, but we chose a path of destruction, and the cost of admission was dehumanization.

"For the next several days, Eva and I barely spoke to each other, and when absolutely necessary, our words were curt and unfeeling. One day, the test showed ninety-nine-point-seven percent efficacy.

We succeeded, and in that moment, when I realized what we had accomplished, I wanted to embrace Eva and kiss her, but instead, I retreated to the back room while she stood next to the workbench with an empty, unapologetic look on her face. I was angry, not because of Eva's untimely news but because the satisfaction and achievement I thought I would feel wasn't there; I felt nothing—empty. I hurried out of the lab for a brisk walk to clear my head. I remember Eva calling my name, but I ignored her.

"Almost an hour later, as I was returning to Glausomon, I noticed an ambulance parked out front. I hurried to see what had happened, and I saw a woman being carried on a stretcher; it was Eva. She lay there crying, her hands pressed firmly against her belly. She saw me and began to scream, 'Why? Why? You did this!'

"I jumped in the ambulance, and we headed to the hospital. For hours, I waited, feeling nauseous and afraid. I realized that creating the neutralizer had meant nothing without Eva. I loved her, and I had to make things right. At that moment of clarity, the doctor joined me in the waiting room and delivered the news I was hoping for: Eva was going to be okay. I took a deep breath, elated that my love was safe and would recover, but after that deep breath came the awful news. 'The baby didn't survive.' I felt cold and stiff. The baby, our baby, was gone. I felt tears welling in my eyes, then streaming down my face. I needed to see Eva, but she refused my visit.

"For days, I worked in the lab, trying to put Eva and our dead child out of my mind. The grief was overwhelming, and all I could do to keep it at bay was work. Then one morning, Eva returned. She entered the lab wearing her white lab coat, looking more beautiful than ever, but something about her was different. Her eyes seemed empty and unaware of my longing for her.

"I got her up to speed on where we were in finalizing the neutralizer for transport, and she recommended another batch of tests to confirm readiness. It seemed like a reasonable request since she had been away for almost a week, and she needed to sign off on the finished project, so I agreed. She insisted on working alone. I felt so guilty and ashamed that I agreed.

"I finally returned four days later when Eva summoned me. When I walked into the lab, she stood next to the workstation looking confident and almost giddy with excitement. She exclaimed, 'We've done it!' Her eyes lit up, and she embraced me. She was exactly as I remembered—warm, familiar, I never wanted to leave her again. That day, we finished our report and left the lab. The next twenty-four hours were the happiest of my life. We spent every moment together, laughing, eating, touching, and making love. I thought we had found each other again, but I was unsure why Eva didn't bring up the baby. I thought about it several times but hesitated out of fear of destroying the moments of pure joy.

"The next day, I woke up to find Eva not lying next to me. She wasn't in my home, so I assumed she'd left early to go home and get dressed for work. I floated into the lab, ready to tell Eva that I wanted us to get married. I was no longer a slave to my ambition. All I wanted was her, and we could try for another child. I loved her.

"In the lab, she was nowhere to be found. I decided to start working with the expectation that she would come whizzing through the door at any moment. Minutes became hours, and I went to the cryostorage unit. There, taped to the door, was a note. It read:

"Alec,

our love so pure, so deep, yet soiled by your selfishness.

Our baby so innocent, so loved by me, yet dead by your thoughtlessness.

So shall be your creation, now my creation.

But alive with no future.

Eva

"At the time, I did not understand what she meant by 'your creation, now my creation. But alive with no future.' I searched for Eva for months but could not find any trace of her. In my grief, I delivered the neutralizer, and as soon as I could get away, I left Glausomon and returned to this place.

"It wasn't until several months into the Great War that the effects of the neutralizer became evident to me. Male fertility and mental cognition had been severely compromised. Upon that realization, I realized what Eva's note meant. She had engineered her revenge into a weapon that took away the power that men need to thrive—their minds and their manhood. I have worked tirelessly to correct this terrible wrong. Since then, I have worked to develop a cure, but unfortunately, I am unable to work the way I used to. Sometimes I have moments of clarity, but more often, my thoughts are confused. I, too, suffer from Eva's vengeance.

"While the women of Dominion celebrate what they call 'the natural occurrence from an unnatural event,' I wallow in shame and guilt for allowing this to happen. Eva created this new human condition through spite and anger toward me. Could you imagine what everyone would say if they knew that the plight of men in today's society is the result of a woman's scorn?"

CHAPTER THIRTY-NINE

The rising sun casts an unusual orange and pink hue across the morning sky; its rays light up every corner of my room as if it were igniting a radiant flame.

I am still reeling from last night's events. First, a near brush with Ambrose's sons and their plan to apprehend Robbie and take him back to Garland in the name of justice, and then Alec's confession. It all seems so fantastic and diabolical. While I wish I could doubt or discount Alec's tale, I know he's telling the truth, and I feel deep sorrow for his suffering.

A knock on the door startles me. "It's Robbie," he calls out.

"Come in."

"Good morning, sunshine," he says. "It's time to pack up, grab breakfast, and head to our next connect.

"I just got up," I say. "I need half an hour to get ready."

"Okay. Meet me in the study," Robbie says.

After a hot shower, I quickly assemble my belongings and head downstairs. I trail my fingers along the grooves of the dark mahogany staircase, but once I reach the bottom step, I overhear raised voices. I stand near the hallway leading to the library to hear more clearly. I overhear Alec's voice: "Robbie, don't make the same mistake I made and entrust your future to your ambition. I understand what you're feeling, as I once felt the same way, but you can't serve two masters. You can't put your cause above all else; it will poison your love for Dani. It will take over and pollute your thoughts and deeds. She will resent you for it, and God forbid, she may strike out in anger or, even worse, abandon you."

Robbie storms out of the library. Luckily, he doesn't see me hidden in a dark corner.

I jet out and run into the library to confront Alec.

"How dare you?" I say. "How dare you presume to tell Robbie to expect the same level of selfishness and callousness from me that Eva showed you. Robbie is not a robot. He is not so consumed by his own ambition that he's unable to love anyone else. You brought about this horror of our reality with your inability to love anyone but yourself. To compare me to Eva is unconscionable. To think that a broken heart would drive me to commit such a vengeful and malevolent act is wrong. That's not who I am. What you fail to realize is that both of you were selfish, and you both made the choice to put your needs above each other. Both of you created this path of destruction. That's not love, Alec. That's anything but love. You suffer, and there's no doubt in my mind that wherever Eva is, she's suffering too. Don't presume to know what Robbie feels or what he will do."

Storming out of the library, I find Robbie standing at the foot of the staircase with our bags. He appears unfazed by Alec's words and proud that I chastised Alec's foreboding.

"Let's go," he says as he gestures to hold my hand. Together, we head to the car where Malchior is waiting to drive us to our next stop.

CHAPTER FORTY

Standing in line at the train station, I am still uneasy about the heated exchange with Alec. This experience is bringing so many feelings and forgotten fears to the surface.

We settle into the stiff seats on the train and make our way east. The ride is very quiet, and Robbie barely speaks to me. Suddenly, with just ten minutes left until we arrive at our destination, he grips my hand. Feeling the warmth of his hand releases the tension from my body. He turns to face me and draws in closer to kiss my forehead and cheek. Then he presses his lips firmly against mine. This is what I need after that encounter with Alec. I need reassurance that Robbie and I are okay, and with that kiss, I feel everything he is feeling—joy, tenderness, and love.

We pull into the station, get up slowly, grab our bags, and hold hands tightly, neither of us wanting to let go.

It's late, and the platform is deserted. The air is chilly, but every inch of the walkway is immaculate. There is no sign of a bustling crowd. Once we're inside the station, I look up to marvel at a fresco on the ceiling. It's breathtaking. The ceiling is very high and painted with a geometric design and the twenty-six republics in quadrels around the butterfly. Scenes of the Great War are used to organize the composition. The narrative begins at the pavilion of fire, where the transformation of the United States to Dominion begins. The first three paintings tell the story of the creation of the eight cabinets: Law, Science, Commerce, Transportation, Religion, Military, Art, and Politics; this is followed by the induction of the governing council of 175 legislators representing the twenty-six republics that make up Dominion; finally, there's the story of the First Ascension. The vectors of Justice, Peace, Vitality, and Honor are painted around these frescoes, and they are accompanied by twenty-six votives, each representing the Dominion Republics. The more I study it, the more in awe I am of this work of art. This place feels more like a museum than a train station.

I'm distracted by a tall woman wearing a puffy black jacket, slim-cut jeans, and dark, weathered combat boots standing suspiciously in the corner of the station. She almost belongs, but not quite. Her hair is slicked back in a pixie cut, but something about her piercing eyes and leering grin makes me feel uneasy. I try to look back up to continue my observation of the fresco when Robbie taps me on the shoulder and motions for me to follow him. We walk past the suspicious-looking woman along a dark, narrow hallway leading to an exit. Once outside, we stand next to a dimly lit sign catty-corner to the exit. The waiting is tiring, and just as I begin to nudge Robbie to express my concern, the woman exits, walks directly to us, and pulls out a vape pen from her jacket pocket. Her eyes are now hidden behind a pair of round glasses with gold trim.

Standing in front of Robbie, she asks, "Are you lost?"

Robbie replies, "No, but do ya know where I can get a burger? I'm starvin'."

She smiles and motions for us to follow her. The faintly lit parking lot is practically deserted. I hasten my pace to keep up with her. Her gait seems almost robotic. She pauses at the fence; the greenery looks dark like charcoal, and the path is fading into the night. She reaches a black EV and motions for us to hurry and get into the back seat. The front passenger seat is occupied with what looks like climbing equipment, rope, carabiners, a harness, rappelling devices, ascenders, and a sling.

"May I ask your name?" I ask.

She turns to me and replies, "Caris. Welcome to Stetson."

CHAPTER FORTY-ONE

The outdoor terrain is tough as it quickly changes from a three-lane paved highway to narrow, hilly dirt roads. When I close my eyes, I can feel the sudden rise and fall of the road beneath us, disrupted by curves and junctions. After almost an hour, which felt like an eternity, we finally reached our destination, a secluded cabin tucked away high up in the hills of Stetson. The scenery is serene, quiet, and cool. Stepping out of the EV, I inhale the scent of pine and honeysuckle. I can almost taste the fresh, crisp air. I hear a small rustle in the bushes around the perimeter of the cabin. The dark, moonlit trees tower high above in a scattered formation, seeming to welcome our arrival. Once inside, Caris shows us to our room, where we crawl sleepily into our beds. The warmth of the wool blanket and goose-down comforter lulls me into a deep sleep, and once again, I feel safe.

Waking up the next morning is uncomfortable. It seems like every muscle in my body aches, and I have a splitting headache. I sit up slowly in bed to discover Robbie on the floor doing push-ups. His T-shirt fits his muscular physique perfectly. His arms are strong and extend outward like menacing weapons from the rippling muscles in his shoulders. My eyes follow his body from the curve of his lower back to the hard roundness of his behind and then linger curiously between his legs, where I see his hardness couched within the looseness of his boxers. I struggle to look away, but the moistness between my legs triggers my insatiable yearning for this man. I glance toward the large window several inches above Robbie's head. The glow from the morning sun stings my eyes and then soothes me with a calming warmth. My body drinks in this intoxicating elixir.

"Well, good morning, sleepy head," Robbie says.

I rise from the comforting warmth of my bed and walk toward the window when my senses are overtaken by the smell of fresh coffee, cinnamon, citrus, and sweet molasses. The smells are intoxicating and lure Robbie and me down the stairs and into the kitchen.

Caris is sitting at the breakfast table, reading her tablet, and drinking a tall mug of coffee. Again, she is dressed in black from head to toe, but I notice a gun in the holster around her hips. She seems relaxed, but why does she have a gun?

"Morning," she says. "How'd ya sleep?" She rises from the table and walks over to the cabinet above the stove to get additional plates and cups.

"Like a log," I say. "You know, for someone we're expected to trust with our lives, we know nothing about you other than your name and that you carry a gun on your hip."

"My full name is Caris, and I'm a detective," she says. "I'm your last Elevator, and I will be guiding you on the rest of your journey to Haven. You need to eat. This journey is not going to be easy. You'll need your strength. Also, take these stun guns. You may need them." Maintaining a clever grin, Caris tosses us each a gun. "I need to go into town to make preparations for our trip and gather additional supplies. Stay in the cabin. We leave at nightfall."

About an hour after Caris's departure, I am unable to contain my curiosity any longer. I begin exploring rooms at the opposite end of the upstairs hallway. The first room is dark. I flick on the light to find an office space. It is very high-tech and equipped with high-definition transmission equipment, a signaler, and a heavy-duty black closet. There's a dark-gray leather jacket sprawled on the chest of drawers directly under the window and a pair of black rubber boots covered in dried mud and soot leaning against the closet door. My eyes are drawn to a red blinking light in the corner of the ceiling. I slowly retreat and make my way to the room at the other end of the hallway.

The door slowly creaks open as my hands, slightly shaking with nervous curiosity, push it forward. This room bears a stark resemblance to the office I just saw. The bedroom is masculine in its design. Unlike the bright and airy hues in the room where Robbie and I were staying, this bedroom is much darker, with a minimalist look. The bed is about six feet in front of the door with a dark, mahogany headboard and footboard. The nightstands on each side of the bed sport identical lamps with tan shades. I trace my fingers across one of the two leather chairs located on each side of a wooden desk, which is positioned in front of a huge window with navy and brown curtains. Peering out of the drawn curtain, I see Caris's EV speeding toward the cabin. This room seems to suit Caris. She seems dark and mysterious, barely saying a word, yet there is something about her that feels restrained, almost tormented.

The faint sound of the EV becomes louder until it stops abruptly, and I hear the sharp sound of a door closing. There's no time to check out the third room, so I rush out of Caris's room and head downstairs to greet her. Robbie is sitting on the floor, nestled on a big comfy pillow next to the fireplace, reading on a tablet.

Caris enters the cabin with two bags of groceries. Bustling toward the kitchen, she carefully places the bags on the counter and heads back outside.

"Caris, do you need any help?" I ask.

"Could you start unpacking the groceries?" she asks. "We'll start dinner soon."

When she returns, Caris starts washing the vegetables while I skin the potatoes and Robbie chops the onions and garlic. It is such a perfectly coordinated effort, with Caris directing every step. The longer we work to prepare the vegetable stew, the more at ease Caris becomes. She adds a wonderful red burgundy to the stew and pours a glass for each of us.

An hour later, as the stew cooks down, the savory aroma of thyme, basil, onion, and garlic creates a perfect symphony with the comfort of rustic potatoes, sweet carrots, snap peas, and mushrooms. After a second glass of the burgundy, I begin to feel a smooth, warm sensation move throughout my body. I feel a little giddy, and without thinking, I blurt out something I wouldn't have asked otherwise.

"Caris, why are you doing this? Every Elevator up to this point has been male. It's clear what their motives are for helping us, but with you, I don't understand why you would risk so much to help us. After all, as a woman who has dedicated her life to upholding and enforcing the ideals of Dominion, helping Robbie and me goes against everything you've sworn to protect."

"I suppose I could ask you the same thing," she says to me. "Why are you helping Robbie? After all, you're a woman too, and you have more to lose by helping him, right?"

"Well, it's different for me," I say. "I never agreed with the flagrant injustice dictating the roles of men and women in Dominion. As an investigative reporter and a woman who loves Robbie, I'm compelled to do everything I can to change this way of life."

"An investigative reporter?" Caris asks, raising her eyebrows and tilting her head slightly to the side. "Are you Danielle Matthews?"

"Yes," I say. "I assumed you knew that."

"I didn't make the connection until now," she says. "Now I'm even more confused by your commitment to this cause. How do you manage your beliefs when your mother is one of the founding perpetrators of this unjust existence?"

"Yes, it's true that my mother created Illegis, but she did not create this horrible situation. She simply developed a way to manage it for the good of society. I, just like you, don't find the status quo to be just, and I support changing society to a more balanced union between men and women."

"Do you really think all your mother did was create Illegis?" Caris asks. "She did much more than that. Your mother knowingly created Illegis to diminish the male role in society, and when she discovered there was a segment of the male population who weren't affected by the war agent, she administered a drug to induce mental decay so that these men would fit the Illegis model. The perpetrators of the male condition in Dominion have to make sure their position won't be challenged, so they prey on the debilitating impact of the war. Haven was founded by the men who discovered this evil and escaped before falling victim to it. Many of the men who found out died of what was described as mysterious aneurysms."

"That can't be true. It can't!" I say. "My mother isn't like that!"

"Sure she is," Caris says with an antagonistic sneer. "How do you think she managed to achieve status as a high-ranking official within the Science cabinet so quickly? Or how she has the ear of the cabinet leader? No other cabinet official wields that kind of power. It's the fear of this secret getting out that horrifies our president. Your father knew the truth, and he demanded that your mother stop perpetuating the lie. She agreed, but obviously that's not what happened. You can fill in the rest."

"How do you know this?" I say as I try desperately to make sense of this.

"Your father, along with a few others, was instrumental in building the Elevator network. He knew the truth and was planning to expose it, but he died before he could do that."

Standing abruptly, I stagger back toward the edge of the kitchen counter and grip it to regain my balance. Something hits me like a ton of bricks and overtakes my senses. The circumstances of my father's death rushes at me, and I remember his sudden and unexplainable death—it was an aneurysm, not a heart attack as I had initially been told by my mother. She was alone with him when it happened. I remember my aunt Delyse, my dad's sister, saying that it didn't make sense because he had just been given a clean bill of health a week before he died. My mother dismissed aunt Delyse's concerns as conjecture and stopped speaking to her. Since the creation of the arbilator, which detects and removes an aneurysm with 99.9 percent accuracy, one causing death is practically unheard of. My father had received an arbilation screening just weeks before he died. It is exactly as I always feared: *My mother caused my father's death.*

CHAPTER FORTY-TWO

I sit on the brown Moroccan wool rug near the flickering flames in the fireplace.

My head is spinning, and my hands and legs are numb from disbelief. Robbie comforts me by wrapping his arms firmly around me. I feel the warmth of his cheek against my face.

"Look, it wasn't my intent to hurt you," Caris says. "I think it's important to face the truth—the whole truth, no matter how ugly. I live this every day, and I suppose I sometimes forget that the truth often has to be delivered in small doses. I'm truly sorry for my callous delivery." She readjusts the belt around her waist.

Robbie loosens his embrace and responds, "I'm sure you didn't intend to hurt Dani. How did you personally come by this information? Surely this is confidential and protected at the highest level of government?"

"My sister is the general consulate and ward counsel to the law enforcement cabinet leader," Caris explains. "She drinks the Dominion Kool-Aid and would never betray the cabinet. I discovered the truth by accident when she was staying here. She sometimes comes here to get away. One night I was here to unwind after a capital murder case involving a woman who had been kidnapped and murdered by a group of vigilante dissenters. I was sleeping in my room when she arrived. While she was downstairs working, she received a call from Selene, the law enforcement cabinet leader. I overheard the entire conversation and learned that Dani's mother, Linda, was seeking to retire and wanted to bring in her replacement to lead Illegis. Judging from my sister's response, Selene was hysterical about it and wanted to find a way to keep Dani's mother in her role beyond her contract. Shortly afterward, Dani's father died, and her mother chose to stay on."

"So you think that someone working for Selene, or Selene herself, may have killed Dani's father?" Robbie asks.

"No," Caris says. "I can't leap to that conclusion, but I will say that the timing of the incident was rather opportune given what Selene had to lose." She takes a sip of her wine and sets her glass down gently. "There's something else you need to know. Haven isn't everything you think it is. Reality rarely measures up to what you imagine. It's true that Haven is the home to the central operative for the resistance, but unlike Dominion, where there is a role for every man, regardless of aptitude, in Haven, only the mentally and physically strong can survive. Escaping to Haven will not be enough; you will have to prove you belong."

"What does that mean?" Robbie asks.

"Gideon, the leader of Haven, will have you tested across a number of areas, and if you fail, he may not let you stay."

"If I don't pass these tests, where would I go?" Robbie asks.

"I don't know," Caris says. "I've never seen a supplicant after I lead them to the Bounty. That's the entrance to a hidden path to Haven. I'm told that no one who has gone beyond the Bounty returns to the outside the way they arrived."

"Well," Robbie says, "I suppose if I was okay living as a Breeder, what you're telling me would scare me away, but it's not. I'm more than what Dominion tells me I am. I won't live as anything less than a man free to choose my own way. No more talk. I'm not turning back." Firm in his resolve, Robbie leaps up from the floor and makes his way to the kitchen. "I think the stew is ready. Let's eat," he says. "We only have a few hours before we leave."

CHAPTER FORTY-THREE

Sitting around the table eating dinner, you would hardly think that just minutes ago, Robbie had been warned that the journey he is risking his life for may not be the salvation he hoped for. Or that my mother may be a co-conspirator in a plan that would artificially perpetuate the bleak outcome of the war through any means necessary. But for now, what I've heard is merely someone else's truth. I will not be able to accept Caris's story until I confront my mother with this horror. For now, I'll finish this meal and prepare for what comes next.

Caris begins clearing away the serving dishes while Robbie and I put the plates, glasses, and flatware in the dish cleaner. The heaviness of the evening has dissipated, and I feel energized and full of anticipation for what comes next. Robbie puts his arms around my waist, kisses me on my shoulder, then grazes his fingers through my hair. Even with Caris standing just a few feet from us, it feels like no one else is in the room.

A dull roaring sound startles us. It's an EV pulling up in front of the cabin. Caris dashes to the front window. Peering intensely through the curtain, Caris whispers, "It's my sister, Ana. I didn't expect her to come tonight. I can't hide you, so just follow my lead." We rush to the tan leather couch, and I sit and lean casually against the armrest while Robbie sits a few inches away from me, picks up a photo plank on the edge of the coffee table, and begins thumbing through it.

Ana stumbles through the door, carrying a large bag and pulling her carrier suitcase. Unlike Caris, her short, petite frame is styled in tailored navy-blue pants and a silky emerald-green blouse with flowy sleeves. A shimmery gold necklace dangles around her neck. She walks carefully into the kitchen, places the bag on the table, sits down, and begins to unsnap the thin straps around her ankles, slipping off her dark spike-heeled sandals.

"You didn't tell me you were inviting guests this weekend," she says in a low, exasperated voice.

"Well, you didn't tell me you were coming at all," Caris says. "I don't understand. You usually tell me when you're coming to the cabin. What's going on?"

"Last-minute change of plans," Ana says. "I needed to get away and clear my head. I wouldn't have come if I knew you had company."

Caris says, "Meet Dalia and Ryan," our aliases. "Their EV stalled on the side of the road nearby, so they walked over to ask for help to the nearest garage. I'm going to take them into town."

"Well, nice to meet you," Ana says. "I'm Ana, Caris's sister. What's your final destination?"

"We're headed east to attend a wedding in Clybourn," Robbie says as he sinks deeper into the couch.

"Oh, I see. I haven't been to one of those in a while. Well, safe travels." Ana unpacks the shopping bag in the kitchen and heads up the stairs, pulling her luggage behind her.

As soon as we hear the sound of Ana's bedroom door closing, we head up to the guest room to gather our things and wait for departure. Robbie is tired. He sits and rests his neck against the cushioned headrest. He quickly dozes off.

I'm feeling much too anxious to sleep. The adrenaline surges through my body, and I start pacing nervously across the floor. My hands need something to do, and my mind needs to be occupied with something other than the journey that lies ahead. I yank my backpack from the corner table, and its contents spill across the floor. At that very moment, I saw it. Yes, that's it. I reach for the weathered cover of the journal I took from Robbie. We were in such a hurry to flee Garland that I forgot about this mental stranglehold that was supposed to persuade Robbie to abandon his plans and remain in Garland. I lay on the bed, prop my head up with a pillow, and trace the leather spine of the journal with my fingertips. The creased pages inside are worn, and the writing looks erratic, almost illegible or shaky, so I have to study each word closely. The first few pages disclose that this journal is a recounting of personal transformation and redemption. I gently turn to the first entry entitled "Capture."

Although a few months ago, every detail was forged into my memory: blood, flesh, and bone scorched by the excruciating pain of knowing that enemy capture would destroy me. Each day, the smell of death was in the air. My eyes were open, but there was only darkness amid a dull light vainly penetrating the narrow opening between the door and the metal walls enclosing me. The only way out was the door, thick and strong. I laid on a bed of stones where the ground beneath me was damp and the pungent smell of death lingered like an impenetrable chokehold.

I heard the sound of footsteps, and then the door creaked open. Two men, their faces as rigid as blunted steel, darted toward me, grabbed me, and tied my arms to a chain. I was hoisted like a piece of meat, my back exposed. Each lash felt like a serpent squeezing and spewing venom in my wounds. Blood ran thick, burning from the heat of the whip. God will give me justice!

The next entry was called "Torture."

Each hour mocked me, and I'd lost all sense of time. I didn't eat the gruel they shoved underneath the door. I spent my days lying on the ground, weak and listless, in the corner of my cell, praying to die!

Then, the door swung open, and the guards threw a limp body in my cell. His shirt and pants, torn and bloodied, hung loosely from his tall, skeleton-like body. His spiny fingers were mangled in blood, and his bald, mottled scalp was caked with dirt. Later, I was to discover his name was Leesin, a soldier from enemy forces. Neglect became my ally.

The soldiers came twice a day, once to collect our excrement and another time to pick up and deliver gruel and water. For what seemed like an eternity, Leesin and I plotted our escape. There were times when we fought like wild animals then would fall out in exhaustion just to hang on the fleeting fringes of life another day. Often, in my suffering, I would beg him to kill me. Death seemed like a welcomed companion.

It didn't matter that we were on opposite sides. In this torment, we were brothers, part of the same race, the human race.

The next entry I read was called "Release."

I was unable to tell one day from the next. Even the check-ins from the guards became less frequent. We would go days without food, and the stench of our urine and feces would become unbearable. But this day was different from any other. Instead of the guard removing and replacing our waste containers, he opened the door and ordered me to exit. I wanted out of this hellhole, but I was afraid. Where was I going? Was this it? Was I going to die? Looking at Leesin, I swallowed the lump in my throat as our eyes met then departed without emotion. "Anything is better than this. Go!" he screamed and laid back down on the damp rocks.

In seconds, I silenced the fears in my mind and let one thought feed my fleeting courage, **Reach your peak**. *I repeated these words in my mind over and over and exited the cell. I was immediately blindfolded by one of the guards while the other jammed a needle into my arm. When I awoke, I was in a bright white room. The smell of disinfectant assaulted my nostrils while the blinding light burned my eyes.*

Still woozy from the drug, I was unable to stand, so I laid there waiting to confront my fate. My countless pleas for death were answered with something I didn't expect. Xavier, my most trusted friend and comrade, walked into the room. He said, "You're safe, my friend. You'll be returning home very soon. Rest for now." I realized in that very moment that I was given a second chance, and I had no intention of squandering it. I was going to make this pain count in some way, and I didn't need to know exactly how right now because **destiny happens whether you're ready or not.**

Before Xavier exited the room, I needed to be sure I wasn't hallucinating, so I asked, "Where is home?"

Xavier smiled and said, "Linda and Dani, of course."

CHAPTER FORTY-FOUR

My mind is reeling from reading my father's words. Knowing what he went through while captured during the Great War fills me with great sadness. I remember when he returned, and he never mentioned the torture he endured. It was his last military assignment before he died. His emotional scars weren't apparent to me, yet I know his memories must've been raw, slicing through him like a razor-sharp blade.

Something within me stirs like a lion awakening from a long sleep. *I, too, have emotional scars—scars from anger, resentment, and regret. I, too, am fighting a biting pain that whips around me, ready to suffocate my spirit and bind me to my suffering. I won't succumb to this darkness. I, just like my father, will overcome my fear and find a way to reach my peak.*

Suddenly, Caris knocks on the door and shouts, "It's time to go!" Robbie struggles to awaken, then jumps up from the chair, still a little disoriented, and I shove the journal in my backpack. We head to Caris's EV with our belongings and wait for her to join us. The stiff leather seats are cold, and the sound of the wind whipping through the bushes is unsettling. Unable to quell my impatience any longer, I exit the EV and head back to the cabin. Before I reach the steps, I hear screaming and then a loud thump. The curtains are drawn, so I rush back to the EV.

"Something's going on in there," I say to Robbie. I rifle through my bag to find the stun gun that Caris gave us, and we run back to the cabin. Peeking through a narrow slit between the curtains of the kitchen window, we see Caris tying what looks like an unconscious Ana to a chair and running upstairs. Moments later, she heads back down with a bag and darts out of the cabin.

We run back and get into the EV. Without hesitation, Caris darts out of the driveway in a panic.

"We have thirty minutes tops before Ana comes to and starts looking for us," she says. "I have her pod so that will slow her down." Caris's laser-focus calm is jarring. As the EV accelerates, Caris begins to explain what happened.

"She knew something was up, and that's why she came up here. For months now, Ana has been searching for information about my activities outside of work. She found a note in my wastebasket several months ago, and while I had a sound explanation for it, she knew there was more to the story than I let on. She has a very keen sense. Since then, she's been relentless with her inquiries and stopping by uninvited to find anything to prove her suspicions. She suspects that I'm supporting the resistance, but she doesn't have proof."

"What exactly did she find that sparked her suspicions?" Robbie asks as he adjusts his seat and leans his head against the headrest.

"It was a name and address associated with one of the aliases of a resistance co-conspirator, Aubach. The address is highly classified. I'm not even supposed to be privy to that. She wanted to know how I came across such highly confidential information and why I had it. I told her I confiscated it from a detainee at a Polix-Five activist rally in Dolvin. I provided the name of the detainee whom I had questioned and released. I thought the matter was over until I discovered that she had pulled the file to discover the reason for the detainee's apprehension. It was robbery, not illegal militant activism. When she confronted me about it, I simply wrote it off as a mistaken recollection, but Ana knows that I have an infallible memory. She knows I would never forget something like that, so now she's suspicious of every action I take."

"I have to ask again," I say. "Why are you helping us? I think there's more to your motivations than what you shared earlier."

Caris pulls the EV over to the side of the road and turns off the engine. She leans back and responds, "I have my reasons. They're for me to know. For now, you have no choice but to trust me. Are we good? No more questions, okay? Just sit back and try to get some rest. We have a long drive ahead of us."

CHAPTER FORTY-FIVE

As the sun begins to rise, it is bright and clear. The window is cracked, and I feel the chill in the air as it whips through the EV. The wide, empty road is bumpy and seems unending. We soon reach an area where the side of the road is covered in a carpet of gold leaves that fell from the trees lining the road. The sunlight makes the leaves glow. Such beauty amid this isolated stretch of road seems to signal hope and an opportunity for change. I feel hopeful in the middle of nowhere because I know life as I know it will never be the same.

Caris exits the road and drives deep into the forest and the mountainous terrain leading to a barren enclave surrounded by very large rocks escalating to a granite peak. She parks close to the side of a deep, dry ravine. My arms and legs feel heavy as we layer on heavy goose-down jackets and backpacks. Caris reaches into the trunk and pulls out ropes, harnesses, helmets, and belay devices. "I hope you can remember how to rock climb because we have a challenging climb up two thousand feet of what looks like complete blankness," she says.

It looks steep and intimidating as I look up to see areas of smooth, sheer granite slabs in between rough, craggy surfaces. I tighten my harness and helmet and grab Robbie's hand as we walk to the base of the mountain.

"I feel uneasy. I could die doing this," I say.

"Are you okay?" Caris asks briskly. She is tall, strong, and lean compared to my more delicate, feminine frame.

I nod unconvincingly.

"You told me that you used to rock climb for sport at Onyx National Park. Onyx is known to have the most challenging mountain in the West. This is no different than what you experienced before at Onyx," she says. "It's tough, but you can make it."

"It's been a few years since my last climb at Onyx," I say. But then I remember the horror of my father's imprisonment and the words that sustained him. *Reach your peak.* I've come too far to stop now.

I squeeze Robbie's hand even harder and then release it with a slow confidence.

"Caris, how long will this climb take? Will we be in Haven when we finish?" Robbie asks.

"We should make it to the entrance in two to three hours. But that will be as far as I go with you," Caris says. "I can't tell you what to expect once you enter the Bounty."

Caris begins to climb. Robbie and I follow behind her. My fear dissipates as I scale the rugged surface of the first fifty feet. I have not rock climbed in a long time. My breathing becomes heavier as I gasp for air, and my muscles start to ache. Climbing up the side of the cliff and looking up hundreds of feet above, I see jagged rocks threatening to end my life. My only security is the rope tied to my harness. With each secure landing of the bolt on the rock, I pull myself up, struggling to keep the cold, harsh wind from my face. It feels like a sharp blade piercing my skin. Each time I get past a ledge and feel the tug of the rope, I think I might actually make it.

"How's it going?" Caris shouts over the wind.

"Okay!" I shout breathlessly.

Robbie follows beside me. He seems to glide over the rough crags and mounds of the mountain. He monitors my progress with each powerful thrust and secure hold into the stubborn surface of the rocks. He turns his head to make sure I'm steady.

"Hold on, Dani, you're doing great," he says.

We reach a ledge with a smooth surface and rest for a moment. My arms are shaking, and my knees feel like they're about to collapse.

I take a deep swallow of water and a deep breath.

"We're about one hundred feet away from the Bounty," Caris says as she tightens her harness and adjusts her gloves.

We begin to climb again. The side of the mountain is smoother, almost slippery in places where ice has formed as the climate grew colder. I begin to feel faint and know that I can't go any further. Caris announces that we will reach the Bounty with our next flight. My lungs are burning, and my shoulders are tense and throbbing. Gasping for air, I pull myself to the top of the enclave. Just after we reach the surface, a wind rushes by and almost knocks me down. I watch Robbie take a deep breath and let out a gasp, then laugh. Somehow, I manage a half smile.

Looking out at the sky, the bright golden light from the sun pierces my face, and I can faintly see the tops of some of the trees below. I close my eyes for a moment and imagine my life in Los Angeles as it was before this moment. I picture me and my girlfriends lying on a beach, sipping lavender martinis, or shopping with my mother and hearing her constant critique of every choice I make. I think of the countless heated debates with my editor about a hot story. I miss it. I miss it so much, and it's this lingering hint of nostalgia that causes my eyes to swell and my throat to tighten. Everything will be different.

"This is where our journey together ends," Caris says as she settles into the corner of the enclave. I will rest for about thirty minutes and then make my way back down."

"Aren't you exhausted?" I ask.

"I'm tired," she says, "but I've made this trip at least a dozen times, so I'm used to it. I'll be fine."

"How will we know where to go once we enter the Bounty?" Robbie asks while loosening his harness.

"Just use this map and follow the signs," Caris says, handing him a small piece of burlap. "The signs are there to guide you. You'll be fine."

"But how do you know?" I ask. "You told us that you've never seen anyone after they enter the Bounty, so how do you know we'll be okay?"

"I know because you and Robbie will have the opportunity to contact me to confirm you've reached Haven. I hear from every supplicant I guide once they reach Haven, but never after that. Rest assured."

"If we won't see you again, maybe you can tell me why you do this? Why help us?" I ask for the last time.

Caris lifts her head and stands up to stretch. She seems even more intimidating than before. She looks intently into my eyes, then Robbie's, and confesses, "Because, my dear friends, I am both woman and man, but woman on the surface for now."

CHAPTER FORTY-SIX

Before entering the cave, Robbie and I study the brown burlap map. The instructions read: "Walk 120 meters north (will see a white eagle with a red beak on the wall of the cave). Veer to the left where you see a narrow chamber. You will notice glittering crystals once you go inside. Follow the shallow brook until you reach the bridge. Do not cross the bridge, but travel beneath it for 50 meters. Veer right at the pillars, which create a wall that slants. Climb over it. Go through the tunnel bearing the seal of the Statue of Liberty. Travel for 200 meters until you reach the falls. Climb the side of the falls and enter through the mouth of the dragon."

The dark, narrow opening is nestled in the rock of the cliff. The stones are jagged, uneven, and concealed by ivy. I feel nauseous with fear. I tell myself that everything is going to be okay. We made it this far, so we have to move on to the next dangerous thing.

I take Robbie's hand in mine. I look for the tenderness that softened my heart, and the warmth of his smile reassures me. I won't turn back now.

Robbie enters first, and I follow. We step into the impenetrable blackness. As I continue to follow Robbie, I watch my shadow engulfed into the surrounding darkness. It is cold and damp. The surface is craggy, with small, loose stones littering the floor, and with each step, the mud and sand covers my boots. Robbie continues to move forward while peering at the sides of the cave for the first sign. We finally reach the wall with the picture of a white eagle with a red beak.

We veer to the left and squeeze through a very narrow chamber. Everything in front of us is still engulfed in a chilling blackness, the only illumination coming from the flashlight in Robbie's hand. The ground beneath us feels less rigid, and the sides of the chamber shimmer in the blackness.

Ahead, we hear the sound of water dripping. I can feel the softened mud squishing under my feet. I see a bridge in the distance; it looks fragile. We carefully move underneath the bridge, our feet splashing in the water around us. In my haste, I fall on my knees and scrape my leg against the sharp rock, creating a tiny tear in my pants.

"Are you okay?" Robbie asks as he turns to help me.

"Yes, just a tiny scrape. Nothing serious," I say.

We walk along the edge of the chamber. My face feels stiff and rubbery. Again, the rocky floor causes me to stumble. I fall to my knees in front of a tall pillar that leans toward the center of the chamber. Robbie helps me over to the side and climbs along the side and then over the protruding stone floor.

Our journey seems like it will never end. We walk, run, climb, crawl, and slither our way through this labyrinth filled with rocks and frigid crevices of stagnant water.

After squeezing through another narrow chamber, we see a round plate embossed with the Statue of Liberty embedded in the wall. First, I am startled; then, I begin to study it. A symbol of freedom and democracy no longer held meaning for Dominion. Instead, it's buried in a cave beneath rocks in eternal darkness. I touch the rim of the seal and press my hand to it. As I begin to trace my fingers along the outer corners of Liberty's face, Robbie jolts me, and I move quickly ahead.

We finally arrive in a large open chamber, and I am astounded to see an enormous waterfall. The water surges over the rocks like syrup and thunders down into the pool as it foams at the bottom. The rest of the pool is so clear, I can see the rocks at the bottom.

I follow Robbie as he climbs along the side of the rocks protruding next to the waterfall. My clothes are drenched in water and mud. I am shivering, and my ears feel frozen. We make it to the ledge near the mouth of the waterfall, about five feet from the ledge we're standing on. Stepping on the stone halfway between the side of the waterfall and its mouth, Robbie leaps. His hand barely grips the edge of the ledge, and his foot slips off the side of the embankment.

"Robbie!" I call out. Robbie pulls himself up and turns back to me with a smirk.

"Come on, Dani. You can do it!" he shouts as he motions with his hands.

My cheeks flame, and I jump to the middle stone while still holding on to the jagged rock above my head. It's so sharp, it pierces my glove, and I see blood trickle down my wrist.

"I got it!" I let out a boisterous scream.

I jump to the mouth of the waterfall and grip Robbie's hand as he pulls me up to the surface of the ledge.

"We made it," I say breathlessly.

Suddenly, he falls to the ground. "Robbie, what's happening?" I scream.

I can't breathe. The air shrieks in my ears as the ground seems to surge beneath me. My heart is pounding so hard that I feel like it's going to explode, and every muscle in my body aches as a dark smoke engulfs me and a falling sensation overtakes my body. I fall to the ground.

CHAPTER FORTY-SEVEN

Everything is a blur as I try to make out my surroundings in the dark haze that lingers. I haul myself upright on the firm mattress covered with a gray and black blanket. There's a small pillow tucked neatly against the wall. The ceiling is so low that I could touch it if I stood up, but I feel so woozy, and I can't get my balance. The walls are bare and dingy gray. A door is located roughly ten feet in front of me. There is a small window at eye level on the door, but it is covered by something on the outside.

My hands feel stiff, but they're warm as I flex my fingers. Looking down, I notice that my mud-drenched clothes are gone, and I'm wearing a set of loose dark-blue cotton pants held up by a tightly knotted drawstring and a long-sleeve white shirt with a scoop neckline. Someone changed my clothes and shoes, but I don't remember a thing.

Standing up slowly, I gain my balance, but the dark haze blurs my vision. I press my ear against the wall, but I hear nothing. Looking around again, I realize that Robbie is not here with me. *Where is he?* Panic sinks into my thoughts, and I wail his name. "Robbie, Robbie! Where am I? Does anybody hear me? Help me!" My ears grow numb from the sharp sound of my own voice.

My voice becomes hoarse, and I feel a dull, aching pain in my throat. I roll my tongue across my upper and lower lips, which are dry and chapped. I'm dehydrated and desperate for water. I sit back on the cot and lean my head against the pillow.

The wait seems endless, and the walls feel like they're closing in on me, so I close my eyes. After drifting into a deep sleep, I'm awakened by a hand pressing forcibly against my shoulder. I'm jolted back into consciousness and stare up at a tall, dark, menacing figure. I scream.

Pressing his hand against my mouth, he says loudly and sternly, "You are in a safe place. Calm down. I won't hurt you, but I can't let you go until you stop screaming."

"Who are you?" I say. "How did I get here? Where's Robbie? Is this Haven?"

"I am Cedren, the squadron leader of the eighth militia. You were found in the gateway, so some of our soldiers retrieved you and brought you here. Robbie is here, and he is safe. You are still weak from the gas, so you will need to rest. An attendant will bring in some water and food for you shortly."

"I want to see Robbie," I say, my throat parched.

"Robbie is also recuperating. You must rest. Then you can see him," Cedren says.

"How do I know he's safe?" I ask. "I don't know you. I need to see him!"

"Why don't you tell me your name?" he says.

"It's Danielle, but people call me Dani," I say, shying away from his intense stare.

Pulling a small tablet from his pocket, Cedren props the screen a few inches from my eyes, and I see Robbie resting on a cot. He looks like he's sleeping peacefully.

"So, rest," Cedren says. "There will be plenty of time for reunions later." He motions toward the door.

"When can I leave?" I ask. "I want to go home."

"Dani, I thought Caris told you. Going home is not an option at this time. You are in Haven now."

CHAPTER FORTY-EIGHT

Waiting outside of my door is an attendant. His name is Siron. He delivered my food and water earlier, and now he re-enters and signals for me to come outside. Still slightly groggy from the dark mist, I exit slowly into a long, narrow hallway. There are several other rooms. While walking, I press my fingers against the wall and glide them against the rough surface. Each door is the same as the next, with a steel plate covering the window. I look up at the circular mirrors placed about six feet apart on the ceiling, and I see myself looking pale and fearful as I walk down the hallway. The attendant maintains a stoic expression as he walks with a militaristic stride. Siron stops and signals for me to enter room twenty-one. There is a man waiting in the room, and he guides me to a bench facing a window.

"Hello, Dani, I'm Dylan," he says in a controlled and deliberate tone. He is not as severe-looking as the attendant, but he is equally intimidating. He wears a black tunic underneath a white lab coat and black combat pants with knee pads. I notice he is holding a tablet.

A window separates my room from a room on the other side. While my room is dark, the other room is brightly lit. In the center is a reclined chair, similar to a dentist's chair. Next to it are a machine and small swivel chair.

I take a sip of water from a tall bottle when I see Robbie being escorted into the room on the other side of the window.

"Robbie! Robbie!" I wail. But he can't see or hear me. "What's going on? What are you going to do to Robbie?"

"Relax, Dani, nothing bad will happen to him. We will simply do an extraction," the man says calmly.

"What do you mean by extraction?" I ask, not liking the sound of the word.

"All Breeders have a microchip embedded in their brains. It contains all of Robbie's experiences since he was indoctrinated into the Breeder class. It's a mental road map of his hopes, fears, and needs. It will help us understand his pure motives and combative resiliency. We need to be sure he can accept and endure the physical, mental, and emotional demands of this commitment. Everyone here has pledged their lives in service of the restoration and protection of our society before its destruction and the creation of Dominion. Robbie must not simply want this change but be willing to sacrifice his life for it. The option is either to become a part of the resistance or leave Haven. There is no in-between."

Robbie reluctantly sits in the chair and reclines far enough that he is looking directly at the ceiling. The bright light floods the room and causes him to squint and turn away from the direct glare. Dylan leaves and joins Robbie in the adjoining room. I can hear what is going on. He busies himself with the machine by Robbie, then attaches a probe to Robbie's forehead.

"Relax, Robbie," he says as he begins to adjust the knobs on the monitor. Letting out a deep sigh, Isaac adjusts the probe further. Robbie starts to squirm as his body tenses up; then he becomes still and motionless. He appears to be unconscious.

Dylan reaches for a syringe and injects it into Robbie's left temple. Still no movement from Robbie. Dylan moves the probe slowly across Robbie's forehead and further back until he stops and digs the probe more intently in one area. Several minutes later, Dylan removes a small metal object from Robbie's head. He stares at it curiously and places it in a round metal container, hands it to his assistant, and returns to the room I am occupying.

Robbie remains in the chair, completely still and unmoved by what just happened.

"Is he okay?" I ask.

"He's fine. He'll be out for the next hour. When he comes to, I will arrange for both of you to join us for dinner in the Great Hall," Dylan says.

I purse my lips and take a deep breath. I have no choice but to wait and trust that we will be safe.

Dylan escorts me to the door and directs Siron to take me back to my room.

CHAPTER FORTY-NINE

After a few more hours of sleep, the effect of the black mist has almost completely vanished. Siron opens the door and motions for me to follow him. The path to the Great Hall is in the opposite direction of room twenty-one. The hallway is narrow, utilitarian, and made of stone. The hallway connects to a dimly lit tunnel that leads to another unmarked path. The further we walk, the more we seem to be descending deeper into a cavern with uneven, sloping ceilings and flooring. *Trace your steps*, I remind myself, but my memory soon surrenders to the overwhelming number of twists and turns.

Siron suddenly stops in front of a large set of double doors, framed and bound by stone columns and the words "Freedom, Equality, Justice" above the entrance. As he pushes the heavy doors open, the stiff silence is washed away by the boisterous flood of loud voices. "This is the Great Hall," he says. "You can go inside." He begins to lead me further into what looks like an enormous atrium. The inside must be at least five stories of formed solid rock. The ceiling is covered in metal tubes mimicking tree roots, and gathering spaces are carved out throughout the enormous space. A dramatic, narrow tunnel with deep ceiling coves leads into the primary exhibition area, where a canopy of wood sticks hover over the center and transform the space into a forest.

Each gallery opening is wrapped in sandstone, and light sconces provide soft bronze lighting. Looking up, I see cavernous galleries and bridges leading to upper levels, each filled with men and women laughing, talking, eating, and drinking. Each level has a variety of fixtures and equipment, such as floating screens, high-top tables, and V/R enclaves. The main floor, where I am, is filled with long community tables and serving stations. The golden lighting at the center of the atrium floods the area and mimics beams of sunlight that create a warming sensation. It's the best artificial representation of sunlight I've ever seen.

There are multitudes of men, women, and children throughout the atrium dressed in the dark military-style clothing of combat pants and boots, vests, and long-sleeve shirts. On the perimeter of the atrium are men with pods and guns. They observe the crowd, poised for action.

There is something so familiar about this scene, yet it's foreign at the same time. Childhood memories invade my mind: children playing, mothers chattering without a care in the world. Since the rise of Dominion, carefree laughter sounds strained and artificial.

"Follow me," Siron says. "I'll take you to the table where you'll take your meals until reassignment." Most people give me a disapproving look. One man leans into the ear of another to whisper; both men look dead at me and snicker. Siron leads me to a table partitioned off from the surrounding tables. There are four men seated. As we get closer, I see Robbie. I'm excited, and my eyes fill with tears. He turns toward me, and relief washes over his face.

"Robbie, I wasn't sure when I would see you," I say. "Are you okay?"

Before he can reply, Siron interrupts, "You'll have time for your reunion later. The commander is making his way to your table."

I look over my shoulder and notice a silence overtaking the room as the sound of heavy footsteps grows louder. I see a tall, menacing, middle-aged man approaching our table. Everyone he passes falls silent and fades into the background. His eyes fixate on me.

"Stand to meet the commander and the leader of Polix-Five. His name is Gideon," Siron says proudly.

"Is he walking with a limp?" I ask.

"He limps from a recent injury during a siege. Stand up," Siron says more forcefully.

Once Gideon reaches the edge of the table, we all rise. I stumble slightly on the way up. Gideon gives me an intense look as if to scold me for being disrespectful.

The longer I'm here, the more unsettled I become about Haven and what, if any, future Robbie and I might have.

"Commander, these are the new supplicants. Lehr, Malcolm, Viktor, Robbie, and Dani," Siron says.

"Welcome to Haven. I trust your stay so far has been satisfactory," Gideon says as he sizes each of us up.

"I know that each of you, as well as many Elevators, made great sacrifices to ensure your safe travel to Haven. And while your dedication is admirable, arriving here doesn't guarantee you will be allowed to stay. Every person around you, including those who are not visible but work to ensure our safety and smooth operations, serves a purpose. Every person, at arrival, did not know what their purpose in Haven would be. It was through challenging our capabilities, strengths, and true nature that our purpose was forged and became a driving force in our destiny to restore this country, this world, to a place where men have the right to choose their own path.

"Our purpose as a collective is clear and must be reinforced with people who have the right set of skills and talents. Over the course of the next few days, you will endure tests and challenges that reveal your true self. These tests will give me and our tribunal the insight to determine if you will stay. Siron will review the details with you. For now, nourish your bodies and commune in fellowship with each other. Your contact with members of Haven outside of your team will be limited, but should you be allowed to stay, you will be welcomed with open arms by every member of the collective. I wish each of you much success." Gideon takes one last look at me before departing. I know that look; it is intense, a lazy exhilaration consumed with sexual tension. I know it well.

CHAPTER FIFTY

I hear a shout and glance over my shoulder. A man with wavy blond hair buries his fist deep into the side of another man with a scar across his forehead. A short, stocky man standing closest to the pillar in front of them reaches out to break up the fight, but he is overpowered by another man standing behind him. The short, stocky man falls as the tall man with a serpent tattoo on his left shoulder smashes his face against the table. Before the fight can get too out of hand, the attendants rush over to break it up.

I feel uneasy watching these men fight.

"Are you okay?" the man sitting to my right asks. He is tall with broad shoulders and a scraggly salt-and-pepper beard. "I am Viktor," he says, offering his hand.

"I'm Dani. I don't think I've ever witnessed a brawl like this before. This is intense."

"I've been here almost a week. This is pretty typical. You'll get used to it."

"Where are you from?" I ask him. "What's your story?"

"I'm a Breeder who escaped from the Colony in the Fifteenth Republic," he explains. "I thought I would be released when I turned thirty, but I discovered they had no intention of letting me go. Apparently, my mental acuity was returning at a rapidly accelerating rate, and they wanted me to stay so they could study me further. I didn't want to stay around for more poking and prodding, so I escaped. I barely made it here alive." He motions to a group of men sitting at the far end of the table. "The guy sitting at the end is Lehr. He was arrested for inciting violence outside of the Dominion Capitol; then he served time at a Dissident camp before escaping. The guy sitting next to him is Malcolm. He escaped a Breeder kidnapping just before they were about to take him out of the country."

"I'm from Los Angeles. I accompanied Robbie here. Robbie escaped from an Ascension event, just before his acculturation. I couldn't let him come here alone."

A siren sounds repeatedly, first faintly then increasingly louder. The boisterous laughter, talk, and movement throughout the atrium starts to die down as the noise of the siren begins to retreat. While everyone around us leaves the Great Hall, Siron turns to us and says in an authoritative tone, "Stay seated."

I feel the mild sweat on my brow and my right thumbnail piercing the inside of my left palm. The silence that remains after everyone leaves is deadening, and I'm fighting my impulse to ask questions. I scoot closer to Robbie, and he glances at me, then fixes his gaze on Siron.

"You will remain together for the remainder of the Becoming," he says. "Tonight, you'll be escorted to the Tunic, where you will reside until your fate here at Haven is determined. Your things have already been moved into your new living area. You will sleep, wash, dress, and rest in the Tunic and be permitted two hours a day for meals and one hour a day for free time to use in the Caldren, which is our activity room. You will be given an additional set of clothing and expected to wash your own clothes. You will be notified when access to your communication devices and personal things is permitted. In the meantime, *do not ask.*" He pauses briefly before continuing. "The Becoming is made up of three phases: the inquisition, the labyrinth, and the battle. You are required to pass all three stages. The criteria to pass each phase is only known to the tribunal. You will find out if you passed at the conclusion of all three phases. Your progress will not be discussed with you prior to the final results, so *do not ask*. Your tasks start tomorrow at eight a.m., beginning with the inquisition. Get some rest, and I will collect you then."

Siron turns away and signals for us to follow him. We form a line with Robbie at the end. I'm directly in front of him. Walking quickly, Robbie grips my right shoulder. His touch is reassuring and calming.

Exiting the Great Hall, we journey even further into the bowels of the interconnected chambers. As we move through each corridor, the lighting changes from a white iridescent glow to more subtle shades of yellow, green, and red. Each corridor disappears into the next, and again I feel like I'm foraging through a labyrinth.

"Here we are," Siron says as he stops in front of a tall, narrow door. "Each of you and the attendees will have access to the Tunic by pressing your right forefinger against the pad like this." He glides his forefinger across the pad to the right of the entrance and invites us to enter.

The room is a large oval shape with a window ceiling that illuminates the entire room. Against the right and left walls are narrow camp beds with metal frames, rolled mattresses, linens, and blankets folded neatly against the head of the bed. Small, midsized, and large storage bins are embedded in the wall between the beds, and black containers are placed directly under the foot of the bed. A wide hallway connects the sleep area with the lavatory, dressing area, and laundry. The accommodations are modest and efficient.

"I'm beat," Robbie says as he plops down on the metal frame of the cot closest to the hallway leading to the lavatory. I settle on the cot next to him.

Each of us begins to make our beds quietly, looking at each other curiously as we tuck and smooth out the linens. Standing against the wall closest to the entry, Viktor asks, "Did anyone know that we have to prove ourselves in order to stay?" At first, everyone is quiet. I look at Robbie for some response, then look down.

"My Elevator didn't tell me there was the possibility that I wouldn't stay at Haven," Lehr says. "And even after what Siron told us, I'm still not sure what the requirements are to stay here." He sits down on his cot and begins to loosen the laces on his boots.

The room grows silent as everyone looks at each other, seeking confirmation of this unsettling reality. "Why would this place be called a refuge for Breeders, other dissenters, and drogans if inclusion is not guaranteed? And further, where do you go if you don't meet the requirements?" Viktor asks as he rises from the cot and walks over to stand in the center of the rest area. "Have any of you ever heard of or seen anyone who didn't stay in Haven?" he asks wearily. Again, there is silence.

"Look, Haven has been a place of refuge for so many of us. Look at the masses of people already here. We know what Polix-Five stands for. We've seen the massive turmoil they've caused in the name of equal justice. Would ya wanna go back to an existence that treats you like nothing more than someone to be tolerated?" Robbie says. "I know I don't. I planned, fought, schemed, and nearly lost my life to get here because there's no other way out of this hell. I'll do whatever it takes to stay, and if you know what's good for you, you will too." He stands up and begins to roll out the mattress on his cot.

Malcolm turns to Robbie with a troubled expression. "No one's saying they don't wanna be here. We're simply asking why none of us knew that Haven wasn't a permanent home. And what happens to people who don't pass the test? Those are fair questions. We can't pretend these issues don't matter."

"No one is saying these issues don't matter," I say.

Robbie cuts me off. "Dani, I can speak for myself. I said all I wanted to say for now." Robbie has an angry scowl, turns away from me, and buries his head in the pillow. Something feels like it's changing between us. *Is this what it's like when a man no longer needs you?*

CHAPTER FIFTY-ONE

"Have a seat, press the probe against your right temple, and place your palms flat on the metal sensors." Maxim, my inquisitor for the day, walks to the front of the small, stuffy ten-by-ten room and turns on the large flat screen. The sound of his heavy dark boots echoes around the hollow walls and the high ceiling. Standing next to the screen and facing me, he looks larger than life. He is a man of tall stature, and his broad, muscular frame is insulated by a tight-fitting black tunic and black combat pants with knee pads.

"Before we can determine your viability as a member of this movement, we must understand your past. This portion of the inquisition will focus on that. I will ask you a question, and you will answer loudly enough that the pulse you see in front of you remains green. A blue pulse signifies that you are not speaking loudly enough, and a red pulse will indicate that you are not being truthful. Should you see a red pulse, do not try and explain why you answered the way you did. Simply restate your response. If you need to ask me a question for clarification, press the black button between the two metal sensors your palms are resting on. You will be given two tries after the first red pulse appears. If your response is accepted, a green pulse will appear. If your response is not accepted, the red pulse will grow larger, indicating that you are still not being truthful. If, after your second response, the pulse doesn't turn green, I will proceed to the next question. Are you ready?"

"One quick question," I ask. "How many red pulses am I allowed before I fail?"

"It doesn't work like that," Maxim says. "There is no pass or fail grade associated with this. You can choose to tell the truth or choose not to. Choose wisely."

The first few questions are straightforward and easy, like "What is your full name?" and "Who are your biological parents?" I rub the back of my neck and switch positions in the hard, high-back chair with the thin seat cushion. We're four hours into this inquisition, and I've had only two fifteen-minute breaks. Questions about my history of trustworthiness, character, and soundness of judgment come one right after the other until my throat grows parched while my fingers and toes feel partially numb from the cold draft in the room.

"It's time for your lunch break," Maxim announces. "You get sixty minutes in the Great Hall. Siron will be here shortly to escort you and your fellow teammates to your seating place." Maxim presses a button that lifts the screen until it is completely hidden within the high vaulted ceiling.

I shouldn't be surprised that Maxim will not be escorting me to the Great Hall. There's something haughty and removed about him. His disdainful attitude toward me is very apparent, and it makes the inquisition even more difficult to endure.

A hard knock on the door is followed by a deep voice. "Ready?"

Exiting the room, Siron waves me forward to join Viktor, Malcolm, Lehr, and Robbie, who are standing in a line. I join behind Robbie, and we continue to follow Siron through a series of empty chambers and narrow passageways over uneven ground. He leads us back to the community table and benches that we occupied last night.

"Isn't it funny how everyone here seems to ignore our presence?" I ask. "Each person I passed either looked away or didn't notice me at all."

Siron gives me a grave look and says, "That is because your status here is *unknown*. After the Becoming, you will either become one with the collective or released. Until that day, you remain *unknown*."

"Well, that sounds very ominous," I say as I pass the water pitcher to Malcolm.

"You know, I understand why Robbie is here, but Dani, why are you here? You're not afflicted by the Dominion status quo, and you don't exactly strike me as the militant type," Malcolm says as he jerks the water pitcher from my hand and gives me a snide look. He quickly fills his glass, passes it to Lehr, and taps his fingers against the table. His hands are rough and chafed with minor cuts and bruises across his knuckles.

"Malcolm," I say, "my reasons for being here are frankly none of your concern." I turn away to grab a slice of bread from the basket. Robbie gives me a deep stare and a gesture that advises me to be a little less callous.

Viktor and Lehr turn away and peruse the room. To divert what is clearly becoming a contentious exchange, Viktor smiles cautiously and exclaims, "The test this morning was brutal." His voice sinks as he looks at Malcolm.

"I wouldn't say brutal, but I suppose it could have been if you had something to hide," Malcolm says, turning to me with a curious glance.

Robbie interjects, "Why's Gideon looking over here? He keeps staring at you, Dani. Even when he looks away, his eyes keep coming back to you with this intense stare."

I glance casually in Gideon's direction. His eyes meet mine, and a wave of heat streams through my body from the top of my head to the tips of my toes. I'm almost put in a trance by his dark, hypnotic eyes. I look down for a minute, and when I look back up, he's turned away from me, and in an instant, the heat that permeated every cell in my body immediately dissipates.

Siron returns and motions for us to follow him out of the Great Hall. "Let's hope we're done with the forty million questions," says Lehr.

Exiting the Great Hall, we walk in the opposite direction from the interrogation rooms. As we approach the first chamber, I hear water crashing against the rocks, and a damp draft brushes against my skin. We approach a narrow bridge towering over a brook. The sound of the water clashing against the rocks is turbulent and unsettling. I try to ignore the uneven walkway as the mist sprays just above my feet.

We finally cross over the bridge and reach what looks like a newly built area. I feel like I am gliding across the leveled, polished floors. The walls are rounded with a silver gloss. The vaulted ceiling extends high, at least eight-to-ten feet, with tiled squares laid in a grid-like frame with actual ventilation. I'm amazed at the intricacies of the security system as we encounter several check-in points requiring security retina scans. Finally, we reach a huge dome with several stories. The atmosphere is very different. The air is fresh and reminiscent of citrus and pine. Glancing ahead, I notice that the walls are bare except for a few kaleidoscope pictures, which lend dimension to the austere environment. The light is so bright, it shocks my eyes.

"Welcome to the Dome," Siron says. "This is where your medical workup will take place. You will be tested for all common medical conditions and those that followed the war, such as latent aphasia, fertility, and nicolysis, to name a few. You will also receive your IQ tests here. You will remain here until four p.m., then be escorted to the Caldren for your one hour of free time. Follow me," Siron says as he checks us in at the admittance station.

The wait feels endless. I close my eyes and try to remember the warmth of Robbie's breath on the nape of my neck or his fingers coursing through my hair. His presence soothes me, but somehow, I'm unable to manufacture that feeling of safety and comfort in my mind.

"Danielle." A tall, slender man in white medical scrubs motions for me to follow him past the double doors. His pace is fast and determined. He stops at an open door just past a room with the word "X-Ray" on the metal plate affixed to the door.

"Go inside," he directs me. "Dr. Messere will be with you shortly." He closes the door behind him and whizzes away.

The room is plain. The walls are an eggshell white and have the antiseptic smell of bleach; the floor is slate gray. I sit on the examination table, press my hands flatly on my thighs, and begin to smooth out the wrinkles in my pants. I scoot back so my feet don't touch the floor. I can hear machines beeping alongside the exam table. My legs are numb, and my eyes are slightly red and puffy from the penetrating chill in the air.

Strangled sounds interrupt the silence in the room as another man enters and approaches me. I scoot a few inches to the left.

"My name is Dr. Messere," he says. "I understand that you are new to Haven and require a full workup. We'll start with the probe, then the body scan to identify any major medical conditions.

"A probe. What do you mean?" I ask.

"I will insert a probe into your bloodstream via injection. It will neutralize your bodily functions so you don't become destabilized from the oxygen modifiers in the air here. Without it, you'll become weaker and develop harsh migraines and nausea. Don't worry. It will be extricated from your body in seven days, after your body has adjusted. Lie down, and we'll begin."

I lie on my back and roll onto my side, facing the wall. The magnetic pulse of the probe seems to penetrate every inch of my body, and the more I squeeze my eyes shut and stiffen my position, the more intense the pulse becomes. I am unable to move my hands or feet. I grit my teeth and grab the side of the table, and then everything goes black.

CHAPTER FIFTY-TWO

"Dani, can you stand up?" I feel drowsy, and my body is limp. The attendant assists me as I slowly get off the table and attempt to stand. My mental haze slowly dissipates, and as I walk down the hallway, I can feel my limbs growing sturdier and my lightheadedness passing.

Siron meets me in the waiting area and escorts me to the Caldren. Walking into the room, I see Robbie sitting alone next to a warming station and watching something on a tablet. "What an unusual day," I say, cozying up next to him and resting my head on his shoulder. "I'm absolutely exhausted but so glad to finally get some alone time with you." He says nothing but tilts his head next to mine, his cheek against my forehead. "How are you feeling?" I ask.

"I'm okay. This place is nothing like what I imagined," he says. "I thought I'd feel a sense of belonging, but I feel like an outsider, even more rejected than I did as a Breeder in Dominion. Every move I make is watched and analyzed for a sign of betrayal or cowardice. And what if I'm not invited to stay? Where will I go? I can't just go back to my old life. Technically, I am a fugitive. I don't know what's beyond this place or where I truly belong."

"You'll be invited to stay," I say, trying to project confidence. "How could they not want you? You're a fighter, Robbie. That's what they need. That's what they want. I know you belong here. You need to stop doubting yourself."

"It's not doubt about myself that I feel; it's the reality of the unknown. We're only one-third of the way through this vetting process, and the most challenging part is still ahead. How do I fight to win? How do I fight for us? The more I learn about this place, the less confident I am about you staying here."

"What are you saying?" I ask, my confident tone succumbing to apprehension.

"I'm saying this place is for those who are willing to put their lives on the line for justice and freedom. Are you willing to do that?"

"I know that I love you and I don't want to live without you," I say.

"I don't want to live without you either," Robbie says, "but the path I'm on requires sacrifice, and I worry we'll have to sacrifice us."

"You may be right," I say, "but for now, let's be in this moment and forget about duty, honor, and reprisal. It's just us now, Robbie, just us."

We sit motionless, clinging desperately to each other. Each moment melts into the next. Our fingers intertwine, and we press up against each other. Somehow, even though our bodies are close enough that I can feel the beat of his heart, he still feels far away.

"Danielle, follow me please," Siron says as he stands in front of me, a very disturbed look on his face.

"Where am I going?" I ask. Robbie starts to nudge away from me. He looks at me and signals for me to go with Siron. "We'll talk later," he says. "Everything will be fine."

I pull away from Robbie and follow Siron into another dark corridor. I look around, trying to note any landmarks along the way. I almost lose my balance a few times on the rocky surface, but it gets smoother as we travel deeper into the interlocking chambers. The hollow silence fades into a dull vibrating noise, which seems to be coming from above us. "You'll need to keep up with me," Siron says. "We're approaching the Divide, and we'll need to cross it quickly."

I quicken my pace and notice a dim light just ahead. It marks the entryway to the Divide. Once I step into the chamber, I see a narrow walkway suspended several feet above a dark hole with no bottom in sight.

"Don't look down," Siron tells me. "Keep your eyes fixed on the landing area in front of you." Staring straight ahead, I see a flat surface about 100 feet away, leading to a large red door. The loud echoes of the siren peak when I've made it about twenty feet across the walkway.

"Hurry and don't look down," Siron says when he turns around and motions for me to walk faster. "The siren alerts him that someone is coming, and the door will automatically open sixty seconds after the siren ends," he explains.

With each step, the siren becomes louder. It's almost deafening. I press my hands against my ears to quell its screeching. I'm moving as fast as I can, but my legs are starting to feel heavy. My heart is beating uncontrollably, and my eyes feel dry and heavy from the cool air that whips across my face.

As soon as I step onto the landing, Siron grabs my hand and whisks me quickly past the entrance seconds before it slams shut. I stumble to the ground, using my hands to brace my fall. The floor feels warm, and before I can regain my footing, someone grabs my arm. His hand is wide and strong, and with one arm, he pulls me up.

"You barely made it. Welcome to my quarters," he says.

His dark brown eyes meet mine, and heat surges through my body. My mouth is dry, so I wet my lips with my tongue and bite the corner of my lip.

"You're Gideon, right?" I ask.

"I am."

"Why am I here?" I ask as I begin to walk further into the chamber.

"Perhaps you'd like a glass of water to quench your thirst?" he asks. "Or would you prefer something stronger?"

"No, water is fine."

I look around and am astounded by the sophisticated décor. The entryway is narrow with a large open light fixture that illuminates every corner. It opens into a large living space. It reminds me of a hotel foyer with high gloss, dark mahogany flooring. A cursory look to the right in this majestic space shows me vintage wall sconces hanging on the cream-colored walls and beautiful vintage tapestries in shades of red and gold. The room is sparsely decorated but very functional, with vibrant cushions sprinkled across the cream-colored sofa and chairs. Glancing to the left, I see there are no VR equipment or AI consoles, but dark, rustic chairs are arranged around a large wooden desk and chair in front of an open fireplace, which leaps with a roaring flame.

"Have a seat," Gideon says as he walks to what looks like a small pantry. He hurries back and sits in the chair next to the sofa where I am sitting.

"Why am I here?" I ask.

"You are here because I don't think you've been truthful about your motives," he says to me. "You say that you're here to be with Robbie, and while that may be true to some extent, there is another reason for your journey to Haven." His intrusive stare strips me bare and frightens me. It's as if there's no life behind those eyes. I look away, invoking my courage to return.

"It seems that paranoia is another one of your steadfast traits. It is not my intention to be disrespectful, but I've sensed some degree of hostility from the moment you greeted us in the Great Hall," I say.

"No, not paranoia," he says, "strong instincts. You see, Dani, unlike most people who question or discount their instincts, I have learned how to master every variance of my instinctual prowess, and I'm sure that your motives go beyond what you're willing to share."

Gideon moves in closer until he is sitting just a few inches in front of me. He strokes my shoulders with the tips of his fingers and then glides them down the side of my arms. He leans in even closer, with just the right look of desire in his eyes. I try to look away, but the intensity of his gaze is like a magnetic pull, forcing me to disarm my inhibitions. Just as I poise my body for his kiss, he presses his lips gently against my ear, the wetness of his tongue grazes my ear lobe, and he asks, "Why are you really here, Dani?" He cups my face before slowly pulling away.

I quickly stand up and walk toward the fireplace. "Let's suppose you're right and I am here for the wrong reasons," I say. "What's next? Do you kick me out of Haven? Kill me? Or find some way to make life here so hard that I beg you to let me leave?"

"Dani, I question if you belong in Haven," Gideon says matter-of-factly. "In fact, you may be released only after I'm satisfied that you aren't a threat to our security."

"What does that entail, exactly?" I ask.

"You will be allowed to continue with the tests, but if I decide you're not here for the right reasons, you'll have to leave Haven. And, before you leave, we will erase the memory of your journey and your time here," he explains. "Once you're released, you won't remember this place, me, or anyone else you encountered while here."

"You can't do that to me! I won't allow it!" I say, standing up.

"Dani, you don't have a choice. This will be done not only for the safety of the people here but for your own safety as well."

"What if I want to stay?" I ask. "I pledged my loyalty and my love to Robbie, and I plan to remain with him. If he's staying, so am I."

"That isn't up to you," he says.

The harsh implications of Gideon's words begin to hit me, and my stomach feels uneasy. I stand up quickly and look around. There's no way for me to escape, and panic has set in.

"Am I a prisoner here?" I ask as I slowly sit back down.

"No, you are not a prisoner," Gideon says. "You're a guest, just as Robbie is. No harm will come to you, but you're not guaranteed a place in Haven here." Gideon picks up my water glass from the coffee table and walks back to the pantry.

I start to stand up quickly, but my knees begin to feel weak, and I'm lightheaded and groggy. I don't feel my skin when I pinch my hand. *This doesn't feel right.* Then everything goes dark, and my body crashes to the floor.

CHAPTER FIFTY-THREE

The ceiling looks fuzzy and appears to be moving both closer and farther away from me at the same time. I wiggle my toes and squeeze my hands together. With my head still heavy and my eyes blurry, I sit up on my cot. Looking around, I can see that I'm back in the Tunic. *How did I get back here?* Everything is so fuzzy. The last I remember is sitting on the sofa in Gideon's chambers; then I blacked out.

"Hey there, sleepy head," Robbie says. "You've been out for more than ten hours." He sits on my cot and begins to sweep the hair off my forehead. "Dani, are you okay?"

"Yeah, I think so," I say wearily. "I don't know how I got here."

"What do you mean?" he asks. "You don't remember coming back to the Tunic?"

"Right. Everything is cloudy," I say. "Robbie, I think I may have been drugged."

"Drugged, are you sure? By who? Why?" he asks, concern showing on his face.

"All I remember is sitting in Gideon's chamber."

"What were you doing in Gideon's chamber?"

"Siron escorted me there," I explain. "You were there when he demanded I follow him. I didn't know where I was going until I got there. I don't remember much. When I try to remember what we talked about, it's all blurry."

"Look, you're obviously disoriented," he says. "Why don't you stay here and get some rest? I need to be in the Great Hall in five minutes, and then I may go a few rounds with Viktor in the combat room. Phase two of the challenge begins at ten a.m. today, so don't be late."

"That's the second phase of the Becoming," I say. "How are you feeling? Do you know what to expect?" I ask.

"I'm not exactly sure what the challenge is, but I do know there's the possibility that at least one of us won't make it," he says.

"Robbie, I'm afraid for you—for us. This place is cruel, and I'm not sure I can endure the darkness and pain here."

"Stay calm," he cautions me. "Everything will be okay. I need you to have faith in me just like you did yesterday—nothing has changed."

"Do you still love me?" I ask.

"Yes, I do," he says. "I never stopped."

With that, Robbie rises from my cot, grabs the backpack from under his cot, and meets Siron at the door.

I struggle to stand and make my way to the lavatory. A hot shower and clean clothes will help reinvigorate my mind, and I can walk without staggering.

The room is empty. Each of the cots is perfectly made up, the corners of the blankets tucked neatly underneath the mattress, and the firm, white pillows pressed gently against the head.

The air is stuffy; I need to move around. I notice that the green security light, signaling that the door is locked, is not on. Siron must've forgotten to lock the door. I grab a water bottle and flashlight and peek outside the door before heading out. I know I'm prohibited from leaving the Tunic without Siron, but this is too tempting to resist.

This time, I have no escort. I have no idea where I'm going. The ground is uneven, and the dimly lit passageways force me to peer intently and move cautiously.

Continuing down the long, narrow footpath, I see a large gold door. It's ornate with a glossy finish. I press my finger against the metal plate, and the door automatically opens into a narrow, brightly lit corridor. My curiosity gets the best of me; I must know what is beyond these walls.

Traveling down the long, winding corridor, I hear voices—mostly women's voices and then the faint sound of children laughing. The walls in many of the transitional chambers are smooth in some places, textured in others. My shoulder brushes against the sharp edge in the wall, and it tears my sleeve. The ceiling light and ornate wall sconces light the winding path to the internal chamber.

The draft that seems to permeate every crevice of this place doesn't exist here. Instead, warmth soothes my body and makes me feel a sense of comfort and familiarity. Unlike so many other parts of Haven that convey only harshness, this place makes me feel welcome and at ease.

Walking into the grand chamber, I feel sheer amazement and a euphoric sense of relief as the smells of jasmine and lilac overtake my senses. The loud sound of children playing brings back memories of my own childhood. I am mesmerized by what looks like a completely different place. The austere furnishings found in all other parts of Haven are gone, replaced by soft, feminine touches and bright colors.

"You must be Dani. I've been expecting you." A woman approaches me from behind. She's wearing a cream-colored robe and satin slippers. Her demeanor is kind and uninhibited. Behind her are four other women, each dressed similarly in light-colored, loose-fitting garments and delicate shoes.

"Yes, I'm Dani," I say. "You've been expecting me. How do you know me?"

"We haven't met, but it is my job to know every person in Haven, visitors and alike. My name is Tshala. I am the spiritual advisor to Gideon. I see what cannot be seen and know what is hidden from the physical world. I bring healing and peace in Haven, during a time of chaos."

"Oh, your role here seems almost supernatural," I say with tempered disbelief.

"Not almost. I do have spiritual gifts, and you will understand that before you leave us. But enough about me," she says. "How about I introduce my companions?" She points at the women standing at her side. "This is Mya, Reyes, Octavia, and Moulin." Each woman stands proud, strong, and unflinching in her purpose. "Maybe we should take a seat in the parlor?" She takes my hand and guides me gently to an alcove opening out of the grand chamber. There appear to be four other sections, each extending from one of the hexagon-shaped corners of the room.

Children play throughout the space, and women go about their daily activities of cooking, reading, talking, and tending to infants. I watch, drinking it all in.

"Tag, you're it!" a child yells as she runs away from her pursuer. The other children flee in different directions, laughing and giggling infectiously. The happiness and carefree ambience here is addictive and renders fear and angst, my constant companions since I arrived here, mute.

The alcove is small and cozy, with fine, textured fabric layering the walls and a radiant crystal and gold light fixture hanging directly above an oval-shaped cherrywood table.

"Have a seat. Would you care for something to drink?" Tshala asks.

"No, I'm fine for now," I say.

"As you can see," she says, "there's a light breakfast buffet and a selection of water, tea, and juice, so help yourself when you feel up to it."

Sitting around the table, each of us holds hands while Tshala prays. "Father, thank you for blessing us with a new day. This day is bountiful and full of wonder. Your blessings overflow and keep us strong, safe, and in eternal gratitude for your goodness and favor. We give you the glory and the praise, now and forever. Amen."

"This is the Solitude chamber," Tshala explains. "It's where the women and children of Haven live." She leans back in her chair and wipes the pastry crumbs from the corner of her mouth.

"We sleep, bathe, relax, and fellowship with each other here. All of our meals take place in the Great Hall, except for breakfast, and there are areas throughout Haven where the children can learn and play in the afternoon and early evenings. The mornings are reserved for the women and children to be together and build that bond of safety and love, which, as I am sure you have found, is not exactly exalted in other parts of Haven. The women of Haven are no different than the men in that we must be strong and work tirelessly to bring back equality to a world that is misguided by bioengineered genetic selection and suppression. This world, our world, is no longer a place where both men and women live as equals with the choice to be who we want without the government defining our futures and controlling our fertility. So, we fight. Just like the men, we fight, but we must also be the primary caregivers and teachers, not only to our children but also to the men whom we love and fight alongside. Every woman here is a fighter. Most fight alongside their men while a smaller number are here to protect their male children from the assignment process. And an even smaller number of women, such as myself, who have no binding commitment to a man or child, fight for equality because it's the right thing to do. Something tells me that you also fall into this category."

The entire time Tshala is talking, images of my journey to Haven, beginning with the day of the Ascension, flash before me. Feelings of courage, conviction, loyalty, and love swirl around in my head. In the wake of all that has happened, I begin to question my feelings about everything, including Robbie.

"What makes you think I have no alliances to a man or child?" I ask.

"I did not say no alliances," Tshala says. "I said no commitment. There is a difference. I know that you traveled here with Robbie, but your bond is transcendental and not of the flesh or even of this world. Your souls are at peace with one another, but your destinies come together for a short time and then diverge again. You are meant to be together as teachers who help each other grow and reach the pinnacles of your destinies."

"I don't understand," I say. "You're telling me that what I feel for Robbie can never be?"

"No, I'm telling you that the love you feel for Robbie will transform into something far more intangible and valuable than what you have now. As a matter of fact, that transformation has already begun. Don't fight it, Dani. You can't win. It is your destiny."

"So I'm supposed to believe what you're telling me?" I ask defensively.

"It's your choice," she answers, smiling.

"Tshala comes from a long line of spiritualists and clairvoyants," Mya says. "Like she said before, she's chief advisor to Gideon and the council. You can choose not to believe her, but that will not invalidate what she says." Mya pushes herself away from the table and walks over to the buffet.

"I'm not sure how to process all this," I say. "I know my heart, and I love Robbie. Your predictions can't change how I feel."

"Dani, you know your heart now, but what you feel will change," Tshala says patiently. "Trust me. You have a higher calling that will require your full commitment, and the kind of life you imagine with Robbie is not in your immediate future. I know it's a lot to take in, but it will settle with you sooner than you think, and you will be at peace with it."

Everything she says feels like daggers in my heart, but in some undeniable way, I feel a sense of relief. Every time I told Robbie that I loved him, there was a tinge of trepidation and a lingering sense of self-doubt, and I pushed it down deep inside because I wanted to believe that I could love someone completely and deeply.

"Tell me," I say. "How did this place come to be? It's unlike any place I've ever been—a place buried deep within a mountain. A place that is dark, rough, and austere, as well as palatial, warm, and comfortable. How does this place exist?"

"Before Haven existed," Tshala explains, "this place was Ace. It existed around 1200 AD and was a much smaller city than its rival city, Cahokia, a heavily populated city of about twenty-five thousand. Now a Dominion Heritage Site, the Cahokian population consisted mostly of farmers and craft specialists who made pottery, jewelry, arrowheads, and clay figurines."

Tshala rises and walks to the console directly across from the parlor. She grabs a scroll from the top drawer and spreads it across the center of the table. Gliding her forefinger carefully against the crinkled, aged paper, she says, "Cahokia sat on what used to be Southern Illinois and was composed of many behemoth earthen mound structures that ran along what used to be the landscapes of the Ohio and Mississippi River Valleys and across the Southeast." I move closer to Tshala, my eyes following her every move.

"The city of Ace was quite different. It existed several hundred miles east of Cahokia. Its founders were the Dissidents from Cahokia who sought to bring more progressive scientific ideas to Cahokia, but they were spurned and cast away. These Dissidents were led by a man named Ahote. He was a man of science and led his followers to their home, which exists within the bowels of this mountain. Ace was the origin of many fantastic scientific discoveries, which were sold to surrounding tribes that feuded with Cahokia. The downfall of Cahokia was finally caused by the great earthquake, which swallowed it whole. The remains were not discovered until several centuries later."

Mya begins toying with her necklace and staring at the ceiling fan that rotates slowly and makes a clicking noise.

"Ace remained a secret city because of its location," Tshala continues. "The eventual demise of civilization was ravaged by the plague. Ahote was a paranoid man, and the internal architecture of the city reflected that. The city was an underground maze that harbored many secret chambers. Surrounding the chambers were large communal spaces with multiple stories and alcoves leading to private and communal living spaces. The rumors about Ahote were known to very few people, and in 2001, Ace was discovered by a group of militants fleeing from prosecution associated with the September eleventh attacks. They were not part of the attack but stood accused because of their ethnicity and Dissident views on blood capitalism."

Reyes and Moulin quietly converse in the background while Octavia revisits the buffet for another muffin and a fresh cup of coffee.

"They resurrected Ahote, and it became a refuge for those seeking asylum from the societal abuse and corruption of what was then the United States. After the Great War and the establishment of Dominion, Gideon was recruited by the ailing leader, Anders, to assume leadership of Ace." Tshala pauses to take a deep breath before going on. "With the establishment of Dominion, the focus of the collective was redirected to dismantle its systemic evils.

"Over the years, Ace has become the legendary Haven to Breeders, Dissidents, and drogans seeking to escape oppression. Gideon has led the charge as we've gone face-to-face with the Dominion government. Our network is expansive as we are part of a global coalition to unseat and replace the Ultra leadership."

I think for a moment before speaking. Finally, I say, "I understand that Gideon must lead with authority and strength, but when I met with him yesterday, there was something dark and insidious about him. When I looked into his eyes, I saw pain and anger. How can you trust someone like that to lead?" I am cognizant of my nervous heartbeat and damp brow.

"Gideon was not always like that," Tshala says. "There was a time when he led with compassion, kindness, and empathy, but all that changed with the mission to Defiance, the first leadership capital of Dominion. His wife, Sasha, was a powerful and highly respected woman. She led several covert missions and was successful until the raid at Defiance, when she was shot trying to retrieve the Illegis headstone. She was rushed back to safety, but she died on the operating table. Gideon's son, Chasen, blamed his father for his mother's death and fled Haven, vowing never to return. In a single day, Gideon lost his wife and his son. His guilt festers in his soul, and he's unable to see anything but what his wife gave her life for—destroying Dominion. Gideon will succeed, and his wrath will be thorough and swift, for his greatness walks hand in hand with his doom. Neither Dominion nor Sasha's executioner will survive."

"Does he know who shot her?" I ask.

"He does, and he is biding his time until it is the right time to strike," Tshala replies while taking a hesitant sip of her coffee.

"Before I left LA, I was investigating death threats against Valentina Cordova," I say. Tshala exhibits no reaction. "Is Polix-Five behind those threats?" I ask, trying to confirm that the Crusaders are to blame.

"Dani, we do not kill unless our lives are at risk," Tshala says patiently. "No, we are not the perpetrators. Dominion leader death threats tend to be the MO of small Dissident groups like the Desperados, Crusaders, or the Myrmidons. Their tactics often involve the threat of violence and conclude with some sort of financial payoff to stop the threat. They were also behind the kidnapping of a high-ranking intelligence officer a few years back." I sigh deeply with relief, but I question what type of revenge Gideon is capable of exacting against the person who destroyed his family.

CHAPTER FIFTY-FOUR

I lie still on my cot in a near catatonic state, replaying Tshala's words over in my head. They were like red-hot irons burning my skin. As much as I want to deny what she'd said, I know she was telling the truth, and it scares me. The love I have for Robbie may not be what it seems; the journey for truth has gone sideways, and I have no choice but to accept what comes.

It's time for me to join the others in the Great Hall for the second phase of the Becoming. I am fearful of what comes next. The moment I lift my head from the pillow, the door opens, and it is Siron, requesting I follow him to the Fortitude chamber. I sit up quickly, grab the backpack underneath my cot, and head toward my next challenge.

"Everybody, line up!" says a man with a bald eagle embossed on the breastplate of his armor. A bright light flickers behind him as a group of other militants stand beside him, watching our every move.

He stands erect and wears a helmet. His voice sounds slightly muffled as he directs us to position ourselves in a straight line, with our heads up, looking directly at the blue light gleaming from the upper section of the chamber.

Robbie's gaze shifts to me and then to Viktor. Each of us takes inventory of the space and possible threats surrounding us. The sweat from my body clings to the back of my shirt, and my legs feel heavy. Lehr is biting his lip and wringing his hands while Viktor moves his head from side to side, slowly releasing the tension in his neck. Malcolm stands motionless, expressionless. He has been the quietest and most reserved of the group—in many ways, a complete mystery.

"I am Keddren, your commander for today's challenge," the helmeted man says. "You have ten minutes to put on the protective clothing and gear sitting on that table over there. Grab a watch, choose a weapon, and meet us at the entrance of the labyrinth."

We run quickly to the service table and begin stumbling through the pile of clothing and gear. I insulate my body with a bulletproof vest, gloves, a fleece bodysuit, and a metal helmet with a flashlight and a backpack. The extra padding on my chest is uncomfortable and hot. Sweat drips down my forehead as we rush to the table a few feet away to select our weapons. There is a knife, gun, spear, rope, crossbow, and ice ax with a leash. I push my way between Robbie and Viktor and grab the ice ax and leash. We run to the mouth of the next chamber, where Keddren and his fellow militants are waiting.

"Where you start is where you will end," Keddren says as he moves closer to us. "Check your watches. They are preset to twelve hours. All you have to do is press the red button when I say, 'Go.' You must make it through the labyrinth using only the weapons you have chosen. At any time, you can steal a weapon from a fellow competitor to make it through. The first one of you to make it out of the labyrinth will receive an advantage in the next and final phase." He pauses briefly, looking at us. "While you are competitors, you are also a team. This challenge will measure your intelligence, ingenuity, and sheer grit to win—all traits you need to thrive here at Haven. Any questions before you start?"

"What happens if none of us make it through in twelve hours?" Viktor asks.

"No one will rescue you," Keddren says. "You must make it out, or you will die. The labyrinth is made up of a series of tunnels and chambers that decline in temperature quickly after the twelve-hour mark, so failure to find your way out will result in you freezing to death. Any more questions?"

Each of us surrenders to the pregnant pause of the moment.

"Ready. Set. Go!" Keddren yells.

The walls of the labyrinth are cold, dark stone covered in moss and towering at least twenty feet above us. They stretch as far as the eye can see and contain numerous passageways. Each wall is identical to the next, with no identifying markers.

"How do we choose which passageway to enter? They all look identical," I say as my eyes try to focus in the uneven darkness.

"Let's choose the one in the center?" Lehr says, uncertain.

"Why that one? The ones on either side seem just as viable," Viktor says.

"It really doesn't matter," Malcolm says. "We simply need to keep our hands in contact with the wall and keep walking. We follow the same wall. We'll need to mark the ground to ensure we aren't in a closed area." He walks to the center passageway.

"How do you know this?" I ask.

"Let's just say, solving puzzles is a passion of mine," he says. "Also, Lehr, since you chose the paint gun, make sure to mark our path every one hundred feet or so. Let's go."

We walk cautiously through the center passageway with our hands pressed securely against the wall. There is something odd about the air. It's thinner and slightly gaseous. These paths go on for what seems like miles before a single split or turn.

Suddenly, Viktor lets out a horrifying shriek before collapsing onto the cold, rocky ground. Before he can get up, the walls of the passageway begin to move in; then one wall drops down into the ground as another rises in its place. Again, the walls close in, shifting repeatedly until we are standing on a ledge overlooking a dark abyss between where we are and the next passageway.

"How are we going to get to the other side?" I ask.

Each of us begins looking around for some way to cross over when a deafening noise pierces our ears and huge slabs of ground begin to emerge from the dark abyss. One by one, they appear.

"We have to leap from one slab to the next in order to get to the other side!" Malcolm yells over the loud screeching noise.

"Okay. Let's go!" Lehr says.

"Wait! Do you smell something?" I ask. "There's a burning smell, like hot ash."

"I don't smell anything," Robbie says.

"Let's stop wasting time here," Lehr urges us. "We have to get to the other side." He leaps to the cratered surface five feet in front of him. He leaps again, each time struggling to maintain his balance.

Then Malcolm leaps, followed by Viktor, myself, and finally Robbie. Lehr is about halfway to the ledge on the other side when another random combustion of flames thrashes the surface, scorching the edges of the slabs, then retreats before reappearing.

I let out a bloodcurdling scream and drop to my knees. The edges of the slab continue to burn as the cinders turn to ash and evaporate.

"Hurry, we have to get out of here!" Lehr screams.

"The flames seem to be coming every twenty seconds. We need to count to twenty after the flame and jump to the next slab. Hurry!" Malcolm yells as he covers his head to avoid the flaming embers.

After each combustion of flames, we leap from one slab to the next. The flames scorch my bodysuit and devour the tips of my rubber-soled boots. Lehr makes it to the other side. Each of us follows until Robbie leaps onto the hot ledge leading to the next passageway.

Our gloves are black from the ashes in the air.

We continue our quest on yet another passageway stretching into an unyielding darkness. The flashlights on our helmets provide some visibility, but we can only see a few feet in front of us. We walk for miles until we see a dim ray of light ahead. Knowing we are nearing the end of this eternal blackness energizes us, and we begin to run toward the light. The light radiates against the walls, and I can feel the warmth filling up the empty cavern. We stop a couple of feet from the entrance to inspect the next phase of our journey.

"All clear," Lehr says after looking around and turns back to signal for us to move forward.

The walls are light sandstone and smooth to the touch. My hands glide across the surface as I walk slowly down the right side with Robbie and Viktor. Malcolm and Lehr trail along the left side. The chamber is quiet and has high ceilings. The light begins to flicker, and then we start to hear a dull roaring noise. It's hard to decipher if the noise is ahead of us or behind us. We move faster toward the exit to the next chamber when the floor begins to shake; then it drops at lightning speed. The sudden weightlessness causes my ears to pop, my eyes to dry up, and a sinking feeling to invade my stomach. I fall to the floor on my knees, pressing my hands against my ears when the floor stops moving with a huge jolt. I try to stand up, but my legs are wobbly, and I feel dizzy.

The chamber we are in is cold, the walls made of ice. Straight above us is a long iron rod protruding from the corner of the ceiling and another ledge catty-corner to the rod. Malcolm, Robbie, and Viktor are still on the floor—their bodies twisted and limp, their faces stunted, looking lost and bewildered. Lehr grabs my backpack and says, "You have the ice ax and leash. We're going to need it to get out of here." He removes the ice ax from my bag and calls Robbie to throw him the rope. "If I can throw the rope over the rod up there and pull it down, we can each climb up the side of these ice walls with the ax. These walls aren't more than twenty feet high; we can do it." Lehr ties and tightens the end of the rope around the paint gun. He tugs on it a few times to ensure it's secure and tosses the end of it over the rod.

"I'll go first since I'm the strongest. I can lift the next person up," Lehr says. "Robbie and Viktor, hold the end of the rope as I scale the wall," he instructs them.

Lehr ties the rope securely around his chest and grabs the ice ax to begin scaling the ice wall. With each dig of the axe, Lehr heaves his body up the frozen, slippery surface.

"I'm almost there!" he yells as he pulls himself up to the sharp edge of the ledge, securing his footing, then throwing the ice ax down for the next person. "Come on, Robbie!"

One by one, we scale the ice wall, trying not to slip. Malcolm is the last to ascend. By now the temperature is well below freezing. My tears turn to frost, and my fingers are numb.

"Now, Malcolm, I'm going to grab the other end of the rope, and we'll pull you up," Lehr says.

With a last heave, Malcolm shimmies his body out over the edge.

We shiver next to each other, trying to distribute body heat among us. The walls of the chamber are covered with vines. I reach out to touch them, but they are hard and impenetrable. They're so thick, we're unable to see a way out.

"Press your ear against the vines to listen for a hollow sound," Malcolm says. "When we get to the hollow area, we start there."

"Start what?" Robbie asks.

"Cutting the vines, of course," Malcolm explains.

We press our ears against the large vines throughout the chamber. Finally, Malcolm calls out, "I think I found something. There's a slight echo here, and I can feel a cool draft through this area. We cut here."

For hours, we grab, bend, and cut the thick vines. I remove my gloves to massage my hands and fingers. My knuckles are bruised, raw, and bleeding. We take turns forcing the blades through the vines until, finally, we have a narrow tunnel to what looks like another chamber, but it's dark, and I'm unable to see much beyond the light through the exit.

"I'll go first to check out the other side, and then you guys follow," Lehr says.

"No," Malcolm says. "I should go first. I'm smaller than you and will be able to get through faster. I'll call out when I get to the other side to let you know if it's safe."

"Fine, just do it!" Lehr says impatiently.

Malcolm crawls into the narrow tunnel, forcing his body forward while pushing dirt and rubble away with his hands. About ten minutes later, we hear his voice: "All clear!"

Tired and sore all over, Lehr goes next. I can hear him bellowing guttural sounds of anger and frustration as he makes his way through. A few minutes later, one by one, each of us burrow our way through the earthen tunnel.

"He's gone!" yells Lehr.

"What? Who?" I ask.

We pick up the pace burrowing to the other side of the tunnel. I push through and fall onto the cement flooring of the next chamber. I stand up to brush the dirt and debris off when Lehr says, "Malcolm is gone."

"What do you think happened to him?" I ask.

"Look ahead," Lehr says. "That's where we started. He knew it when he got through and raced to the goal."

Looking down at our watches, we notice that we have twenty minutes until time runs out.

"So we're done?" I ask.

"Not yet," Lehr says. "We need to make it to the goal. I think it's just through that oval cavity ahead. Let's go!"

Hungry, dehydrated, exhausted, beaten down, bruised, and bloody, we make it to the goal where Keddren and the other militants are standing. Malcolm stands coyly against the wall, a clever grin on his face.

"You made it just in time," Keddren says. "Now the hard part begins."

CHAPTER FIFTY-FIVE

Steady bursts of water stream over my head and down my beaten frame, soothing every bruise, cut, and laceration. The steamy water is calming; it washes away the struggle, betrayal, and grit of the day. My mind swirls with images of desperation, hope, courage, and love intertwined into a confusing yet exhilarating cadre of emotions, and as quickly as these images appear, they are carried away by the purifying effects of the waterfall. I want to remain here, naked and standing in my truth, exposed and unguarded by pretense, duty, or honor. The water feels so good, but it can't last; I know that now. I step out of the shower, my toes flinching once they meet the cold ceramic floor. With my mind in shreds and my body ravaged by the struggles of the day, I make my way to the changing room to find something warm to wear. Like a butterfly, I will emerge from my cocoon, my mental armor restored and my mind ready to do battle.

The sound of loud, angry voices fills the room, and I rush back to the sleeping area. Lehr, Robbie, and Viktor surround Malcolm. Lehr's hands flail as his face contorts from anger to rage, and he balls his fists, ready to throw the first punch. Viktor is holding his composure while he yells and turns away in disgust, then turns back to send more verbal daggers at Malcolm. Robbie stands behind Malcolm, jabbing him in the back with his fist, hard enough to force Malcolm to the floor. Everyone is yelling, and it is impossible to decipher what's being said.

"What's going on?" I yell, exasperated from the confusion and anger wallowing in the room.

"We're talking to Malcolm about his betrayal during the labyrinth challenge," says Lehr. "He's a coward, disloyal."

"How am I disloyal?" Malcolm asks. "It was a competition. Someone had to be first, so I took the opportunity when it presented itself. What I did is no different than what you would've done under the same circumstances."

"That's where you're wrong," Robbie says. "I would have never abandoned the tribe the way you did. You left us vulnerable."

"I'm done with this snake," Viktor says, turning away. "As far as I'm concerned, you're dead to me. You're nothing!" He walks to the edge of his cot and sits down to compose himself.

Robbie and Lehr retreat to their cots while I remain standing, bewildered by Malcolm's shaming and exile.

"Don't tell me you feel sorry for this loser," Robbie says as he sees the expression of pity on my face.

"No, I don't feel sorry for him," I say. "Just disappointed. He represents so much of what is wrong with our society today—putting self ahead of everyone else—and for what? To be first in the hopes of getting something that no one else can have? People like him are the reason why we're here. No, Robbie. I don't feel sorry for him. I feel sorry for us."

CHAPTER FIFTY-SIX

The bright lights of the Tunic sting my eyes as they wake us up. Every muscle in my body aches, and the bruises on my side are tender to the touch. I lift my broken body out of bed to face another brutal day. Thankfully, it's the last phase of the Becoming.

"Robbie, are you ready for this?" I ask, whispering softly.

Turning on his side, he looks up at me, his neck straining to hold up his head, the rest of his body contorting to stretch into a comfortable position. "As ready as I'll ever be," he says. We make haste to prepare for the next challenge.

Siron arrives at our chamber promptly at 8 a.m. "Today is a special day. It marks the last day of the Becoming and, for some of you, the start of a new life, your rebirth. Follow me."

Following closely behind Robbie, I ask, "I wonder who he meant when he said, 'some of you'?"

"Yes, well, they did say someone wouldn't make it," Robbie says. "I'm guessing it's either Malcolm or Lehr." Robbie hastens his pace to keep up with Siron on his way to the Great Hall.

When we enter the Great Hall, all eyes are on us. It's as if they can all see the sheer terror each of us is harboring. Whizzing by the rows of communal tables, we return to our designated area and sit anxiously on the bench.

My stomach is in knots. All I can keep down is orange juice and two bites of dry toast. Robbie is quiet as he slowly eats a bowl of oatmeal while Lehr devours eggs, toast, and a side of fruit. It's like he's eating his last meal and refuses to relent any portion of his food in the event that it has to last for a while. Malcolm sits quietly, eating and playing with his toast and cereal. He seems content to be ousted and almost relieved that he no longer has to contend with the bullheadedness of Lehr, the ever-inquisitive nature of Viktor, or Robbie's contempt for him. He can live in his bubble of self-righteousness and look down at all of us mortals with abhorrent disdain. And of course, there's me. Malcolm seems neither affected nor concerned about me, as if I am inconsequential. Maybe he knows something I don't, or maybe, like most men, he underestimates the power of a woman.

Siron hurries back to our table. "Time to go to your next challenge. Follow me," he says. I am jittery with anticipation and fear. Not knowing what comes next is mind-numbing. As I walk through the Great Hall toward the exit, it feels as if I'm moving in slow motion. Every muscle in my body feels weightless, and my consciousness doesn't seem to be in my body anymore; I feel like I'm floating above everyone. My body in motion looks one-dimensional and flaccid while the bodies around me are vivid but vulgar. Once we reach the exit, my consciousness re-enters my body, but I still feel pale from the reality that is swallowing me whole.

CHAPTER FIFTY-SEVEN

"I am Xander, leader of our armed combat squadron. You have entered the third and final phase of the Becoming, which involves hand-to-hand combat and advanced weaponry. You are not expected to be an expert in anything we show you today, but should you remain in Haven, you will be expected to gain functional capabilities in hand-to-hand combat, ranged weapons, biological and chemical weaponry, and explosives. The degree of those capabilities will be based on your natural skill set, interest, and the needs of the collective."

Xander removes a handgun from his holster, points it at a human-shaped target outlined on a white canvas, and shoots a bullet clean through its left eye. Then he shoots the target again in the right eye, then through the center of its head.

"If any of you are questioning your desire to stay here, now is a good time to step out so you don't waste your time or mine." He walks from one end of our line to the other, peering intently into our eyes and scrutinizing our reactions.

"Before we get started," he says. "Who was the first to reach the goal from the labyrinth challenge yesterday?"

Malcolm takes one step forward. His demeanor is calm and collected, mixed with arrogance. Xander stands in front of him and looks him up and down. "You'll be receiving an advantage in this final phase," he says. Malcolm puffs out his chest and glances sideways at the rest of us.

"Your advantage," Xander continues, "is that you will not have to participate in this phase of the Becoming."

Malcolm releases a sigh of relief and a shallow smirk.

"You will not be participating today because you have been cut from the tribe," Xander says. "You will not be staying in Haven."

Malcolm's haughtiness turns to terror, his knees buckle, and he falls to the floor.

"You failed the challenge yesterday by choosing yourself over your tribe," Xander explains calmly. "Such blatant disregard for your fellow teammates will not be tolerated at Haven. No one person is more important than the collective. Simply put, you don't belong here." Xander signals for the attendants to help Malcolm to his feet. Malcolm's head remains bowed, and his arms stay limp at his side as he is led toward the exit.

"What will I do? Where will I go?" He sobs, then lets out a scream. "You can't do this to me! You can't do this!" The sound of his voice fades from a high screech to a dull murmur as he's taken from the combat room.

We stand numb, processing, each of us questioning which one of us might be next.

"Now we can start," Xander says. "You will go to several practice sessions with our instructors. We will measure your aptitude and assign you a grade based on your performance in each category. Each grade will establish the additional level of training needed to meet each category's minimum performance standards." Xander signals for the four instructors to join him as he walks us through the schedule for the day.

"Combat and Defense Rotations start in fifteen minutes and will end at nine a.m. Then you will have Guns and Explosives from nine to eleven a.m., followed by lunch from eleven-fifteen to twelve noon. You will have Hand-to-Hand Combat from one to three p.m., then Chemical Warfare from three to four p.m., and finally, Simulations will last until six p.m. After that, you will be released for dinner and free time. You will learn if you will be invited to stay tomorrow morning between eight a.m. and ten a.m. If you are chosen, you will remain, but if you do not make it, you will be removed immediately from your quarters and prepared for reintegration. For those of you remaining, the Rebirth Ceremony will commence tomorrow at noon sharp."

"I'm Quentis," the instructor says. "Follow me!" He guides me to the shooting range. "Have you handled a gun before?" he asks.

"Yes," I say, "but it's been a while. I'm a little rusty."

"Well, today you're going to learn how to handle and shoot a gun," he says. "This is a GISM, which is essentially a semi-automatic revolver with a built-in tranquilizer cartridge and tear gas mechanism." Quentis forces the gun in my hand and motions for me to follow him to the quarry just below the main level of the combat room.

Holding the soulless hunk of metal in my hand seduces my senses and makes me feel powerful and in control. It reminds me of the way I felt when I saw my first published article in the *Beacon*. Seeing those words, my words, memorialized for the world to see, made me feel powerful, like what I had to say meant something. The only difference was that my mouthpiece was the keypad, and now it's much more lethal. The weight of the gun grounds me in the realization that power can protect or destroy. I press the trigger. The harder I squeeze, the steadier my grip and aim become until the rapid release of the bullet startles me, and my hand retracts.

"Very good. You aren't too rusty," Quentis says. "You have a steady aim and a raw instinct for anticipating the next move. Let's move on to weapon assembly and disassembly." Quentis walks over to the gun lying on the sturdy oak table beside the target. He flips the gun in his hand, points it to the ground, presses the release, and unloads it. He puts on safety glasses to dismantle the slide, removes the barrel in seconds, then repeats the steps in slow motion. I follow his eager fingers as they glide, pull, turn, and twist the slide and barrel. "Now you try."

My hands seem to have muscle memory because they move faster than my thoughts, and before I can blink, the gun is completely disassembled.

Feeling confident in my skill, I request another round of shooting. I go back to the target shooting area of the quarry, pick up the gun, and face the target. The sound and power of the bullet escaping the chamber titillates me, and I fire again and again, each time hitting my target.

After two more rounds, my hands fall to my side while the throbbing ache between my thumb and forefinger fades. I have not felt this alive in years, and I love it. I can't remember why I stopped shooting years ago. All I know is that I feel strong and in control of my life, and more than ever, I understand what I have to do.

My next rotation is explosives. The trainer, Alexei, is much more talkative than Quentis. He shares his entire family history with me, ending with how he came to Haven by way of the Russian collective, which had been advancing into the West and Southwest regions of Dominion. He is tall and pale, with ice-blue eyes and blond hair.

Alexei escorts me to the zero chamber and introduces me to chemicals, nitroglycerin, and ammonium nitrate explosives. We study how to detect and defuse explosives. I watch and listen as Alexei walks me through each type. His hands are so precise, and his eyes remain glued to each edge, groove, and wire as he removes them and reinserts them into the exact position. His movement is fluid, patient, and careful, his expertise undeniable.

"Believe me when I say you will have plenty of time to learn this stuff," he tells me. "Most people who come to Haven know nothing about explosives, so it's a slow and iterative process of studying and practicing."

I nod, trying to take in everything he tells me and watching his eyes carefully.

CHAPTER FIFTY-EIGHT

"It's time for lunch," Xander says. "I will escort you to the Great Hall, then pick you up at one p.m. to bring you back here for the Hand-to-Hand Combat portion of your training. Let's go." He motions for us to follow him.

My fingers feel raw, and the throbbing in my palm remains. I am absolutely famished. I stack my plate with fruit, greens, potato chips, and a sandwich made with thick, crusty bread. Robbie, Viktor, and Lehr overload their plates, and we sit next to each other, quietly devouring our food.

"So, how did weapons and explosives go for you?" Lehr asks Robbie after a few moments.

"I think it went as well as could be expected for someone with no shooting or explosive experience," Robbie answers. "Violence of any kind was not permitted in my family, and I was drafted to the Colony at twelve, so there was no need for me to learn about combat."

"How about you, Dani?" Lehr asks, turning to me. "You seemed to be rather comfortable with a gun."

"It was good," I say. "I've handled a gun several times before in my line of work as a reporter. It's been a while, but after a few rounds, everything started to come back to me. I guess shooting is like riding a bike," I reply as I squeeze my shoulders together to stretch my back.

"Well, for the first time, it felt like home for me," Lehr says. "My dad was an ex-US military guy, so he trained me how to shoot when I was very young, and I stuck with it until I was sentenced to the camp, but I never forgot. Dani's right. It's like riding a bike. You never forget. Whether it's the feel of cold, hard steel between your fingers or hard times as a Dissident, you never forget." Lehr spoke softly, recalling a memory from his past.

"How about you?" Robbie asks Viktor.

"This is all new to me as well," Viktor says. "You're right. There's no use for this at the Colony." He pauses. "I guess no one is going to bring this up, so I will. Surely, all of you are wondering what's going to happen to Malcolm." Viktor looks at each of us, eagerly anticipating a response.

"Of course," I say. "But I have no idea. Everyone here is very close-lipped about what goes on and severe about asking questions. They prefer to tell us only what we need to know and nothing more." I look to Robbie and Lehr for additional comments, but they just nod in agreement and continue scarfing down their meals.

Again, there is dead silence until Xander reappears to take us back to the training room. We rise from the table, sore and weary from the last three days, and follow him to what we hope will be the final challenge.

CHAPTER FIFTY-NINE

"You will spend two hours reviewing what you learned in hand-to-hand combat training, and then you will fight!" Xander's eyes light up at the prospect.

With my belly full, I am appreciative of the opportunity to shoot and review explosive protocols, but in the back of my mind, I'm terrified of what's to come. It's been a long time since I have been in a physical fight. I regret not paying closer attention in self-defense classes. My hands are cold, and my mind is restless. Refusing to let my anxiety get the better of me, I begin stretching. My delicate feminine form feels stronger, and I can see that my abs and biceps are becoming more well-defined. The words *girly* or *princess* don't describe a body like this. This body is fearless, like a weapon, ready to take on whatever comes its way. The only feminine feature about me now is the ponytail that dangles down the middle of my back. My eyes survey the room for possible threats as I stand upright, in my black-on-black uniform and combat boots, ready to pounce like a lion on my prey.

Finishing this morning's refresh and the Hand-to-Hand training, I walk confidently toward the open fighting ring. Xander stands in front of the ring, his fingers interlocked in a prayer position below his chest. "The very first thing you need to know before you step into this ring," he says, "is that you're going to be nervous at first. It's perfectly normal, so don't let that feeling defeat you; it will pass. The more you refuse to let it consume you, the faster it will retreat. The second thing you need to know," he continues, "is that no amount of scenario planning in your head will prepare you for what's to come. Sure, practice and sharpening your skills are important and will keep you standing, but your mind will keep you alive. It's just as important to think fast as it is to act fast, so don't let one dominate the other—you need both. Dani, you're up first!" Xander says as he paces back and forth in the ring.

I approach the ring slowly, feeling intimidated. It feels larger-than-life, and the closer I get to it, the bigger it appears. Before I climb into the ring, Xander hands me a set of black gloves. I slip them over my already bruised and scraped hands and enter the ring. My opponent is instructor Carlyle. He assisted Alexei with parts of the explosives training. His shoulders are broad and muscular, and his arms look like massive cannons. I can see the veins in his neck bulging as he grits his teeth. I am beyond terrified at this moment, but I do as Xander instructed and force fear to retreat while my courage emerges.

Carlyle approaches me. "Don't worry," he says. "I won't hurt you too badly." Then he gives me a sinister grin. He steps back for a moment, then throws a quick jab. I feel his fist connect below my chest. Pain erupts from the point of impact, and I immediately buckle. He walks over to help me up, and I grasp his side, bring my knee up to his crotch, and throw my entire body weight behind it. I force a heavy thrust to his groin. He bends over for a few seconds to recover, then draws his fist back again and plows it into my stomach; it feels like my guts are smashed together. Stars burst in my vision, but I clear my head and throw a sloppy kick. We stumble apart for a few seconds. He jabs me again in the stomach, but I repay this by punching him in the face, and pain blazes up my arm. I feel a sense of accomplishment to see blood leaking from his nostrils. I guide my knee back to his groin, and this time, with even more force, I kick him repeatedly until he hits the floor. He quickly rises, then falls as he gasps for air.

"Well, I think that's enough," Xander says. "Clearly you have some basic self-defense skills. With practice, you can sharpen those skills and increase the impact at the strike zones and hasten the time it takes to incapacitate your opponent. Now Carlyle will take you outside of the ring to review some combat strategies. Robbie, you're next!" Hammond, the other weapons instructor, joins him in the ring.

The entire time I'm working with Carlyle, I catch brief glimpses of Robbie in the ring. I didn't see who threw the first punch, but when I look over, I see Hammond slamming his fist into Robbie's side. They stumble apart for a second to catch their breath, then dive back at each other. The kicks and punches look brutal. By the time they're finished, Robbie is staggering to the corner of the ring. I take a break and walk closer to see and hear him. His knuckles are bloody, he has a bruise above his left eye, and blood is streaming from his nose.

"Is that all you got?" Hammond asks with a menacing grin.

Robbie snarls, then rushes back into the center of the ring. I see the determination in his eyes as he continues to ram his fists into Hammond. Each blow looks more forceful than the one before. Hammond returns a forceful kick to Robbie's side and delivers a punch to his face.

"Okay, that's enough!" Xander steps into the ring and motions for Robbie to return to the corner. Hammond stands up, gripping and rubbing his side. Robbie limps back, more blood streaming from his nose and mouth.

"You two are done," Xander says. "Why don't you head back to the Tunic and get cleaned up. Viktor, you're next!"

CHAPTER SIXTY

The walk back is painful and unending. With each step, I can feel the sharp pain of Carlyle's fists digging into my side. We limp into the Tunic and head directly to the showers.

Standing under the showerhead, every muscle in my body begins to melt as thousands of lukewarm droplets cascade over my battered frame. I gently press the loofah to my skin, making sure not to aggravate the cuts and bruises all over my body. I lean against the cold tiles as my knees begin to weaken. With the stinging and throbbing pain still rippling throughout my body, I leave the shower stall and walk toward Robbie's. The floor is cold and slippery, so I walk slowly.

Stepping into Robbie's shower, I feel the hot steam ravage my body. Robbie is slumped against the wall as the water beats furiously against his skin. I reach for the loofah and begin to gently dab his cuts and bruises as his blood trickles down his back and arms, then scatters down the drain. With each stroke of the loofah against his skin, my eyes close, each time imagining every intimate moment Robbie and I have had since we began the journey to Haven. The feel of his fingers gliding across my face as the smell of lilacs filled my nostrils in Alec's solarium, the secure grasp of his arms around my waist as we scaled up the side of the mountain in search of Haven, and the feel of his legs intertwined with mine while we lay on my cot talking about our future. All of these thoughts occupy my mind and invoke a passion unlike anything I have ever felt before. I release the loofah and rub his body with my hands, each stroke gentle, caressing his aching muscles. I kiss his arms and chest, invigorated by the steamy rivulets consuming our meshed bodies.

His response is slow and intense. He begins to stroke my hair and massage the back of my neck. Pressing intently against my lower back, he pulls me in even closer, kissing my shoulders and tracing the tip of his tongue around my nipples. I guide my hand between his legs to gauge the intensity of his excitement. He drops to his knees, putting his tongue directly on my clit, rubbing it softly until it swells and my legs are weak. Grabbing my wrists, he turns me around and presses my body against the shower wall. My nipples are hard and erect against the slippery tiles. He slides inside of me, thrusting slow, hard movements. My lips quiver as I inhale deeply with each thrust. Our pain and pleasure become one, and when I explode, my body evaporates and succumbs to an unyielding pleasure. Engrossed in the water cascading over our bodies, he holds me still and kisses my neck, then slowly turns me around to face him. I stand naked, knowing that the ingenue I was a few weeks before is gone, and a woman with ambition, flaws, and fears stands in her place. I am ready to become who I am meant to be.

After the shower, I slump onto my cot and lie there, reliving the moment again and again while watching Robbie slip into a deep slumber. Unable to relax into the warmth of the blanket wrapped around me like a cocoon, I get up and walk down the dimly lit passageway. I have no particular destination in mind, yet I find myself standing in front of the Sanctuary. I enter the inner chamber, still unaware of my purpose, when I see Tshala.

"Dani! Welcome back," she says. "I've been expecting you."

"You have?" I ask. "Why is that?"

"Like I told you before," she says. "Your destiny is becoming clear to you now, and you will understand what you must do. I believe you already know what you must do. Am I right?" Tshala leans in and smiles.

"What I know is that I truly do love Robbie, but there is something pulling me in another direction," I say. "It haunts me at night and chides me during the day. I try to ignore it, but it's relentless."

"Dani, don't fight it," she says. "It's a part of you struggling to the surface, and it must be acknowledged and revered. It is who you are becoming, and that can never be denied. I believe that what I am about to say to you will be received the way it is intended. Your place is not in Haven. You are part of our struggle, but your role is to be exercised outside of this place. You will become a key figure in closing the Divide between Dominion and Haven, and to do that, you must leave. Do you understand that, Dani?"

"Yes," I say. "I do, but how can I be this go-between if I'm unable to recall my experiences and what I learned here? Gideon told me that should I leave Haven, my memory would be erased."

"Gideon refuses to acknowledge your value the way I do," Tshala says. "In time, he will realize it, but for now, he sees you as a potential liability should you disclose the location of Haven and its operations."

"I would never betray Haven," I say. "I would never betray Robbie."

"I know that. Do you trust me, Dani?" Tshala scoots closer.

"I do," I say, realizing as I say it that it's true.

"You will leave Haven today," Tshala says. "When Gideon discovers you are gone, I will reason with him not to send anyone after you. It will take some convincing, but he will understand. He always does. In the meantime, go back to the Tunic and prepare for your departure. I will arrange everything. Just follow the instructions of your attendant, Siron. He will not know that he is helping you escape, but he will facilitate your departure. And one more thing," she says, looking me in the eye. "You can't tell anyone, including Robbie, of your plan to escape." Tshala is composed as she calls for one of the attendants to escort me back to the Tunic.

I am conflicted. "He will never understand," I say.

"You have no choice here, Dani," she tells me. "If you tell him, he will become complicit in your escape, and Gideon will punish him. Not telling Robbie is the only way to protect him from something that will surely destroy him."

"Before I leave," I say, "I must know. What happens to the people who are turned away, people like Malcolm?" Tshala turns away as if to dismiss my inquiry. "Tshala, I must know," I say again. "If I can trust you, you can trust me. What happens to people like Malcolm?"

Tshala looks into my eyes and presses the palm of my hand between hers. Her somber expression intimidates me as the lump in the back of my throat hardens. "You must understand that with great achievements come great sacrifices," she says. "Many of us who left Dominion for a life at Haven came with limited resources, financial and otherwise. While we're growing in numbers, we have to continue to find ways to build the financial resources of the collective. One of those resources includes selling and, in some instances, bartering the unfit to other nations around the world. Dominion is among the more fortunate countries to have an abundance of fertile males. Many other countries are far less able to ensure ongoing survival through their current supply due to the ravages of chemical warfare. We supply them with Breeders. In the case of supplicants who are not Breeders, we offer able bodies for scientific testing. There are other uses as well, but those are the most common."

I tremble, and my eyes tear up at the prospect of Robbie facing such a horror. Anger floods my body, and I can feel the saliva thickening in my throat. "You're telling me that Malcolm has been sold, and if he's found complicit in my escape, Robbie will be as well?" I ask.

"Yes," Tshala says. "I know it seems harsh, but it is what Gideon refers to as the casualties of war. Please understand, Dani, that Gideon will achieve victory by any means necessary."

I have no choice but to trust that in some way and at some time, Robbie will understand what I had to do, not only for myself but for him as well. And if he doesn't understand, I will have to be content knowing that my choice was the best choice for me and for Dominion. My stomach is in knots. I have to do the same thing I did eighteen years ago—let Robbie go and don't look back.

All the way back to the Tunic, I feel like I'm walking in a trance, unable to hear, feel, or smell my surroundings. It's as if I'm wandering in the unknown and unable to communicate that I'm lost because no one sees me.

"Dani," a voice echoes in the chamber. "It's Gideon."

I turn around to find him walking quickly toward me. His confident stride is striking. With each step, his arms move with a controlled swing. He has the strong body of an athlete, the clever brain of an intellectual, and the emotional intelligence of an artist. He has a daunting presence, and he is handsome, from the depth of his eyes to his commanding voice.

"Are you in a hurry?" Gideon asks.

"Not at all. Just heading back to the Tunic," I respond.

"Great, I have something for you. Let's head to my quarters," Gideon says.

On the way to his quarters, I can't stop imagining what he wants to give me. Would this be a continuation of our attraction to each other without the innuendo about my true motives?

Sauntering into his quarters, I decide to stand near the couch.

"So then, bourbon? Or something lighter?" Gideon points to the bar area.

"Bourbon," I say, because it's going to take something strong to get through this.

"Neat, on the rocks?"

"Sure."

He darts to the bar. Moments later, I hear doors closing and glasses clinking.

He's taking a while, so I wander around his living quarters, peeking into rooms, wondering if I will come across the bathroom.

"Dani, try this drink. It's called a Sonic Twist. Also, I want to give you this." Gideon motions close to me and rests his left arm on my shoulder while cupping my chin with his right hand. He says, "There's something different about you. You're not the same woman who came here several days ago. Of course, I see the physical transformation, but your spirit is unleashed and ready to soar. Dani, this is for you."

Gideon reaches inside his pocket and places a thin bracelet around my wrist. It is woven with vivid hues of purple, green, and gold threads shimmering under the light.

"This bracelet symbolizes strength and your commitment to our cause for freedom. The gold hue represents fire, which can bend any object to its will, the green hue represents eternity, which promises longevity of purpose, and the purple hue represents dignity, independence, and power. I see all these attributes in you, Dani. You remind me of my late wife, Sasha. She was a *rebel with a cause.*"

He kisses my forehead and strokes my hair. I am not sure what to make of this. "What do you want?" I ask.

"Right now, nothing." Gideon takes my hand and guides me to the doorway. I am mesmerized by his mystery. I don't understand him, but maybe that's okay. Right now, I have to focus on leaving Haven.

CHAPTER SIXTY-ONE

By the time I reach the Tunic, my panic has surrendered to a placid resolve. I know what I have to do.

"Dani, where have you been?" Robbie asks anxiously.

"I was restless, so I had to take a walk," I say, giving Robbie a pensive look.

"The determinations are in, and I got in! Lehr and Viktor are in as well. Your determination is on your cot. I didn't read it because I know you'd want to know first. Quick, open it!" he urges.

I rush to rip open the carefully folded notice. Looking excitedly at Robbie, I yell, "I'm in!" and throw my arms around him. He gives a huge sigh of relief and squeezes me tightly.

"I was anxious waiting for you to return," he says.

"Now, let's get some rest. Tomorrow's a big day."

Snuggling under the covers, I use the flashlight in my pod to continue reading my father's journal. There's still so much I don't know about what happened to him after he returned home. Thumbing through the worn pages, I find an entry entitled "Sacrifice":

I discovered the price of my freedom, and it sickens me. Linda is now part of the Dominion machine in the worst way. Her work is now a weapon to force men into accepting mediocrity. They call it Illegis, and it is a destroyer. She defends her choice, and now I know why. She had to agree to Allura's demands to use Illegis for the Singletary assignments. In return, Allura agreed to deploy troops to rescue me. I question if my capture was part of Allura's plan to manipulate Linda.

Now Linda seems to have lost her way. She doesn't see the error in her ways. Instead, she believes that Ilegis can help pave the way to peace and prosperity.

I can't let this deception continue. I need a plan.

Safe and cocooned within this quiet space, I wonder about the conflicting choices my father had to consider. Just like me, he chose to do what was right despite the repercussions from Dominion and my mother. His pain was the internal compass that led him to his purpose. Living in your truth can be lonely.

CHAPTER SIXTY-TWO

"You have to get ready for the Rebirth Ceremony. You have about ten minutes before Siron arrives to take us there," says Robbie.

I rush to gather what few belongings I have, stuff them in my backpack, and carefully place it underneath the foot of my cot.

"Hurry, you don't have much time," Robbie chides me.

Within moments, Siron arrives with a box secured underneath his right arm. "The time has come for your rebirth," he says. "Everyone, line up. I will guide you to the ceremony. You must follow me closely until we reach the Harken Chamber; then you will be required to wear a hood for the remainder of the journey and during the majority of the ceremony." Siron adjusts the box against his side. "Follow me!"

Once again, we are guided through another dark passageway. This one is different from the others. The ground is unusually warm and growing warmer still while the air above is cold. Every step we take creates a shallow echo as the darkness transitions to a smoky haze that camouflages our path.

"Keep walking straight ahead," Siron urges. After a moment, he calls, "Stop here." The sudden stop causes me to bump into Robbie from behind. "Each of you, put on your hood. Your guide will accompany you inside."

I put on my hood and stand quietly. I can hear the others being taken into the Harken Chamber as the large double doors swing open and they walk in, one by one.

I feel an empty space in front of me as Robbie is guided inside, then a sharp tug on my left sleeve.

"Come with me. We must leave now," Siron says as he removes my hood. "You have been summoned to the lab. Don't worry, you will return when it is time. Follow me."

Our walk to the lab is short and swift, and we run from one interlocking chamber to another. By the time we reach the lab, I can feel beads of sweat on my forehead, and my heart is beating erratically.

"We are here. Go inside. The doctor will tend to you," he says.

"Doctor?" I ask. "I don't understand." Instead of answering, Siron shoves me into the room and slams the door closed.

The glare of fluorescent lighting suspended from steel rafters assaults my eyes. I stumble awkwardly across the white tiled floor toward the gray recliner. The room has a stagnant smell of disinfectant and lemon. There are stands for monitors, dispensers for rubber gloves and syringes, trays of assorted microchips, and an electron microscope and mini portal.

I sit in the chair, leaning my head back against the headrest. I close my eyes and clench my fists, trying to force myself to relax, but the throbbing pain in my limbs makes this futile. The faint sound of footsteps seizes my attention, and I lift my head to watch the heavy metal door as it opens and Tshala appears.

"Stand up. Hurry," she says. "We only have a few minutes to get you out of here. You are scheduled for a memory erase, and that can't happen. Follow me." She grabs my hand and slips a magnetic card into a security panel next to the side door, and we exit. The dimly lit passageway leads to a large chamber containing a massive power generator and scores of long, intricate pipes that seem to stretch to infinity. "The only way out of Haven undetected is through the HVAC system, which is accessible from this room," she explains. We scurry along the fringes of the room, carefully maneuvering across the floor grid. Beads of sweat are streaming down my brow from the steam and exhaust in the air. Our pace quickens, then slows as Tshala temporarily disables each of the security monitors hidden in the walls with the touch of her magnetic card. My breathing becomes shallow as we approach the entrance of a narrow tunnel encased by a metal fence.

"This is where we end our journey together," she says to me. "You will escape through this tunnel." She hands me the backpack I had packed and a metal monitor. "This monitor will help you navigate through the vent. As long as the signal is green, you know you're going in the correct direction. If you make an incorrect turn, the signal will flash red, and you'll know to change your course. It will be simple to follow. Also, press this red button if you encounter any warning of what's to come. There is a nerve gas that will repel them immediately. The vents are cleaned every twelve hours. You have two hours before that happens. You must exit the vent before then, or you will be incinerated by the heat. You should be able to get to the exit within forty-five minutes, so use the monitor to pace yourself. You'll know when the cleansing is about to start if you hear a siren. It will sound three times within five minutes before the heat is released. There will be someone to meet you on the other side, so go quickly." Tshala smiles briefly and pushes me to the gated entrance to begin my quest.

CHAPTER SIXTY-THREE

The sharp edges of the cover of the air vent scrape and cut my fingers as I remove it and maneuver my body into the narrow passageway. It is dark, with a small glimmer of light illuminating the rough, concrete walls as the tunnel snakes away. I crawl on my elbows and knees through the winding duct, constantly checking the monitor to make sure the signal is green. My dilated pupils scan the joints, flared parts, and rough edges of the airway as I crawl to safety. I shudder and feel numbness in my limbs. My eyesight begins to blur as I search for a way out. The darkness robs me of my senses, and I am fleeing against time while trying to suppress a paralyzing fear. Distance is all that matters. I am not stopping for anything, my eyes glued on the passage ahead. The hiss of the air over the hollow vent is lost under a repeated pounding noise. My clothes are perfect for gliding along the surface, but I feel the rough edges scraping against my knees. The repeated release of bitter cold, then warm air blurs my vision even more and causes me to stop and wipe the tears welling from my eyes. A sudden rip of the polyester fibers near my right knee exposes my skin to the icy condensation underneath me, and my body heat drains away, leaving me cold and shivering, my muscles cramped and unable to move. Again, tears roll down my face and crystalize before reaching the corner of my mouth and leaving frozen tracks on my cheeks.

For just a moment, I close my eyes to alleviate the pressure of straining to see through the impenetrable darkness, but when I open my eyes, I feel dizzy from the struggle. Exhaustion overtakes my body, and I stop moving. The realities of the past few days feel like shackles weighing me down. I can't escape it, I can't forget it, and the pain is slowing me down. Just as quickly as this thought enters my mind, it retreats, and I begin to move again.

The tension in my temples moves to my throat and turns into a thick knot that nearly chokes me. I gasp for air and scurry toward what feels like a warm section just above the jagged surface of the lower level. I grab the edge of the upper ledge to pull myself up when I feel tiny beads covering my hand. Unable to raise my head high enough to see what is prickling at the joints of my fingers, I harness the force of my body weight to heave myself up and onto the upper shelf. One by one, I grip the side grooves of the surface to elevate the lower half of my body onto the upper level. Before I can regain my focus, I feel a flood of creepy-crawly insects around my hands, crawling over my sleeves. They are not the harmless, housebound kind but instead are armor-plated with little needles that poke through my sleeves and deliver sharp stings as they move with incredible speed. I lower my head and press the raised red button on the side of my sensor, which will release a foul-smelling gas. It was the only thing I could think of that might thwart this mob attacking me. Seconds later, I raise my head cautiously and see the ants retreating and dispersing into the dark corners of the duct.

Recognizing that my time is quickly running out, I scramble furiously through the hollow vent. Within moments, the green light begins to flicker, signaling that I am within fifty feet of the exit. At almost the same time, the first siren sounds. My knees are raw and bloody, yet I hasten my pace. The second siren sounds, and I begin to feel a suffocating heat penetrate the air around me. Sweat rolls down the sides of my face, my eyes water, and the joints in my hands are stiff and cramped. Less than ten feet away from the exit, the third siren sounds, and I can feel a rumbling sensation. Then the light ahead brightens as I reach the exit. I heave my head out and feel a sharp pain piercing my chest. My knees feel like rubber as I drag the rest of my body out of the vent. Seconds later, the vent exit closes, and through the glass panel, I see a blaring orange and red blaze overtake the vent. Despite my exhaustion, my eyes close, and my lips curl into a smile as I realize that I've made it. At this very moment, I understand what my dad meant when he wrote, "Destiny happens whether you're ready or not."

I barely have time to feel relieved or smug about my victory when I look up and see Caris standing over me with a curious scowl. "Well, I see you made it," she says. "Let me congratulate you on becoming the first person to escape from Haven. That I know of, anyway. That's quite an accomplishment."

"How did . . . who . . . what?" I'm confused and dehydrated; my thoughts are a jumble. My lips are dry as my tongue peels from the top of my mouth. I can barely believe I've accomplished this feat.

"I can answer all your questions later," she says. "For now, drink this and follow me."

We rush to Caris's EV, which is parked next to the same ravine we encountered when we arrived at Haven a few days ago. The sky has a milky glow, and the horizon is pink and gold. The trees are evergreen and tower in the distance, and I pause to take in this majestic beauty.

"Hurry, get in!" Caris yells as she grabs my backpack and nudges me toward the door of her EV.

The omnipresent trees grow smaller as we speed away from the mountainous path to Haven. The highway is just as I remember: long, desolate, and unwelcoming. The uneven pavement occasionally delivers a jolt that disquiets my thoughts. Images of the endless dark duct scraping and bloodying my knees, the multitude of warrior ants hungry for my body, and the near miss of incineration assault me repeatedly. I am held captive by the harsh shackles of my mind, but the soft current of the crisp, clean air streaming across my face reminds me that I am back on course and ready to face my purpose. I lean my head back against the soft leather headrest while the dull purr of the EV lulls me into a quiet slumber.

The muffled humming of the EV ceases as we approach the cabin. I am startled by Caris's blunt tap on my shoulder as she steps into the bitter cold and races toward the front door. I follow behind at a slower pace, squinting and huddling in the blanket she draped around me. My jacket and pants are torn and spattered with blood, and I wreak from the smell of refrigerant and burnt plastic. My hair is disheveled and partially matted across my forehead, and like a newborn pup, my limbs are shivering all over, incapable of masking my pain. Besides being a little testy, Caris appears to be completely unfazed. Sporting her standard black jeans, shirt, jacket, and cap ensemble, her stride is quick and confident. She's mastered her role as an officer of the law and an Elevator, which means being alone and reducing fear to nothing. When the fear is gone, the only thing that remains is focus and the ability to become whoever you need people to believe you are. Right now, Caris is my savior.

Upon entering the cabin, the warmth of my surroundings and the smell of cinnamon serenades my senses. Everything is just as I remember. The breakfast table with the yellow-and-green floral tablecloth nestled in the corner is burdened with shopping bags and a tray of cookies.

"Come on in. Sit by the fireplace so you can get warm," Caris says. "You must be hungry. We were on the road for several hours." I follow her to the spacious living area with the dark brown leather couch, the chairs around the cobblestone fireplace, and the cherrywood coffee table. I sit on the couch, unable to do anything but stare emptily at Caris.

"Why don't I take you upstairs?" she says after a moment. "There's antiseptic and bandages in the bathroom, so help yourself. I also have clean clothes laid out on the bed."

I follow Caris upstairs. I climb each step like my limbs don't belong to me. My aching muscles burn and feel like worn-out rubber bands, thick and twisted. Once I step into the room, I stumble wearily to the bed. "Thank you," I say. My eyelids droop, and my limbs feel like jelly.

Caris helps me sit on the edge of the bed and removes the blanket from around my shoulders.

"Get some rest," she says. "We'll talk in the morning."

CHAPTER SIXTY-FOUR

The smells of cinnamon and vanilla awaken me from a deep slumber. I'm starving, and despite the throbbing muscle soreness, I waste no time changing into the pair of jeans and an oversized sweatshirt Caris laid on my bed the night before. My shoes are coated in dry mud, and the soles are worn, so I step into the pair of slippers nuzzled against the foot of the bed. I pull my hair up in a ponytail and follow the sweet and spicy aroma as it seduces me down the stairs and into the kitchen.

"Well, good morning," Caris says as she prepares a cup of dalgona coffee in a glass mug. "I trust you slept well. Have a seat. We have cinnamon vanilla coffee, honey-butter pecan pancakes, and fresh fruit."

My eagerness to sit down at the breakfast table is surpassed only by my ardor to dive into the stack of pancakes lathered with maple syrup and warm butter. I can hardly slow down to take a breath or digest my food comfortably. I'm like an engine consuming fuel systematically and unapologetically. The warmth of the sun grazes my cheek, so I release my fork and glance through the narrow opening between the yellow curtains. Looking at the way the sun glistens atop the tall trees and highlights the flowers as they bathe in its soft, nascent rays fills me with an undeniable sense of gratitude. Unlike so many previous mornings, this one seems to invite my attention.

"So, Caris," I say. "Tell me how you knew where I'd be."

"Tshala reached out and informed me of the plan for you to escape Haven. Honestly, I've never seen a supplicant after I've led them to Haven. As I told you and Robbie before, the only contact I've had with supplicants is a brief call informing me of their safe arrival. I was stunned to learn you were returning."

"What else did Tshala tell you?" I ask.

"She said to tell you that you are not to worry about any interference from Gideon. She'll inform him of your allegiance to the cause and commitment to supporting Polix-Five from the outside. Your contacts will be invaluable to the collective."

"How exactly do I support the cause?" I ask. "I don't have direct contact with them now, and we never discussed my role."

"Don't worry about the contact issue. For now, I will serve as the intermediary between you and Polix-Five, at least until your loyalty is acknowledged by Gideon. Until then, all you need to do is take my call when it comes." Caris rises from her seat and grabs a gray pod from the kitchen counter. Handing it to me, she says, "Hang on to this. I'll communicate with you via this pod. It's untraceable and programmed to operate only with your commands. Should you lose it, you can contact me, and I will ensure a replacement. Just know that when it rings, you must be ready to take action."

"I understand, but I'm still baffled about why you're doing this," I say. "Before you left Robbie and me at the Bounty, I asked you why you were helping us, and you said something puzzling. You said that you are both man and woman. What did you mean by that? What happened to make you turn against your official pledge of allegiance and commitment to Dominion? Should your true loyalties become exposed, the punishment will be total destruction of your career and certain jail time, or even death. It seems like such a high price to pay for an effort that doesn't appear to benefit you in the long run."

"I could say the same about you," Caris says. "You stand to gain nothing by supporting Polix-Five either."

"That's not entirely true," I say. "There's my belief that the Dominion way of life is fundamentally flawed. As a reporter, my primary job is to ask questions and expose the truth whenever possible. What I've learned since I embarked on the journey to Haven confirmed what I've felt for quite some time. And of course, there's the love I have for Robbie. Both of these things have sealed my fate and make my choices clear."

"My choice is clear as well," Caris says. "Each day, I grapple with the truth in a different way." She takes a sip of her coffee and gently places her mug on the table. Her hands appear stiff and her eyes sullen and empty. She looks at me, then turns her attention to the sun-drenched world outside the window. She lets out a sigh as tears well up in her eyes, then trickle down the side of her perfectly smooth, unblemished face.

"When I was born," she begins, "my parents and my sister lived a fairly normal life. My parents were civil servants. My dad was a police detective, and my mom was a district attorney. Both deeply believed in living by the rules and functioned well when the rules were clear. But when the rules were murky or nonexistent, they faltered. I am the undeniable example of their failure to function outside of the rules. Back then, the typical birth plan consisted of baby delivery plans and possibly a pre- and post-care plan should there be an underlying physical condition that could harm either mother or child. Now birth plans serve as biogenetic road maps to determining gender, genetic traits, and the future livelihood of the unborn child. Children are bred by scientists seeking political recognition rather than through the natural love between a people. Everything about human creation is controlled, including biological imperfections." Caris scoots her chair closer to me. Her voice gets louder. "I was born with a physiological imperfection, and when my parents were alerted to it, they failed to take action because there weren't any rules about what they should do. So, they chose to do nothing. I live with a daily reminder of their failure to act."

Caris stands up and walks to the stove. She glances at the cookies resting on the warm cookie sheet. She struggles to decide which cookie to choose. She sits back down and licks the foam around the brim of her coffee mug.

I'm perplexed and completely riveted. Caris continues, "I was born with both female and male genitalia. When given the choice to determine my sex, my parents chose to do nothing—not because they wanted to give me the choice later but because they couldn't acknowledge that I wasn't what they expected me to be. As a result, I grew up always knowing I was different, not because of how the outside world treated me but because of the way my parents and my sister did. They chose to project the appearance of a perfectly happy little girl, knowing that I would have to live with the confusion of being both male and female. When Dominion was instituted, they reinforced the charade and told me I could never expose my truth and that the right to live as anything other than a woman wasn't a right I had. So, I continue to hide who I really am. On the outside, I look and act like a woman, but I am a man. Dominion makes it impossible for me to live my truth without losing my freedom to choose. Isn't it ironic how the failure to choose eventually led to the inability to choose? The downfall of Dominion is my salvation to a better way of life, and that is why I am part of the Polix-Five movement." Caris looks away. It's hard to tell if they're focused on the beauty of the world outside or the burden of their truth.

CHAPTER SIXTY-FIVE

The train is on time, and I hear the screech of its arrival as it glides slowly into the station and comes to a complete stop. Turning to Caris, I hug her, then release her thin, muscular frame. "You are a true warrior, and I am honored and privileged to know you," she says. "We will do great things together. I know it." She holds my hands firmly in hers.

"Thank you for everything you have done for me," I say, releasing her hands yet still feeling her warmth on my fingertips.

I board the metal train steps. The transition from fresh, cool air mingles with the scent of sandalwood and peppermint as I peruse the semi-crowded seating area for the perfect spot. I want to be close to the aisle, have extra legroom, and be near the lavatory. I pass by a woman engrossed in a paperback book. It's been a long time since I've seen one of those outside of a library. A few rows behind her sits a man with a distinguished gray beard and a woman with long strands of gray hair mixed with raven black, loosely gathered on her shoulders. They are holding hands while he whispers in her ear. She blushes and kisses his neck. They continue to ogle at each other and appear to be completely unaffected by the little boy sitting behind them and kicking the back of the man's seat while licking a lollipop. I make my way even farther away and discover seat 21B a few feet from the lavatory. There's plenty of legroom and no one else sitting in the row on either side. This will be fine.

As the train pulls away from the station, I lay my head comfortably against the headrest and close my eyes. Just as I start to feel my muscles relax and my breathing become shallower and steadier, I am startled when someone says, "Excuse me." A man edges by and sits beside me next to the window. Even though he is wearing a heavy jacket, I can tell he has a broad, muscular frame. His arms protrude beyond the armrest that separates us. He sinks into the corner of the seat and leans his head against the window.

Hours later, over the intercom, I hear, "We will arrive at Lennox station in ten minutes." My legs are stiff, and my lower back feels strained, so I get out of my seat and walk toward the back of the compartment. I am looking straight ahead and imagining what I might buy at the concession stand when I feel a strong jolt and then a push into a dark, secluded corner, with no visibility to the main walkway. I am pinned against the wall, my face smashed against the cold, steel surface with a hand covering my mouth. "Scream and you die," he says. "I won't hurt you. Just listen. You are not to utter a word about the existence, location, or people of Haven to anyone. Don't attempt to return to Haven or contact anyone at Haven, including Robbie. When we need you, we will reach out to you. Remember, we have allies everywhere, and we will be watching you. Do you understand what I am saying to you? Squeeze my hand if you understand." My hand is cold and numb, but I manage to squeeze his thumb tightly. "Good. Now, when I step away, you are to remain facing the wall for sixty seconds. Turn to look at me, and you die." He slowly releases the forceful pressure against my back and removes his hand from my mouth. I can feel him stepping away slowly, and I remain facing the wall with my eyes closed and my fists clenched tightly.

"Fifty-eight, fifty-nine, sixty," I count to myself. My heart feels like it's about to burst out of my chest. Carefully, I turn away from the wall and stagger back to my seat. I'm shaking, and my mouth is dry. I lean my head back against the headrest as hard as I can while my hand clenches the armrest.

Lennox station is announced, and the train begins to decelerate and come to a slow stop. I am still shaking and beginning to question whether I did the right thing by escaping Haven instead of getting my memory erased and leaving peacefully. The idea of someone watching me and having to jump at Gideon's beck and call seems absurd. What was I thinking? Panic sets in, and I start to question if I can do this. Seconds later, the panic begins to dissipate into something forceful and unrelenting: courage. Whenever I panic or feel anxious, I think about all the times in my past when I've faced challenges, experiences I never thought possible. Then, I find comfort in knowing that each time, I succeeded. I don't know if it's my own sheer will or luck, but I know that just like so many times before, I will make it.

I gather my backpack and slip on my jacket, eager to get off the train, when I pause for a moment and look toward the window. On the seat is a note with a picture of a bald eagle and the words *We are watching.*

CHAPTER SIXTY-SIX

Entering my apartment feels like a more high-tech endeavor than I recall. The biometric and retinal scanners lodged in the outer corners of the door release an inconspicuous buzz that automatically unlocks and slowly swings the door open. The stale air is warm from the radiant golden-red glare coming from the windows. The quiet feels unfamiliar as I enter my gentle space, my home. The twenty-foot-high white ceilings that once loomed over the first floor of my duplex apartment and sometimes made me feel like it could swallow me whole now feel just right.

Even though the walls are painted a muted light gray, the light streaming through the windows and dispersing throughout the room gives the appearance of a smaller space. *What is this place that intoxicates me with a familiarity of my new self—strong and resilient yet comfortable and celebrated?* The sharp edges of the room feel softer and are smooth to the touch. I take off my shoes and socks and allow my toes to meander across the plush, textured rug that stretches along the outskirts of the room where my couch, chairs, and cocktail table are located. The off-white olefin upholstered couch that faces the fireplace is smooth to the touch, shiny, and bright. I fling myself onto it and immerse myself in its warmth and protection. This feels more like home than ever before.

I tilt my head back into the bosom of the couch. The quiet calm begins to lull me into a tranquil slumber. I pull the wool blanket up from the corner of the couch and gently curl my body into an S-shaped cocoon to begin what feels like a long-awaited hibernation.

The moments fade into hours, and then dusk disappears quietly into a veil of darkness, thinly illuminated by the pearlescent moon. I move slowly, stretching my mildly aching limbs and shedding my cocoon. I feel reinvigorated and energized from the nourishing slumber. I can still recall the images of my dreams. The sense of foreboding I felt after my encounter with the stranger on the train is diminished and replaced by a sense of purpose and determination, reaffirmed by my father's words, my deep love for Robbie, Tshala's wisdom, Caris's confidence in me, and the peaks and valleys of my journey to find, survive, and escape Haven. I am meant to be here, in this very moment, living in this righteous struggle, but there's no time to waste. I pick up my pod from the rug. Uncertain of what I will say but knowing the words will come when I hear his voice, I place the call and sink slowly back into the couch.

"Well, hello, stranger, it's great to finally hear from you," he says. He sounds jovial and welcoming.

"Hi," I say. "I know it's been some time, and I apologize for waiting so long to reach out. I would love to see you."

"I'd love to see you as well," he replies seductively.

"How about tomorrow night at seven p.m.?" I ask, envisioning the makeover it will take to get me looking the way I did when I left.

"Sounds great!" he responds enthusiastically.

"Good. I'll call you later with the details. Talk to you later, Colin," I say and hang up.

CHAPTER SIXTY-SEVEN

It's 6:30 p.m., and I'm fluttering around the kitchen, putting the finishing touches on the lemon dill orzo and roasted eggplant salad and prepping the swordfish with tangerine and jalapeno for grilling shortly after Colin arrives. The bottle of Chablis is chilling on the marble countertop while the roaring blaze of the fireplace and the mellow, soft jazz echoing throughout the apartment make everything feel cozy and warm. The spicy, tangy aroma of the roasting wild mushroom kabobs seduce my senses, and I begin to slow my hurried pace as I admire the décor of the dining area. The cream walls and tall mullioned windows showcase the elongated table with a white and gold tablecloth and the polished silver cutlery and crystal glasses shining brightly in the early evening light. The chairs are minimalist yet elegant, with high backs and curved armrests. I refold the napkins that match the runner and head upstairs to slip on my dress and touch up my makeup.

The doorbell sounds at seven on the dot. I can see Colin standing in front of the door, straightening his collar, and unzipping his jacket. I slip on my open-toed black heels and float down the stairs carefully, brushing back the wisp of hair near the corner of my eye. I press the button near the console in the hallway, and the door swings open. Colin steps in confidently, but before I can finish greeting him, he scoops me up in his arms and squeezes me tightly.

"It's been at least a month. I missed you," he says as his hands softly cup my face and he looks intently into my eyes.

"Yes," I say. "I didn't mean to go this long without contact, but my assignment took much longer than I expected."

"Do your assignments typically take you away for long stretches of time?" he asks.

"No, not often," I say. "More often than not, I'm gone for no more than a few days, but this was a special assignment, and I knew far less about what to expect than I typically do." I pull away slowly, leading him into the living room and pouring us glasses of wine. "I'm sorry I wasn't able to uncover any information behind the threats to your mom. Detective Monahan should investigate Dissident groups like the Crusaders," I say.

"I will let her know that. Thank you for looking into it," Colin says.

"Did Detective Monahan uncover anything?" I ask.

"The tests she ran on the letters were inconclusive. We still don't know where the threats came from. In the meantime, they've beefed up my mother's security. It's around-the-clock, and she absolutely hates it," he tells me.

"You know, I'm still not quite finished with my article," I say. "I still have some unanswered questions. I'm hoping you can help me fill in the blanks." I hand him a glass of wine. "Have a seat on the couch, and I'll grab the appetizers."

Returning to the couch, I notice Colin looking around, searching for something.

"You once told me that on a Breeder's thirtieth birthday, he has a choice to stay at the Colony or be released. You also said that most, but not all, Breeders choose to stay at the Colony, but you never told me what happens to the Breeders who choose to leave," I say, my tone light.

"Well, the Breeders who choose to leave go through a six-week transition program to prepare them for living outside of the Colony," Colin explains. "Upon successful completion, they're free to go to a residence and a job that's been set up in advance."

"Do you stay in touch with any of the Breeders who left?" I ask.

"Breeders who leave the Colony are required to discontinue contact with those who remain, and friends and family outside the Colony, for a period of one year. It's called *disconnection*. It's my understanding that barring contact enables a smoother transition to the outside. They're challenged to build an entirely new life in which no one knows about their past. Once they're secure in their new identities, they can reach out to people from their past. But it's discouraged."

"What about after that one-year period?" I ask. "Surely there must be someone who left but remains in touch?"

"Dani," Colin says, "so few Breeders actually leave, and I'm told that when they do, they're given new identities and livelihoods to prevent possible exploitation or something more sinister, like kidnapping."

"I don't understand," I say, setting the wineglass on the table and studying Colin's reactions more closely.

"When a Breeder leaves the Colony," he explains, "he's vulnerable to people who may want to exploit his fertility by using him to breed outside of the national reproduction guidelines. In some cases, Breeders are kidnapped and forced to breed in foreign countries in dire need of males for reproduction. It can be a scary business out there, which is why so few Breeders actually choose to leave."

"So, you're telling me that you haven't reestablished ties with any of the Breeders following the disconnection?" I ask.

"That's right, Dani," he says. "None of my friends have left. Life at the Colony is comfortable and safe. I want very little, and what I don't have, I learn to live without until, eventually, it doesn't matter anymore."

"That sounds almost tragic," I say. "The opportunity to live life on your own terms is taken away from you at the age of twelve, and then it seems like when you do have the opportunity to break free, you're manipulated into relinquishing your freedom for fear of exploitation. The way I see it, whether you choose to stay or leave the Colony, you're bound to something that's nothing more than a form of indentured servitude. The only difference is that the devil you know seems better than the devil you don't." His facial expression grows more perplexed as his eyebrows merge together. He stares at me.

"I don't see it that way at all," he says. "Is this what your assignment was about? Learning about the inner workings of the Colony and the lives of Breeders?" His posture stiffens, and he shifts his position on the sofa.

"No," I say, "that's not it. I'm simply trying to understand your choice to stay in the Colony versus living more freely outside of it. I don't mean to agitate you. I'm trying to get to know you better. And I can't help but wonder if what you and I are building is sustainable since your choice is made and you're bound to stay at the Colony. What if we choose to partner or marry? Would I have to live in the Colony?" I ask.

"Marriage and partnering are forbidden for Breeders," he says. His tone indicates that he's growing frustrated with my line of questioning.

"Oh, that's right," I say. "You did tell me that before. And that's okay with you?"

"Dani, marriage is an antiquated social structure that limits the full potential of men and women. Can't we simply accept each other for who we are and enjoy our relationship for however long it lasts?" he asks.

"Colin, I don't want my romantic relationships to be only casual fun. That may have been okay a few years ago, but I know that love between people can be so much more than that, and I want more." I look at him and then turn away. Awkwardness fills the air. I get up and motion for us to begin eating.

The conversation, once energetic and flirty, has turned polite and stilted. With each morsel of food I eat, I become more uncomfortable with the tension between us. I place my fork on the edge of my plate and say, "Look, it was not my intention to insult your lifestyle choices. Your sacrifice is a noble one, and I was wrong to suggest otherwise. I just have to be honest about my needs, and unfortunately, what we want doesn't seem to align. I'm sorry."

"Dani, no harm, no foul," he says, smiling with, I think, relief. "I appreciate your honesty. It's very difficult to date women outside of the Colony because of the limitations it imposes. It's okay. I've enjoyed getting to know you, and if I had to do it all over again, I wouldn't change a thing. You're an exquisite woman in every sense of the word.

Dinner was amazing, but I think I should leave now," he says and pushes away from the table.

I follow him to the door. Before he can open it, I grab his hand and he stops and turns toward me. I see regret in his face, and he moves closer and grips my waist. I can feel the sexual tension between us. His hands move up from the small of my back to my shoulders. He kisses my forehead, then my cheek. I want to pull away, but the warmth of his breath seduces me for a moment, and I give in as our lips press together gently and then slowly part. My hands quiver, and I lean my head against his chest. I love the way he smells and the strength of his body against mine, but I step back and release his hand.

"Goodbye, Colin," I say.

The door opens, and as quickly as he entered, he leaves. There's nothing left of him but the lingering scent of sweet, honeyed musk.

CHAPTER SIXTY-EIGHT

The morning sun creeps through my window, causing a feeling of apprehension and fear. Today I will join my mother for brunch, her favorite meal. She will undoubtedly be dressed in something exquisite, her makeup done to perfection, with not a hair out of place. Brunch will be served in the solarium; it's the perfect day for it. Every detail, from the fresh-squeezed orange juice chilling in a white ceramic pitcher to the waffles sitting in the sterling silver warming tray, will be perfect. She'll have the Wallingford china, flawlessly polished eating utensils, and, of course, her favorite set of glasses that were given to her and my father as a wedding anniversary gift by the Wilkinsons. The stage will be set for a perfectly respectable exchange between my mother and me.

I begrudgingly roll out of bed. My head aches slightly from the four glasses of Chablis the night before. I'm still reeling from Colin's goodbye. It felt abrupt, incomplete. Nonetheless, I shake off the feelings of unease and begin to mentally prepare myself for what lies ahead.

The hot water from the shower christens me for the task ahead. The scared little girl, who once couldn't exist without her mother's approval, is washed away. Stepping onto the white tiled floor, the quivering sensation that immediately assaulted my body when I turned off the hot water dissipates, and I feel warm and fortified with an inner strength I've never known.

The face I see when I look in the mirror is new. It has known pain, desperation, courage, and love. My eyes are still soft but sultry, and they speak of a quiet wisdom. My complexion radiates a confident glow. The need for makeup is minimal. I need nothing more than eyeliner to create a cat-eye effect, a dab of blush, and flesh-toned lip gloss for that luscious full lip. I feel unstoppable today, but there's still an unresolved hesitation inside me that wonders if I can really face the potential outcome of the day.

Instead of the perfect dress and heels, I slip into my favorite blue jeans and a bright yellow blouse with puffy sleeves. I grab my vintage high-top sneakers and head downstairs for a quick glass of juice before heading out the door. Like a soldier going into battle, I am ready.

CHAPTER SIXTY-NINE

The smell of lilacs and pine fills the air as I make my way up the walkway to the door of my mother's house. Bright white pillars on each side of the door loom over the entrance and give the house an aura of impenetrability. But in reality, they don't protect, fend off, or even deter possible assaults; they simply look big and intimidating. My knock is loud and determined. I look down at my sneakers as if to instill the same level of confidence I had as I put them on.

Like every beginning, it's the debut that is the scariest. The last fleeting breath you take before the inevitability of what is to come overwhelms you. In that split second, you have only two choices: to retreat or to step into your destiny, a moment that you have trained, fought, and even bled for. I take my cue and step into my moment.

"Hello, sweetie," my mother says as she opens the door. She welcomes me with a hug while holding a glass of wine in one hand. Nearby stands a man. I hadn't expected anyone else.

"Dani, this is Alias Briggs," she says. "He's the head of security for Illegis Labs."

She turns to him. "Thank you for the update, Alias. Contact me immediately following the interrogation."

Alias nods in agreement and exits swiftly.

"Interrogation?" I ask with a curious tone.

"Yes, do you remember meeting Linus Graves, the lead cognitive development scientist for Illegis, at the Ascension ceremony?" she asks.

"Vaguely," I reply.

"Well, his partner reported him missing two days ago," she says as she ushers me in. "He was discovered on a park bench, unconscious and severely beaten. The police think it may be a mugging, but nothing about the incident makes sense, like why he was in a park roughly thirty miles from his home while his EV remained in the parking garage of Illegis Labs."

I set my jacket and purse on the table against the wall in the foyer, and we head to the solarium.

"We have to be sure that this was not a kidnapping attempt to compromise Illegis security," my mother continues. "Illegis is constantly under siege from Dissident groups. It's exhausting." The aroma of cinnamon rolls, freshly brewed coffee, and savory cheese and jalapeno biscuits fills the room. I sit at the round glass table and pour myself a glass of water.

"I take it that Illegis security extends to you as well, right?" I wait for her to confirm what Sam told me about the threats.

Mother responds, "Well, yes, but there's nothing to worry about. If I'm not worried, you shouldn't be." Mother looks away, attempting to change the topic. It's unusually warm, and the glare from the sun is strong. "It's so good to see you, Danielle. How did the assignment go?"

"I accomplished what I set out to do," I reply as I shift positions in my chair.

"That's good to hear. I can't wait to read it. I'm sure it will be great like all your other articles." My mother tries her best to smile, her face never really exuding any joy.

"I'm not so sure you're going to feel that way after you read it," I say as I turn away and look at the buffet.

"What do you mean by that?" she asks.

"Well, Mother," I say. "I don't think you'll approve of the subject matter. It's about Dominion and the abuses within the government."

"What do you mean 'abuses'?" she asks, her tone curt while she pours a cup of coffee.

"Mom, what do you know about the Breeders who choose to leave the Colony and transition into mainstream society?" I ask.

Calmly buttering her biscuit and looking at me with a placid expression, she says, "Their contribution to Dominion is recognized and rewarded quite handsomely. Breeders are given the necessary resources to continue a productive and successful life. They're assigned jobs that afford them a quality of life comparable to what they had in the Colony. Their home, livelihood, transportation, and living provisions are included in their release package as well."

"What you just said sounds like it comes directly from a Dominion press release," I say as I begin to tap my fingers on the table.

"What it sounds like is not the point," she says. "What matters is that it is the truth."

"And that's exactly where I'm going with this. The truth. Mother, the Dominion rhetoric we hear all the time about the high level of respect Breeders are given is a lie. Breeders are nothing more than indentured servants brainwashed into accepting their plight. And the very few who choose freedom are not lavished with some sort of compensatory inheritance. They're sold! Sold to foreign governments in need of young, fertile males. They're punished for the audacity to seek their freedom. But that doesn't sound as good as a Dominion brochure."

A vein near her left temple begins to throb. "Where did you hear such nonsense?" she asks. "I don't believe it!"

"It's not nonsense," I say calmly. "It's the truth, confirmed by very reliable sources, one of whom is a member of the elite Dominion police force. There are close to thirty unsolved missing person cases of Breeders. It's difficult to connect the dots because their legal names are changed once they're released from the Colony, but it's true nonetheless. Released Breeders are required to disconnect from everyone and everything they know. Even contact with their families and friends outside of the Colony is discouraged for one year. They're told that starting a new life requires complete immersion and that anything that represents ties to a prior life can deter their progress. It's a cover to facilitate an easier transaction on the black market. I know this is true. I was told about this by a Breeder who was sold and managed to escape before he was transported abroad."

She returns the half-eaten biscuit to her plate and stares out the window. Still composed and determined to stand her ground, she says, "You know, we have so few days like today when the sun manages to break through the heavy, gray clouds and hold back the rain. But we know that, regardless of its attempts to fool us into believing the sunshine is here to stay, the next day comes, and the clouds and rain return, stronger and more determined than before."

"I hate when you speak in riddles, Mom," I say. "Just say it!"

"It's obvious, Danielle," she says. "Things are not always as they seem. No matter how welcome they are." She turns back to me and resumes eating her biscuit.

"Mother, there's more. Did you ever question exactly how the neutralizer, which was under development and tested for several years, miraculously became the center point that pivoted the balance of power? There's no way the Defense Department knew what would happen. You know what I found out? Not even the scientist who invented it knew. But you know who did? The person who worked alongside him. The side effects of the neutralizer were planned, Mother. They were planned by a woman."

I examine her reaction for any sign of disbelief or confusion. She is still and quiet. Her jaw remains stiff.

"Before you ask," I say, "my source for that information is Dr. Chavin." The name strikes a chord for her. She rises from the table, walks over to the window, and resumes staring outside.

"Since you appear to doubt what I'm telling you, I have more. And this is in your own backyard. Mother, Illegis, your masterpiece, is not the sole determinant of the assignment results. Men are not assigned according to their natural cognitive abilities like you think. They are predisposed to drugs that compromise their performance on Illegis. This is done to perpetuate the falsehood that all males alive today or their male offspring are cognitively impaired. The leaders of Dominion need to retain power. That is only possible as long as the belief in male infertility and cognitive impairment continues. Predisposing males to a cognitive decelerator results in Illegis assignments that align with the planned workforce distribution. Mother, Illegis is part of a sinister architecture built on lies and deception." My voice quivers as I speak. "Everything I'm telling you is true. Whether you choose to believe it or not, I have a credible source to back up everything I'm saying. Mother, Dominion is a house of cards, and eventually, it's all going to come tumbling down, either by the sheer will of the people when they learn of this deception or by its own faulty construction. Either way, you have to find a way to get out of this machine."

Unable to maintain her stoic composure, her hands begin to shake, and I see a reluctant tear streaming down my mother's face. "Dani, I tried to leave years ago," she says quietly. "When your father was still alive. But when he died, I buried myself in my work and have not been able to pull away." She grabs a tissue and blots her eyes.

"I was so young when Daddy died," I say. "You never really talked about how it happened other than to say he died of a heart attack."

"Well, what else is there to say?" she asks.

"Maybe that when you tried to leave before, you were clear that you wanted to spend more time with Dad. I was not as much of a factor since I was scheduled to go away to boarding school that year. I remember you were always busy with work, and I remember the arguments you and Daddy used to have about your work schedule. Didn't it strike you as strange that Daddy died right after you conveyed your decision to leave your job? Daddy had just received his medical clearance, which included the arbilation screening within four days of your announcement to leave. There could not have been an aneurysm, Mom. That test was clear."

"What are you saying?" she asks, peering at me with her sharp eyes.

"I'm saying that Daddy was murdered," I tell her. "They couldn't afford to let you go, so they got rid of your reason for leaving. Dominion falsely induced an aneurysm but told you it was a heart attack to make sure you wouldn't question his death. After he died, you did exactly what they wanted you to do—devote your life's work to priming the machine. Do you think you'd have the will to leave now? Mother, Dominion robbed you of your husband and your life. Your work and the web of lies supporting Illegis killed Daddy!"

Once I stop speaking, the silence in the room becomes almost deafening. She reaches out her hand as if beseeching me for comfort. I walk over to embrace her. In that moment, the little girl who cowered when sensing an ounce of her mother's disapproval emerges like the sun as the new me: confident, strong, determined, and ready to stake a claim to my rightful existence.

The embrace between a mother and daughter that symbolizes acceptance is the centerpiece of almost every Declaration of Independence. It serves as the axis upon which the balance of power and the leveling of new roles turns. To pull off this tremendous coup requires perfect synchrony. The daughter, once a girl, now a woman, must be willing to give, and the mother must be willing to receive. Both parties must see their roles as converging and begin to heal. But the embrace is just the beginning. The constant call and answer of balance can change on a dime, so to stay in sync, each woman must be willing to sacrifice who they are to become who they are meant to be. Each woman fighting for something bigger than both of them, a relationship that will evolve into the butterfly each of you long to be. And in its execution, only three things matter: the *love, trust,* and *respect* between the two of you. But this new beginning is fragile, as with just one seed of doubt or incidence of betrayal, the perfectly balanced teeter-totter collapses, and everything that was once perfect can disappear for the struggle to start all over again.

CHAPTER SEVENTY

The drive home is quiet as the wind blows through my hair and whistles gently in my ears. I am riddled with emotions, elation and anticipation, while weighed down by uncertainty and fear. This tug-of-war wages an aggressive attack, and when I get home, I'm exhausted. I step out of my EV and onto a piece of glass. The cracking beneath the sole of my shoe reminds me that no matter how fragile the truth is, its true nature must be exposed, and the pressure of that truth shatters its very existence. That sound is like music, a battle cry for social justice that I can't ignore. I begin to walk boldly and with purpose to the front door, where I know the actions will change my life. The time to retreat is over, and nothing is left but the truth. I feel cold, alone.

As the night folds its darkness and hugs the stars, I type furiously. Each word flows from something within me that burns for justice. The truth about Dominion is also the truth about myself—born of a union between man and woman, transformed under the dictatorial power of a woman, striving for independence that seems unattainable, and finding the courage to claim who we truly are and become the best version of who we can be.

Dominion's truth is shocking and at times painful. But the truth is also the key that will unlock the moment when power will not be hoarded and defiled by opportunists. Dominion and I, our journeys of discovery, are kindred spirits as we seek to untether our minds and hearts from the seduction of power and deceit.

Exactly 2,500 words comprise this article. I look away for a moment only to see a sliver of light piercing the fading darkness. Dawn is upon us, and a spark of exhilaration enlivens me. Dominion's story, my story, is far from over. In fact, it is just beginning. I carefully read my words, tears streaming from my eyes, and just as I am ready to click "send," the gray pod rings. It must be Caris. I am ready.

GLOSSARY

8 Cabinets—The political order led by Dominion upholding egalitarianism, social equality, the protection of the environment, and the strengthening of the sociopolitical safety of every human being through the eight cabinets: Law, Science, Commerce, Transportation, Religion, Military, Art, and Politics.

Acculturation—One-year period following a Breeder release, which allows for lifestyle adjustment to life outside of the Colony.

Allura Yakubu—Dominion's first president.

Alzaiec wine—Full-bodied red wine that is made from hybrid grapes.

Arbilation—Full-body scan used to detect physiological abnormalities, including aneurysms.

Ascendant—The person who is part of the collective known as "the elevator" and is designated next in line to assume responsibility for the safe travel of the escapee.

Ascension—The anniversary of September 23, the national celebration of Dominion's nationhood. It commemorates the day women achieved absolute power. 2050 is the twentieth anniversary of the birth of Dominion and honored by the Ascension ceremony.

Aqua Screen—A three-dimensional TV experience that displays visual content with no structural boundaries.

AV—Self-driving car is also known as an autonomous or automated vehicle (AV).

Body-glam dial—A miniature compressive device embedded in wearable shapewear designed to shape and support the torso. Simply press and release the device to attain the desired silhouette.

BioGenome—To produce high-quality (chromosome level) genome assemblies for all eukaryotic life on the planet.

Breeder—Singletary classification (S5) designates fertile males assigned to live and work in national communities known as the Colonies. Their primary function is to support the genetic targeting and propagation of Dominion offspring.

Climens—Clear, thin twenty-four-inch rope that serves as handcuffs. Binding is simple and provides the restraint strength of steel handcuffs.
the Colony—Lifestyle community for Breeders.

Carousel—The official Dominion matchmaking app.

Couche—The French word to describe furniture used for lying down.

Coventry—The interview room at the Transformation where Dani interviews Tobias.

Defiance—The capital of Dominion.

Descendant—The person who is part of the collective known as "the elevator" and shelters the passenger prior to the next destination.

Desperados—Militant Dissenters.

Digi pens—Next-generation stylus.

Dissenter—Anyone engaged in activities to overthrow Dominion.

Dominion—Established in 2030 and led by a female president and eight cabinet leaders governing twenty-six unified republics, previously known as the United States.

Dominion Anthem—The Pledge of Allegiance was written in August 2030 by Dominion Minister Delenya Paul (1978-2045).

Dominion Flag—Butterfly with twenty-six quadrants.

Doyennes (a.k.a. the Collective)—A body of female administrators who unified the country following the Great War.

Drogan—Modern-day term for "prisoner" but exclusively references a male legally held in prison for crimes unrelated to political dissension.

Echelon microbeads—A small device that fits in the ear to amplify sound.

Effigent (Vanguard) Award—Recognition given annually to those who have "done the most or the best work for the creation and sustenance of Dominion national order."

Great War—It involved several of the world's superpowers, forming two opposing military alliances. It ended with a bilateral surrender following the release of chemical warfare and its effects had global impact. Most males became cognitively impaired and infertile. As a result, new governments were formed with their leadership firmly in the hands of women across the world.

Harken—Seal of the Harken, the Dominion's federal symbol of incarceration.

Illegis Headstone—The nerve center of the Illegis testing platform.

Illegis Test—A form of IQ fencing, that determines the appropriate Singletary group to which each male is assigned. Once assigned, a male will be given priority status to obtain jobs in that group. A male can change his assigned Singletary group by passing additional test hurdles for IQ reassignment.

Infinity—A drug that delivers a "functional high" that produces enhanced cognitive acuity and elevates feelings of euphoria and self-confidence. This "functional high" lasts several days, and then ends with depressive episodes (highly addictive and corrodes mental function over time).

IQ Fencing—An assessment that measures a range of cognitive abilities and provides a score that is intended to serve as a measure of a male's intellectual abilities and potential in Dominion society as denoted by the Singletary classification.

Israe—Man-made infectious disease caused by a synthetic parasite.

Keelan—The location of the Transformation Center where all twelve-year-old males, newly assigned to the Breeder class, are sent for training before moving to the Colony.

Licon—Pods, the modern-day term for cell phones, are made of this lightweight, biodegradable metal.

Malism—The belief that the world is evil has evolved to include powerful discrimination against men.

Myrimidons—Militant dissenters.

Osmanthus tea —Made from the fragrant flowers of the Osmanthus tree. It is therapeutic for promoting relaxation and calm.

Photo plank—A tablet containing three-dimensional photos.

Pleasure seeker activities (PSA)—Coupling services provided by males in the S6 Singletary classification.

Release tribute (a.k.a. the Reckoning)—A ritual ceremony held at the annual Dominion Ascension Gala honoring the dedication and contributions of the Breeders who have reached their thirtieth birthdays and chosen to end their assignment as Breeders and live outside of the Colony.

Sandicists—Modern-day purists who live simply and peacefully outside of Dominion's social, political, and economic strata.

Singletary Classifications—Males are defined within a caste system made up of six core Singletary groups:

- **S1: Benignants** (white bands) social workers/religious leaders/ teachers/ childcare professionals
- **S2: Assiduites** (purple bands) artists/athletes (e.g., dancers, writers, singers, performers, athletes)
- **S3: Formalists** (brown bands) service works (e.g., nail techs, clerks, hair stylists, fitness, admin)
- **S4: Expeditors** (green bands) public works (e.g., construction, public, transportation)
- **S5: Breeders** (black bands) lives and works in breeding colonies)
- **S6: Seducers** (red bands) also known as pleasure givers.

Skizzer Ball—A new form of racquetball played with three-dimensional ball images and a short-handled probe in an eight-walled skizzer court.

Standards—Educational level through high school (matriculation 1-12).

Supplicant—Person seeking refuge at Haven.

Transformation Center—Place where Breeders are trained and transitioned to meet their obligations to Dominion.

www.ingramcontent.com/pod-product-compliance
Lightning Source LLC
LaVergne TN
LVHW091625070526
838199LV00044B/946